About the Author

Poli Flores Jr. has been a criminal trial attorney, professor of criminal justice (San Diego State, IV), and superior court judge in Southern California for over forty years. His first novel, *In the Shadow of the Sun,* received critical acclaim, including a finalist for Book of the Year in fiction, 2023, from the American Book Awards and the International Latino Book Awards. He resides in Calexico, California, with his wife, Mercy.

The Nickel Choir

Poli Flores Jr.

The Nickel Choir

Pegasus

Dedication

To the Flores Five, plus.

Acknowledgments

A special thanks to Brian McNeece, retired professor from Imperial Valley College, Raul Ayala, Esq., and Vicky Ross for your excellent insights in reviewing my initial drafts.

PROLOGUE

Nicolas Meza, facing life or death, peers downward, his weighted head drooping like a wounded dog, staring morosely at the ground, searching for the gates of hell as the devil's taunting whispers tickle his ears.

"Counselor, are you ready for your final summation?"

"Yes, your honor. Thank you."

The defendant awaits his fate of life or death before twelve strangers—his peers, his jury.

By the trial's third day, the jury avoided eye contact with him and his attorney. Surrendering to providence like a pre-written eulogy, the defendant quit taking notes halfway through the trial.

The packed courtroom is eerily silent and dour, like a morgue weighed down by the heavy ambiance of shadowy death. Blackness. Distant honks from the L.A. rush hour and dusty sunlight filter into the courtroom, the only reminders of the world beyond the courtroom. Meza's head rises furtively to glance at the prosecutrix, a Deputy District Attorney for the County of Los Angeles who seeks his death. For one fleeting moment, their eyes lock.

The prosecutrix slowly rises from her table, sighs, adjusts her black dress, and casually approaches the podium before twelve jurors and six alternates. In the legal vernacular, these jurors are *death qualified*—meaning they have taken an oath before jury selection to impose the death penalty if the facts and the law support the verdict. Death. Blackness. The jurors' collective eyes, bloodshot and haggard, lock onto the trial attorney as she clutches the podium, glances at the victims' family in the audience with a slight nod, then glances at the defendant, who doesn't reciprocate. She reminds herself always to *look a defendant in the eye*. She's in no hurry—the courtroom clock is now running on *her* time.

The prosecutrix carefully adjusts a large color photo on a nearby stand, an image of a gleaming mother holding her small boy with a cheerful tooth-gapped smile. The defendant only hears the drumbeat of his heart, now in sync with the collective heartbeats of the jurors. The defense attorney clutches Meza's drooping shoulder with a faux embrace—like a distant relative consoling a widower.

The confident prosecutrix clears her throat and slowly peers down the two rows of jurors with eyes expressing deep reverence for their solemn duty. "Ladies and gentlemen, thank you for sitting through this trial these past six weeks. We began this trial on March 10, 2023, but it feels like we've been here longer. I can speak for many others when I extend my deepest appreciation for your work in this case. But your commitment is not over.

"In the first phase of this trial, you found Mr. Nicolas Meza guilty of murder in the first degree. Now, it is your solemn duty, a duty that you each swore to affirm, to consider whether we proved special circumstances to you beyond a reasonable doubt under section 190.2 of the California Penal Code. You heard testimony that Amelia was trying to end the relationship, a five-year relationship that was a living nightmare of abuse of every kind and every degree. She fought back; we know that from the scratches on the defendant, a two-hundred-and-twenty-pound man and a two-hundred-and-twenty-pound coward," she says, pointing to Meza. "He then covers up his crime by burning down the house. A coward." She pauses to catch her breath, approaching the jurors directly, away from the podium, locking her eyes on each of the twelve.

Juror number seven in the front row, a retired schoolteacher with thick glasses, removes a handkerchief and delicately wipes her left eye, glancing furtively at the defendant.

"As I speak to you today, do not listen to the sound of *my* voice or the voice of attorney Holder. No, listen to the sound of the defendant's ten-year-old son, Little Nicky, as he burned to death in his home on the horrible evening of February 2, 2021." She clutches the photo of the young victim. "I know the defendant heard that sound as he watched that house engulfed in flames. He heard only the outward cries—but not the soulful anguish of his boy, his blood. *You* must also hear those same sounds from little Nicky—not sounds of pain, but an anguished plea for justice. Nicky's plea. Please take a moment and close your eyes so you can see and hear that ten-year-old child." She stands away from the podium for a few seconds, allowing the jurors to ponder that image. Some spectators emit quiet sniffles.

"I honestly cannot think of any other more important and challenging decision a jury must consider. Thoughts of morality, religion, anger, vengeance, or even sympathy might guide your judgment. But as this court will instruct you, these delicate and profound thoughts should not dictate your ultimate decision. Justice. Simple justice is your guide. Justice will guide you from the deep, dark wells of your souls and into the light, where you will see the only verdict in this horrendous case." The voice of the prosecutrix is calm, with a controlled pace, almost soothing.

"Your verdict, reduced to its most simple form, should be based on a few basic questions you must ask yourselves and ask yourselves honestly.

"One: Will I uphold my duty as a juror as I listened and weighed the evidence in this case?

"Two: Whether the facts presented in the guilt and penalty phases have established any special circumstances enumerated under section 190.2 of the California Penal Code. Did this defendant murder these two victims—his own son and his mother—during the commission of an arson? And whether this crime was especially heinous. The law defines *heinous* as a *conscienceless or pitiless crime that is unnecessarily torturous to the victims*. The facts we presented are clear. Amelia and little Nico died a slow, burning, tortuous death. Meza's conduct defines the very essence of the word *heinous*.

"Finally, defense counsel will argue that mitigating factors call not for death but life without parole. Listen not to the attorneys. Listen to Little Nicky. His voice is your guide. He is crying for justice for his life that the defendant brutally scorched from this world at the age of ten. He calls for justice for his mother, who saw her son's life extinguished as the last thing on earth.

"When you enter that deliberation room, close your eyes to listen closely to Little Nicky. Mr. Nicolas Meza does not deserve life for the simple reason that he placed no value on the lives of two others. Why should you value his? The victims' sisters, nephews, and cousins who witnessed this trial and testified before you also seek justice. The only memory the mourners had left at the funeral were two sets of teeth. The victims' ashes remain in the rubble of the burned house. That's their gravesite. But Amelia's and Little Nicky's spirits survived. Little Nicky is crying for justice. Amelia is *begging* for justice.

"Do your job, ladies and gentlemen, and impose a verdict of death. Thank you."

***

Sitting at their favorite Spring Street deli, three blocks from the Foltz Criminal Justice Center, Edward Ross said, "Linda, that was a quick deliberation, only two hours. Even the judge took little time to certify the jury's decision to impose the death penalty. Damn. Hell of a job, Lin."

Sanchez clutched her glass of cold water and said, "Thanks, Ed, appreciate it."

Weighed down by internal conflicting emotions, Linda Sanchez slumped in the booth in the café with a sullen look and said, "Somehow, it doesn't feel satisfying. I used to feel victorious when I put bad guys away. That's why I went to law school—cleaning up the street. Putting away the bad. Here, we were lucky when forensics recovered the defendant's cap at the scene. I don't know how we missed the cap the first time. At one point in the trial, we were starving for evidence. That L.A. Dodgers cap was like manna from heaven. That cap sustained our case and brought it to life." Sanchez's thoughts seemed to drift, and she took a deep breath.

Edward Ross, her supervisor and likely the future district attorney for the County of Los Angeles, stared at her with a confused look. Tall and distinguished-looking at age forty-five, Ross was slim, with specks of thick grey hair, and he took pride—without too much vanity—in always looking his best with custom-tailored dark three-piece suits. His photogenic smile would bode well as an aspiring politician, but in private, Ross was usually serious and a good listener and carefully chose his words. Before becoming a supervisor, Edward Ross was an outstanding trial attorney who worked his way up the ranks of the Office of the L.A. District Attorney. Ross said, "Be proud of yourself. You're one of our best; it took our best to get this conviction." She looked away from him and stared at the slow-moving traffic outside in the late afternoon.

"Ed, you ever had a small pebble caught in your shoe?" Linda asked.

"What the hell are you talking about? You just convicted a horrible person who snuffed out his son and wife." Ross scooted to the edge of his seat and said, "And you're babbling about a pebble stuck in your shoe. What's wrong?"

Linda said, "Yeah, it's a pain when you get that small pebble stuck in your shoe and can't get it out. Maybe I dreamed it; I don't know. But this conviction feels like something is stuck in my mind, and I can't get it out. Like that damn pebble."

"Forget about it. You're just exhausted. Take a vacation."

"No, Ed, I need to work. I've got a vacation coming up in two months. Maui."

Ross said, "I'll get the check. Oh, by the way. I also need to congratulate you on something else."

"What?"

"You, Miss Linda Sanchez, are the newest member of the Nickel Choir."

"Huh?"

"This is your fifth death penalty conviction. As fighter pilots say, you have five *confirmed kills*. You have joined an exclusive club. Five death convictions—you've joined an exclusive club.

"Miss Linda Sanchez, welcome to the Nickel Choir."

CHAPTER 1

The American courtroom is an insular world of immense power, a malleable breathing creature created and shaped by the mighty hands of idealism, nourished and sustained by the frail hands of mortals—but ultimately cursed by both.

***

FROM LINDA

I am a donkey.

Since grammar school, I never felt like the smartest, wittiest, or prettiest person in a room. I still don't.

I have one secret pleasure—my hidden tattoo that's protectively nestled in a secret place on my body. Only two other people on this earth have seen it: the Berkeley tattoo artist, Kodiak the Bear, whom I visited in a drunken spree after law school finals, and my deceased husband. The only other person likely to ever see it is a pathologist when I'm lying on a freezing slab, but that pathologist would have a hard time finding it. Indiana Jones and his crew of Hovitos tribesmen couldn't find my tattoo.

Anyway, the tattoo. OK, well, my tattoo is a miniature donkey. A small, simple, bland, harmless donkey. When we see a plain, featureless donkey, we assume the donkey is a simple-minded creature. These creatures carry unbearably heavy loads. Dumb. Ornery.

But that impression is deceiving. Most people are not keenly aware of—or fully appreciate—their other, more valuable traits. Donkeys have excellent memories. For example, they can remember complex routes they've previously taken. They also have a keen sense of logic compared to other animals. Unlike their cousin, the horse, donkeys respond well to pain, illness, and fear. And their sense of impending fear is more acute than other animals'—they sense when bad shit is around the corner. People think donkeys are stubborn when they dig their legs into the ground, but they do so because they sense fear. And a child would want a small pony rather than a donkey, right? I'll take the donkey any day over a pretty white horse.

Sorry, let me hop back onto this runaway train of thought. I went off-rail. I am a donkey.

Some colleagues, attorneys, and judges might see me as that donkey in a professional setting. Bland and featureless. That's OK. On the legal battlefield, my outward looks will lure some of my professional adversaries into a false sense of security when they deal with me. Like the donkey, my other attributes reveal themselves later after they spend time near me. I succeed in court because I'm not afraid to fail; I'm impervious to the pain of setbacks in my cases; I think and speak logically, and my memory is superb.

I am a donkey.

My entry with the Los Angeles D.A. in the spring of 2000 was bumpy. Then, I heard the whispers of—token, diversity hire, no experience, too bland, and she won't cut it. Twenty years later, some of those same whisperers are constantly seeking me out for advice. The rest couldn't cut it.

Then, cocky defense attorneys on the other side of the table often smirked when they saw who the prosecutrix was. A simple, unobtrusive donkey. Now, those smirks vanish when they and their clients hear the guilty verdicts announced.

Then, some judges seemed dismissive whenever I addressed them. Now, most seem to pay closer attention. In the criminal departments, I know the law better than most black robes on the bench before me.

Then, the quiet misogynistic comments I heard would bother me— especially from female lawyers. Now, I don't hear them. It's only white noise—muted, bereft of substance or effect.

Here's another embarrassing admission: I'm not a very good or typical millennial, and I wasn't born with that intuitive grasp of technology. The I.T. guys in my office are on my speed dial. A poster of all those friggin' computer icons for reference hangs on my office wall.

Traveling is not something I do in my free time. I've been outside of California only three times in my life. Besides alcohol, I'm also addicted to work. I have few friends, and I avoid social networking. I tried

Facebook but couldn't think of meaningful shit to post, like photos of my dog, a photo of my shriveled rib-eye at Applebee's, or random biblical quotes. I have a dog, Wallie, but he's not too photogenic. He's a mutt, part Chihuahua and part of some unknown breed— maybe an unknown species. At his age, he can't hear, he's moody, and he sleeps and farts all day like an old man on his deathbed. His only senses that remain intact are smell, taste—and time.

He knows when it's time to eat and not a second later. But he sleeps near my bed and comforts me. Hardly anyone wants to 'friend' me. I don't like texting or the ubiquitous emojis. Because my Mayan blood passed into my D.N.A., my fingers look like plump wieners, which are not conducive to the dexterous act of simple texting. So, between my Mayan-chubby fingers and the mysterious A.I. intruder on my cell phone, my text messages are incomprehensible to the average reader. Just get on the damn phone and talk to me!

My roots: Boyle Heights. East L.A.

The invigorating Pacific breezes drifting from the L.A. coastline never seem to reach my childhood home in East L.A., as if an invisible wall blocked them. The west-side folks retain the purified ocean air, and we get the dusty smog on the east side. But that's OK. The sultry sounds, the vibrant aromas, and the breathtaking ambiance within East Los Angeles are uniquely beautiful.

Sometimes those sounds are haunting, and sometimes they're soothing—helicopters whirling at night with their sharp laser lights splashing down onto the city like flashlights from the heavens, like menacing U.F.O.s hovering over the earthly urban landscape. And the shrill sirens, screaming trouble nearby. And sometimes, the gunshots pop nearby. One can distinguish the various weapons from the sounds. "Small caliber, probably a .22."

"That one sounded like a .38 cal." The automatics were the ones you never wanted to hear and what kept you up at night. Even worse— multiple sounds of automatic weapons because that meant a street battle, baneful exchanges of death. Children with a warped sense of masculinity engaging in a mutual slaughter.

Those sounds I cannot suppress, but I still can muffle them with the other soothing soundscapes and undulant wafts from East Los Angeles: the laughter of children, the rich music of Santana, corridos, and hip-hop

*during those muggy L.A. evenings when East Los Angeles moves outdoors
to cool off. Rich Mexican music blasting from Mariachi Plaza. Kids
splashing in their front years with water hoses during muggy days. The
teenage cruisers crawling along Cesar E. Chavez Avenue, what we call
La Brooklyn. The viejos in quiet conversation with their viejas, laughing,
gossiping, and crying. Someone cooking carne asada, or my favorite place
where they serve vegan posole. Neighbors talking. And oh, that mole from
the Tenampal on the First Street Corridor. The myriad of extraordinary
murals that grace the urban landscape around East L.A. add to my home's
astonishing texture.*

*After my father left us, we moved to East Los from the San Fernando
Valley in 1985, when I was ten and my brother, Julio, was eight, four years
after the summer of the "Night Stalker," a serial killer named Richard
Ramirez. His reign of terror ended three blocks from our home when Boyle
Heights citizens cornered him and detained him on August 31, 1981, after
a nationwide manhunt. Like the old West, the brave citizens of Boyle
Heights took matters into their own hands to protect the community—
until L.A.P.D. arrived.*

*I didn't want to move, but it slowly became my home. It is home. So
long as someone looked after you and steered you away from violence,
drugs, and pregnancies, you could survive and make it out. My mom
struggled, holding two jobs in the garment district stores and
McDonald's, and brought leftovers. I could not eat another stale Big Mac
for the rest of my life. With only a sixth-grade education, that's all she
could get. But I sometimes got some excellent used clothes. "This nice
dress only has some loose stitches, but it's easy to fix, and look at these
jeans, brand new, with just a new zipper-like new!"*

*High school was tough. Lots of stuff was happening at home. My mom
constantly struggled in one form or another. Julio began his youthful
troubles. The rent was always late. Dad left us, and I never knew why.
Adults keep their marital problems sequestered behind closed doors as if
their children are too weak to understand toxic parental dynamics. Julio
and I knew they wouldn't last before they did.*

*But I was fortunate. My mother always protected me and always saw
something special in me. The sparkle in her eyes warmed me inside when
she looked at me. She always told me to be tough and let no one or
anything drag me down. And I took that to heart all my life. Be tough. I*

always had uncles, aunts, and cousins around me like a thick shield to protect me from all the dangerous elements; they nurtured me like mothers and probably saved my unknown future. They were rough on Julio and me, but they had to be because they knew the existential dangers lurking beyond our home.

My mother squeezed every dollar to ensure we had food under a protective roof. She shocked me when she pulled me out of public school around seventh grade and enrolled me at St. Mary's Catholic School, five miles from my neighborhood in Cypress Park. How could she afford it? So, I left my friends and started St. Mary's until I graduated from high school.

My grades were good, but in my wildest dreams, I never thought Loyola University would accept me. Those nuns from St. Mary's pushed me and pushed me and pushed me. The old "hard work pays off" maxim used to sound like a corny platitude, and it sounded silly when I first heard Sister Olivia say it. But she made me believe in that old mantra and made me believe in myself. If I wrote a term paper, she made me rewrite it until it was polished. If I misspelled or mispronounced a word, she made me rewrite it or repeat it. I practiced my cursive writing until my fingers were numb. When I was down, she brought me up. She wiped my tears.

When I first met Sister Olivia, I thought it was a mistake to come to this school because of her. My first impression of her—not good.

I first saw her as a stern-looking spinster. But later, my eyes refocused, and I saw a warm, vibrant smile.

I first heard a voice belching submission and fear. But later, after I listened closely, I heard her speak with a soothing tone, an elixir.

I first saw a person who was distant and reserved. But ultimately, she graced my life with compassion and joy. The most important things she taught me were not writing, math, and reading. Instead, she taught me the most important things: self-confidence, inner grace, and raw tenacity. Then, being accepted to the U.C.L.A. School of Law was another shock. But Sister Olivia told me, "I knew you had it in you. U.C.L.A. is lucky to get you." Sister Olivia and my mom were my special guests at my graduation. A future lawyer. The law. Justice. I, Linda Sanchez, would make a difference in the world.

Thank you, Mom. Thank you, Sister Olivia.

After passing the California bar in July 2000, I started my career where I dreamed about

— the District Attorney of Los Angeles County—the largest prosecutorial office in the United States. Its prosecutorial jurisdiction extends to 4,083 square miles, serving 10.4 million people.

Its mission statement says, in part:

"The Los Angeles District Attorney's Office will advance an effective, ethical, and racially equitable system of justice that protects the community, restores victims of crime, and honors the rights of the accused."

I began my career with L.A.D.A. on the lowest prong of the totem pole, looking upward at hundreds of other attorneys. Like a Sherpa climbing Mount Everest, I began trudging uphill in the spring of my career, never looking down:

Year1: Arraignments

Years two to three: Low grade misdemeanors. Ten convictions, two acquittals. But who's counting? (All my supervisors, that's who.)

Year four: Focus on domestic violence cases. Five convictions. One hung jury. No acquittals.

Years five to ten Gang cases and violent crimes. This assignment coincided with my first concealed weapons permit, a Glock 19.

Years ten and following: Special circumstances cases or death penalty cases. Cream of the legal crop.

Being assigned to these most challenging cases wasn't easy. Along the way, I heard snickering, "She's only a token." "Not tough enough." "She's snobby." "Won't last past probation." Even some of this crap filtered into social media. So, after having one of the highest conviction records in the office, I proved those pricks wrong, and more importantly, I proved myself wrong.

After a few years of successful litigation at the highest levels of the D.A.'s office, the nicknames around me changed from harpy, lightweight, dowdy, mediocre, and bland to shark, she-devil, chingona, and brilliant. Pejoratives can be badges of honor.

Yeah, I was not the brightest. Maybe my public speaking skills weren't the smoothest. I'm not as physically packaged as those supermodel actresses on TV who play glib lawyers in those fantasy court dramas on TV. I'm only 5'3" and retained all my baby fat. My hair: always dry and stringy. My fashion sense: dowdy. And I have a small gap in my front teeth that creates a whistling sound when I sleep.

But what accounts for my professional success is simple: I OUT-WORKED, I OUT-STUDIED, I OUT-PREPARED EVERY LAWYER IN MY OFFICE, EVERY COURT OPPONENT, AND MOST JUDGES. I never missed seminars to improve my skills. I left my pride aside when I asked questions incessantly from experienced attorneys. Like Sister Olivia, Edward Ross became my prized mentor. Like Sister Olivia and my mom, Ed saw something in me that others didn't. My tenacity never wavers, my intensity never wanes, and my self-confidence never escapes. I cannot relax until I hear the words of a court clerk: "Guilty." Guided by Sister Olivia's stern voice, I rewrite my opening and closing statements half a dozen times until I think they're polished like silverware. Even after I got married, I worked fourteen hours a day.

But the work has its rewards, 'cause I'm a badass donkey armed with a California attorney bar card.

CHAPTER 2
July 8, 2005

A chocolate milkshake—the last thing her husband and child enjoyed before they died. After a relaxing Italian meal in Westwood, Linda, five months pregnant with a girl, craved a chocolate milkshake.

"Lin, how the hell can you eat so much? Do you have room down there?" Her husband, Robert, rarely teased her about her eating habits, and with Linda's burgeoning pregnancy, he knew she ate healthy foods. So Linda and their unborn girl deserved a reward. Their demanding child, who would enter the world in four months, had favorites: pasta, strawberries, peanut butter, and chocolate milkshakes. Robert took Linda after dinner and picked up her chocolate milkshake as they headed onto the 405 from Pico Boulevard. A chocolate milkshake was the last thing her husband and child enjoyed before they died.

As they merged onto the 405 freeway on-ramps, a nineteen-year-old boy sped through a red light at fifty miles an hour, distracted by blaring hip-hop music and his girlfriend. The boy's black S.U.V. plowed into their car, directly smashing Robert and toppling their vehicle onto its side. Right after the impact, Linda felt Robert's last frigid breath on her left shoulder as her child no longer kicked gleefully from the last taste of her chocolate milkshake. After the deadly impact, Linda still clutched her milkshake, its sweet aftertaste lingering in her mouth, but the light fetal tingling in her womb stopped. Time stopped. Her world stopped.

When Linda regained consciousness at the hospital, she felt pain down below as trickles of blood oozed out. Her mother and Julio were at her bedside with frozen pain on their faces. Her mother clutched her hand like a warm vice, and Julio sniffled quietly in the corner of the hospital room.

"Ma…"

"No, *mija*, they didn't make it. They're gone."

"I know. I should've gone with them. I want to go with them, ma," Linda said meekly. "Please hold me, ma. Hold me."

"Linda, I'll never let go. I love you."

In the ensuing weeks, Linda recovered with just a broken collarbone and returned to work, facing a busy schedule. The work was cathartic and helped her sharpen her focus in court. Sympathetic—and well-meaning—gestures from friends and colleagues partially mollified her black despair and horror.

But during lonesome moments away from work, her pain returned, her loneliness endured, and she sought refuge in vodka, wine, and self-loathing.

Because she never lost a step in her work and continued to progress as a superb lawyer, few around her noticed or pretended they didn't see that her drinking was slowly rotting her insides. When she could no longer camouflage her drinking with wads of gum, eye drops, and fake smiles, her supervisor, Edward Ross, directed her into his office.

His ultimatum was short and direct: Curb the drinking or leave the District Attorney's Office, along with her career.

"Lin, you're a great lawyer. You're also an alcoholic. You can't be both. I will authorize time off for you to get into rehabilitation. There are some fine programs through the California Bar Association. Alcoholics Anonymous is an option or the church. I don't give a damn which one works for you, but *you* need to fix this. I will support you with whatever you do to curb your drinking, but you cannot go further down this hellhole."

Ross squinted his eyes and glared intensely at Linda and said, "How dare you excoriate drunk drivers and spousal abusers who come into court and tell the judge they couldn't help it because the drinking was beyond their control. You didn't show too much empathy to those defendants you sent to jail or prison. And I will not show any empathy to you."

Sanchez knew Ross well, so she didn't call his bluff, went cold turkey, entered a two-week rehabilitation facility, and crawled back to work. The support of her mother and brother, the candid talks with Sister Olivia and Ed Ross, and her reservoir of internal willpower buoyed her spirits and saved her. She stepped to the edge of a deep black precipice, looked down to emptiness, and stepped back to safety. But she also sensed that the dark cliff was always nearby as she tip-toed along its steep edge for the rest of her life.

The young boy who crashed into them pled guilty to manslaughter, and Sanchez spoke at his sentencing hearing.

"Your honor, I lost a part of me that day, and this boy was responsible for my unbearable loss. My husband and child will never return, except maybe in my dreams. That will not change. What little I know of this boy shows a decent young man with great promise for his future. He wasn't drunk. He was reckless." Turning to the young defendant, she said, "Most of us at nineteen were probably guilty of some kind of recklessness, weren't we? God knows I was.

"I am here before this court to speak not for myself but for my husband and the daughter I will never know. They would say the same thing if they were here. Sending this boy to prison will not assuage my loss. Sending this boy to prison will not return my family. Sending this boy to prison will not send any message. What's the message? I don't know. If he's half the decent human being I think he is, he will punish himself for the rest of his life for what he's done. Those prison bars won't add to that punishment. Those prison bars will only turn him mean, hard, and soulless. I will try to return to my life; let him return to his. Please don't send him to prison. Thank you, Your Honor."

The boy received probation. Five years later, when Sanchez visited her husband's and child's graves, she saw a lone figure, a young boy, standing by those same graves, talking to the headstones, crying.

As Sanchez returned to work with youthful vigor, she refined her legal skills and soon became recognized as one of the finest prosecutors in the D.A.'s office. She volunteered to prosecute the most demanding legal cases—death penalty cases.

***

Sanchez attended a week-long seminar on death penalty training in Chicago early in 2010 to prepare for her new assignment. She listened to and spoke with a *who's who* of death penalty prosecutors who sauntered throughout the various workshops like rock stars. She digested their information, presentations, and suggestions like a starving child in a free buffet. Only five district attorneys had put over 300 men and women on death row. Those elite prosecutors shared their collective insight, and Linda soaked that information into her psyche.

If there were a Babe Ruth of death penalty prosecutors, it would be

25

Ron Lacy from Oklahoma. Linda learned he had put over fifty people on death row in his thirty-year career. Not without sartorial flair to highlight the zeal for his work, he only dressed in black. At 6'4" and 300 pounds, he favored oversized Yosemite Sam Black Stetsons, a black vested suit with boots of black lizard skin, and a black bolo tie with a black ebano-encrusted stone. Linda guessed (correctly) that his undershorts were also black.

Booking photos of all those he convicted to death were placed on his office wall like collaged wallpaper, and a miniature paperweight of an electric chair was propped on his oversized desk connected to an A.A. battery. His side gig included a pastorship in his local church. He sermonized scriptural references copiously into his closing statements during his trials. The pious congregations of twelve—the jurors—loved him.

Lacy had a signed photo on his wall of one of America's deadliest prosecutors: Joe Freeman Britt of North Carolina. Britt compiled thirty-eight kills. The photo also included a quote from Britt:

"... within the breast of each of us burns a flame that constantly whispers in our ear, 'Preserve life at any cost.' It is the prosecutor's job to extinguish that flame."

Batting behind Babe Ruth Lacy in this murderers' row was Stanley "The Killer" Miller from Alabama. To a casual observer, he resembled a dull bookkeeper. Only 5'5" and weighing 130 pounds with thick glasses, he looked harmless with no outstanding facial features except a tiny beak nose. Facially flat. Nothing. Hairless like an albino hairless sphynx cat. Blank eyes. His face looked two-dimensional. Linda thought he looked like an insect. He worked like a dry bureaucrat in court as if he were adjudicating small claims cases. However, he wasn't trying fender benders and neighbor disputes; he put human beings to death with dry flair and clinical precision.

During an illustrious thirty-year career, Killer had a pretty good batting average, forty death penalty trials with thirty-one convictions. Mookie Betts would kill for those stats. During each execution of those he convicted, he always tried to get front-row seats because he didn't like the bleachers; you couldn't get a close-up of their faces as they exhaled their last breath. According to Miller, his patriotic duty was to seek the death penalty with God's guidance. Rumors persisted about him, which he did little to quell. For example, as a child, he collected various bugs in a shoebox and burned them with a magnifying glass. This activity eventually progressed to household pets and feral cats.

So, over ten days, Linda listened to zealous speakers extolling the virtues of the penalty of death—the ultimate sentence of an advanced democracy. Even though she was a seasoned attorney, she felt like an ingenue, intimidated by this new world she was entering.

Some speakers bemoaned the growing use of drugs to execute the condemned. *Too painless, unlike their victims.* A few reminisced about those halcyon days of electrocutions, hangings, and firing squads. To the untrained ear, the lectures sounded clinical. *Research the special circumstances in your particular case. Empathize with the victims' families and offer something personal and touching about the victim. Having a young child of the decedent testify before the jury is always a plus. Jurors eat that up. Be selective with the photos you present.*

Prom photos. Make sure the vic is smiling and happy in the photos. Recuse any liberal judge who might have philosophical reservations about capital punishment. After ten days of bloated egos, endless iterations, and morbid humor, Linda Sanchez was completely exhausted, utterly fascinated—and slightly horrified. This area of law was like entering a dark forest for her, and nothing in ten years as a prosecutor prepared her for this. But she saw this new assignment as a challenge.

Linda caught Ron Lacy one early morning on the fourth day of the seminar at the Holiday Inn lounge.

"Hi, Mr. Lacy, my name is Linda Sanchez. I'm a deputy district attorney from L.A. May I sit down and join you for coffee?"

"Miss Sanchez, is it?"

He adjusted his Stetson respectfully. "I don't know of any attorneys in our specialty like you. Hon, want some coffee?"

"Sure. I have so many questions, but I'm embarrassed that my mind is blank." Sanchez adjusted her dark coat self-consciously.

"Sure, Hon, lemme git the waitress." Turning to the young waitress, he said, "Hey, Hon, get this little lady a coffee and me too. Add a shot of Macallan 12 in the coffee, will you?" The waitress looked at her watch in case this beastly mortician didn't realize it was seven in the morning.

The waitress said, "Sir, our bar isn't open."

Brandishing two $20 bills, Lacy asked rhetorically, "Is the bar now open?"

"Was that a double Macallan 12?"

"Thank you, precious."

As a recovering alcoholic, Linda couldn't ignore Lacy's drinking; however, she only wanted to pick his brain and learn from him. Under normal circumstances, Linda would have excoriated Lacy for calling the young waitress *Hon*. She held her tongue to squeeze out any relevant information about Lacy's extensive death penalty experience. After listening to two hours of Lacy's copious belches of advice, pontifications, crass jokes, platitudes, and empty bullshit, Linda's conflicting emotions left her both exhausted and energized. Life and death.

After his second loaded coffee, Lacy finally ended with some sage advice. "You can't do what we do without actually seeing the result at the end of the deadly road."

"What?" Sanchez caught the implication, but she wanted to make sure. "You mean—"

"Linda, you got to see an execution in person. Otherwise, your work in court is an abstraction. That defendant is a real person. Court battles are like real battles. When I was in 'Nam, we didn't think our enemy were actual people, actual human beings. They were V.C.; they were gooks. They were *Charlie*. They were nothing. Because if you saw them as human beings, you might hesitate to kill them. You can't hesitate or overthink in combat. That's just the psychology of war. Any war. When I killed a bad guy in Vietnam, I felt nothing—like I killed a rabid dog." He shoved a wad of chewing tobacco in his mouth and continued, looking pensive.

"But in this business, you *must* see the defendant as a person. Unlike actual combat, it's OK to hesitate because there might be other alternatives. Life without parole. Give the guy his life, you know? Once you go for death, you must face the consequences of your decision. You need to see a condemned man die for yourself. The viewing removes the abstraction. They are no longer an empty specter in prison garb but actual human beings. It will make you a better lawyer and, I think, a better human being. Shit, I need another scotch." Sanchez said nothing, as she was laser-focused on this man sitting across from her, mesmerized.

"You're suggesting I view an execution before I start death penalty assignments?"

"Look, you came to this convention for a reason, for an education so that you can be the best in court. I've asked around, and I hear you're one of the best in the L.A.D.A.'s office. That says a lot."

Lacy slurped his loaded coffee, then continued, "I tried a guy about three years ago, Marlo Crawford, who tortured then killed a young girl. He kept her alive for three days, beat her, then strangled her. Crawford dropped the girl like garbage in the Arkansas River. When her father viewed the body for identification, he couldn't believe the corpse was his daughter. After a few days, those submerged bodies look like fat reptiles, all bloated with few human features— tough case to prove. No DNA, no blood. Everything circumstantial. The guy had no violent record and a low I.Q. But a few shady eyewitnesses placed him near the scene of the abduction and the river at the time of the murder. Defense counsel supposedly had a strong alibi witness but never called him.

The defendant never testified to explain his whereabouts, and the jurors we spoke to after the trial talked at length during deliberations about the defendant not testifying. As you know, they can't do that— discuss a defendant's right not to testify. There was no motion for a new trial, so I guess the defense attorneys felt that those discussions during deliberation weren't important. I never question a defense attorney's strategic mistakes. I just want convictions.

"Anyway, we tried to talk to the alleged defense witness, but he disappeared. We will never know, I guess. The vagaries of trials. We got lucky." He chugged the scotch and quietly burped. "His execution is next month, and I can get you a viewing spot, front row."

Lacy slowly rose and left cash on the table. "Well, Linda, got to go. Another lecture. This Crawford case was my last death penalty, and after forty years of this, I'm getting too old. I keep that Toby Keith lyric as my mantra: *Don't let the old man in.* But after a tour in Vietnam, forty years of this crap, ulcer, diabetes, and one divorce, I call it quits. I am an old man. I need to catch up on my hunting and fishing. Linda Sanchez, I think you'll be a great lawyer in this realm of death. But don't let this business steal your humanity. We're an extraordinary breed of lawyers. I'll contact you about attending that execution, Hon."

Sanchez looked away for a second, trying to process this bombardment of information, and quickly finished her coffee. "I'll be there."

Oklahoma's "Big Mac" doesn't serve hamburgers and fries; they serve justice and death. Oklahoma's death row inmates are sent to the prison in McAlester, Pittsburg County,

Oklahoma, "The Big Mac." The condemned inmates are housed in Unit H of the facility. Named and founded by James J. McAlester, a Confederate captain who made a small fortune in coal, McAlester is a quaint town in southeastern Oklahoma, about fifty miles south of Tulsa, within the Choctaw Nation of Oklahoma. Old brick buildings dominate the commercial area, which has changed little since the Civil War. Nearby, Talawanda Lakes 1 and 2 and McAlester Lake offer abundant largemouth bass, black crappie, and spotted bass. McAlester lingers in a time warp, a Rockwellian nineteenth-century Americana postcard.

When Linda planned her trip to witness the execution in June 2010, she found a few points of interest in the town. A *Trivia Pursuit* buff, she discovered McAlester was the location of the Terry Nichols trial related to the Oklahoma City bombing in 1995. Relating to the prison, she was astonished to find information about the *Inside the Walls* sporting event in the prison that ESPN once covered—an annual rodeo by the institution that included inmates as participants.

She cynically wondered if death row inmates could participate as a last wish. In the novel and movie version of *The Grapes of Wrath,* the opening scene depicts Tom Joad's release from McAlester Prison. Woody Guthrie immortalized this event in the song "Tom Joad:"

Tom Joad got out of the old McAlester Pen; there he got his parole

After four long years on a man-killing charge, Tom Joad came a-walking down the road, poor boy

Tom Joad come a-walking down the road

Tom Joad he met a truck-driving man; there he caught him a ride

He said, "I just got loose from McAlester Pen on a charge called homicide. A charge called homicide…"

She entered the prison a few hours before the scheduled execution of Marlo Crawford, an African American age thirty-six, with a sixth-grade Mississippi education. Lacy greeted her at the reception area. Oddly, he wore lighter apparel—including a white Stetson. *Lots of psychological baggage to unpack there*, she thought. Prison officials gave all observers a brief orientation once they were in the public viewing area. She observed Lacy hugging some people, presumably the victim's family. Very little was said.

Crawford, the condemned man, had been on "death watch" for three days pursuant to the execution protocol, which meant close monitoring of Crawford to minimize any suicide attempts. Sanchez was seated next to Lacy, who whispered to her with a smirk, "I'm always curious what their last meal request is. Mr. Crawford ordered a Big Mac, fries, and a glass of milk. A Big Mac, damn. He was eating a Big Mac inside 'The Big Mac.'" He elbowed her in the ribs to make sure she caught the pun.

The last person to be executed here by electrical shock, by "Old Sparky," was in 1966. Linda would observe a lethal injection. The year before, Oklahoma was still tinkering with the most effective manner of execution after a few embarrassing malfunctions.

(Years later, in April 2014, Oklahoma executed Clayton Lockett, but not without logistical complications. The drug of choice for Lockett was midazolam, a sedative that some anesthesiologists have said is not strong enough to induce unconsciousness. For fifty minutes, the medical personnel had difficulty setting the intravenous execution line in his arms and legs.

According to the Tulsa *World,* the condemned man helped the executioners look for a good vein. The horror show continued as the handlers misplaced the line in Lockett's groin. Lockett continued to writhe in pain on the gurney in a pool of blood, and thus, the executioners aborted the execution. However, he still died. The Oklahoma legislature then expanded the execution options to include nitrogen asphyxiation, i.e., gas.)

For his death, Marlo Crawford chose an injection.

Crawford lay on a hospital gurney that was slightly inclined; a white sheet covered his body up to his heaving chest. Firm straps secured his stomach and chest. His arms extended from the gurney like he was dropping free fall from a plane, with empty eyes searching to the heavens for a God that wasn't there. Linda Sanchez couldn't look away after the needle was stuck into his throbbing vein. Hundreds of fleeting images bombarded Linda's brain, pounding her skull like a violent lightning storm: her mom, law school, boyfriends, food, East Los Angeles, running on the beach, her first sex experience, eating ice cream as a child, walking in a courtroom, having a drink with colleagues, graduation, her father. The fleeting imagery dissipated, and only one remained: a dead man.

On June 12, 2010, at 12:21 a.m., Marlo Crawford was officially pronounced dead.

***

Sanchez's trip to Oklahoma in 2010 profoundly impacted her professional and personal life, giving her a powerful impetus and direction for the former but triggering new moral, philosophical, and religious questions for the latter. After a highly successful ten-year career as a prosecutor, she was ready to commit herself to death penalty cases after returning from that memorable trip.

Her assignment placed her in the upper echelons of her profession, and when she secured the most recent death penalty conviction in 2023 of Nicolas Meza, her fifth, she became revered in and out of her office. Lawyers glanced at her differently. Judges treated her differently. She noticed law students on field trips to the courthouse point at her. News crews knew her on a first-name basis. Her quotes appeared in news periodicals. The California State Bar often requested her insight at their mandatory training seminars. She was proud of herself while she worked hard not to let these accolades get to her head, but Sanchez just wanted to continue what she had loved—work, work, work.

After her trials concluded, she would always review her cases with her investigator and legal assistants to prepare for the inevitable appeal and analyze possible trial errors. She never wanted to make the same mistake twice.

Did she fail to anticipate legal issues in the trial?

Did she research the legal motions thoroughly?

Were her examinations and cross-examinations compelling?

Did she ask the jurors the right questions during voir dire?

Were there any grounds for a new trial?

Was there any juror misconduct during deliberations?

Linda sat in her office one late afternoon two months after the Meza trial with her primary investigator, Raymond "Mon" Santos.

32

The D.A.'s office hired Santos right after he retired from the L.A. Sheriff's Office, and Sanchez used him almost exclusively, especially in death penalty cases. Santos, only five feet and nine inches tall, resembled a human vending machine——all square, mainly aging muscle and hard fat that forms in an ex-marine. He was in the First Division of the U.S. Marines that spearheaded the fight through Kuwait and Iraq in the 1990-1991 Gulf War—Operation Desert Storm. After his deployment ended, Santos joined the L.A. County Sheriff's Office. After twenty years with the Sheriff's, a bullet to the right hip during a domestic violence call triggered an early retirement. The L.A.D.A.'s Office then quickly snatched him. Santos had one lingering souvenir from the war: an onset of Parkinson's from sucking up the toxic chemicals in the air as the Marines worked their way through Iraq. He hid the condition, but Linda was aware of it.

He looked younger than fifty, with soft grey eyes and a calm disposition. Sanchez liked that part of his persona because he could extract information from reticent witnesses, not through brute force and intimidation like some of the other hotshots in the office. He was straightforward with people and garnered trust quickly—something that was difficult in the streets of Los Angeles. Growing up in the San Fernando Valley, this veteran knew all of L.A.'s dark corners, alleys, bars, and assorted hangouts, and the large amalgam of people who inhabited those worlds. His hairline began to recede at eighteen, so he shaved the skull but kept a manly mustache. He felt as comfortable talking to street thugs as he did with attorneys. Santos had a vast network of contacts in the legal world and the L.A. underworld; he knew people in high and low places. Raymond Santos was also trilingual—in English, Legalese, and Chicano street slang.

Standard English: *Nah, you're wrong about that.*

Legalese: *I take umbrage with your position and respectfully disagree.*

L.A. Chicano street slang: *Vales verga, guey. Pinche baboso!*

Her bottom line: Ramon Santos was indispensable to her success, and she trusted him immensely.

Linda peered out her office window at the grey smog settling smugly into the L.A. basin like a heavy blanket diffusing the sunlight and befouling the air.

Santos said, "Hey Lin, that Meza trial. I thought those jurors might go the other way. Lots of avenues for them to hang up the case."

He looked out the window at the Civic Center and stroked his mustache. "I mean, he had a bad record, all right. The only violence was with his wife, but he had no other convictions involving violence. What got him into prison before was a load of meth in 2010 and small stuff before that. Meza's parole agent said he was OK and always reported. Some alcohol and drugs, but the parole agent liked him. Then this."

Linda said, "Mon, you never know. Domestic violence brings out the worst. 'Member that guy? I think his name was Benny Garcia a few years ago. Hawaiian Gardens, I think. A loving husband. Then he whacks his wife with a dull machete 'cause his baloney sandwich had too much mayo. You never know." She stared at her computer screen and said, "I heard he didn't last too long at CDCR (CA Department of Corrections and Rehabilitation), but he got shanked out there in Calipat. A beef over Raman noodles or pruno or some crap like that. Those guys kill themselves over anything. You never know."

Santos said, "So, Meza burns down the house. It's just something a guy with his background wouldn't do. I've been around guys like that all my life. If he got ticked off, why not just run? He did before when he beat her up. Just run. She probably wouldn't have called the police. Let it go. And you know another thing? He really liked his kid. He fought for custody in court. We saw that family law file. When we talked to the vic's family, some had to admit he was a good father. The kid witnessed their fights, but I bet he loved his dad. Why burn down the house?"

"Damn, Ramon. I'm glad you weren't on that jury. Second thoughts about the conviction?" Linda asked.

"Nah. I'm just thinking out loud, Lin. The jury got it right."

Linda sat up in her chair with a pensive look. "I have to be honest, Mon. Of my five death penalty cases, I thought this might be the hardest to convict. I mean, this was my first death penalty arson case, where the strategy is to rule out any accidental fires. You have to prove a negative, that it was *not* an accident." Santos looked at her with a severe face and nodded in agreement. Linda continued and said, "And those experts. I thought Holder, the defense attorney, had a pretty good forensic pyro expert. And those terms they use. I thought the jurors might think it was all gibberish. *Multiple points of origin* or *V patterns*. I saw two jurors nod in agreement when the defense expert was testifying. Anytime a juror nods, he's buying everything they're saying. For a while, I had my doubts during the trial."

"But that L.A. Dodgers cap got him. It was his calling. That got him convicted because if the forensic experts negated themselves, Meza's precious cap placed him there at the time of the fire like a blue fingerprint," Santos said.

Nicolas Meza was never without his Dodgers baseball cap. He thought it brought him good luck after he used the cap to snatch a home run ball in the left field bleachers from Andre Ethier's line drive, who later autographed the inside bill of the cap. Meza sometimes slept with it.

"It bothers me a little that we didn't locate that cap in the house until *after* we went through it a few times," Linda said.

"Lin, I went through that house at least three times with the arson guys. One officer posted at the house found it right in the living room, where the investigators found Amelia's corpse. With all that rubble, I can see how we could've missed it. There wasn't much left in that house. Honest, professional mistake, Lin. Don't kill yourself over it. Sometimes, we just get lucky in this business."

Sanchez felt that small pebble gnawing in her gut. She slowly rose and grabbed her briefcase. "Gotta go, Mon. Mom promised some homemade tortillas and carnitas. I'll pack some for you for tomorrow."

"Cool. Make sure you pack her green salsa."

"And Mon, you said finding that cap before the trial was luck. I don't get convictions with luck."

CHAPTER 3

"I know in my heart I didn't do this."

Meza and his lawyers, Jeremy Holder and Wallace Whitten, sat in a holding cell a few days after the verdict, staring awkwardly at one another and discussing the guilty verdict.

Meza had two able attorneys: Jeremy Holder and Wallace Whitten. Holder was the lead counsel and one of California's most experienced death penalty defense attorneys. Also, licensed in Texas, Florida, Missouri, Oklahoma, and Arkansas, the Meza case was his third death penalty case in California. Holder trained lawyers and judges nationwide and wrote several treatises on the death penalty.

Meza was breathless and spoke slowly in staccato tones, "I… I can't believe this is happening. I know I didn't do it."

Holder, trying to reassure him, said, "Nico, that jury went on emotion. I'll file the appeal quickly, I promise. The appeal is automatic, but I wanted to clearly outline all the appellate issues. I expect to remain your counsel and the appellate team the court appoints."

Whitten added, "I feel we have some grounds for a new trial motion before your formal sentencing."

Meza asked, "What things can you argue?"

Whitten said, "We can simply argue insufficient evidence. Also, the judge should not have admitted your statement to the police. Your rights were arguably not clearly explained to you, and they used intimidation. The jury instructions were not helpful either. We asked for valid special jury instructions, but the judge ignored us. We can raise these potential appellate issues in the appeal."

Meza asked, "Wallace, can you stay on my appeal?"

Holder interrupted, "Since I was lead trial counsel, I will be the only one that will remain at the appellate phase. I agree with Wallace. We have lots of potential issues.

"First, the trial judge might have messed up some of his rulings. Your statement to the police was not properly Mirandized."

"But I spoke to them voluntarily. I had nothing to hide. When I learned what happened, I went to them to give a statement." Meza said.

Holder shook his head and said, "Yeah, but you admitted to fighting with Amelia and hitting her a few times in the past."

"But I tried to explain that to the cops and the jury. I told them they were just normal fights like all couples have—nothing too serious. But that lady D.A. just twisted that around."

Holder said, "Well, anyway, that might be an important issue on appeal. Also, we will continue to interview the jurors to see if there were any improprieties during deliberations. For example, some may have read about this case in the newspapers. Your case received a lot of press coverage. Sometimes, jurors talk about the case with others during the breaks when they're not supposed to."

Meza became frenetic and said, "I still don't know about the cap. Mr. Whitten, you told me once that you would follow a theory that someone planted it at the house. Holder, I told you I was at that bar."

Holder said, "I know, but that bartender was no help and couldn't remember the days you were there." Holder turned to Whitten and shook his head.

Meza said, "I go nowhere without that damn cap. I thought it was my good luck charm.

Nothing bad ever happens to me when I wear that cap. I would never have left it behind anywhere. I just know in my heart I didn't leave that cap there! I left a day before with that cap. Some luck, huh? That lucky cap is gonna get me clipped by the government.

"My mom knows I always keep it hidden in my bedroom drawer. I still think someone planted it there to set me up, man. Maybe the cops. L.A.P.D. don't like me. Too many run-ins with them. I even punched one of those pricks. That felt good. They could have done it, man. I explained all that to those jurors, but they never listened."

Whitten: "We couldn't find anything along those lines. The jury assumed you accidentally dropped it at the house the night of the fire."

Holder waited a few seconds until his client calmed down and said, "The automatic appeals will take years. The California governor put a moratorium on executions in 2019, and you'll remain on death row in San Quentin. I just got a feeling that your appeal has a good chance." Whitten's subtle facial expression showed a question mark.

Holder added, "Nico, because of the governor's moratorium, there's also a bit of good news. CDCR might transfer you from San Quentin to a better facility with more liberties. San Quentin sucks, man. You're in a small cell twenty-three hours a day. The California voters passed Proposition sixty-six a few years ago to allow transfers of death-row inmates elsewhere so they can work in the facilities to help pay restitution for victims."

Meza said, "Shit, I never worked outside of prison—you think I'm gonna work inside?"

CHAPTER 4

En route from downtown to her mom's house in Boyle Heights, Sanchez welcomed the L.A. traffic. Driving at the maximum rush-hour speed limit during L.A. rush hour—five miles an hour—gave the lawyer time to reflect as she cranked up Taylor Swift and Lizzo anthologies, singing along the way. Hopping onto the 101 Freeway and snaking eastward, the L.A. Civic Center faded away like an old photo in her rear-view mirror—along with work, lawyers, and courts. She could smell and taste home-cooked Mexican food that would greet her at her mom's house.

Her mom, Rita, didn't want to move from Boyle Heights. "All my friends are here, Linda. The markets are near. The bus stops are nearby. We've been here thirty years. I raised you here, *mija*. You always talk to me about the crime here. Don't you think I get scared? But that's the way it is here. We live in Los Angeles. Crime is all over. No more talk about moving!"

Linda Sanchez lived most of her life in the Boyle Heights sector of Los Angeles, located on a small bluff east of the Los Angeles River. "Boyle" replaced its historical name, *Paredón Blanco* ("White Bluff"), after Andrew Boyle purchased 22 acres on its bluff and grew and sold wine ("*Paredón Blanc*") in the nineteenth century. Notably, in the early twentieth century, Boyle Heights did not share a common feature with other communities: racially restrictive housing covenants that excluded people of color. Thus, the culturally diverse community thrived as a center of Jewish, Mexican, and Japanese immigrants. The community still retains its Japanese cultural influence, with Japanese churches, schools, and temples sprinkled within the community. The Jewish influence still remains in the form of the Breed Street Shul.

Linda accepted her mother's rationale as sound. Where would she move? Linda had no alternative to offer. She lived in a small 2-bedroom apartment three blocks from Santa Monica beach. Her and her mother in a small apartment? No way. Even with her solid income, buying a house in Los Angeles was out of her reach. And her mom would feel isolated.

Her mother greeted her with a comforting hug and a slobbering kiss on the cheeks. "You haven't come around in three weeks! And you look skinny. Something wrong?"

"Ma, I'm good. I eat well. I smell carnitas. Gimme a tortilla with butter!"

"You still going to A.A.? And Sunday mass? Don't miss. I think it helps you. It's cheaper than therapy. Even though you look thin, your face looks healthy. I saw you on TV, but you never talk about your work."

Rita Ayala Sanchez bore her two children at seventeen and nineteen. Linda was her first, and then baby Julio followed. She never complained about working two to three jobs to support her children, especially after their father left. The only specious explanation she offered for his departure was that *he didn't love us anymore and found another woman.* Nothing further. The fatherless void in Linda's life never filled. Linda and Julio wanted to know the real reason for his departure but never found the right time to ask. So, the subject lingered like acrid air over the years.

"So, has Rob visited you lately in your dreams?" Rita's face showed concern.

"No, Ma. But I'll talk to him soon. I miss him, and I know he misses me."

Rita said, "I miss him, too. Tell him Hi, for me, OK? Hey, Lin, do you know the secret to these carnitas? Milk. I add milk to the lard when I fry the meat. Somehow, it makes it sweeter. Don't know why."

"Well, Ma, milk caramelizes at about a hundred and twenty degrees and releases sugar compounds to the meat. It also tenderizes the pork."

"Gorda, save that information for your Trivial Pursuit *chingadera.* I spent all that money on your Catholic school. You have too much stored in that head." She passed a fresh tortilla from the *comal* and pointed to the butter. "And don't get that on your jacket. It looks expensive. And the cleaners always charge too much."

With a worried look, Linda said, "Mom, you sure you're doing OK here? If you need more money, just ask me." She placed the buttery carnitas on her plate and packed it with green onions, lime juice, guacamole, and a stout jalapeno. Her nimble fingers wrapped her burrito, and she asked, "Don't you need a new washer?"

"No. I'm good." Rita walked away from the stove, sat near her daughter around the Formica table, and said, "*Mija,* Julio's out."

"When?"

"A few days ago."

"Has he come by?"

"Two nights ago. He looked healthy; he had put on some weight. He hasn't had good Mexican food in a long time."

Linda swallowed the last piece of her burrito and sat back, bracing for the bad news. "And his plans?"

"I told his parole officer he could stay here for a while. He had no other place except the streets. I couldn't see him at one of those homeless camps on Skid Row, *mija.* He needs to be safe. He will look for a job. He learned how to cook in prison, and he said he liked it. Maybe he might find work as a cook."

"Ma, he needs to get his place. You know he attracts bad things, bad people. You don't want to put yourself in danger because of him. Julio needs to grow up."

"*Mija*, because of what happened last time the police arrested him, *you* also attract danger here in my house. Please don't take that the wrong way. That's the way it is." She clutched her daughter's hand and stroked her hair.

"I understand, Ma. I need to go. Lots of work," Linda said. "Take some food. I have some wrapped tortillas for you."

"It's OK, Mom, I lost my appetite."

Julio Sanchez spent five years in state prison, mostly in administrative segregation—*ad seg* in the prison parlance, relative isolation reserved for sex offenders and snitches. He pled guilty to drug sales, two hundred thousand dollars' worth of meth.

Connected with one of the most powerful street gangs, the Sunshine Projects, gang members instructed Julio to stash the drugs before the subsequent street distribution. The Sunshine Projects gang originated in the Sunshine Projects in Montebello in the late 1960s. Eventually, it grew into one of the most powerful gangs in Southern California, with a firm grasp within the California State Prison system. Julio breached gang protocol, hiding the gang's stash in his mother's house. Linda discovered the drugs one day while helping her mom clean the house and had no choice but to report it. This decision tormented Linda for the rest of her life.

Offered probation by the prosecutor in return for naming associates,

Julio refused to cooperate, pled guilty, and the court sentenced him to five tough years.

Under normal circumstances, Julio would be a dead man as soon as he entered the gates of state prison. A *green light* from one of the gang's lieutenants was tantamount to a death warrant. He only survived Corcoran State Prison because he placed himself in *ad seg,* and the green light never flashed. A gang lieutenant, Hector "Foster Boy" Allen, put the word out not to harm Julio. Even the correctional officers treated him well. From a business standpoint, it was a wise decision for the gang; Allen did not want to draw attention to the gang if someone murdered Julio because the law enforcement compass would point directly to "Foster Boy" Allen and the Sunshine Projects crew. But Julio still had a debt to pay, and the Sunshine Projects would be waiting for him upon his release to collect the two-hundred-thousand-dollar debt in cash—or in kind.

One prison would replace another.

***

"Miss Sanchez, you're pathetic."

A month after the Meza trial, Linda spoke to third-year law students at her alma mater, the U.C.L.A. School of Law. During her time with the D.A.'s Office, she maintained a close rapport with the law school through volunteer programs she initiated, like presentations, mentoring, and training. She was now in a grand lecture hall before fifty third-year law students, months away from the California bar exam and their golden ticket into the legal profession.

"Excuse me, miss, what did you say?" Linda heard the comment in the rear but wanted to offer the declarant, a young Hispanic female, a chance to explain herself. The lecture hall shut down into silence. "And what is your name, miss?"

"First, I don't go by 'miss.' I prefer the neopronoun 'ze; it's gender neutral. Miss Sanchez, do you go by 'Miss'?" she said in a tone dripping with sarcasm.

"Ze, 'Miss' is OK. You can just call me Linda. It won't offend me, and I don't need to crawl to a safe space if you call me any other names, derogatory or not." A few students giggled in the back. "I was about to speak about potential employment with the Los Angeles District

42

Attorney's Office, but you wanted to say something, Ze? Why do you think I'm pathetic? The last time I heard someone call me that was a serial pedophile that I convicted before he went to Pelican Bay for seventy years."

Linda waited for the nervous laughter to abate among the students and said, "So, Ze, I will respectfully yield the floor to you."

"I don't appreciate your sarcasm. That sounds like a microaggression, Sanchez. This'll be the last time you come here, Miss Sanchez."

"How does one cancel another person, Ze? Do you wave a magic wand, then, POOF!

"CANCELLED! Now that sounds like a microaggression, Ze, or it might even be a macro or maxi aggression!"

"What the hell is a maxi aggression, Linda?" said Ze, scribbling notes.

"It's nothing. I just made the friggin word up, Ze. So, Ze, why do you think I'm pathetic?"

"Yeah, Linda, I think you are pathetic because you send people to their deaths, and most of them are people of color and poor. I read somewhere that you belong to this club called *The Nickel Choir* because you have five convictions that sent human beings to death row. You are nothing but a *vendida*, a sell-out to your own people." A few students nodded their heads in tacit agreement. "How do you live with yourself?"

"Well, Ze, technically, I do not send convicted defendants anywhere; a trial judge does that. You should have learned that in your first-year crim pro class. Perhaps this law school can invite those judges who imposed death penalties so you can call them names. And you could also invite those jurors who voted for death so you can have your way with them, Ze.

"But let's digress to your first comment about me being pathetic. Ze, you're partially correct. I am pathetic. Every time I wake up and see myself in the mirror, I see a pathetic, broken human being. A person who almost committed suicide by drinking a half liter of vodka daily after her husband and unborn child died; a pathetic person who nearly lost her bar license; a pathetic person who has nightmares of those she's convicted awaiting execution and their victims; a pitiful person who spends eighty hours a week working with no semblance of a social life. From my Catholic background, I grapple with the death penalty philosophically and morally. Yeah, I'm pathetic." The rest of the class sat nervously in rapt attention, and some closed their laptops and notepads.

Linda said, "But Ze, I will also tell you why I am *not* pathetic like you think. I am not pathetic for convicting those defendants who committed heinous acts that are beyond the imagination or comprehension of most people. My first death penalty case was a guy who sliced open his young wife's womb with a box cutter after she left him. She was six months pregnant and lived for a few seconds long enough to see her in-utero baby dead in her womb. It was a girl. Quite a fucking gender reveal, huh? I don't feel pathetic for convicting that prick.

"Ze, I know GEN X, millennials, or GEN Z—or whatever generational sticker you attach—talk about microaggression. What kind of microaggression did that guy commit? Answer that one, Ze. As you young women will soon learn, I've faced all forms of aggression my entire career: bitch, sell-out, spic, and the C word that rhymes with punt. It just dissipates into white noise.

"What's that other term or phenomenon? Safe place? Someone needs to go to a safe place if he/she/them/they feel mean people attacked them. Is that right, Ze? You seek a secure place like a terrified five-year-old. When I was a student here, my safe place was my old Toyota. I slept in it four days a week in a Westwood parking lot because I couldn't afford those expensive apartments along Gayley Avenue. I commuted from Boyle Heights. Later, I had another safe place at the bottom of a vodka bottle. But I survived, and I'm stronger from the experience. I haven't had a drink in seventeen years, two months, but I'm tempted every day. Right now, in February 2024, I'm still tempted. If any of you offered me a bottle of scotch or vodka, I might grab it.

"But you know what, Ze? Someday, when you grow up, pass the bar, and enter the real world south of Wilshire Boulevard, the best thing you can do with your priceless bar card is challenge me in court. I know you will be a formidable opponent. Become the best damn defense attorney who can represent those defendants facing the death penalty. Work on the various innocence projects. Use that bloated, pent-up anger you have stored inside you for something good and decent because calling people silly names accomplishes nothing and gives the name-caller a warped sense of satisfaction. Now, *that's* pathetic, Ze. Let's get back to the reason I came here and discuss future job opportunities with the L.A. District Attorney."

Some students rose with a vigorous standing ovation. Ze remained seated but respectfully nodded her head at Linda.

***

Plopping down on her old sofa and tossing her shoes, Linda opened a window that invited the cool waft of the salty Pacific Ocean to drift into her tiny apartment. Wallie found his usual place curled up near the sunny window. She found this place off Santa Monica Boulevard five years ago and hoped to live here forever. Within walking distance to a few small cafes and delis, the apartment was within a smelling distance from the Santa Monica beach. Collapsing onto the sofa, she dove into a heavy slumber.

Hi babe, I missed you. Had a long day.

We haven't visited in a long time. Lin, I wish I was there with you.

Rob, you are. Every day. Every night. Time is different since you left. The days are short because of my work. But the nights are long when we talk and longer when we don't.

Your mom said you're too skinny. Have you been eating well? Remember when we started a vegan kick? That didn't last too long. You have too much Mexican in you. You need your mom's food. Me too. I wish I could have some now. Little Linda would have been an adult by now. She would have all your good qualities. Your easy smile. Your rich chocolate eyes. That's what got me hooked on you, the eyes—they hypnotized me when I saw you that first day in law school. When I sat behind you in torts class, even the back of your head was beautiful. Little Linda would also probably inherit your fearlessness, attacking something directly without worrying about consequences. That's you. You fuckin' argued about anything in class. You even challenged the profs, you pain in the ass. Little Linda would have been a brilliant lawyer like her mom. I'll visit again soon.

"*Rob, wait…*"

When she woke the following morning, it was nine. Although deaf and arthritic, old Wallie knew when to eat. Seven o'clock sharp. Linda never slept past five. Wallie, after four attempts, jumped onto her bed to wake her. It was breakfast, and Linda forgot to close her blinds when she fell asleep. The California sun splashed her face with abrasive heat like a warm shower.

45

Things to do on Saturday morning:

Jog along the beach. Build up to five miles without stopping. Buy groceries.

Laundry. *I need clean chonis.*

Then, a few hours back at the office. Trials were coming up. More motions. More death.

***

After entering the courthouse, Ramon Santos hopped onto a squashy leather chair. "Mr. Santos, howya doing?"

"Good, Eddie. Make these wingtips shine. I wanna see myself in the reflection. I have to go in front of a jury today, and I gotta look good from head to toe. One of the first things the jurors see is how the cop dresses."

Edward "Shoeshine Eddie" Hager had worked near the entrance on the bottom floor of the criminal court building since Jimmy Carter's presidency. He was the courthouse answer to a Walmart greeter. An anachronistic profession, his shoeshine business thrived because there were few active competitors. He made it a point not to draw too much attention to himself, and his looks didn't stand out—seventy-three years old, sinewy, bald with no facial hair, a gap tooth, but with a non-threatening, easy smile. These features were conducive to an essential feature of his business—trust.

The genesis of Eddies' nickname—along with his profession—goes back to 1968, Long Binh Post, South Vietnam, when he was part of a dangerous *Dust-Off* unit that would retrieve soldiers from hot landing zones. One day after a harrowing rescue operation, Private Hager returned to his base camp in a foul mood after retrieving five wounded U.S. Marines, one dead Marine, and a few body parts of others. As he headed to his Quonset hut to sleep, drink, and cry inside, Hager passed by a junior captain who had been in-country only two days. The young captain's uniform was still military crisp, bereft of sweat, dirt, blood, or wrinkles, like he was in a Fourth of July parade. The cherubic Captain formally saluted Hager, but the latter reciprocated not with a stern military salute but with his erect middle finger. For this breach of military protocol, the baby captain ordered Hager to polish officers' boots for two weeks. *You will lick some boots for a while, Private!* Hager's *boot-licking* assignment was the most relaxing part—and the only cherished memory—of his Vietnam deployment.

After the war, Hager spent the next ten years in the throes of a heroin addiction, spending most of his civilian life in jails, in hospitals, on the streets of Pico Rivera, and in the criminal courts. After a court appearance one day in 1980, Hager spotted the empty shoeshine chair that invited him, climbed on, and took a nap, trying to ward off a hangover. Hager didn't realize that the previous shoeshine guy had passed away a week before. Eddie woke up as a patron approached and asked, "How much?"

Eddie—waking from his nap—responded, "Ten dollars," and started to shine. Eddie cleaned up his life, became an enterprise squatter, and inherited the shoeshine stand along with its accouterments, horsehair brushes, polishes, and the prized inheritance—a 1940s tufted, exquisitely plush leather chair for his new customers, some who napped during the shoeshine. No one asked questions about the previous shoeshine guy— Hager just started shining shoes and has continued ever since. At seventy-three years of age, his fingers are now as nimble and strong as they were when he was a *boot-licking* private at Long Binh Post, South Vietnam.

But shining shoes was not his only enterprise. In the gutters of the murky world of lawyers, cops, investigators, and the myriad criminal elements lurking around the courts, some knew him as an independent professional—a paid informant. To a small coterie of trusted clients, he provided valuable information.

There are certain professions where clients become too comfortable and inadvertently divulge private information: psychologists, barbers, hookers, priests—and shoeshine workers. To most clients, Eddie was just a court jester, a dumb, happy dork whom no one took seriously. Who would? He shined shoes for a living. *The poor dude saw too much combat. Just a dunce!* But those who knew him as a snitch knew that his memory was phenomenal, and his information was usually sound. He worked on consignment only if the info was worth something. No one within the group was aware of the other. Only Shoeshine Eddie knew. And Ramon Santos was one of his trusted clients.

With no one nearby, Eddie said, "Hey, Santos. Maybe this is nothing, but I was shining this guy's shoes a few weeks ago. He was on his cell phone talking to someone. He never mentioned the other guy's name on the other line." Lowering his voice, Eddie inched closer and said, "I picked up bits and pieces. But I could connect the dots. My Spanish is good. Santos, the two were talking about a Dodger cap and a house fire. Something about people dying and a trial. They were both joking about the incident. It seemed like, but I'm not sure, the other guy was saying he was at some house and put a cap there. They didn't mention names or places. Maybe it's nothing. But then I remember that case you worked on a few months ago. Came out in the L.A. Times. I gotta have a few copies for clients, but I also read the paper, mainly the sports pages. I don't know if it's connected, but parts of the conversation might have fit. Maybe not."

Santos asked, "What did this guy look like?"

"Nothing distinctive, maybe about thirty. Chicano. Thin. A black mustache. Not much else."

"That probably narrows it down to about five million people in Los Angeles?"

"Hey. Don't be insulting, man. I was busy. He probably had Court. It was a busy morning, and he was in a hurry. I had customers waiting."

"Nothing else?"

"Nah. Sorry." Santos took out a twenty and began stepping down. "Oh shit, I remember. Shit, his shoes. Santos, his shoes."

"What about them?" Santos asked. "You ever see *Zoot Suit*?"

"Yeah. I saw the play at the Taper in '96 with Esmerelda. The movie was wonderful, too. I'm an Edward James Olmos fan. *Ganas*! Member? *Stand by Me*."

"OK, I guess that's a yes. But the point I'm making is that the old-time zoot suiters wore very distinctive shoes. That's what this guy had. A 1920s dress shoe in zoot style, two-toned, white, and grey. Partial wing tip. You don't see those around anymore. When I was a kid on the east side, I remember lots of the *chucos* wore them. I saw an old photo of my Mexican grandpa from Monterey Park in a zoot suit. They looked cool. *Toda madre,* Santos. Old school. Anyway, the ones I saw this guy wearing were nice, and I had to charge him extra because they took longer to shine, being two-toned."

"OK. Eddie, call me if you see this guy again. You have my cell. *Ganas!*"

CHAPTER 5

After the trial, Nicolas Meza's defense team attempted to contact jurors, searching for a legal *Hail Mary* to raise on appeal. The trial court admonished the jurors that they did not have to speak to any of the attorneys. Sometimes, attorneys would find improprieties during the jurors' deliberations that might be the basis for a new trial or other grounds for post-conviction relief.

The five jurors who agreed to speak with them all had variations of the same point: although they may have harbored doubts at the trial's early stage, the defendant's baseball cap sealed his fate. The cap, with burn marks and smoke residue, put him in the home at the time of the arson and was as good as a fingerprint. The attorneys found no juror misconduct.

Holder told Whitten, "Our guy's appellate case is all shriveled up like burnt bacon. We have few appellate issues."

Jeremy Holder was also well-known for hosting an annual barbeque every fall before Thanksgiving at his gorgeous Spanish-style home in Pacific Palisades overlooking the Pacific Ocean. He took pride in preparing the center of attraction: Texas-style beef brisket. At least three-hundred attended in the past—attorneys, judges, administrators of the California Bar Association, and a sprinkling of minor celebrities and politicians. Some invitees came not so much for the beef brisket but to gawk at celebrities amidst the beautiful grounds that were a featured cover in *Los Angeles Homes Magazine.*

Linda only went after Santos encouraged her to do so. "Let your hair down, Lin, as long as you don't talk shop with Holder. You need to relax more."

Sanchez was agoraphobic at these large social gatherings and drank some cold tea at the party's periphery. Small talk was not in her. A blues band belched endless tunes of love, hate, loss, and sadness. The sun was an hour away from setting as Sanchez sat alone and enjoyed the view of the Pacific, now placid and deep blue in late afternoon.

"Hey, Miss Sanchez. How are you doing?" Holder startled her.

"Where's your drink? I don't want these two bars going to waste."

"Thanks. I'm not drinking tonight. Splendid party. What a lovely home. Did I just see Jay Leno?"

Holder said, "Yeah, we share our love of cars. I have a few. Not as many as he does. I sometimes go over to his massive garage and see him tinker. I want Jay's Cobra, a perfect piece of machinery." He looked at her intensely, like he wanted to analyze her mannerisms, trying to figure out what lay beneath her thick exterior. *She is a tough nut to crack,* he thought.

Jeremy Holder was in his mid-forties, thin and wiry, a few inches over six feet. Specs of premature grey hair on the sides of his scalp gave him a faux aura of erudition and wisdom. He had the ubiquitous hipster-West-L.A.-ultra-cool six o'clock facial shadow with a $300 haircut that looked like he woke up in a tornado. Linda envied his elegant manicure and trimmed eyebrows. No socks—just ultra-soft Italian loafers. Sanchez guessed Holder's daily health regimen: he drank his gluten-free swamp-green smoothie while exercising at forty percent on his Nordic after an hour of level 5 Pilates, finishing with an hour of Buddhist chanting and capped with avocado toast and organic, range-free egg whites. Or maybe the guy just ate *Fruit Loops* in his robe for breakfast.

Armed with self-deprecating humor and a Matthew McConaughey-Texas twang, his charm could dismantle most. He loved to surf and tinker with his precious cars whenever he could. He seemed easygoing and overly polite and was starting his third marriage to a former model, Sara. "So, Linda Sanchez, what's your story? How the hell did you get into the death penalty business?" His theatrical Texas twang wasn't as pronounced as in court, where it was endearing to the jurors. She couldn't tell if he was flirting with her or interrogating her.

"Don't you feel guilty putting people to death?" Holder asked.

"Mr. Holder, I'm enjoying this beautiful view. Do you think I'll let you lasso me into a needless colloquy about the death penalty? I've never been a big fan of *The Godfather*. My boss is always quoting it until I finally saw it recently. I get it. Great movie. A character in the movie says *this is the business we've chosen, and we have to live with it.*"

Holder said, "Hyman Roth."

"Yeah. This is the business we've chosen, and I don't have to explain it to anybody, especially an attorney who represents some of the worst human beings."

Holder dismissively swatted away her last comment like a pesky fly, pivoted, and said, "Lin, you know what the key is for this beef brisket? It's the wood. In Texas, it's the oak 'cause it burns slowly. And that smell. Can you smell it? Oak and barbeque, nothing like it. I make my sauce, and I'm thinking of producing it commercially. I make it a little heavy with chile powder; it kicks it. It's gonna be dope, Linda. I'm gonna name it *Legally Insane Texas Barbeque*. What do you think, Linda?"

"Sounds catchy," Linda said.

"Make sure you get plenty and take some home. I see Judge Winford—gotta talk to him." "Thanks, Mr. Holder."

"Jeremy, please."

"OK, Jeremy."

Linda took a generous bite of the melted brisket with a smoky taste that lingered deep past the tongue, down through the throat, and below. Heaven. Holder was a charmer, and his *Legally Insane Texas BBQ* was as good as he promised. But she still didn't like the guy, Texas charm and all.

***

"My name is Linda, and I'm an alcoholic." From the A.A. group, "Hi, Linda!"

"Linda, you've been with us for several months, and we finally get to hear you. No pressure, but you can say anything within your comfort zone."

Encircled by five strangers, Linda rose and said, "I started drinking a lot a few years ago. I don't blame my work, which is high pressure for most. I have to admit I like the pressure. I love my career, and my job keeps me sane and stable. I became an alcoholic after my family suffered a tragedy on July 8, 2005, at 7:21 in the evening near Interstate 405. I will not share the details, but that made me an alcoholic. I know we all have excuses to drink ourselves to death. But that's mine."

Linda paused to gather her thoughts, then continued, "My mom saved my life. She told me I would soon lose everything and end up pushing a Von's shopping cart under a bridge. She did something she'd never done before, even when I was a kid—she slapped me hard across my face. That slap woke me up on different levels. Anyway, I took a month off work with her and my boss's support, and I forced myself into rehab. My mom

51

saved me. I've never taken a drink since. Thank you for listening."

"No, Linda, we should thank you."

***

Joe Gomez sat at his kitchen table eating breakfast in his small Culver City apartment.

When his cell phone rang, he rose and went to his bedroom, away from his wife, to take the call. On the other end of the call, a voice said, *"Sup, Ese?"*

Gomez whispered, "Hey, homes."

"Whatcha doing?"

"Eating breakfast, dawg. My *ruca* made me *papas* and eggs. Again. That's all the *vieja* knows how to make. *Papas* and anything left in the kitchen. *Papas* and chorizo. *Papas* and hamburger helper. *Papas* and spam. *Papas* and *Top Ramen*, man. Torture, bro. The other day, I was eating my Frosted Flakes, and I thought she might put some in the friggin' bowl. She thinks we're *pinche* Irish, all potatoes. Even when I take a dump, my crap looks like a brown russet."

"Listen, guey, don't talk about that other thing too much. I heard you were saying stuff about it. I won't like it if I hear you talking more. Anything. Facebook. Phone. Especially to the viejas. You know how they gossip."

Gomez said, "*You* were the one who called me last time, *puto.* I was in the courthouse when you started fuckin' bragging. Getting my shoes shined. Nobody heard nothing. *La neta.*"

"You were in the courthouse during our conversation? People can— what's that pinche word? You know a lot of words, like El Guapo from The Three Amigos. He liked that pinche word—plethora. Órale! So, what's that word again I was thinking about?"

"*Eavesdrop,* homes. *Eavesdrop,*" Gomez said as he took a bite of his eggs and potatoes burrito with a side of hash browns.

"Yeah, eavesdrop. That's righteous, man. Someone can eavesdrop into conversations; know what I'm saying?"

"Nah. When I talked to you at the courthouse, no one heard. Shoeshine Eddie was working on my shoes, homes. That *vato* just shines shoes. The dude's not *metiche*. Doesn't talk much until I give him the ten *lanas* for the shine. Not too much upstairs, know what I mean?

Probably saw too much combat in Vietnam. PTD. He got PTD; I read about those guys. They got messed up from the war."

"That's PTSD, pendejo. I think PTD is a sexual disease homes. Anyway, you gotta be careful, man. I got the feria for the job, bro, 'cause you helped; I'll cut you some. I got a thousand dollars, and I can cut you two hundred bolas. Easy money, dude. Just to put that baseball cap there. The dude told me never to contact him anymore. He scares me. Let me get that feria to you, OK?"

"Nel."

"Why not, Bro?"

"'Cause I don't, man. Just no."

"OK, bro, righteous. I respect that. Check this out: 'I want to avoid a plethora of more phone calls.' Pretty chingón, eh?"

"OK, Guapo." Gomez hung up and returned to the kitchen to finish his potato-infused breakfast.

***

A lazy Sunday morning.

Sanchez was groggy when she woke and felt like those long-ago hangovers. In the bathroom, she stood on the body dysmorphic apparatus—her bathroom scale—and stared at it for a few seconds. The same stubborn number stared back at her, mocking her. Maybe it was stuck. She shifted her weight to her left foot on the scale; she lost half a pound. Reaching momentarily for a towel, she lost two pounds for a few seconds. She held her breath for five seconds, then quickly exhaled. Same number. Crap. Does air weigh anything? Let me take a quick pee, then weigh again.

She changed, peed, tiptoed onto the scale, and held her breath. Exhaling, she peered down at the digital reading, waited a few seconds, and kicked the scale, stubbing her big toe.

Damn scale. Maybe it needs new batteries.

After her morning run on Santa Monica beach and Sunday mass, Sanchez was back in her office. Solitude. No phone calls. No interruption. No water cooler gossip. Just her and her work. Inhaling the crisp Pacific air gave her lungs a deep clean and exfoliated some rough spots in her

53

mind, smoothing out some bad memories. She reviewed the Meza reports that she had read dozens of times, but she just wanted to look for any clues that might explain the oversight of the cap. *How did we miss it? Trained investigators and forensic experts, not to mention the defense team, had combed through that charred house, and a rookie cop guarding the house finds it?* She briefly interviewed him, and he told her he wasn't looking for anything. He saw the bill sticking out from some ashes in the living room and retrieved it.

She kept suppressing the nagging thought that someone planted the cap after the fire.

No, that's not possible. *But hypothetically, could one of our investigators or street cops have put it there? Why? A beef with Meza?* He had a track record with cops. He even had an assault incident involving an officer from the L.A.P.D. about fifteen years ago. Her imagination and fear were running ahead of her intellect and common sense. Think logically. Think rationally. No one planted that cap. Meza was there. He did it. And justice prevailed.

That vexatious pebble, however, was still there.

***

Monday mornings at the Clara Foltz Criminal Justice Center are the busiest. Ramon Santos was rushing to the fifth floor to testify at a preliminary hearing. Following the large herd of human cattle trampling through security, he didn't want to be late. One of the most important lessons he retained from the U.S. Marine Corps—be on time.

As he cleared security, he spotted them—the shoes. Two-tone grey/white zoot suit shoes that contrasted with other shoes in the crowd like technicolor in an old black and white movie. Santos thought, *who wears those shoes after 1960*? The shoes scampered ahead of him, approaching an elevator. (Santos later told Linda he could hear the soundtrack to *Stayin' Alive* in his mind when he saw the shoes.) Attached to the zoot suit two-tones was a skinny Hispanic kid with a thick beard, about six feet tall. He wore a navy-blue pressed shirt and dark slacks courtesy of the Salvation Army Thrift Store. But those shoes—a piece of sartorial art that deserved to be in a museum, encased behind glass.

The shoes exited onto the fifth floor and Department 33, criminal.

Santos scanned the court calendar to check for names and entered the courtroom. When the clerk announced the name, *Joe Gomez,* the shoes approached the judge. Attached to the shoes was Joe Gomez, en route to his sentencing. He picked up his second felony, both second-degree burglaries, and the court put him on probation.

Santos then noticed Gomez's probation officer, Dan Fuller, outside court, speaking with him like a teacher chewing out a truant. Fuller and Santos were casual friends from his years with the sheriff's office, and the former was a year from retirement with the Probation Department.

After the shoes departed, Santos approached Fuller and asked, "Hey Dan, that guy Gomez you were talking to."

"What about him? He's a nice kid, but I can't see him avoiding prison in the future with two felonies, but he's been OK with compliance."

Santos asked, "Can you show me his jacket?"

"Sure. Is there something I need to know? Mon, you mostly handle homicides."

"May be nothing. I'll call you, thanks."

As he left the courthouse, he passed Shoeshine Eddie, who made a subtle hand gesture to stop and whispered, "You see him?"

Santos nodded and said, "Yeah, that was the guy. Cool shoes, huh? I owe you, Eddie."

"No time for a quick shine? I'll give you a freebie. Mon, your shoes look like they've been slogging through a field of cow shit. In my profession, that's called *aggravated footwear abuse,* bro. Look it up in the penal code."

***

Linda sat impatiently in her office, waiting as her three o'clock appointment arrived.

"Hi, Officer Ganz. Come in. Please sit down. I know we spoke before the Meza trial early last year. I'm doing a routine follow-up that helps me and my investigative staff. There is no such thing as a perfect jury trial, even when you get good results. I never want to make the same mistake twice." Sanchez closed the office door and began pacing, making the young officer nervous.

With a glowing Huntington Beach surfer tan, Ganz sported a cropped

55

military-style peroxide-blond haircut and exuded a casual, laid-back persona. Three years removed from the police academy, he looked like he was still playing high school football, hanging out at rowdy keg parties on the beach, and dating cheerleaders. Linda remembered watching 1960s surfing movies with her mom, who had a crush on the popular teenage heart-throb Troy Donahue. Ganz could have been Troy Donahue's grandkid. Strenuous efforts to stimulate facial hair were likely abandoned, although a few nubs squeaked out. But he sported a tiny tattoo on his forearm that he hoped gave him some street and beach cred. It was either a rattler or a fat, menacing worm.

"OK. I thought I did something wrong. That was my first time testifying in court and in a death penalty case." Ganz said.

"No. You did very well. Your testimony was an integral part of our success."

"Thanks. That means a lot coming from you, for sure. Man, I thought the defense attorney would grill me more. In the back of my mind, I thought that lawyer dude might accuse me of planting that cap at the crime scene. You know how those defense attorneys are, always planting some bullshit idea in the jurors' minds. But he was pretty mild. I thought I did well, for sure."

"Officer Ganz. Wow, you have such keen insight for your first trial. You're likely to get tougher lawyer-dudes in the future, for sure."

"Call me Paul."

"Officer Ganz. Tell more about your assignment monitoring the house where the arson occurred. Let me be more specific. How long were you on this assignment before you found that cap?"

Ganz licked his dry lips and said, "Well, let's see. They put me on that rotation for a two-week shift from six p.m. to six a.m. I got lots of comp time—I'm saving my money to buy a '68 black Barracuda. That's a four-barrel with two-hundred and seventy-five horsepower!"

Linda said, "Gnarly! Good for you. That's a bitchin' ride, Paul, a chick magnet. Anyone ever tell you that you look like Troy Donahue?"

Confused, Ganz asked, "Who?"

Linda said, "Never mind. According to my notes, your assignment started about three months after the homicide, correct?"

"Yeah, that's about right. Yeah, I remember 'cause I just returned from my Costa Rica vacay. I went surfing there with buddies from Redondo

Beach. Those beaches got righteous curls! You ever surf at midnight, Miss Lawyer?"

Linda said, "No. Why don't you hop off your surfboard for a sec and return to this case?" Ganz said, "OK, cool. The home looked pretty messed up. Poor kid."

Sanchez quit pacing, sat down, and stared out her office window. "So, how many officers monitored that house after all the investigators and forensics people left?"

Now Ganz stiffened, wondering what she was after. "No, I couldn't know. I just got my weekly assignment at the station."

"Did you ever come across Nicolas Meza on the street?"

"No, ma'am. I'm assigned to the west side. Westwood, Santa Monica. It's pretty chill there. Nothing like this. Never met Meza."

"Did his name ever come up that you know of?" "I never heard of this dude until the trial."

"How *did* you hear about him?"

"Just station talk. All gossip. Nothing really. But I heard he got into a beef with some off-duty officers at a bar in Montebello. Nothing serious, for sure. All innocent."

"So, what cop did Meza have a beef with?" She asked.

Ganz looked down at his feet and slowly inhaled. Sanchez had seen that look before when she grills a nervous witness. "Well, this is just gossip. And I don't have any personal knowledge about this. But the cop's name is Ordoñez. He might be in the Metro Division. But really, what I'm telling you is hearsay. I don't know Ordoñez too well. I'm sure he's a good brah. I'm sure it was nothing. He may have worked in the Rampart Division in the late nighties."

"Wait, Ordoñez worked in the Rampart Division in the late 1990s? You sure?" "Again, that's what I heard."

"So, my next question is not a reflection on your capabilities. But how closely guarded was this house? It's obviously in a residential neighborhood, and there's a lot of traffic in that area. Tell me what you would normally do on your shift."

"I would park the patrol car in the driveway to ensure any criminal dudes would know my presence. Lotta baddies out there, for sure."

"Would you stay primarily in the car during your twelve-hour shift?"

"Yeah, but I would never nap if that's what you're suggesting."

Feeling like a hostage, Ganz said, "Can I have some coffee or water?"

Linda ignored his plea and said, "Just a few more questions, Officer. You indicated you never napped. I never suggested you did. But how many times did you exit your patrol car and walk around the exterior of the house?"

"At least every hour. I never saw or heard anything unusual. But in that neighborhood, there's always noise—music, sirens, helicopters, especially at night. Several times during the night, patrols came by to see how I was doing. We always watch our backs."

Linda asked, "Besides the yellow tape around the burned house, were there any other barriers to prevent anyone from entering the house to look around?"

"No, the yellow tape usually keeps out bad guys, and with the police presence, no one would dare enter the house."

"So, bottom line, only cops, forensics, and the defense investigators entered the house?"

"Yes. I heard that the defendant's attorneys were there during the day a few times, but I was not present when they were there."

"And you didn't hear from any of the other officers regarding any incidents with trespassers?

"No, ma'am, none. There's a large homeless camp in a nearby canyon, but as far as I know, they weren't a problem."

"How or why did you enter the house before you found the cap?"

"I was just curious, you know? I had never been to a homicide crime scene. If you're worried I may have moved something around, don't worry. I didn't."

"And the cap was just there? Clean as a whistle?"

"Well, as I testified, I saw the blue bill partially sticking out around some other debris.

And there it was! Pretty lucky, huh?"

"Yes, pretty lucky. Thank you, Officer Ganz. And Officer Ganz, even though this discussion is just a routine follow-up, this conversation is highly confidential."

"Cool, Miss Sanchez. Copy that."

CHAPTER 6

West of downtown Los Angeles is the Rampart Division of the L.A.P.D. When Sanchez was in law school from 1998 through 2000, her crim law professor scrutinized the Rampart scandal within the Los Angeles Police Department. What is now referred to as the Rampart scandal began to emerge in the news in the late 1990s involving police corruption. This area was a gang-infested, high-crime area, and most of its residents were Black and Latino. The L.A.P.D. created an anti-gang unit called *The Community Resources Against Street Hoodlums (CRASH)*.

To say that many of the officers and supervisors of CRASH were overzealous in law enforcement was an obscene understatement. The CRASH unit became a gang but with blue uniforms, badges, and its own sub-culture.

Investigators eventually implicated several CRASH officers with perjury, planting false evidence against gang members, robbery, unprovoked shootings, and dealing and stealing drugs. The scandal came to light after the arrest of Officer Rafael Perez, who stole from an evidence cookie jar—$800,000 worth of cocaine. On September 8, 1999, Perez brokered a deal with prosecutors: In return for a five-year plea deal, Perez provided information that implicated seventy other officers from CRASH with a horrific picture of misconduct. After a lengthy and thorough internal administrative review board, the board eventually sanctioned twenty-four officers.

Perez pried open a shuttered window to the hellish underworld of CRASH and released a stench of corruption like a rotting corpse. Tarantino could not have created an unbelievable story like this. CRASH officers kept spare guns to plant on a suspect. They would gather at the Short Stop bar near Dodger Stadium to celebrate their illegal exploits. CRASH officers received rewards for some of their shootings.

The net result was one-hundred-forty civil lawsuits, over $125 million in settlements to victims, and one hundred and six criminal convictions overturned.

Officer Jaime "Jimmy" Ordoñez was in the Ramparts Division as a young cop, the same cop who had an altercation with Nicolas Meza. Ordoñez was then a young cop, and after reviewing the lengthy reports on Rampart, Linda concluded that he had no direct contact with the CRASH unit or its conduct. This scandal was over year years ago, and she did not want to draw any adverse inferences. Maybe there was no connection between Rampart, Meza, and the CRASH unit. Perhaps it was just another meaningless coincidence that amounted to nothing. A lot of trial prep leads nowhere. Or maybe Ordoñez retained some bad habits from Rampart. He was near retirement and was unlikely to risk his retirement to do something dumb, like plant evidence. While he might not have been part of CRASH and its activities, he was a young rookie learning the ropes from some dirty officers and may have picked up bad habits. Bad habits developed early in a cop's career can harden later.

***

After a late-night visit with her mom in Boyle Heights to pick up leftover enchiladas and rice that Julio cooked, Linda returned to her car parked on the street two blocks away. The moonless evening was quiet, with a cool Mediterranean breeze.

Linda saw the shattered window on the driver's side.

Someone must have disabled the alarm system. Damn vandals. Or dopers looking for quick cash. Someone spray-painted *Puta* on the driver's door.

Hearing a noise on the passenger's side, she yelled, "Hey! What the hell!" A skinny teenager quickly stood up, startled, and glared at her from the street's greyness. In his hands: a black spray can and a tire iron. He fumbled, trying to pull something from his waistband, but Sanchez was quicker as she aimed her Glock 9 directly at his torso twenty feet away. Even in the darkness, her target was clear.

"*Mijo*, don't even think about it. My first shot will be right through your chest and then in your brain. But you probably don't have much of a brain if you're doing this. Did someone send you?"

With his arms up, he said nothing, still trying to process his options with a steady Glock quickly pointed directly at him. "No one. Let me go. It was just for fun, you know?"

Linda said, "Wait! I know you from the neighborhood. You're Felipe, right? They call you *Flip*. I used to hang with your mother, Elsa, years ago, back in the day." Looking confused, the boy turned and sprinted away down the street, swallowed by the black night.

Ten minutes later, two black squad cars pulled up with red lights lit up like a pair of Christmas trees and parked in the street next to Linda. L.A.P.D. Four officers carefully approached her, looking around like nervous soldiers on patrol in hostile territory. Two female officers from the first unit drew their black pistols like *Charlie's Angels*. From the second unit, a male and female officer emerged. The alpha male in charge asked her with a phony, commanding voice, "Ma'am, we got a call about someone in distress. Is this your vehicle?" Sanchez nodded.

Visibly annoyed, she said, "Officer, my name is Linda Sanchez, and I'm a deputy district attorney. I have a concealed weapon in my side holster and my identification and badge in my coat pocket. May I produce both?" She slowly raised her open palms and put them down at her sides. "Officer, you don't need to put that flashlight close to my face. What's this, the friggin' *Blair Witch Project*?" She carefully opened her blue blazer, revealing her holster, weapon, and badge. "May I remove these officers?" He nodded yes, and she handed him her Glock and badge. The other three foot soldiers maintained a 360-degree vigilance like they were looking for rooftop snipers. Hostile territory. Brown people lurking in the shadows, ready to slit their throats. The alpha male's partner, a young female, illuminated the car's interior. Sanchez guessed that she was a trainee.

He said nothing and nodded. "Ma'am, are you OK? What's going on here?"

The young trainee alerted him, "There's an empty wine bottle in the front seat."

"Miss, have you been drinking?" His flashlight went from her head to her feet, like he was inspecting a strange specimen.

She squinted at his nameplate and said, "Officer Bronson, is it? Officer Bronson, I haven't had a drink in ten years, three months, and six days. All I drank recently was my mother's wonderful *horchata*. You can ask her if you'd like. And if you think I'm under the influence of alcohol, you will pick up nothing unless your P.A.S. device can detect chorizo, refried beans, red salsa, and tortillas. Give the F.S.T.s officer, but make sure your hand-held camera is on.

"And while I'm performing those balancing tests, you must know my left knee is weak. One of the bad guys L.A.P.D. arrested six years ago kicked me in court during an arraignment. Partially dislocated. And I haven't driven this crappy Corolla for two hours." She turned to the trainee and said, "Officer, as part of your training day, you might learn something. Touch the hood of my car, and you'll notice it's cold. Go to my mother's house; she will show you all her videos from her ring. Grab the empty wine bottle and run prints. Make sure you preserve its evidentiary integrity. When you take the bottle to forensics downtown, you ask for Percy Matthews, tell him it's for Lin, and he'll run it for you expeditiously, miss. God, these rookies are getting younger." The male Officer overlooked one of his colleague's hand-gesturing him to abort this. He finally motioned them to retreat.

"Did you get a look at the individual? Was he a gang-banger?"

"What do you mean, a *gang-banger*?"

"You're from here. You know what I mean."

"You mean a male Hispanic? Is that what you mean, a *gang-banger*?"

"Yeah, I guess."

"Officer, he was a big guy, probably over six feet tall and over two hundred pounds. He had a thick goatee. I couldn't see any tats on him. Just a tagger. He didn't look familiar."

"Why would he throw a bottle of Merlot in the car?" he asked.

"Maybe he preferred a Chardonnay. That's the wine of choice for gangbangers." The rookie cop giggled. "I don't know, Officer, he probably just needed something to break the window. He probably was looking for any valuables."

He said, "Ma'am, with all due respect, it looks like you were in a dangerous situation. I'll write a report on this. Do you need a tow truck or a ride someplace?"

She retrieved her possessions and said, "No, I'll take care of it. Hey, Officer Bronson. I must commend you guys. Your response time was excellent, faster than most other times out here. I don't think even the *Paw Patrol* could've responded quicker."

"Good evening, counsel." The young trainee offered Linda a mock salute with a smile, and the patrol retreated from hostile territory.

***

"Wow, that's a beautiful view," Meza said.

The driver in front of him ignored him. Nicolas Meza peered out the rear window of a generic white van with *California Department of Corrections and Rehabilitation* emblazoned on its sides. Meza had never been to San Francisco; for a second, he felt like a tourist. But the van was not a *hop-on-hop-off*; he would only hop off into a small cell on San Quentin's death row.

His panoramic view of the San Francisco Bay, Alcatraz, the Transamerica Building, and the Golden Gate was stunning. Anecdotes from inmates who had served in Alcatraz long ago recounted how, when acoustical conditions were ideal, the San Francisco sounds would taunt them—music, laughter, and cable car clangs. This phenomenon was unintended torture. Meza would preserve this wonderful image during his incarceration like a snapshot, pending the years of appeal, until the end.

A misty cloud of fog began to settle in from the west as if the Gods were looking for a soft landing. "Hey, can you roll down the window for a second? I wanna smell the ocean. Just for a second." The driver glared at his passenger through the rearview mirror, ignoring him.

They drove past quaint cottages that housed employees of the facility. Finally, they entered the prison:

California Department of Corrections San Quentin James T. Gordon, Warden.

The facility placed Meza in the "East Block," an old edifice built in 1927. The institution housed the worst inmates in the "Adjustment Center." Death Row comprises five floors; each single cell is four feet by ten feet, described as *sardines in a can* stacked up in five rows. Meza would have a metal bed and a sink, twenty-three hours without sunlight, and a fifteen-minute shower. Most condemned inmates hope to be housed in the North Segregation portion next to the East Block, where they have a sweeping view of the San Francisco Bay and beyond. CDCR transferred many death row inmates to other facilities after California voters passed Proposition 66 to allow inmates to work and pay victims' restitution, which they could not do while on death row in San Quentin. Meza prayed his stay in this hellhole would not be too long.

After processing, Meza entered his cell on the third floor, shut his

63

eyes, and visualized the glittering San Francisco Bay; he heard the cable cars ringing up in Chinatown ten miles away; he smelled garlic and crabs from the Wharf and almost tasted some North Beach carbonara.

His sanity began to hemorrhage.

CHAPTER 7

FROM JULIO

My big sister taught me to ride a bike without training wheels.

Before I entered Kinder, I would follow Linda to school on her bike every day at seven.

Elementary school was only five blocks away. That bike was so cool. My dad got it at the Pasadena Swap Meet one Sunday and fixed it like new: He replaced the front tire with a new chain and seat. He painted it blue. "Gordita's favorite color," he told my mom.

I wanted a bike, too, but Dad said I was too young. Five years old is too young? So, after Linda returned from school, I went into the garage with her, hopped on, and pretended I was riding like those kids in the movie "E.T." up in the sky, beyond the clouds. As a kid, I always wondered what was above the clouds. I still do.

So, one day, I waited to have the garage all to myself when no one was home. I snuck in and tried to learn. After a few days on the bike, this badass five-year-old would be ready for a Harley. I could ride with Dennis Hopper and Peter Fonda across the country, beyond L.A., eat by a campfire, and laugh all night. I could spend all my life on that Harley.

I tried to ride the bike out of the garage but couldn't. I thought I did everything exactly like Linda, but I must've done something wrong. I sat on the seat, put both feet on the ground to get balance, kicked the stand, placed my feet one at a time on the pedals, and then tried to push myself out of the garage. My legs were longer than Linda's, even though she was older than me. The Gods cursed her with stumpy, plump legs. So, I thought riding would be easy. If Linda could do it, I could do it better.

Plop! I fell on my side. My knee hurt a little, but I hopped back on the bike and tried again. OK, not too bad. I'll get better with practice.

Plop! This time, I landed on my left hand, and it hurt. The pain on my left side began throbbing, but I thought the pain would go away once I got the bike moving.

Third time. Why not?

I dusted myself off and got back on. My balance felt good and strong. This time, my weight shifted too quickly, and I fell on my right side. Now, both sides of my body were throbbing. I had traveled about one foot forward and one foot to each side when I fell. Before I went cross-country with Peter and Dennis, I would eventually have to leave the garage.

Suddenly, my dad grabbed my shoulder like a vise, picked me up, dragged me inside like the morning trash, and gave me a nalgaso, a spanking so hard I can still feel the waves of pain vibrating deep in my butt today.

"That will teach you a lesson, menso! You can barely walk. Do you think you're old enough to ride a bike? That garage is not safe! I have so many things in there that might hurt you. Stay out of there. Please, Julio."

Linda heard the scolding, so she entered my bedroom that evening and said, "Tomorrow is Saturday. Dad and Mom are going to run errands all day. I'll take you to the park and teach you how to ride. There's a big parking lot there, and it's a good place to learn. Be ready by seven, Mr. Easy Rider."

The next day, with Linda leading the way, we walked with the bike about five blocks to the nearby park, and Linda parked the bike in the middle of the parking lot, empty at this early hour.

"OK, let's do the basics. See how I get on and move my legs. Once you get your balance, just peddle. You will just feel it in your bones, that balance." With patience in her voice and kindness in her eyes that I had never seen in her, she continued softly, "You can do this, Julio. Just believe in yourself. No one here will laugh at you. I promise I won't."

She brought a bike helmet and knee pads and put them on me. "Linda, I've never seen you wear a helmet when you ride."

"I can't," she said matter-of-factly. "Why?"

"Dad bought it for me when he fixed the bike. But it won't fit me, my head is too big. Haven't you heard Dad say I have a humongous Olmec head? When he's not calling me Gordita, he calls me Cabezona, big head." I thought about what she had just said and burst out laughing, holding my knees together so I wouldn't pee. She made a circular motion around her head, laughing.

"Julio, just watch how I get on and peddle. Easy." She quickly hopped on that bike with no effort. I never saw the athlete in her until that day,

but she got on the bike with silky agility and confidence. That was the first time she amazed me—it wouldn't be the last.

With a stern voice, Linda told me, "Don't think—get on the bike, and just push forward!"

On the second attempt, I began riding that bike like a pro. "Julio, you did good. Now you can ride. You can do anything! No matter what happens to us, everything will be all right."

Linda was the big brother I never had. She protected me from the bullies lurking in the school hallways' shadows, taught me math, and helped me with homework daily. A year after our riding lesson, she gave her precious bike to me.

I depended on her more than my parents. When they divorced, Linda consoled me and told me everything would be all right.

When we moved to Boyle Heights in 1985, Linda told me everything would be all right.

When I started messing up in school, I dropped out of Roosevelt High, and she told me everything would be all right.

But when she left for another school, she abandoned me. I lost her. Everything was not all right. I love Linda, but sometimes I don't like her.

CHAPTER 8

"So, Linda, you know this tagger?"

Santos was driving his black S.U.V., going south and threading light traffic on the 5 freeway through downtown L.A. The Santa Ana winds were springing to life, and the temperature was ninety-five degrees by late morning. Glimmering heat waves bounced on the L.A. skyline, and the cloudless sky looked dusty and grey. On the far eastern horizon of the city, they could see white smoke-wildfire plumes.

Linda caressed her pumpkin latte coffee and said, "The tagger's mom, Ester, and I grew up together during elementary school before I transferred to Catholic school. I have seen her a few times since then. Her kid, the one I caught tagging, was a cute little kid, always smiling. She showed him to me a few years ago when I ran into her at the market near my mom's house."

"Why didn't you identify him to the officers?"

Sanchez turned to him and said, "One, I don't want to get him in trouble for now. And two, he might give us some information. I don't think his tagging was random. He's a street kid and must've recognized my car. He, or someone else, wanted to send me a message. Let's get off on Whittier Boulevard, and we'll pay him a visit. I'll take you to *El Mercadito* for some *birria* if we have time afterward. And I'll even treat."

"You're going to treat? Lin, I know how stingy you are. When you pinch a penny, you squeeze so hard, Abe Lincoln screams like you're grabbing old Abe's nuts."

With Linda directing, they exited on Whittier, traveled about a mile within Boyle Heights, and then pulled into an empty alley scattering a clutter of filthy feral cats. The streets were quiet as sunset was an hour away. Sanchez opened her door and entered the rear seating area. "All right, I think I know where to find him. There's a small park four blocks ahead where he probably hangs out. It's not really a park, but a small vacant lot. It used to be a thriving Korean market before the Rodney King riots, but they torched it and rebuilt nothing. Julio and I used to get

Korean candy and sweet rice cake there."

They cruised slowly near the lot and parked two blocks away. Linda whispered, "Look, that's him, Little Flip, hanging out with his boys. Let's wait to get him alone, and then we'll chat with him." They could see a group of about six kids, none older than sixteen, standing in a circle. Flip was smoking a joint and laughing about something they said. Finally, after an hour, they broke up, and Felipe walked away alone like a defenseless gazelle separating from the flock.

Santos followed him discreetly for about five blocks and then pulled over behind him.

Santos then quickly exited, ran behind the prey, grabbed him by the neck, cuffed his bony arms from behind, and escorted him to the car. Sanchez opened the rear door and motioned Santos to place the young man beside her.

"Hey, what the… Wait, aren't you? Shit, man," the boy said.

Linda scooted near him, saying, "Listen to me, and listen good, son."

"Hey, you can't do this. *Pinche placa. Pinche vieja.*"

"I guess you're not listening. We're going to have a little talk here. You know who I am, right?"

"Yeah, you're that district attorney bitch. You can't do this! I know my rights!"

"Correct. I'm that district attorney bitch." She winked at Santos in the front seat.

"And yeah, I know you're Julio's *carnala*. I heard he's out on parole. No one wants him around here. The *vato* is a dead man walking 'cause he owes some people."

"Look, I'm not here about Julio. I'm here about what you did to my car the other night, remember?"

"Don't know what you're talking about, Miss District Attorney." He tried to loosen the handcuffs and squirmed in the seat.

"Look, Flip. I know you and your family. I saw you when you were crapping in your diapers. You were a cute little kid, and your mom was so proud of you. I'm not here to mess with you. I just need some information that has nothing to do with you, OK? By the way, how's Ester?"

"Dead. Last year. Fentanyl. I found her sitting on the toilet, all foaming at the mouth like a dog. She kept staring at me before she died. Even after." He paused a second to catch his breath and said, "Her stare went right through me. I have nightmares over that shit. Damn cops, they thought I gave it to her. I think it was her boyfriend. I don't touch that stuff. Let me go! What the hell, you want?" He turned away from her, staring at the empty streets, sniffling. Dusk would soon arrive.

Linda said, "I need to know who got you to mess with my car. You must've known it was mine. And then you put a wine bottle inside to set me up with the police. They got there fast."

He glared at her and said, "Nobody. I just wanted to tag, that's all, lady."

"You know, Flip, the one thing that really pisses me off is when someone calls me lady. I can live with bitch, 'cause I am, but I'm not a lady." In the front seat, looking through the rear-view mirror, Santos nodded in agreement. "I don't have time for your *pendejadas*, your stupidity. Just answer me. I'm not going to snitch on you about the tagging. Turi at the body shop took care of it."

"Turi. He's my uncle! Dude's good with cars, man. He can fix anything."

"Who told you to tag my car?"

Felipe squirmed, turned his back toward her, and defiantly extended his middle finger. "Fuck you. You're a *pinche vendida*, a sellout. Putting your own people in prison. Hell with you!"

Without hesitation, Linda turned the boy round and shocked him with a lightning-quick slap across his soft cheek. "*Mijo*, here are your two options, and there's no third. And you need to give me your choice in the next few seconds.

"Option one. Give me the information I want, and we'll let you go. Two, if I don't get the info from you, I will put the word out that you're a snitch for the L.A.P.D. Then, I will have L.A.P.D. put a closer watch on your boys. Everything: stop and frisk, parole checks, welfare checks, jaywalking, overdue library books, gangbangers not paying their PBS dues. And this will piss off your boys even more. And I'll have my office go ballistics in prosecuting anyone you know for everything in the California penal code: shoplifting, littering, loud music, truancy. *Chota* will be all over you. I *need* to know why you tagged my car, son."

The boy's countenance changed from defiance to confusion to fear.

Flip said, "I heard about you on the street. You don't act or talk like a lawyer or a cop. You don't play fair. Look. They were gonna jump me into the gang. But before I could do that, they needed a favor. They wanted me to send you a message. That's all. Someone said you're getting into our business here, that's all. That's all I know. Maybe it's about your brother; I don't know, lady. I'm not gonna mention names."

"Did they mention anything about an arson case?"

"A what case?"

"Arson, a burning house."

Looking perplexed, he shook his head and said, "Nah."

"Anything about a Dodger cap?"

Looking even more perplexed, he shook his head and said, "Nah, lady."

Linda paused, looked at Santos, and said, "OK, I believe you." Removing his handcuffs, she lowered her voice and, with a motherly tone, said, "You know, I really liked Ester. She told me she thought you'd make it out of here and that you wanted to be a teacher. Do you think she would be proud of you? Her only child? She told me she prayed you might go to college. I'm not gonna mess with you anymore. We're good. Where can we drop you off, Felipe?" Linda wanted to salvage this soft boy and did not want to toss him onto the rugged streets of Los Angeles. She thought he might be an angel who got his wings clipped early in life, but he could still grow them back.

"I got a place at a homeless camp near Hollenbeck Park."

"Why are you homeless?"

"When my mom died, I got evicted. The social workers couldn't do nothing except put me in crappy hotels. No foster homes wanted me. So, I got out to the streets. It ain't too bad. I'm a survivor."

"Look, Flip. You'll be dead before you turn eighteen. Where's your father?"

"Nah. He don't want nothing to do with me. Haven't seen him in a year. He's up in Merced. He's too strict, works for the fire department, and thinks he's a big shot with that blue uniform and shiny badge. He's a loser. He and my mom only had a one-night stand."

"Flip, listen to me. These streets will eat you up. I was one of the lucky ones to get out 'cause I got help. If the streets don't kill you, prison will. Those guys there are just waiting for a skinny, soft guy like you. You're raw meat to them. Your bony arms are just tasty chicken wings.

"I know a social worker, a great person. We will take you to her right now. She will find you a safe place to stay, and then she'll find your father. All this will be off the books, so there will be no record of the social services helping you. Your friends won't know what happened to you. Maybe they'll figure you disappeared somewhere or are in some unmarked grave. You didn't jump into the gang, so you owe them nothing. You need to try it out with your father, understand? Choice number two is you will die like a dog on the streets—nothing but a dirty, faceless dog. Think of your mother. She had hopes for you."

She shifted closer to him and gently tapped his face. "Do you understand?"

Sniffling, he looked down and said, "Maybe I'll try."

"Flip, I'm sorry I slapped you. Don't worry about my car. Your Tio Turi fixed it. Good as new."

She turned to Santos and said, "Santos, I got hungry talking about skinny chicken wings.

Let's take this boy for some birria, and then we'll get out of here. You like birria, Flip?"

Felipe wiped the snot from his nose and nodded, "Fuck you, I mean fuck yeah! How 'bout Fat Burgers instead?"

Ten years later, Linda would receive an envelope from Merced, California. There was only one thing in it: a photograph of a skinny young man with peach fuzz along his upper lip and chicken-wing arms in a black graduation cap and gown with a yellow sash that read *WITH HONORS*. He proudly smiled and stood beside a young girl with a newborn baby in her arms.

On the back of the photo was a simple *Thank You*. Flip would graduate from the University of California at Merced with a degree in social welfare. The angel grew his wings back. She would gingerly place the photo back into the envelope, careful not to spill her tears.

***

Sanchez arrived at the courthouse early, rested outside on a wooden bench, and indulged in her morning ritual: an iced white chocolate mocha with a pumpkin scone. She was an hour early for her pre-trial motion hearing in Department Five and wanted to enjoy a quiet moment. Closing her tired eyes, the incessant drone of L.A. traffic disappeared as she listened to the cool   melodies of Eddie Harris streaming through her earbuds. The generous heavens delivered a sensory feast to the Angelinos: Winter air, crisp and redolent, massaging the lungs; Pacific breezes, sharp and saline, crackling the senses, its airy saltiness leaving a warm aftertaste. The San Gabriel Mountains gleamed with a heavy blanket of snow, glistening like a million tiny candles, majestic, divine, and gorgeous.

She felt a shadow on her, blocking the morning sun and its soothing warmth. The source of this partial eclipse was a beefy police officer hovering next to her, glaring, saying nothing. He was about mid-fifties, six feet, with a small gut cascading over his belt. *Sergeant 1* flashed on his insignia along with his name tag: *ORDOÑEZ.*

Ordoñez said, "Miss Sanchez, I do not appreciate my name coming up in the Meza case. What are you after?"

"Sergeant Ordoñez, please have a seat. I'm enjoying my coffee. It's a gorgeous morning. Look at those mountains. Please don't fuck up my day." Linda scooted to her right to give him room on the bench. He sat stiffly, and his peering eyes locked in on her without blinking. "Your name came up in a routine interview. Mr. Meza will get an automatic appeal, and I want to explore potential appellate issues. These death penalty appeals go on forever, and I will assist the Attorney General with the appeal. Defense attorneys will leave no stone unturned and look for anything they might raise on appeal. We never want to get surprised."

Ordoñez growled, "Again, lady, why did my name come up?"

She turned to him and said, "Well, is it true you had an off-duty altercation with Nicolas Meza a few months before the homicide?"

Ordoñez shook his head dismissively and said, "You're a piece of work, lady." He leaned close enough for Linda to catch a rancid whiff of stale garlic and coffee on his breath.

"Officer, my name is Deputy District Attorney Linda Sanchez. Do not, and I repeat, do not address me as *lady*. Let's have an understanding. You will not call me *lady*, and I will not refer to you as a *former Rampart Division cop, Ordoñez.* Are we good?"

Ordoñez bit his lower lip and squinted painfully like he couldn't focus. "Rampart, huh? That's where you're going? That's the play here? Shit."

"Officer Ordoñez, part of my job is to make sure these cases, especially death penalty cases, are ironclad." She took a leisurely sip of her chocolate mocha and offered him a piece of her scone. He grabbed it with his meaty paws and chomped it in one bite, never taking his glare off her. "If a defendant in my trial has had a beef with a cop, I need to know about it. It's probably nothing, right? So, you tell me, what was the beef about?"

"It was nothing. The guy was a punk and mouthed off to me while we were playing pool. I had never seen him before, but I think one guy knew him from the streets. I don't think he even knew I wore a badge. We exchanged a few punches, but nothing serious. He got a bloody nose, and I got a few hits. No biggy. One guy I was with knew his name and maybe mentioned it."

Linda said, "OK. Anything more?"

"No, counselor. Nothing more. You look skeptical. You think I planted evidence in the case? That's where you're going with this, right?"

"I frankly don't know if someone planted evidence. All right?"

"You must have checked my file and found I had nothing to do with the Rampart fiasco. I was a young cop then but never hung with those CRASH guys. The investigators cleared me, and I didn't testify because I knew nothing about their actions. I was a low guy.

"Yeah, some of those CRASH guys mentored me. Most of them were brave and dedicated cops—at one point in their careers. But they went to the other side.

"For over twenty years, I cannot rid myself of that connection: *Officer Ray Ordoñez, former Rampart Division cop.* I lost promotions because of that dead weight, Miss Sanchez. It almost broke up my marriage because my wife and kids thought I was a dirty cop. I still get those side stares from other officers. I have that scarlet letter 'R' on me. *Rampart.* I'm a damn good cop, Miss Sanchez. You can look at my personnel file—no major complaints. I retire in two years, three months, and six days. And then you bring this up. You probably thought that the *ex-rampart cop must have done something crooked here, maybe even planted evidence, right?*

"That's fucked up, lady. You could mess with my career, especially since I'm near pension."

She stared at him pensively and shook her head. "Officer Ordoñez, I respect you. I do. I can't say that about all cops. I commend you. You know why? Because over twenty years ago, you were a young, impressionable police officer surrounded by all that abysmal corruption and stinking rot at Rampart. And I'm sure you could've taken that dark road. Temptation is the devil, officer. Alcohol. Drugs. Graft. Money. Sex. No human being is immune."

She turned to face him squarely and said, "I should know. I deal with those devils every day." Linda handed him the last piece of her scone. "But you had the integrity and decency not to succumb to those temptations. That's a testament to your character, Officer Ray Ordoñez. No, I know you were not involved in the Meza case. You're off my radar. Have a good day, and enjoy your well-earned retirement."

Ordoñez exhaled like he was holding his breath, quickly rose, adjusted his uniform, and extended his meaty hand for a handshake. "Thank you, counselor. Good scone."

***

The next day, Santos called Linda and said, "Lin, can you meet with me at Dan Fuller's office? You know him at the probation department." Santos rarely called Linda before work unless it was urgent.

"I've got a fairly light schedule today. How about three?" Linda said. "Cool. See you then, Lin."

At three-thirty, Joe Gomez and his shoes strutted into Dan Fuller's office as the latter sat behind a desk. Ramon Santos stood to his right, and Linda Sanchez, dressed in a dark business suit, sat in front. Fuller motioned to him, and Gomez awkwardly sat next to Sanchez.

Santos broke the silence. "Hey, Joe. How's it going? Or would you rather I call you that ridiculous street moniker? What is it? Oh yeah, Joe *Little Rambo* Gomez. Where'd you get that nickname?" Gomez glared at him, scanned the room nervously, and said nothing.

Gomez finally spoke, looking at Fuller. "Hey, Dan. What the fuck? Who are these clowns? Are they here only to insult me, man?"

"Joe, my name is Ramon Santos, and I'm an investigator with the D.A.'s office." Gomez turned to Linda and asked Fuller, "And this *vieja*? Does she talk?"

Linda politely extended her tiny hand and said, "Good afternoon, Mr. Gomez. My name is Linda Sanchez, and I also work for the district attorney's office. And yes, I talk a little, but your shoes blinded me momentarily like a deer caught in headlights, and I was speechless. I

75

looked at your rap sheet—wow, you're an industrial-grade idiot, but I think we can work together on something." Gomez looked even more confused.

Gomez said, "Who's this Latina princess? Why did they bring a secretary from the D.A.'s office here? What's going on?"

"I'm an attorney with the district attorney." She showed him her badge, and he glanced at her Glock sticking out under her business jacket.

"Damn, girl. A friggin' district attorney, huh? You don't talk like no lawyer. Where you from, sweetheart? You're too fine to be one of those *pinche* prosecutors. Most of those *viejas* I see in court don't do it for me. But you—I could get into." Linda motioned to Fuller to leave the office, and he stepped out, closing the door.

Santos casually sat in Fuller's chair and said, "We believe you might have some valuable information for us."

Gomez sat up nervously. "I'm listening, man. What kind of information? Hey, I am not a snitch."

Santos said, "It's about a baseball cap."

"Don't know nothing about no Dodgers cap."

Santos smiled and said, "I didn't mention it was a Dodgers cap, moron. Play dumb all you want. But we have information that you drove someone to a location two years ago so he could leave a Dodger cap at a crime scene. A burned-up house, to be exact."

Gomez tried to stand as if to leave, but Santos stood and walked near Gomez, grabbing his shoulder and slamming Gomez back into his chair. "Why you messing with me, *ese*? I know nothing about a cap. You saw my jacket—mostly burgs, dope, and auto theft. What's this about?"

Santos said, "Little Rambo, we can connect you to a frame-up in a homicide, dude, and you don't wanna get in trouble. Now, who is the guy you drove?"

"Fuck you, Santos. And fuck you too, Miss District Attorney. *Pinche vendida.*"

Linda slowly turned to Gomez and said, "Maybe we can discuss this in terms you might understand, Mr. Gomez."

"Fuck you, lady."

"You know, you're the second guy this month that's called me a *lady*. Joe, you need some water or coffee. You're sweating, *mijito*," Linda said.

Gomez said nothing as a sweat globule crawled down his forehead.

"Lady, I got nothing for you. Nothing! So, you can—"

Linda interrupted and said, "OK, Joe. I've been around guys like you all my life. You're all the same. Talk shit on the street. Kill yourselves around *pendejadas*. Most of the time, your talk is empty. The louder your talk, the smaller your balls. Those homeboys in CDCR are going to like you, Joe. And you'll give it up to those prison predators. They're gonna *rambo* you until you can't feel anything below your waist."

"I ain't going to prison. The judge put me back on probation."

Linda said, "Now, Mr. *Rambo*, you'll give us this information, OK? If not, your P.O. will prepare a petition to violate your probation again, and I will handle your violation myself. Your last pee sample came out positive. Meth. Boom! Violation. You're consorting with other known gang members. Boom! Another violation. You got a long jacket, Mr. Gomez. And you got what, a four-year suspended sentence? It might not sound too long. However, CDCR has a better gossip network than Facebook. Word might get out about that child molesting case of yours back in 2017. Four years isn't a long time. But four years for a pedophile, accused or convicted? That time drags. *Tic Tock, Tic Tock.* Every day, you'll wake up in prison with a big target on your back. On your anus, to be exact."

"You guys never convicted me. The little bitch didn't show up to court. It was all bullshit. No conviction."

Linda said, "You think those guys in CDCR care or know the difference? Arrest or conviction? Those big boys in the CDCR won't know, or care, if there's a difference. All they'll hear is *pedophile*—nothing before or nothing after. Just *pedophile*, just *Chester. G*ive us the information, and you can leave here now. No violation. And I might even consider recommending early termination of your three year probation period. I'll cut that long tail of yours in half, *cabrón.*"

"Damn, girl! You can take the *chola* out of the barrio, but not the barrio out of the *chola.*

"You got a rough mouth, worse than my *ruca.* You're nasty, lady. You don't play fair."

Gomez fidgeted in his seat and nervously scanned the office as if others besides these three were present. Biting his lower lip and lowering his voice, he said, "OK, some guy I met in a homeless camp near the Maravilla handball courts asked me if I wanted to make some easy money. All I had to do was to drive him to a house so he could leave something. I

had no ride, but getting one would be no problem. You saw my jacket—
two convictions for auto theft. So, I pinched an electric Toyota—no noise,
man. Those suckers are quiet, *toda madre*.”

“Anyway, about two years ago, he said he could cut me in on the
feria. Good money for a simple *jale*, in and out. So, I got the car and
picked him up.”

“Where?” Linda asked.

“Some bar in West Hollywood. I didn’t get the name. So, we go to
Monterrey Park to a house that was all fucked up, burned up. He knew the
location. We got there about two in the morning. All quiet. I scanned the
neighborhood and cruised around for a while. I wanted to take off ’cause I
saw a police cruiser in front, but the blond cop was on his cell phone, not
doing *ni madre*, know what I’m saying? So I went behind the house in the
alley, and the *vato* pulled a cap from his pocket and went past the police
tape for about thirty seconds.”

“What kind of cap?”

“Dark blue, L.A. Dodgers. *Pinche* Dodgers. Did you see that playoff
game against the Padres two years ago? The Padres kicked their asses.
Embarrassing, man. The fucking Padres. I lost fifty *bolas* on that bet.”

Santos said, “I’m a Boston fan.”

Linda said, “Boys, tuck your baseballs back in your scrotums, and
let’s get back on point. So, Mr. Shoes, what happened next?”

“That’s it. I dropped him off somewhere in Montebello. Then I
ditched the car. I think he only had a burner phone. So he called me one
last time and wanted to split the money with him. I said no. I had a funny
feeling about this, and I saw you guys here and realized I might be in deep
shit.”

“OK, what was the guy’s name?”

“He didn’t say much. But he told me his name was Panchito. No other
name, just Panchito.”

“What did he look like?”

“Kind of tall, about thirty years old. Skinny. There’s not much about
how he looked except this—his hair was long and spiky, like one of those
cartoon guys, you know, the ones with that spiky colored hair. Looks
fucked up if you ask me, but I don’t judge. Yeah, like a troll, a *gnomo*.
Brown eyes. Over six feet. We didn’t talk much, but he often used the
word *righteous man*. Like *this car is righteous man*.”

"Any idea where he was from?"

"Nah. But he mentioned his mom lived near Mex. A border town, yeah, Calexico. She lived in Calexico."

Santos asked, "Anything else… something to identify him? OK, he has family in Calexico. Never heard of it."

"I can't give you more, man. No last name, just Panchito. Oh yeah, the dad died a few years ago, and he owned a gas station in Calexico."

"Did he say he might contact you again?" Linda asked.

"Nah, we're done. The thing's over; I didn't want any of his money. So, he don't need me no more."

Linda interjected, "Hey Joe, you've been a big help. We'll keep in touch if we need anything more. We'll put in a good word for you with the P.O., but you must keep this conversation tight. Confidential. Understand?"

"I can do that."

Linda said, "OK, get the hell out of here. We know where to find you. We'll just follow those shoes." The shoes then left, and Little Rambo trailed behind.

CHAPTER 9

"We gotta go to Calexico."

A week after the Gomez interview, Sanchez planned a trip with Santos to Calexico, California, to track down Panchito, a link to this mystery. Only she and Santos knew of the developments, and they would go to Calexico on their accrued vacation to camouflage their intent. These developments could all amount to nothing, and they needed concrete information before notifying their superiors and the defense team. The *Brady Rule* required her to provide information to the defense that could arguably exonerate a defendant, so she wanted to follow this new lead.

The lingering concerns in Sanchez's gut remained—*that pesky pebble.* Like reading a book in reverse, she wanted to review some salient factors that led to Meza's conviction and investigate backward. She also wanted to contact the victims' family ostensibly to see how they were managing after the trial.

Amelia Meza had two loyal sisters, Grace Gonzalez and Patty Escalante, who never missed any court hearings, including the lengthy trial. Little Nicky and Amelia lived with them periodically during Amelia's tumultuous marriage. Nicolas Sr. was not welcome in their homes, so neither sister observed any violence first-hand. They only saw the aftermath—Amelia's bruises and scratches and Little Nicky's despondency. Both sisters briefly testified through victims' impact statements in the trial's penalty phase. The jurors appeared moved by their poignant description of their sister as a loving mother and Little Nicky as a wonderful little boy. Sweet, funny, and happy.

Linda met them for coffee at Patty's apartment near the U.S.C. campus to check on them. Both sisters were in their mid-forties with shy dispositions. During these follow-up trial reviews, Sanchez often discovered something new.

Sanchez told them about the endless appeals that invariably follow death penalty convictions, beginning with an automatic appeal to the California Supreme Court. Further, she outlined the 2019 moratorium on executions in California imposed by the governor of California. The sisters' expressions mirrored one another—confusion and frustration.

Patty Escalante spoke first. "You mean, they might never execute him for what he did?"

Linda said, "The short answer is no, but I cannot predict the future. I truly appreciate all your help in this case. You were brave throughout this ordeal, and all your background information helped me and my staff."

Escalante looked at her sister and said, "I'm a Christian, but I wanna go to his execution and see that monster die. I wanna be in the first row." Both sisters made the sign of the cross.

Grace said, "Praise God. Do you think he has a chance on appeal?"

"I don't think so. The state and federal appellate courts will scrutinize it, but I think it was a clean trial. But you never know."

Escalante looked at her sister and said, "I'm not a lawyer; all this is new to me. But wasn't it lucky that you guys found Nico's cap at the house? How did you guys find it after all those others looked through the house? I thought Nico's lawyer would convince the jury that one of your guys planted it like something from a movie. I watch a lot of those crime shows. I think there was an episode like that where some cops would plant evidence on people. But that would be unbelievable. Wait, that happened a while back here in L.A."

Linda interjected, "Rampart."

"Yes, Rampart! Those dirty cops planted evidence, didn't they? That's why I thought the jury might believe a cop could frame Nico." Both sisters shook their heads.

When Amelia and Little Nicky stayed with them, the sisters periodically received calls from a social worker who monitored the case. According to the sisters, Amelia never contacted the Child Protective Agency because she distrusted them, and they were too *"metiches, too nosy, always looking into personal stuff."*

Although the sisters never thought this was odd, considering the violent nature of the marriage, they also understood that Amelia was extremely private. Sanchez only guessed that the child support services received information about domestic violence from mandatory reporters, possibly a schoolteacher. The social worker, Melissa Strickland, left her business card with the sisters, which Sanchez took.

"Thank you once again. You can contact me anytime if you need anything day or night, do you understand?"

"Miss Sanchez, thank you so much for all your work."

***

The L.A. Office of the Department of Children and Family Services was near MacArthur Park. Sanchez did not want to alert the social worker, Melissa Strickland before the former arrived. It was late in the workday, so she hoped to catch Strickland in her office.

"Miss Strickland, my name is Linda Sanchez, and I'm a deputy district attorney. Thank you for seeing me without advance notice."

"Don't worry; I routinely arrive somewhere without notice in my work." Sanchez nodded her head. Linda thought, *Good, she has a sense of humor*. Strickland escorted Linda into a small, cluttered office resembling a filing room.

"I prosecuted Nicolas Meza."

"I know. I followed it in the papers and through courthouse scuttlebutt. Frankly, I am surprised you just realized any connection with the case and D.C.F.S."

"All I know is that you monitored the household for a few months before the homicide."

"Miss Sanchez, you must know some of the information about our work is confidential, and I'm uncomfortable talking to you about the Meza family. No one ever filed an 827 petition to see the confidential juvenile records." Strickland nervously parsed her lips.

Linda said, "No. I didn't even think of filing one in this case since there was no record of a petition filed by the Office of the County Counsel in the juvenile dependency court. Until recently, I was unaware of your intervention in the case." Linda paused for a few seconds as if she was trying to study the social worker. "And that's why I'm here. I was reviewing the case to ensure we left no stones unturned. Endless appeals are still pending. And when I spoke with the family, I learned of your involvement for the first time. I just need to ask you a few questions."

Strickland shook her head and raised her palm. "Miss Sanchez, I need to cut you off right here. You're getting into a confidential area. You know that. You're an experienced lawyer. I can't tell you anything without that 827 petition, but I'll verify that with our county counsel. You get a judge

82

to sign off on the 827, then the juvenile records are yours. When our department does not initiate formal proceedings in the juvenile court, we keep the reports in confidential files and monitor the family informally." After a long, awkward silence, the social worker closed the office door. In a more subdued tone, she said, "Listen, I'm surprised that neither you nor the defense attorneys contacted me or attempted to file the 827 petition."

Sanchez leaned forward. "Oh? Without a formal juvenile petition, the defense attorneys were likely unaware that D.C.F.S. was even involved. Neither was *our* office."

"Well, I can't tell you too much, and I can guess why, strategically, you would not want to file a petition anyway. But I can tell you this off the record." Strickland cleared her throat and tried to choose her words slowly. "You know, the dad, Nicolas Meza, seemed like a reasonably good father. He tried to spend time with his son—they would go to the park, the beach, and even Disneyland. The parents' fights were mutual, and they gave each other good licks, but the dad was much bigger. As far as I understand, they never hurt each other too seriously.

"But the kid saw and heard all their fights. I'm not a psychologist, but the kid developed pyromania because of his exposure to their violence. Some people, especially young children, lash out differently from stress. Their psychological anxieties manifest in different ways, like bedwetting, introversion, and anger. Burning stuff can also result from acute anxiety. Pyromania. We often stereotype pyromaniacs as adults who have a fetish with fire. But some children also burn stuff because of stress. I've seen it in my work.

"Little Nicky displayed this. On at least two occasions, he tried to start a fire inside the house shortly after he saw his parents fight. He lit some curtains. There was minor damage, and the fire didn't spread, so Amelia never called the fire department. My sister never liked to draw attention from law enforcement. I'm sure you checked. Dad didn't know, but we asked Mom to take the boy to therapy, but she was dismissive of that idea and never took him as far as we know.

"We did not file a formal dependency petition. Our department seals internal reports that do not result in a formal petition. So, when I read about the case, I did not reach out to you because I heard they found Dad's cap in the house and connected him to the arson and murder. Maybe he knew about the kid's tendencies and thought he could blame it on Little Nicky. But I guess his cap got him convicted, huh?"

Linda said, "Well, yes, that cap was the linchpin. But do you really think this kid started two other fires?" Linda said, biting her fingernails.

"Yes, Mom told me. But she still didn't want to send him to therapy. One last thing, Miss Sanchez—I gave you this information in the strictest confidence. You still should have filed the 827 petition to get this stuff. And if you ever say you received this confidential information from me, I will vehemently deny it. So, do we understand each other?"

"Understood. Thank you." Under her breath, Linda said to herself, *Dear God. The boy may have started this fire.*

CHAPTER 10

FROM ROBERT

I first noticed Linda Sanchez during our first year at the U.C.L.A. School of Law in 1998, sitting two rows in front of me in my torts class. I didn't see her face until a few weeks into the semester, and I teased her later that her rear head was sexy. No, there was no "Hallmark" music in my mind, just the drone of an old professor lecturing about comparative negligence. Love doesn't always happen "at first sight." More often, deep love sets in somewhere between the first and hundredth sights, in small, savoring bits and pieces. My first impression of Linda was—standoffish, shy, blunt, intelligent, rude, moody, and confidently opinionated in and out of class. Her brutal sarcasm could be offensive. As time passed, I found her—the real her.

The first time I saw her closely was one early morning when I was walking in Westwood near the campus after my usual caffeine stop. Taking a shortcut to the campus, I crossed through a parking lot and spotted her in the back seat of a Toyota Corolla. She slept in it. Curious, I stopped, observed her from a distance like a perverted stalker, and followed her.

The U.C.L.A. campus has a women's gym near the sorority row on its far eastern side. I learned that Linda would commute to her mother's house in Boyle Heights every Friday through Monday. She would shower and change in the women's gym during the week, and no one questioned her. So, Mondays through Thursdays, her home was the back seat of her car.

She never knew I was aware of her housing situation until we married two years after law school. I honestly don't know how she maintained this for three years. I never knew someone as resourceful and driven as her. If she faced a problem—any problem—she analyzed her options and then fiercely attacked that problem with little compunction. Any problem. Money problems. Bathroom mold. Family problems. Courtroom problems. Housing problems.

But tenacity was her astonishing strength and her pernicious curse. She attacked a problem headfirst without fear, almost to the point of recklessness—cautious, strategic recklessness.

During our third year, we were in the same study group, and the same study group stayed intact when we studied for the bar exam. Our relationship was platonic, but I gradually fell in love with her.

Her practical approach to the law attracted me intellectually. She knew how to quickly apply abstract legal concepts to the real world, which set her apart from many of our peers.

But that's not why I fell in love with her. I adored her simple smile, warm embrace of life, and raw honesty. She was so beautiful without trying to be, and I don't think she realized how beautiful she was—that flawless olive skin, those deep, rich brown eyes that glinted hazel, that shy smile with a small gap in front. Her humor was self-deprecating. And when I started to compliment her, she retreated inside like a turtle. We began to spend more time together studying for the bar. OK, that doesn't sound like a Hallmark rom-com love story. But we created an emotional bond, relying on each other during the pressure of the bar exam. When we got the results that we passed, I finally kissed her. When I kissed her the first time, an angel grabbed my heart and hurled it toward the heavens. That kiss followed me to the netherworld, where I am now.

We eloped in Las Vegas in the spring of 2002 and then went to Boston, where she met my parents. They instantly adored her for the same reasons I did.

We started our careers immediately. I began as an associate with a downtown business firm, and she had already started with the district attorney's office. On July 8, 2005, we were returning to our apartment in Westwood after dinner and ice cream when a speeding car T-boned us on La Cienega Boulevard. My side bore the brunt of the collision, and I died instantly. I felt nothing. The impact did not injure Lin too severely. But she was five months pregnant with our beautiful daughter. A womb provides warmth, nourishment, and protection. But it couldn't protect our daughter from a speeding car.

Oh, by the way, I'm dead.

I don't exactly know where I am. But I hear Lin talking to me now and then. I still feel that first kiss. I still see that gorgeous smile and boisterous laugh. Our daughter and I will wait for her until eternity.

CHAPTER 11

Sanchez and Santos sat down and carefully reviewed the situation. They suspected someone, or some persons, may have framed a condemned man. But they needed more corroboration before they revealed this to anyone—their department, the defense attorneys, or the L.A.P.D. It was still conjecture. The picture was incomplete.

"Santos, what do you think?" Sanchez and her trusted investigator sat in a quiet booth at a Denny's near the civic center. It was late afternoon, before the dinner crowd. "My gut told me something stunk about this case, but I didn't know what. I even told Ed, my supervisor, that it felt like I had a friggin pebble stuck in my shoe, and I couldn't get rid of it."

"*A pebble stuck in your shoe.* That's funny." After nibbling a few healthy bites of his cheese omelet, Santos said, "Several other possibilities point away from planted evidence, and we must eliminate them all. But the little pyromaniac and this cap thing is interesting. And, if someone planted that cap and the boy started the fire, then who or why would plant evidence that gets a guy convicted?"

"Rampart brings L.A.P.D. into the realm of possibilities," Sanchez said as she sipped her iced tea.

"Lin, you think cops could have framed this guy?" Santos asked.

Sanchez said, "Don't know. Maybe. That kid who tagged my car seemed to say someone wanted to send me a message. Cops? Those two sisters also wanted this guy to go down. They wanted front-row seats to his execution, not the bleachers. Maybe somehow they're connected. My imagination is running away from me. Damn."

Santos added, "Meza was not gang-connected, so that we can remove that variable from the equation."

"Mon, I don't want to rule out anything." She moved closer to him across the dining table and murmured. "I trust you. We've worked together for over fifteen years. Never have I doubted your professional abilities and your ethics. Our careers are on the line if we mess this up and make false accusations about anyone. And I think we need to keep this to ourselves until we have more concrete information. You can bow out. I'll understand. And let me be blunt. We can't rule out one of our own might be involved. Our beloved L.A.P.D. But I must go as far as possible on this thing until that pebble is gone."

Santos took the last bite of the omelet along with his thick coffee. "Look, these leads might point to Meza's innocence. But have you considered letting this whole thing drop? It might be a can of worms. The jury convicted him, and he got a fair trial. He had two competent attorneys. And his cap was at the scene. He was a bad guy with a history of domestic violence."

Linda said, "No, I need to pursue this. Are you in?"

Santos swallowed his food, breathed, and said, "Yup. I'm with you, Lin. So, what's next? What's our play?"

"We need to do three things. I want to go to Meza's home in Compton to talk to his mom. She might tell me if her son had any enemies. Second, I must go to Calexico to look for the mysterious Panchito. He's the key. Someone might have paid him to plant a key piece of evidence that led to a death verdict. I don't trust Joe Gomez and his shoes. And three, let's get the cap re-analyzed to look for anything other than Meza's D.N.A. We know it's his cap, but we don't know if anyone else handled it. I'll talk to our forensic people."

Santos said, "We gotta keep our stuff under wraps. At some point, we would, at the very least, let the defense attorneys know we might have *Brady* information. At first, I questioned your instincts, but when you look at all the odd things we've seen, there might be a problem with the conviction. There are too many questions, and the answers might mean Meza is innocent. I'm with you, Lin."

Santos nervously extended his fist to Linda for a fist bump in solidarity.

***

Nicolas Meza spent all his life in Compton, never traveling north of the San Fernando Valley or east of Montebello. Entering San Quentin was the first time he saw San Francisco. Through her trial preparation, Sanchez knew his background superficially in two dimensions. Only child. Two felony convictions. He lost his father after a random attack near Wilson

88

Park. Somehow, he managed to avoid gangs, even though he spent most of his waking moments surviving the unforgiving streets of East Los Angeles. His mother attended most of the pre-trial hearings and the jury trial. A solitary figure, she always sat alone in the back of the courtroom's grey shadows. Sanchez once saw her outside the courthouse, praying the rosary to herself.

Attempts for an interview by local writers failed. During the trial, Linda felt her stoic gaze follow her in the courtroom like a portrait moving its eyes.

Linda arrived at the Meza home around one 1:00 in the afternoon to avoid the 3:00 traffic. She did not want to give her any advanced notice of her visit in case she received a frosty reception. Arriving at the porch of the Meza house, Sanchez passed a beautifully simple garden. Manicured green hedges, healthy white roses, and bright red bougainvillea adorned a cracked stone path leading to the front door. A mature Jacaranda tree bursting with bright purple flowers stood proudly in the yard as heavenly breaths blew its petals onto the ground like snowflakes. A Saint Francis statue acted like a sentry in front. The ubiquitous black metal bars on the windows reminded Sanchez where she was.

As she was about to knock on the door, Mrs. Meza opened it slowly.

"I saw you drive up. I know who you are, Sanchez. Should you even be here?"

Sanchez began speaking in Spanish, but Meza interrupted her after the second word. "I speak English. I been here all my life. Born in Texas. What do you want?"

"Mrs. Meza, may I come in, please?" Sanchez shuffled her feet and wiped some sweat off her brow. The abrasive winds brought upper-ninety temperatures all week.

Mrs. Meza looked at her closely for a few seconds, as if trying to read her mind. She carefully opened the door and allowed her in. "Please sit down. I just made coffee. Do you want some?"

"Please. Mrs. Meza, I won't take up too much of your time. I am just following up on some information."

Sounding harshly, Meza asked, "Except for my son's execution, isn't the trial over?"

Cradling the cup of coffee, Sanchez asked, "Did your son have any enemies? Maybe someone who would want to harm him?"

Meza looked confused. "You're asking me now? After the conviction? Well, look where we live. He had problems on the street. About six years ago, someone tried to shoot him in front of our house, but he wasn't hurt. He told me he didn't know who it was and ignored it."

"Did you ever find out anything more about that incident afterward?"

"No. He don't talk too much—especially about his street business."

Linda said, "Tell me about his L.A. Dodgers cap. Did he always have it?"

"You people know all that about the cap. That's all you talked about in the trial. Yes, he always had it. He thought it gave him luck. Some luck, huh?"

"Around the time of his arrest, did he have the cap on?" Sanchez asked.

"I don't know. I wasn't here when the police first came to arrest him. *Dios mio*, I heard they had a full swat team and helicopters. He always wore the cap."

"Where did he keep it in the house?"

"I'll show you." She led Sanchez into a small bedroom that was neatly and sparsely furnished. Surrounding a small wooden bed were miscellaneous sports posters. Lebron. Fernando Valenzuela. Al Pacino's Scarface. She opened an old wooden drawer and pointed. "There."

Linda looked around the bedroom and said, "How many times did the police enter your house after the arrest?"

"They came two times. The second time I let them in—they didn't need a warrant and so many cops. I begged not to break anything."

"Do you know if the cap was still in the drawer when they came?"

"I don't remember the last time I saw him with the cap?"

"Was anyone else in Nico's bedroom besides the police?"

"His two lawyers came about three times to talk to me about Nico and the case. They were really nice. I think the tall guy, Mr. Holder, came alone one time. I remember because he brought me *pan dulce*."

"Did they look around the house?"

"Yes. They went around the house like they were snooping to find something that might help Nico's case."

"Did any of the police leave their names? Or could you recognize any of them?"

"I don't see their faces, only their black uniforms."

Linda rose and said, "Thank you, Mrs. Meza." The host said nothing, opened the door, and gave the visitor a slight nudge to the blazing Compton sun. A powerful gust of the blistering wind sliced into the house. *A bad omen*, Linda thought as she passed the wandering eyes of St. Francis.

From the porch, Mrs. Meza said, "*Gracias*, Miss Sanchez. You think I should hate you because you convicted my son. You saw me in that courtroom during the trial every day. But I had heard that you were a good and fair lawyer. I never saw you do anything during the trial that I thought was bad. You acted like a professional, but who am I to judge? I'm just an ignorant old woman. I know you don't understand my son, and you don't know his other side. But he has good in him. I pray every day that his appeal will succeed." Linda didn't react and returned a nervous smile.

***

"That's the last time I saw Panchito."

Snuggled on the Mexican border in the far southeastern corner of California, Calexico is home to thirty thousand people. Its eastern neighbor is Arizona. While the County of Imperial is rustic with an agricultural-based economy, its Mexican counterpart, Mexicali, is a sprawling modern metropolis of nearly one million. The unique juxtaposition of these two disparate communities presents a dynamic glimpse into the lives of its residents. Many who live in this unique part of the state do not see the boundary on the maps. Geographically, culturally, and politically, the border between the two countries is not a solid black line; it is transparent, sometimes non-existent. Mexicali and Calexico share a symbiotic relationship like close cousins. Many Calexicans share dual residences in each city, with families divided in both countries.

Businesses in both communities depend on each other. Calexico is an American town that's Mexicanized, and Mexicali is a Mexican city that's Americanized.

Sanchez and Santos needed to locate Panchito in Calexico to follow the leads. Still, they did not want the trip to be an official part of their job, so she went on Labor Day weekend in 2023 to burn up some of her accumulated vacation time and camouflage her intentions from the prying

91

eyes of her office. Their only guides were instinct and shallow leads.

An hour east of San Diego, they crossed mountains, then passed a strange primeval landscape of monstrous boulders, and, near sunset, they finally reached the balmy floor of the Sonoran Desert—the Imperial Valley. The prickly ocotillo cacti, with beautiful red flowers, spread out to the desert horizon among the multi-colored wildflowers that had burst to life after heavy winter rains. Grey shadows from Mount Signal to the south began to slowly crawl eastward onto the desert floor as the nocturnal choir of desert life began to howl, sing, and chirp—owls, coyotes, sparrows, cicadas, prairie dogs, and crickets. Tremendous white windmills sprouted from the desert floor like sleek iron cacti, their graceful arms slowly twirling with the wind like giant fronds. The stark beauty of the desert mesmerized Linda as she gazed out the open window, breathing in the desert's dry, unspoiled air.

Panchito's mother lived in Calexico, so Sanchez deduced that the mysterious Panchito had lived here most of his life. Seeking anonymity, they did not want to alert the local police of their visit. As they entered Calexico, they cruised around the city to feel it at ground level.

Santos said, "My dad and I drove through here as kids. He loved off-roading just east of here at the Glamis sand dunes, heaven for off-roaders and motorcycles. Man, it was fun. My dad refurbished this V.W. into a dune buggy, and we also spent one Thanksgiving out there in the dunes." Santos looked out the window, daydreaming.

Linda asked, "How the hell could you guys eat? I mean, all that sand in your turkey and pumpkin pies. Doesn't sound too comfortable. I need hotels on vacation, Mon. Where's the fun?"

"Yeah, I know what you mean. But I was closest to my dad on those trips. And riding those cycles was so cool. Nothing like it." They entered the Calexico city limits and drove south on Imperial Avenue toward the international port of entry.

Linda said, "I wanna see Mexico."

Santos looked incredulous. "You've *never* been to Mexico?"

"Mon, I have lived in L.A. all my life. I rarely left. My mom used to mention her cousins in Mexico City and Matamoros. But we never visited. Not even for weekends in T.J. Why is that so hard to believe, Mon?"

"It just seems weird. You're a Latina, but you've never been to

Mexico, two hours away from L.A. No offense, Lin.”

As they approached the International Port of Entry, Sanchez looked out the passenger window. “Is that the wall?” Linda asked.

“Yup, that’s the wall that’s gotten so many excited about.” Santos parked the car, and both exited on foot along the international fence.

Linda said, “The fence looks like miles and miles of black prison bars. Damn.” A green and white U.S. Border Patrol car crawled by them, the driver giving her an extra look. Behind the fence was Mexicali, Mexico, the largest city in Baja California. Sanchez saw families speaking with each other between the bars. What she read about in the news was an abstraction. Now she was seeing the real thing.

She approached a young teenager on the U.S. side, speaking with an older woman on the south side behind the black bars. In Spanish, she greeted him and said, “Hi.” Sanchez wore a professional outfit: a dark skirt, black pumps, and a matching blazer. The boy looked at her with suspicious eyes and said nothing. She pointed to the elderly lady and asked the boy, “Who is this?”

“*Mi abuela,* my nana.” The elderly lady smiled demurely. “Why are you speaking to her here at the fence?”

“We’re doing nothing wrong. My family is getting papers pretty soon, but we cannot cross until the customs people approve the paperwork. And my nana cannot cross. She has no papers. My father said in about three months, we get approval.” The boy turned squarely to Linda and said, “Are you *migra*? Are you police?”

“No, *Mijo.*” Sanchez turned to the lady and wished her a good day. They continued strolling to the Port of Entry, where they gazed at hundreds of border crossers entering Calexico, a human amalgam of shoppers, visitors, students, and professionals. Like spectators at a parade, Linda and Santos sat for a few minutes and watched the rivers of humanity crossing north and south. They finally returned to their car and proceeded to the Calexico Police Department three blocks away. Entering the police station, they introduced themselves and displayed their identifications to a young cop. The cop peered through the plexiglass in the lobby. “L.A. District Attorney, eh? What brings you down here?”

Santos said, “May we speak with your chief or someone from investigations?”

The cop nodded respectfully and ushered them to an interior office where they met Calexico Chief of Police Victor Legate. He extended a warm hand. "Sit down. How can I help you guys?"

Santos introduced themselves and said, "We'll get to the point. We're investigating a case from Los Angeles, and we think there might be an individual from Calexico who might have information. It's a weak lead, but we need to check it out."

Sanchez chimed in, "Chief Legate, this is highly confidential since the investigation is still in flux. We would appreciate it if you did not reveal this to anyone."

Legate looked perplexed. "OK. How can I help you, Miss Sanchez?"

Linda said, "We only have three clues of this guy's identity. We know he lives with his mother here. His nickname is 'Panchito,' so I assume that's short for Francisco. We learned he has distinctive hair like a cartoon troll—those creatures with spiky hair that stands straight up. I used to collect those as a kid. I still have the one with the purple hair. And third, we heard his father used to own a gas station some time back."

Legate looked sternly at both and said, "Oh crap. Francisco Gutierrez, Sr., long ago owned a gas station on Imperial Avenue. He was a lousy businessman, and he lost the station to alcohol, gambling, and womanizing. His son, Panchito, is the guy you're looking for. When he grew up in Calexico, they called him *El Gnomo*, the troll. He always had that style. Everyone in Calexico has a nickname."

"Can you take us to him? I assume you know where he lives."

"I can take you to see him 'cause he's not going anywhere—he's dead. An unknown assailant murdered him three days ago, and I have investigators looking into it."

Santos and Sanchez looked at each other in disbelief. Legate continued, "We found him in the All-American Canal, snagged in the river bushes. The assailant shot him twice with a nine-millimeter and beat him. The body was bloated, making it more difficult to analyze it forensically. When the divers recovered the body, they were in luck because we think they got the gun used in the murder. I have it in the evidence locker; I'll show you."

Legate returned with a sealed, transparent bag with a handgun inside. Legate said, "It looks relatively new, but I'm not familiar with this model. I'll check it out further." Santos and Sanchez inspected it, and their eyes widened. Legate said, "You guys looked a bit startled."

"Look, chief. We want you to keep this thing under wraps for a while." Santos kept peering at the gun and continued. "This is a nine-millimeter, model FN 509 MRD-LE."

Legate looked intrigued. "OK. It's a nine mil, so what?"

"This new model is a new duty weapon… for the Los Angeles Police Department. How, or why, did the shooter lose it?"

Legate said, "The banks along the All-American Canal are dangerous. The currents are fast and deceiving. At night, the footing is treacherous, and the shooter probably slipped and dropped it."

"Can we see the body?" Linda asked.

"The pathologist has scheduled the autopsy in two days, but you can view it now if you like."

Sanchez said, "Let's go now."

After a quick ride, they arrived at a local morgue. They approached a metal slab with a corpse lying on it, covered with a white blanket up to the decedent's forehead with the only body part that was exposed—the spiky hair. Linda saw the spiky hair sticking out and said, "No other deceased trolls in here, so this must be our guy." Legate was still trying to process the visitors' humor.

"How could the troll's hair maintain that stiffness after being submerged in the All-American Canal for hours?" Santos asked as he peered closer to the body. "You can't tell he was in the water for a long time. Unlike the rest of him, the hair is in good shape, with excellent follicle texture and superb shine."

Inching closer to the corpse, Linda replied, "Probably used *TRESemmé* extra-hold hair gel. I use it when those friggin' Santa Ana winds are blowing. If that gel can beat the Santa Anas, it can beat the All-American canal."

With an ambivalent frown, Legate was trying to find the humor as he uncovered the white blanket and said, "As you can see, he suffered two gunshot wounds. One on the knee at close range and the headshot. We can still see that he has facial injuries that tell us the shooter also beat him."

Santos said, "First, they punched him, then they blew out his knee. Then, they fired the last one into the brain. They were trying to get information from him. Or they were just trying to keep him quiet."

Visibly frustrated, Sanchez shook her head and said, "He's quiet, all right. Can we talk to his mother?"

"We couldn't get anything out of her," Legate said, "and our investigators spent a lot of time with her. She saw him two nights before we found the body."

Sanchez asked, "Who found the bodies?"

"A young kid, Mark Campos, and his crew were frog gigging along the canal."

"What the hell is *frog gigging*?" Sanchez asked.

Legate said, "Frog gigging—it's basically spearing the frogs with this special spear on a bamboo pole called a gig. I used to do it when I was a kid. It's a fun sport. So, you need a two or three man hunting crew and go along the canal banks at night with a searchlight. When you see a frog, you blast the light on it, and it will freeze." Legate then stood like an Olympic javelin thrower and said, "Then the other guy spears it with the gig."

Santos said, "That's how they shank a guy in prison: a two-man crew. One guy distracts the victim while the other guy shanks the guy from behind. Classic."

Legate said, "OK."

Looking away from and ignoring the spikey corpse before her, Sanchez was now fascinated by frog gigging. "Is Calexico full of javelin throwers? After they spear the little Kermits, then what?" she asked.

"Then what, what?" Legate asked.

Linda asked, "What do you do with little Kermit once you shank it with the gig?"

"Well, you cook them. The frog legs are what you're after. They're a delicacy. You brine them in salt water for a day, then cook them any way you want. Barbeque, deep-fried. Damn, I think I'm getting hungry."

Santos turned to Sanchez and said, "Well, I'll be damned—frog legs. You know, that doesn't sound too bad. Sounds like something they would do in the deep South, like the Mississippi version of *chicarrones*." Linda started whistling the banjo medley from the movie *Deliverance*. "But I prefer Miss Piggy over Kermit."

Linda asked, "You're a Muppet fan, Santos?"

"No, Lin. I prefer eating Miss Piggy, not Kermit. *Carnitas* Lin! Pork—not frogs. *Carnitas* Lin!"

Linda said, "OK, Santos, I get it." She turned serious and said, "Chief Legate, we can't tell you the nature of our case or why we're interested in Panchito. But we can still work together." Legate nodded.

Legate drove them to Panchito's home on the west side of Calexico, a pleasant older neighborhood of well-kept wooden homes and gardens that reminded Linda of home.

They entered the house, and Legate introduced them to Mrs. Gutierrez, a petite woman with grey hair in a tight bun and purple bags drooping under her bloodshot eyes. Linda guessed she was about sixty, and the lady reminded Linda of her mother. Beneath the woman's shriveled face, her baneful life was visible to Linda: a life of endless suffering, constant tragedy, and profound anguish. Sanchez saw a woman slowly dying in the endless winter of her life, hoping for a glimpse of a spring that would never arrive. She offered her guests coffee and *pan dulce*, which the three visitors respectfully accepted.

Legate removed his hat and told Mrs. Gutierrez, "*Señora,* I'm very sorry we have to talk to you again. I know my investigators and have already spoken to you at length. We recorded your interviews, but these two individuals must ask you additional questions. This is Ramon Santos, an investigator with the Los Angeles District Attorney's Office." Santos nodded. "And this is Miss Linda Sanchez, an attorney with the District Attorney."

Mrs. Gutierrez peered closely at Sanchez and whispered, "You're an attorney? Hm."

Linda said, "*Senora,* we think there's a connection between your son and a case in Los Angeles, and we're trying to clear up some information. We are not accusing Panchito of doing anything wrong; we just want to learn a few things. Thank you for the *pan dulce*." Sanchez relaxed and sat down on a sofa next to the host. "This neighborhood is lovely. I like Calexico. It reminds me of East L.A. but of a small-town version—except for the police helicopters, incessant sirens, smog, traffic, and the occasional sounds of automatic weapons."

Mrs. Gutierrez smiled nervously and said, "What do you want to know that I haven't already told the police?"

Santos said, "Well, you must have known your son lived for some time in Los Angeles. How long was he gone?"

"My son would come and go. He's an adult. I don't ask. But he lived up there for the past two years, and he used to call me to tell me he was doing good, working; I didn't know where. He even sent me a little money now and then. I don't know where he lived. He never had a job for

long. He dropped out of school in tenth grade but was still a good boy."
She turned and blew her nose, sniffling.

Sanchez asked, "Did he ever mention a blue baseball cap?" Both Legate and Gutierrez looked puzzled at the question.

"No, nothing."

Santos asked, "When did he return?"

"He surprised me a few weeks ago and said he would visit family in Mexico. We have family in Rosarito, in Baja California. But it's funny 'cause we're not close to that side of the family. Panchito had only gone there a few times. Before he left the house the last time, he would stay up late, and I noticed he would look out the window a lot like he was expecting someone. He seemed very nervous.

"He has no friends here in the neighborhood. After he left high school, he wandered around in San Diego, San Francisco, and finally, Los Angeles. He was a loner. And when he came this last time, he was very quiet. We used to talk a lot, especially after my husband died five years ago. But this time, he was different, *Dios mio.*"

Santos pressed her. "Did he ever say anything about any problems in L.A.? Anything."

"Nothing."

Santos asked, "The last night you saw him, tell us about that."

"Well, I think he got a call on his cell. That's another thing: he would never give me his cell number. He would always call me here at the house. So, he got a call, got dressed, and then left. That's all I know. That's the last time I saw my Panchito."

Legate said, "Miss Sanchez, we never recovered Panchito's cell phone. It may have washed away in the All-American."

Sanchez asked, "Could you see where he went? Or did you see if someone picked him up?"

Chief Legate said, "We canvassed the neighborhood. We picked up some images from the neighbors' rings of Panchito walking about two blocks, and then he entered a vehicle. The images couldn't pick up the make of the car; it was out of view."

Sanchez then asked, "You mentioned he would send you money occasionally. When he came this last time, did he seem to have more money than usual?"

"You know, Miss Sanchez, that's an unusual question. You're the first person who's asked me that question." She rose and escorted the visitors to her son's bedroom, spartan with only a wooden bed and a rickety drawer with an old lamp. She opened the drawer and showed them a wad of twenty-dollar bills totaling over nine hundred dollars hidden under underwear and undershirts. "When I washed his clothes, I found this. I loved my son dearly, but he never had this much money in his life. I know he didn't earn it legally, but I would not ask him about it. It's his business."

Sanchez gingerly clutched the lady's hand and said, "*Señora, perdón*, but we must take this money because it might be evidence. Let's put this money in a sandwich bag." Gutierrez nodded in agreement. "Mrs. Gutierrez, I will give you my business card, and I promise to return this money or the same amount out of my pocket. Promise."

Sanchez then embraced her in a warm bear hug. "Mrs. Gutierrez, I know how difficult all this has been. He was your only son and didn't deserve this. We will try to sort this out. I'm sure he only wanted to return to Calexico to care for you."

Gutierrez sighed wistfully and said, "*Que Dios te bendiga, mija*. May God bless you, child."

Upon return to the Calexico Police Station, Sanchez reminded Legate to keep the visit confidential and told him that they would share any relevant information with him in the future.

Sanchez then asked Legate if he could show them Mexicali and have lunch there. Santos turned to Legate, rolled his eyes, and said, "She's never been to Mexico."

Legate said, "Really? Let's go. I know a place where we can get some of the best Chinese food this side of Hong Kong." Sanchez and Santos looked utterly confused. "You guys are from L.A., and you can get the best Mexican, Cuban, Puerto Rican food and anything in between. But Mexicali has the best Chinese food anywhere. The Chinese settled the place."

Sanchez said, "I'm gonna visit my ancestral land for the first time and eat the best Chinese food. What the hell? Let's leave the troll in Calexico, and let's roll to Mexicali!"

Santos asked, "You think they serve frog legs?"

CHAPTER 12

Cruising westbound on Interstate 8 east of San Diego, Santos and Sanchez were absorbing the relevance of their Calexico trip. Two days in Calexico offered more questions, created more theories, and provided more leads—but furnished no clear answers.

Holder was connected to the incident in Calexico. Random events can morph into disparate clues, evolve into a discernable pattern, and unfold into a clear picture. Panchito Gonzalez's premature demise provided no additional clues, and there were no leads about the now-famous Dodger cap. Maybe he had other problems here. Panchito Gonzalez entered a dangerous world of his own volition and likely had enemies in that unstable world. His crimes were the price of admission, and his death was the price of his exit. He had substantial cash, consistent with the information extracted from Joe Gomez. Someone or something spooked Panchito in Los Angeles. The weapon recovered was a newly issued duty weapon for the Los Angeles Police Department. *Was L.A.P.D. involved?*

"Hey Santos, what do you think? Was this trip a waste of time?"

"Nah, except for the dead troll. You also got to visit Mexico, your homeland. And you ate some terrific Chinese food."

Linda said, "OK. You're right. But I meant the investigation we're looking into. Any thoughts?"

"I know. I'm just messing with you. The clues we learned in the past few days don't point toward a theory of a frameup. But they don't point away from it either. I don't believe in coincidences too much. There's a chance Panchito planted that cap to frame Meza. But why? The guy's not a genius. Whoever paid him that money is the guy we're looking for. And when we find the persons responsible, then the next question is, why?"

Chewing her fingernail nervously, Sanchez said, "Panchito's murder was not random. Someone silenced him. If that's the same person who framed Meza, then we can assume we are dealing with some nasty people. Meza was an insignificant lowlife. Why would someone go the extra mile to set him up? If someone set him up, those behind it have lots of resources."

Santos said, "Maybe I'm getting too old for this. I was in combat during the Gulf War in 1992, and I've been around some pretty bad people as a cop and investigator. This case gives me the creeps, Linda. What did I hear you say about a pebble?"

"I told my supervisor right after the Meza verdict that I felt like I had a pebble stuck in my shoe, and I couldn't ignore it. Something about this case just keeps bothering me," Linda said.

In the darkness of their sedan, Sanchez could see that Santos was biting his lower lip. "Linda, I think I feel that same pebble. Crap."

"Wake me when we get to L.A., Mon." Within a minute, she was softly whistling in her sleep.

***

Passing the Irvine off-ramp, Sanchez woke up and imagined her cozy, warm bed in Santa Monica waiting for her in thirty minutes. She looked forward to a warm shower, snuggling into her worn pajamas and slowly cruising through a pint of Ben & Jerry's cookie dough flavor.

There was a lot to process, and a sweet pint of decadent ice cream greased the cogs of Linda's brain. Then she dozed off again.

The 405 freeway between Irvine and L.A.X. is one of the most congested in the United States, but the city looks haunting and surreal at one in the morning. Los Angeles slumbering before dawn: soft undulating sounds of traffic creating a soundscape of soothing white noise, shimmering lights crackling like ambers upon an urban basin framed by a light glow on the eastern horizon, a city's pulsating heart beating to life, breathing in a new day. Flickering headlights crawled along the 405, snaking like a thousand-legged centipede in unison. Glittering lights from the Culver City skyline offered a sparkling reflection of the stars above.

Linda woke as they passed L.A.X., and she rolled down her window, inhaling cool, salty air, tasting the Pacific Ocean with a hint of rain. Looking westward, Linda saw no horizon or sky—only deep, thick blackness, as the sun would creep up over the San Gabriel Mountains to the east in about three hours. Grey silhouettes of the Santa Monica Mountains and silent skyscrapers in front of them began to form like ephemeral shadows rising from the depths of the L.A. basin as if they were reaching for the darkness above. She turned to see Santos, who seemed to be daydreaming, probably about fishing with his father long ago or sitting in the cheap seats in left field at Dodger Stadium.

They arrived at Linda's Santa Monica apartment just past two.

Linda slurred, "I've got a busy morning schedule in court. But let's meet during the week."

"Hey Lin, when should you tell your supervisor of all this stuff? Not to mention, you also need to tell the defense attorneys. I'm not a lawyer, but even I know about your *Brady* obligations."

"I know. Soon. We gotta make sure we have this case secured. I just need some sleep."

"Hey Lin. We might be in some serious shit."

"I know. Let's keep on rolling. See you later."

***

"Been a long time, Lin. I missed you."

"I know, Rob. I've been busy. I have this thing I'm working on, and I can't sleep too well. Sorry. I miss you. I think about that time, the night before I lost you and our baby. You wanted to go up to Mendocino for a few days. I've never been up there. You said we would do nothing, just walk, sleep in, clear our lungs, maybe walk on the beach. You would grab some wine and save it after the baby was born. I always thought that once my pregnancy advanced, I would look too fat, and you would not look at me the special way you used to."

"Yeah, you would look fat and beautiful. Too beautiful for my eyes."

"Rob, you always knew how to spit out a good line of bullshit, but thank you. We should have gone to Mendocino. It's one of the million things we never did. We could have had an entire lifetime to do those things."

"Yeah. I remember. I went there during my undergrad with some guys in my fraternity."

"You friggin frat boy!"

"Guilty as charged. I was a frat boy. When I first went to Mendocino, I imagined coming back with someone special like you. I envisioned a girl just like you. Mendocino would have been great.

"I think I'll go up there myself, and you'll be with me. And our little

102

girl, too. She'll be with us in Mendocino. We can show her the ocean's moods, the sunsets' astonishing colors, and the coast's peaceful quiet. We can show her beauty."

"Lin..."

"And maybe we could take her to the redwoods on the—"

"Lin!"

"On the way back—"

"LIN!"

Sanchez burst awake from her deep slumber by a muffled sound in her kitchen. Her clock displayed three thirty. The heavy curtains suppressed the streetlights, and she heard Wallie's soft, rhythmic snores. The foreign sound grew louder—careful steps were creeping toward her bedroom.

Slowly retrieving her Glock from the dresser, she waited quietly in bed. She felt the soft staccato of her nervous heart, heard her breath grow louder, and the synapses of her brain snapped to life. Her hands began to sweat, but she was calm. Her eyes adjusted in the dark like an animal in the jungle. Survival. A vague silhouette emerged at her bedroom's threshold, a slowly moving spectral moving cautiously toward her. They were two living creatures in this shadowy realm. Survival.

"Hey babe, is that you?" Linda asked, thinking she was still dreaming.

As the intruder raised his right arm, his outline grew clearer, like a ghost morphing into human form. As her brain fog cleared, she could see a face—and the unmistakable outline of a handgun pointed at her. The simultaneous explosions from both weapons created a tremendous echo chamber that throbbed in her ears. She fired two more times. A heavy thump. She smelled burnt cloth a few inches near her head—her pillow. Slowly turning on the light switch, she rose and saw a quivering body on its back, his mouth ajar, his dead eyes bulging open in shock. She could hear a light guttural moan. With two holes in the upper torso and one in the jaw, the young assailant looked like a hideous creature from another world; his body contorted in odd, unnatural angles. In her frigid bedroom, she saw and felt a weak puff of his last breath dissipate out of his gaping mouth like steam from a dark gutter on a winter night.

She slowly placed her weapon on the night dresser, forcefully breathed in, and called 911.

Her voice was calm and clear, her palms dry and steady, and her heartbeat slow.

She whispered, *"Thank you, babe, for the warning. I love you. Stay with me for a while."*

Wallie finally woke up, impatiently waiting for his breakfast. The acrid scent of the gun smoke lingered in her nostrils, briny and sharp, reminding her of the first time she smelled the ocean when she was five.

***

"The S.O.B. missed her head by inches!"

Sanchez, Santos, and Edward Ross waited outside Linda's apartment as paramedics removed the body on a gurney into a white van. The paramedics had finished treating her and prescribed some sedatives. Linda wrapped herself in a heavy wool blanket, cuddling Wallie like a newborn.

Ross said, "Linda, take off a few weeks. You have enough vacation time stacked up. I'll sign off on any extra time you need. How did you wake before the shooter entered? I assumed your dog woke you."

Linda said, "This deaf mutt slept during the shooting. I'm good. Do we know who he was? Santos, run a check on this bastard. Let's see who he is. I just need a day, and I'll be back. I want to get to the bottom of this."

"Lin… Santos, is there something you two aren't telling me? I am assuming this was a random burg. The perp probably knew you were away," Ross said.

Santos said, "Yeah, it's probably random. I heard from an officer that there's an uptick in break-ins around the area these past few months."

Ross said, "Look, I'm no fool, guys. This guy was no burglar. He didn't break in just to take your jewelry."

"Hey, Ed. Lin has no expensive jewelry. She buys that cheap shit from Old Navy and the Rose Bowl flea market." Linda giggled and nodded her head.

Ross said, "Guys, I'm trying to be serious here, OK? He was no burglar, and the guy entered with that weapon drawn and knew you were here. He knew how to use those burglars' tools; there were no entry marks. And Lin, he missed your head by inches in the dark!"

Santos said, "Ed, look at Lin's colossal head. Stevie Wonder couldn't have missed that thing. She was the fuckin model for those Chitzen Itza sculptors."

104

Ross said, "Not funny, Santos. You know, Lin, I never noticed that head of yours." Sanchez forced a nervous smile and shook her head. "But I hope you two are taking this thing seriously. If a deputy district attorney is a target, we will use all our resources to figure it out. Linda, when you first saw this guy, was his gun already out?"

"Yeah. But I didn't see the handgun when he first entered my bedroom. He might have had it in his waistband, but I shot when I saw it pointed at me. Robert warned me."

"What, Robert, your... deceased husband?" Ross asked.

Santo stepped in. "Ed, leave the questions for internal affairs. Have an officer take her to a motel and get her protection." He saw Linda shake her head. "Maybe it might be better if I took her to my house in Costa Mesa. My wife would like the company." Ross nodded.

Santos raised his hands to the paramedics to stop. They unzipped the body bag and asked Lin if she recognized him. She approached and saw the face of a young boy, probably twenty-five, with facial tattoos. Dry blood caked around his mouth. She said, "He looks like the thousand guys I've prosecuted. He looks like one of my cousins. He looks like my damn brother. He looks like my father used to. I know them all. I don't know this one." She convulsed and began sniffling. Santos and Ross said nothing and gave her some space.

***

"His name was Enrique 'Kike' Escalante," Santos said, hovering over his kitchen stove.

After sleeping in for a day at the Santos residence, Sanchez felt rejuvenated, but her head throbbed like a hangover. She sat in Santos' kitchen with coffee and scrambled eggs.

"Esme lets me cook on weekends. It's relaxing. I didn't know what you eat, so I made something simple."

"Thank you. This is perfect. I didn't know you had other skills, Santos. Where's Esmerelda?"

"She wanted to give us some time to talk, so she went to buy groceries and visit her mom at the convalescent home. Dementia, poor thing, she barely recognizes her own daughter." They both sat quietly for a few minutes, eating.

"His name was Enrique 'KiKe' Escalante," Santos said. "He's got a long rap. He was twenty-eight years old and grew up in Culver City, but he's been on his own since he was thirteen. He practically lived in the Central Juvenile Hall until he turned eighteen." Santos looked out the kitchen window as the morning sun began to show the top of its head. Its brown aura hinted at another hot, dusty one.

Santos continued, "But his record becomes interesting when we see his adult rap sheet. He has some pretty heavy arrests: drive-byes, carjackings, and at least one shooting out in your neighborhood, Boyle Heights. The bastard was good with a gun.

"What makes it interesting is this. With all these arrests, this guy should be in CDC by now, but he had a few convictions and hasn't done substantial time. This shooter has some guardian angels looking over him."

Linda banged on the kitchen table. "The shooter was a snitch!"

Santos nodded and said, "Yup, sure looks like it. No one can get this kind of criminal rap with dozens of arrests and few convictions unless he's playing ball with law enforcement."

Linda asked, knowing the answer, "L.A.P.D.?"

"That would be my guess."

"And this guy likely met our Panchito out in Calexico on the All-American canal."

"That would also be my guess, Lin."

"And the shooter is probably working for the person, or persons, who set up Nicolas Meza."

Santos pushed another warm plate of eggs and hash browns to her and said, "That would also be my guess. I'll check around to see if he was an informant and who his handlers were."

"Santos, we're getting warm. I always said to follow the leads to see where they go. But when we get to the end of this damn trail, I don't think we'll like what we find."

Sanchez returned to work after taking off a week. Upon her return, she received uncomfortable glances from anyone she encountered. Most wanted to ask her about the incident or morbidly ask how it felt to kill someone. Death followed her. But she also felt stronger for the incident. The shooter wanted her for a reason, and Sanchez instinctively knew she was getting closer to the trail's end, but the donkey in her could sense more danger lurking around the corner.

***

The next day, Sanchez completed her interviews with the L.A.P.D. investigators and the Internal Affairs Division. Her story was consistent, although she was vague when asked about anyone having any other motives to kill her. There was no mention of baseball caps, Panchito, or investigating a closed case. She was still reluctant to mention anything to Ed Ross about her lingering doubts and needed more time to continue her investigation. Now, she no longer feared where the dangerous path might lead.

***

A few days later, Sanchez walked to one of her favorite delis near her office on East Temple Street. The weather forecast was pleasant, with a mild Mediterranean breeze sweeping out the smog with a dark blue sky. The San Gabriel Mountains hovered over the L.A. skyline with postcard beauty. As she was about to devour her Reuben sandwich, she noticed Wallace Whitten, one of Meza's attorneys, entering the deli and peering at the menu on the board.

Whitten was forty years old and a well-respected African American attorney within the legal community and beyond. A solid trial attorney, he had a terrific working relationship with the district attorney's office. The attorney garnered respect among judges by avoiding courtroom histrionics, thoroughly researching his cases, preparing meticulous motions, and never misleading the court. Within the L.A. legal world, they called him affectionately *a bland vanilla version of Johnny Cochran.* Running a small practice, he specialized in criminal defense cases and appeals. On a personal level, Whitten was polite, composed, and respectful of all his adversaries. Juries loved him, and his humble charm was a plus. An L.A. native, he enjoyed a home-court advantage in trials since he intimately knew the disparate L.A. neighborhoods.

Whitten spoke to jurors on the ground level, not hiding behind a podium, and framed his defense so jurors might empathize with his predominantly Black and Latino clients.

Linda cupped her hands and yelled at Wallace, "Hey, Wallace! Try the

107

lobster bisque. It's great!"

"Nah. I'm allergic to shellfish. I'll try just a simple B.L.T. May I join you?" She nodded yes, and he sat across from her after he picked up his B.L.T. and water.

Linda asked, "Got a busy schedule today?"

"Not too bad. It's just a suppression motion in front of Judge Early. He's tough, but I have a chance."

Linda asked, "Who's the Deputy D.A.?"

"Marla Anderson."

"You got more than a chance." Whitten grinned and took a healthy bite. "Wallace, I'm not going to talk shop about the Meza case, but I just remembered that I had not tried a case with you in over twenty years. You were in the Public Defender's Office, and I was a newbie just out of law school."

"Yeah, Anthony 'Wilo' Tafoya. What a guy. That was also my first trial. The nimrod goes into a store in Koreatown with a semi-automatic in broad daylight during a busy morning. He forgot to put on a mask, but it was still a weak I.D. I had never prepared so much for any trial, and I couldn't sleep just thinking how I would screw it up."

Linda said, "That was also *my* first jury trial. I felt devastated when the jury walked him. The facts were pretty straightforward. But that's our jury. I learned a great deal from that loss."

"How so?" Wallace asked.

"Well, it's one of those things they don't or can't teach you in law school. I prepared that case as thoroughly as anyone could."

Whitten interjected, "I remember."

Linda continued, "I researched all the possible trial motions. I prepped for my witness examination. I researched all the elements of the charges. I prepared the jury instructions. I spent countless hours preparing my opening and closing arguments. I thought I would dazzle those jurors with brilliant oratory about the U.S. Constitution, sprinkled with bombastic quotes from Judge Learned Hand.

"Well, Mr. Whitten, Mr. Vanilla Johnny Cochran Jr., what I learned from you is just to talk *to* those jurors, not talk *at* them. There's a difference. Those jurors have to like you. But it's more. They need to know you're not insulting them with fancy multi-syllabic bullshit. Just talk to them. As trial lawyers, we understand that we're transparent and the jurors see right through us, right down to our heart and gut. We're no different from a used car salesperson selling a Honda. If the potential buyer likes you, the attraction to the product they're selling will follow."

"And I saw you in that trial, Wallace. You were honest with that jury. I even saw some of them nodding like bobbleheads, agreeing with you. That was a bad sign for the prosecution. You made me change my approach to trials, and I became a better trial lawyer observing you."

Whitten put his BLT down and said, "Wow. I'm flattered, Miss Sanchez."

Linda asked, "The Meza case was your second death penalty case, right?"

"I received death penalty certification four years ago and asked Jeremy if I could sit as second chair. He was gracious, and I learned a great deal from him. He handled most of the Meza case, and I felt like I was a neutral observer. But it was a good experience. I probably would not try another case with him, though," Whitten said.

Sanchez looked curious and said, "Why not?"

"Nothing concrete." Whitten paused to collect his words and said, "Linda, you and I grew up in similar circumstances, you in Boyle Heights and me in South-central. We go through life instinctively picking up certain messages. Sometimes, we use those instincts on the street, at a store, etc. We also need to rely on those instincts within our esteemed profession."

Whitten continued, "Maybe it's subtle. A fellow attorney might look at you in a certain way. For example, when I'm speaking casually to attorneys, they might start using more street slang than they normally would. Other attorneys often greet me with, *Hey, Bro, how ya doing, man*? Why can't that attorney use standard English? I pride myself on a well-developed vocabulary. Often, they limit conversations with me to sports and music. I *do* have other interests.

"Don't get me wrong. I have thick skin, and all those slights brush off me. I don't look for racism around every corner, but I still keep my antenna up." Whitten rose to leave and said, "But Lin, I will not work on the same case with Jeremy Holder because of those instincts. I won't say more. By the way, this B.L.T. is fabulous."

Linda said, "OK, Bro, right on Brotha!" She crossed her arms over her chest and yelled, "WAKANDA FOREVER!"

"Not funny, Sanchez." Whitten gave her a toothy smile, savored his last bite, and left, shaking his head, laughing.

CHAPTER 13

"Linda! Do you know how worried I got?"

Linda was at her mother's house three days after the shooting to mollify the latter's maternal worries.

Rita said, "It came out in *La Opinion*, and the shooting also came out on TV. How are you, *preciosa?* I called you a thousand times, but you never answered your phone." Both then heard the toilet flush.

Linda asked, "Julio? I thought he was going to find his own place, ma."

"I told you he would be here for a little time until he found a place. He's been doing well, looking for work anywhere, and his parole officer checks up on him. He's nice."

Her brother entered the living room. "Hey, sis. You OK? I heard about that shooting. That fucker almost got you, huh?"

"Julio, I'm good. I have to see a psychologist to make sure I'm OK up here," she said, tapping her head.

Julio said, "Hey, ma, how did the shooter miss her big head?"

"Mijo, that's not funny. I'm just glad she got him. Do you know who he was?"

"No, we're checking him out. He might have connections with Boyle Heights, but we don't know." Julio looked away for a moment. "We'll get more information soon. It was probably just a random burglary. I was not a target, ma, so don't worry; he was probably just some doper who noticed I was gone a few days. That's the price of living in Los Angeles."

Rita asked, "What do you mean, *gone?* Where were you?"

"My investigator and I are working on a case, and we had to go out of town for a while."

Rita said, "But Santa Monica? You moved there to avoid crime. The only criminals in Santa Monica are stoned surfers and drunken college kids pissing in the alleys—but a guy with a gun? You got to move out of there, *mija.*"

"Ma, I moved there because that area is safe, especially for someone in my profession. I'm good. So, Julio, what are your plans?"

Julio said, "You mean, how long will I be here? I dunno. I'll find my place soon. Are you sure you're good, Linda? I read people involved in shootings can get P.T.S.D., even a long time after."

Her brother's honest concern was soothing to Linda. They weren't close for many years, but his concern was genuine.

Julio said, "Linda, look, I hear a lot of stuff on the street. I don't know who the shooter was, but he might be from around this neighborhood. I don't know why. You and I have always had good instincts. As a kid, you always told me to trust my instincts. I don't think it's safe for you here. I can help take care of Mom. I wanna show off my cooking. We've been here for over thirty years and survived OK."

Linda nodded and said, "Mom, I have to leave now. I have a lot of work. I'll keep my phone line open. Call me anytime. I'll check on you. Julio, maybe staying here for a while is a good idea, OK?" Julio and their mother nodded and hugged her goodbye. Sanchez returned to her car and took a deep breath, clutching her Glock under her coat.

***

Linda arrived at her office the following day at dawn. Her priority today would be to check the results of the forensics exam on the cap and the money they brought from Calexico. In addition, Santos would give an update on the shooter. That a known informant came into her apartment to kill her was something they needed to investigate quickly. The L.A.P.D. connection was frightening to her. She thought, *Rampart again*?

While the Meza investigation was critical, there were always new murder cases on the horizon. And she had not given Ed Ross the complete picture. He might discourage her and tell her there was little to pursue in the Meza case. *Let it rest*, he would probably tell her.

At around ten that morning, she received a text from Ed Ross. He wanted her and Ramon to meet with him at one o'clock in his office.

***

Before her scheduled meeting, Sanchez went to the forensics lab to meet with Carl Mason, the forensic analyst, who had examined the cap and the

111

wad of money.

"Hey Carl, what ya got for me?" Mason had a cluttered office that looked like a blind five-year-old had ransacked it. He closed the door.

"Lin, is this an open case you're working on? I need to catalog it. It's the Meza case, but I thought that case was closed. You convicted the guy, right?"

"Carl, I'm just doing some follow-up. The investigators did not analyze the cap since it was very distinctive, and we knew it belonged to the defendant—the beer stains and the Adrian Ethier autograph. And the officers smelled smoke on it. The defendant also admitted ownership to the police and in court. So, there was never any point in analyzing it. So, what can you tell me?"

"First, we picked up multiple prints from some dollar bills. Nothing conclusive, and we'll continue to pursue that analysis. But the cap. I found microscopic indicators of smoke, as you might surmise. The arson started in the boy's bedroom and spread to the living room. So, you would expect to find indicators of that material on the cap."

Linda asked, "And?"

"The smoke residue was not from curtain or furniture material. It was likely from wood. Probably oak." Sanchez nodded and showed no response.

"There's another thing. I need to show something to make a better point. I thought it was my imagination when I opened the evidence bag, but I wanted to show it to you directly." Mason brought the sealed bag to his cluttered desk and carefully opened it after placing his initials and date to preserve the legal chain of custody. As he opened the bag, he gestured for her to come closer. "Put your nose in there. What do you smell?"

Linda said, "It smells like barbeque beef. Damn."

"I found something else on the cap. Another substance on it appeared to be barbeque or tomato sauce. That stuff doesn't decompose quickly, and I could still smell it. Do you know what it might be?"

"Carl, that smell might be *Legally Insane Texas Barbeque*."

***

Santos and Sanchez arrived at Edward Ross' office shortly before one o'clock. You never want to keep your boss and possibly the future Los

Angeles District Attorney waiting.

Ross entered the office and commanded them to sit.

"Linda, let me cut to the chase. Why are you two still working on the Meza case? I heard you guys were in some border town asking questions about the case. The appeal will take years, probably long after you have retired. You worked hard to convict this bad guy and don't want to blow it."

Sanchez went first. "Ed, you know I always review my trials to ensure I covered everything. That's all."

Santos said, "Mr. Ross, we just need to cover some loose ends from the trial, and they all might not mean too much, anyway. There's no point in briefing you with nothing. We know you're busy with a future campaign and all."

Ross said, "Ramon, I'm not thinking in political terms right now. If, and it's a big if, I run for the vacancy, that won't be for another year. Right now, I want to ensure that one of my best lawyers and one of our best investigators are not going rogue."

Linda said, "Ed, if Ramon and I receive information about the Meza case, you'll be the first to know."

Ross said, "By the way, Linda, have you been attending your therapy sessions? What you've been through can trigger P.T.S.D. That was a close call. Also, is this shooting incident related to the Meza case?"

"Yes, to the first question, and no to the second."

"All right, that's it for now. Get back to work and keep me briefed."

Santos said, "Yes, sir."

***

Sanchez woke early the following morning for a quick jog along Santa Monica beach. She passed by a few joggers, some fishermen, hungry seagulls, and a misty fog rolling in from the Pacific. Los Angeles in the fall doesn't offer color foliage, but the change is palpable in a west-coast way: cooler winds, clearer skies, and the San Gabriel mountains sometimes show early snow framing the L.A. basin. The chilly temperatures along the beach keep the non-locals away. The ocean's immense beauty made her feel like her problems were minuscule, and the beach helped her remove clutter from her head and think clearly.

Her problem was the *Brady* case. She reached the point in the Meza revelations that might require her to reveal this information to the defense attorneys. But this created a *Catch-22*.

All prosecutors have grappled with the ethical demands of the *Brady* case. In a pivotal case in 1963, the U.S. Supreme Court succinctly outlined the ethical obligations of a prosecutor:

"... the suppression by the prosecution of evidence favorable to an accused upon request violates due process where the evidence is material either to guilt or to punishment, irrespective of the good faith or bad faith of the prosecution," Justice William Douglas.

Prosecutors must do something that might seem counter-intuitive to some—providing information that might get a defendant off. Convictions have been reversed for *Brady* violations. *Brady* violations can trigger legal sanctions for prosecutors. Defense attorneys are constantly sniffing around for any potential *Brady* issues to exploit.

The words of Justice Douglas were gnawing at her psyche, and she might be obligated to reveal this exculpatory information to the person she now suspected of setting up his client, Jeremy Holder. But she still did not have enough to accuse Holder of misconduct or firmly say this information was exculpatory. Justice Douglas was looking over her shoulder.

She pulled out her cell phone. "Hey Wallace, how are you? Oh, I'm at the beach. Those are seagulls you hear. Yeah, lucky me. Wallace, can we meet at our favorite deli this evening around seven? Ramon Santos will also join us. Great. Thank you, see you then."

***

Sanchez and Santos arrived before Whitten and ordered him a B.L.T. on wheat with unsweetened iced tea. She had her usual Greek salad with water. Santos sat beside her, clutching a cup of black coffee and a sugary bear claw.

Whitten saw her and the B.L.T. and joked, "You must need something from me with that B.L.T., Linda. What's up?"

Sanchez took a deep breath and outlined her theory of Holder's activities. "Now, Wallace, I realize this sounds far-fetched, but here goes."

"Your co-counsel, Jeremy Holder, for unknown reasons, set up his own client, *your* client, to shove him onto a path directly to San Quentin."

114

"Holder hired a guy to place Meza's cap in the house several months *after* the murders. The same guy, Panchito Gutierrez, who planted the Dodger cap on the premises, winds up dead in Calexico, California, shot with a nine-millimeter Glock. The shooter probably dropped it by mistake, but that Glock is the newest service-issued weapon for the Los Angeles Police Department. There is also evidence that Nico Jr. started the fire. We didn't know he had a history of setting fires; it's some kind of anxiety-driven pyromania.

"You guys would not have known about it, Wallace, since the Social Services Department channeled the reports into confidential files. My office certainly was unaware of it."

Wallace said, "Son of a bitch. Nico didn't start it. You think L.A.P.D. set up my client?"

Linda said, "Maybe they were involved, but we don't know. Lots of maybes. Maybe both Holder and the LAPD were in on it. Holder wanted to ensure there was smoke residue on the cap, so he placed it in his barbeque smoker. You've been to his famous barbeques, right? There's residue of wood smoke and barbeque sauce. Holder called it *Legally Insane Texas sauce*; he has some flair."

Whitten interjected, "Man, those ribs and briskets he cooks. It's better than anything I've had in South-central."

Linda said, "Yup. That was a damn good brisket I ate at his house. But back to the point—we think the same guy that killed Panchito Gonzalez in Calexico was the same guy who tried to kill me."

"Wasn't that guy only trying to burglarize your place?"

Santos said, "No, it was an assassination attempt, not a burglary. The shooter in Lin's apartment was a guy named Enrique 'Kike' Escalante. We think he was a snitch with the L.A.P.D., but we can't confirm that. And this will be news for both of you, but guess who represented both Panchito *and* Kike?" Santos looked at both and raised his eyebrows.

Whitten asked, "No shit, Holder?" Santos nodded; Whitten stood up for a second, then sat down. "Damn, I don't think I want iced tea; I think I need a double scotch, and I don't drink much!"

Santos said, "I don't know if the defendants' family retained Holder or if the court appointed him. He was probably retained since most appointments are random. But he sure knew both and represented both on at least four or five cases. And if Kike was a snitch for the LAPD, then Holder must have brokered those deals with the LAPD. Logically, one can assume Holder knows some of those cops well. Mr. Whitten, do you know how Holder could have retrieved that cap?”

Wallace said, “Well, we visited Nico’s home at least twice for background information. And I remember Nico mentioned to us once that he kept that lucky cap inside his bedroom dresser. But I never saw Holder with it. We looked around the house both times but only took a photo with his mom to use as a prop in the penalty phase, garnering sympathy from the jury. But that’s it. Jeremy went alone to the house once before I went, ostensibly for some follow-up information from Mrs. Meza.”

Sanchez looked frustrated and said, “We don’t have enough concrete evidence, just a lot of loose dots to connect, but those dots are getting clearer and closer.”

Santos said, “And we don’t have any motive. What’s with this guy? Who would set up his client? A conviction needs a motive. Did Holder have a beef with Meza? Something personal?”

Whitten stroked his chin, staring into space. “While we’re thinking about some far-fetched theories, I’ll give you one. The University of Texas at Austin School of Law.”

Linda said, “OK, I know he went there. He always brags about that friggin mascot, *Bevo*, the longhorn steer. So, what about his law school?”

Whitten said, “Well, one time, we were prepping for the trial at his office, and Holder mentioned an incident while he was in college. I don’t know why he told me; it was probably during one of his drunken episodes. Jeremy is a lush, but he calls himself a *social drinker*. Anyway, Jeremy mentioned nothing more except that he got into some kind of trouble with a Black student there. That’s all I know. I told you, Lin, a while back that I got bad vibes from the guy.”

Sanchez said, “It’s unlikely there’s only a racial element to this, but you never know.”

Whitten said, “I’m not shocked at these developments. I’ll talk to Nico and check out the law school thing. I know some people. At some point, we have to reveal this information.”

Linda edged closer to Whitten and said, “Wallace, I’m sorry for dragging you into this crap. And I realize your awkward position. But you might have some insight that can shed some light on this.”

Whitten quickly finished the B.L.T. and left. “I’ll keep in touch, Linda.”

CHAPTER 14

FROM RITA AYALA SANCHEZ

I don't know where to begin about my family or me. Linda is my pride and joy. Don't get me wrong; I love Julio just as much, but he took another path. That was his choice. He's an adult.

The worst thing that happened to us was the breakup of my marriage. My husband, Marcos Sanchez, was a good man. We met when I was seventeen, working in a San Diego restaurant. I had no papers, but we fell in love. He fixed my immigration papers, and we married. At first, I thought I was in the American dream. A loving husband. A good house in the San Fernando Valley. Marcos had a good job with decent money.

The dream faded over time, and the reality of life began. I had two kids and more expenses. I think I was too demanding. "Get another and better job!" "This house is too small!" "I need more help with the kids!" Marcos worked two jobs, and they were good jobs. He drove a truck with a construction company in Ventura and worked part time as a janitor in a hospital. Everything seemed promising, but I still never had enough. My husband didn't want me to work, so I devoted all my time to raising the kids. But we grew apart. We hardly discussed family things except rent, doctor visits, and the kids' school. After a while, we slept in separate bedrooms. Although I know he loved the kids dearly, he saw them less and less because he was always working. I still have good memories of him and Linda taking walks around the neighborhood, throwing a baseball, or riding bikes with Julio. The kids worshiped him.

I found out he was seeing someone at the hospital. The signs were there. A scent on his shirt. Daydreaming. He spent more time at the hospital than necessary. He finally left us. I told the kids he didn't love me or them anymore, and we divorced. He left the kids to me, but I know he loved them, and I know I pushed him away from the marriage and the family.

He still supported us after he left, but it wasn't enough. My sister said the houses in East L.A. were cheaper, so we found a home in Boyle Heights in 1985 when the kids were little. At first, I missed the San Fernando Valley, but over time, I got used to Boyle Heights, where I raised Julio and Linda. This is my home. Linda wants me to move, but I won't. I can't.

I had to get two jobs to pay the bills, even though Marcos still sent support payments. He was really a good man. The kids did well in school. Julio made a lot of friends, and Linda was the opposite. She spent her time studying while other girls her age were out having fun.

I had to make an important decision about their school. My dream was for them to go to Catholic school. I did not want them in the public schools in Boyle Heights. I felt the Catholic schools were much better—and much safer. And my kids would stand a better chance of success.

But I couldn't afford to send them both. I thought Julio was stronger and could survive Boyle Heights. He was tough and quickly made many friends. He was book-smart and street-smart. Linda was like a frail flower who needed protection. Little did I know then how tough she was.

So, I only sent her to Catholic school and lied to Julio that he would soon follow her. He knew I was lying—I could never afford both. I lost Julio to the streets. Those streets welcomed him. I blame myself for that. I failed as a mother. He changed after Linda left for Catholic school, started skipping school, and never did homework. He came and went whenever he wanted. His father was no help. Julio hated him for leaving. I lost Julio. I cry every day for that. Dios mio!

When Linda did well in school, I was so happy. She saw me cry at her law school graduation but didn't realize I cried because Julio could not attend.

He was in jail.

As I saw Linda grow, I never realized she was so strong. Failure was never something she accepted. She took on a problem without wasting her time thinking about it. I met some of her co-workers at the district attorney's office, and I could tell from their faces that they respected her deeply.

I even saw her on television as her cases got bigger and bigger.

I have no regrets in my life. I wish some things could have turned out differently. I go to church every Sunday and find comfort in my Bible. I pray the rosary daily, and I pray that Julio will come back to me for good. And I pray that Linda will always be safe.

CHAPTER 15

"What the hell you doing here, Wallace?"

Wallace sat down before his client across the plexiglass and said nothing.

Meza stood up and said, "I'm not sure I wanna see you, man, unless you're bringing me good news and telling me I'm getting out of this shithole! I been here only six months, and I don't think I'll make it. One hour of daylight. That fucking cell is smaller than my closet. It smells like death in here. The guards are assholes. There are some crazy bastards in here on both sides of the bars. Lots of these guys kill themselves waiting, always waiting. Maybe that's the way to go. I don't like waiting. I keep hearing I might get a Prop 66 transfer, but I don't think that's gonna happen soon, man."

The sight of his client shocked Whitten—Meza seemed to have aged ten years since he saw him six months ago with a ghostly complexion and angry, bloodshot eyes. Wallace noticed a few more grey hairs sprouted. Dull redness around his left cheek suggested a previous altercation. Meza's eyes were lifeless, like a dead fish on a shore.

Meza paused a few seconds and said, "Sorry, man. You've always been cool with me. You're a good attorney. So, why the hell are you here? Is it about my appeal? Have you seen my mom?"

Whitten would not tell Meza he was here without Holder knowing, so he needed to talk with Meza around the edges. "I just want to review some things. You will be communicating with your appellate attorneys soon, and I just wanted to go over some things that might help your appeal."

Meza calmed down and said, "OK. You came all the way from L.A., so it must be important."

"It might be. Let me ask you this. As you know, I was the second chair in this trial. Holder had more experience and took the lead in the case. I was not involved in all aspects of the case."

Meza looked annoyed. "Where's this going, Wallace?"

"Well, Nico, let me ask you this. When you spoke with Jeremy, was there anything you may have told him that you didn't tell me? Don't get me wrong; he always filled me in on all the trial developments, and I learned a lot from him. He's one of the most experienced lawyers in the state in death penalty cases."

Meza then reviewed most of the information he told Holder, and nothing seemed unusual in Wallace's mind.

The conversation invariably returned to Meza's lucky cap. "I still can't explain that cap, man. I never leave it anywhere. It's my luck. I know I would not have left it at Amelia's house. I remember telling you guys I always put that cap inside my bedroom dresser. Even my mom knows not to touch it. She once wanted to wash it, but I wouldn't let her." Meza parsed his chapped lips and said, "I'm too superstitious about it. When the cops came to arrest me, I knew that cap was in the dresser."

Wallace asked, "Could they have grabbed it?"

"Nah, I don't think so. Afterward, I thought my luck had run out because I didn't have the cap on. Sounds stupid, huh?"

"Nico, no, it's not stupid. Do you remember visiting any public places after leaving the house that night? Maybe somewhere, a witness might have seen you with the cap?"

Meza said, "Wait, I told you guys about the alibi! I know you were there with Jeremy when I told you. Yeah, I told you guys that after I fought with Amelia the night of the fire, I went to a bar, Eddie's Bar, right off Whittier Boulevard in Montebello. And when I left the house, there was no fucking fire." Meza squinted his eyes like he was trying to jog his memory and said, "It's about five miles from Amelia's house. I know the bartender. It's a hole-in-the-wall, but it's quiet. Never any hassles. That's how I like it. And I went there again the night after. I left the house pissed; that's it. No fire. I've always been consistent with that point."

"What did you do at the bar?"

"It's a damn bar, Wallace."

Wallace said, "No, what I mean is, did you meet anyone there those nights?"

"I like that place because everybody keeps to themselves. I might have thrown some darts and played a little pool. But I don't remember seeing anyone I know except the bartender, Arnie, Arnoldo. I've gone there for about five years, and he's always behind the bar. Cool guy.

Quiet.”

“The fire happened around ten o’clock when you say you were at the bar. Do you remember what time you got there?”

Meza said, “I usually get there around eight. Arnie leaves a small spread of munchies on the bar at nine, like clockwork. I never knew why he set out the munchies at that specific time. It’s just a habit, I guess. You know, salty nuts, chips, salsa, sometimes fresh guacamole. You know I’m a fucking alcoholic. I rarely leave the bar before closing time at two. And that’s when I left both nights.”

“So, just so I’m clear, you went to Eddie’s Bar both nights between six and two, the night of the fire and the day after? February second and the third of 2021? And you had your cap on?”

“Yeah, that’s about right. I told you guys that, or maybe I just told Holder; I don’t remember.”

“Nico, I wouldn’t have forgotten that information. Do you know if Holder followed up on that lead?”

Meza said, “About two weeks after I told him about Eddie’s Bar, Holder came to see me at County Jail and told me he checked out the alibi, but he got nothing. Holder told me the bartender couldn’t remember anything, and there was no proof I was even there on a specific night. So I thought that’s gone nowhere. Holder seemed honestly frustrated that the alibi didn’t pan out. I liked Holder, and I believed him.”

“OK. Holder’s very thorough, so he must’ve checked it out. Another question: Do you know a guy named Panchito Gonzalez?”

“No. Never heard of him.”

Meza stroked his whiskers on his chin and asked, “Why?”

“It’s probably not important. How about a guy named *Kike* Escalante?”

Meza paused and said, “I don’t know him—I don’t wanna know that dude. He’s a known independent hitman—a professional. There’re lots of stories about the guy. He’s like an urban legend in East L.A. I heard he’s a snitch for the L.A.P.D., so he’s Teflon—no one can touch him. I heard he does jobs for some drug cartels on both sides of the border. Is he somehow involved in my case?”

“Maybe. I was just trying to follow up on some information, that’s all.”

Meza asked, “What do you know about Escalante?”

"He's dead. And Nico, you mustn't tell Holder about this conversation, OK?"

With a confused face, Meza said, "OK. Hey Wallace, so who capped Escalante? The guy that killed him must've been a badass."

"Yeah, she is."

***

"How are you really, Linda?"

Linda sat in the office of her assigned psychiatrist, Dr. Sofia Chambers, in Culver City. "I'm doing well. I can't wait to get back to work full time."

"This should be our last session, and you can return full-time to work. I'll sign off on it. Keep going to A.A. because I think it's good for you. It's probably better and cheaper than therapy with an expensive psychiatrist like me." Both chuckled. "My clients who have gone to A.A. or N.A. rarely regret attending."

Linda said, "I know. I like it. I understand why I drank too much, and I quit feeling sorry for myself. I also stopped blaming myself for what went wrong in my life. I still go to mass as often as possible, which helps."

Dr. Chambers said, "But Linda, I'm still not convinced you have completely dealt with this shooting incident."

"What do you mean?" Linda asked.

Dr. Chambers said, "Well, those that are involved in shootings like yours—it might be cops, or victims, or spouses—have a difficult time processing the shooting. Instead, they might become victimized again by the memory of the violent event. It's a form of P.T.S.D. Some outward manifestations resemble combat vets, like the use of alcohol to suppress the memory, not talking about it, or even some sense of guilt, as if the incident was the victim's fault. I once treated a defendant in therapy before her jury trial. Her charge: murdering her boyfriend after he raped her. But with a twisted and perverted sense of logic, she blamed herself. She felt the breakup was *her* fault, and she felt his anger and wrath were *her* fault. She felt his constant mental abuse was *her* fault. So, the logical endpoint of that twisted logic was that the rape was also her fault."

"How did she turn out?" Linda asked.

122

With a dry monotone, Dr. Chambers said, "She committed suicide before her trial."

"Doctor, I feel good, really," Linda said.

"Do you still have conversations with your deceased husband?"

"Yes, mostly in my dreams. But I also talk to him when I'm awake. Is that messed up?"

"To most people, it might seem odd. But therapeutically, it's actually beneficial and healthy—to a point. It might be a way to tell your late husband things you never had the chance to do so before he left this earth. And it's also a chance to deal with the loss of your unborn child," said Dr. Chambers.

"I've accepted the fact that I lost my husband and my child, and they're never coming back. I'm not delusional, but I feel a soothing calm when I talk to him."

"Good."

"But Doctor, about the guy I killed. I have no regrets. Yeah, it's messed up. That son-of-a-bitch tried to kill me. I can still feel the heat of that bullet near my head. I can still smell the smoke. I can still see and smell his last breath. And when I fired those three shots at him, it was not just a mindless reaction. In slow motion, I was fully conscious of what I was doing. I wanted that bastard dead. You hear stories about people in shootings who describe a surreal, out-of-body experience. No, hell no, I knew exactly what I was doing and where I was, and I would do it again a million times. I wanted that guy dead. And I feel good about it."

Dr. Chambers embraced Linda's hand and said, "I don't think I can follow up on that point. Linda, you're good. This will be our last session. Get back to work. You know where to find me if you want to talk again. Maybe we can get a coffee."

***

Wallace Whitten reviewed his options. His co-counsel, an esteemed lawyer, might have set up his client. That possibility was difficult to fathom. While Whitten never felt comfortable around Holder, that feeling did not mean the guy would set up his client, especially if the consequences were so extreme—death. He could not imagine any scenario where this might be possible except in a far-fetched movie. Tarantino

123

would laugh his ass off at this script.

But Meza was no dummy. Although he was homeless and had a sixth-grade education, his memory was good, and he could recall details of his activities around the time of the fire. Maybe he made it up to sound credible, like many of Wallace's clients.

However, Holder never told Wallace about the potential alibi Meza mentioned. Why not? It made no sense. Wallace was deep in these thoughts as he took the off-ramp onto Whittier Boulevard. His Google Maps didn't show *Eddie's Bar*, so he used an old-school method: an actual paper map. Near eight p.m., he parked a block from the bar, a nondescript building that could have been a small warehouse. A small sign and window were the only indicators that this was, in fact, a bar that was squeezed between a tire shop and a Mexican bakery. He wasn't sure if it was open as he pushed the door and entered.

Two lonely patrons sat at the bar, clutching their beer bottles, alone in their thoughts. The muted sounds of Vicente Fernandez blared from an old-fashioned jukebox in a dark corner. Thick air trickled into his nostrils with a strong hint of urine, sweat, and stale beer. The two turned to him in unison and stared at him up and down, then returned to comfort their beers.

Wanting to blend in, Whitten discarded his expensive business attire and donned what he thought were blue-collar—barely—employed—but—not—homeless street clothes: worn jeans from Nordstrom that came with holes off the rack, a work shirt he often wore when he pruned his roses, a black Raiders cap worn backward with a faux-gangster vibe, and capped with $500 Air Jordans. He couldn't suppress his innate nerdiness and fooled no one in that bar except himself. He stuck out like a zebra among black stallions. The bartender thought: *This guy's an undercover cop, a dumb nerd who wandered into the wrong place, someone casing this place for a quick score, or a dumb tourist who got lost off the L.A. freeway.* As Whitten approached the far end of the bar, the patron gulped his beer and quietly left. The other glanced at him sideways, protectively clutching his beer.

Whitten said, "Get me a cold draft, please." The bartender appeared distant yet friendly and placed the frosty mug before Whitten. "This place is nice and quiet. I like it." The bartender was in no mood for mindless banter and returned to the other end of the bar to view a soccer match on a small TV.

Whitten wanted to make the lone drinker uncomfortable, so he kept staring at him. The lonely guy chugged his beer, dried his lips, glared at Whitten, and left. The bartender, visibly annoyed, told him, "You made these guys uncomfortable. Are you L.A.P.D.? If you are, that's cool. Anyone is welcome here. I just never want any trouble."

Whitten ignored the question and didn't realize how thirsty he was until he sipped the beer. He quickly drank the mug and asked, "Can you get me another one? That's good. Damn, it was hot today. Must've been at least ninety-five."

The bartender locked eyes on Whitten, then slowly placed another cold brew on the bar and said, "Thanks for the weather report. You gonna give me a barometer reading? Hope you like this one, and I hope it's your last. No offense. We close soon."

"I thought you closed at two." There was no response from the other side of the bar—just a curious stare that turned into an icy glare.

"Tell me what you want here. You didn't just randomly wander into this place. I don't think you're a cop. You sound too smart. You're more like an I.R.S. agent. What, I checked off too many deductions?"

Whitten giggled and said, "You're Arnold, Arnie, right?"

"OK, so you know me. Who the hell are you? Did my ex-wife send you? Tell her she'll get the money next week."

Whitten extended his hand across the bar. The bartender kept both hands clutched to the bar without reciprocating the gesture. "My name is Wallace Whitten, and I'm a lawyer."

"Lawyer. Worse than an I.R.S. agent. What do you want from me, Mr. Lawyer?"

"I was the trial attorney for Nicolas Meza, Nico."

"Isn't that trial over? Heard your guy went down pretty hard—death penalty. You can't go down harder than that. Nico was a good customer."

"Yeah. Nico told us he came here often. He was right. It's quiet. No one bothers you. And he felt comfortable here, especially with you. He said you were a good guy."

Arnie's voice relaxed, and he said, "I remember Nico. He was like clockwork. He usually came right before I put out the munchie tray— nothing too fancy: chips, salsa, beer nuts. Every so often, I would have my old lady make something special, like tiny quesadillas or deviled eggs.

I got repeat customers that way, including Nico. I put out the spread at nine. Nico usually stayed till closing."

Arnold looked annoyed. "I told the other guy all this stuff. You're asking me the same questions. Why?"

"What other guy?'

"His other lawyer. Tall white guy. Hold something."

"Holder."

"Yeah, that's the guy. Holder. Seemed cool. Gave me a good tip. Anyway, he asked me about three specific days and if Nico had been here those days. And, oh yeah, he kept asking about Nico's cap. I told Holder I would never see that dude without it. Nico told me the whole lucky cap bullshit story. I'm sure he believes in luck. I told the lawyer I vaguely remember Nico coming here those days because some of my regulars had this informal dart tournament going."

"You sure it was the three days in February 2021?"

"Yeah, during COVID, but business was actually good. People just wanted to get out and get drunk during Covid. I remember the time 'cause he quit coming right after he got arrested. I even told that guy Holder I kept security tapes from that month. I keep tapes for a few years, then dump them. I got two cameras; see that one behind us? Then there's another one pointing to the entrance. This is mostly a cash business, and I post signs so everyone knows we have those cameras. We got robbed about six years ago. Crapped in my pants. But L.A.P.D. got the moron a few months later."

Whitten said, "Did Holder see those tapes?"

"Yeah. I showed the tapes to the guy and gave him a pen drive that recorded the three days. But he never came back. He never called me to follow up. I don't read the papers. I get most of my news on my old lady's Facebook. Was this important for his trial?"

"Maybe. Do you have those tapes?"

"Let me close up the place. Let's go back to my office, and I'll get that pen drive, the copy, just like the one I made for Holder." They entered a cramped office behind the bar, and the bartender inserted a pen drive. On the computer screen, Whitten observed what he hoped not to.

According to the timestamps on the videos, for three consecutive nights, one day before the arson, the day of the arson, and the day after, Nico Meza entered the bar at about eight, sat at the bar, slowly drank beer, ate the free munchies around nine, and left around two a.m. like clockwork. The only times he left his seat were to play darts and pee. On all three days, there was one unassailable consistency—Meza wore his lucky Los Angeles Dodgers cap. Whitten could clearly discern the distinctive beer stain on the bill of the cap because the video quality of both cameras was good. The unique beer stain was as good as a fingerprint. Whitten remembered what Linda told him—*the pebble stuck in her shoe.*

Nico Meza did not start the fire. Nico Meza was wearing his lucky cap before and after the fire—the same lucky cap that was recovered at the crime scene months *after* the incident and after his arrest. And Nico was on death row because his attorney may have set him up. But Holder's motive remained a mystery.

***

Whitten nervously rode the elevator to the tenth floor of the Century high-rise. He exited the elevator and entered office 128:

Law Office of Jeremy Holder

Attorney at Law

"Hey, Wallace, what's happening? We haven't talked in a long time, man." Holder greeted him in the reception area with an overly zealous bro hug. Let's go into my office. "We haven't talked in a long time. Need some coffee? I just got a new expresso machine. It's dope. Good stuff."

"No, Jeremy, I'm good. I have to be in court in two hours for a prelim. You didn't tell me over the phone what this was about."

"Right. I'll get to the point. Have you been speaking to Linda Sanchez about the Meza case?"

Whitten knew he couldn't hesitate to answer with a guy like Holder. He had seen Holder in court dozens of times with hostile witnesses, and he could chew them up in tiny pieces.

Hesitating to answer a question would allow a witness to deflect or avoid the question. Whitten quickly blurted, "No. I ran into her a few weeks ago at a deli, and we had a quick bite together. But there was no discussion about Meza. That would be inappropriate. Why?"

"I'm just checking."

"Jeremy, if I had any substantive discussions with her or anyone else

127

about the case, I would let you know. Look, you asked me here for a reason. What is it?"

"Nah, bro. I just heard rumors she's snooping around the case, and I just need to know why. Did she mention anything at all to you?"

"She just asked if you or I will work on the appeal. I only told her you were on the appellate team. I don't think she was probing. She knows me better. Besides, what the hell would she be doing looking into the case? She got her conviction. There's probably nothing to those rumors. Lawyers are the most prolific gossipers I know, even more than elderly Black women like all my aunts."

Holder chuckled and said, "I'm sorry I wasted your time here. You're probably right, and there's nothing to those rumors. But here's another thing I know—she spoke to Nico's mother."

"Why?"

"I was told she was asking general questions about Nico and the cap. She wanted to know how often we were at her house before the trial. And how many times the cops were there."

Whitten said, "That's strange. She probably already had that information during her trial prep."

Holder said, "Mrs. Meza told me she was polite, and there was nothing unusual about her visit." Holder paced nervously and said, "But I don't like it. She can't be talking to our client's mother. It's almost like talking to *our* client. I need to put a stop to this. She can't communicate with our client's family. Wallace, can you guess what Sanchez was doing there?"

Wallace quickly answered, "A burglar almost murdered her, and maybe she thought Nico's mother might know something. That's too farfetched, I know, but I can't think of any other reason. Your guess is as good as mine. It's probably nothing to worry about. We know Sanchez is very thorough and probably just wanted to cover herself."

Holder said, "Well, bro, I'm still pissed that she might be communicating indirectly to my, our, client, a client she just sent to his execution. I don't want her playing any games." Whitten said nothing and left.

CHAPTER 16

THE HOLDERS FROM WESTLAKE, TEXAS, 1985

Their glittering lives flowed beautifully along a golden river toward a bright tomorrow, a future of glamorous vacations, summer homes, outdoor barbeques, and a bounty of grandchildren buffeted by wealth, Texas wealth. They say everything is bigger in Texas, including money. The father cultivated a prosperous business—an expanding law firm in Fort Worth. The mom no longer worked as a cardiac nurse and retired to full-time motherhood to raise their only child, a vibrant and outgoing boy. Freckles dotted the child's adorable face, topped with thick, curly, light brown hair.

Living on a sprawling ranch-style home of five thousand square feet on five acres, their ten-year-old child had plenty of room to play. Grand oak and pecan trees proudly surrounded the manicured landscape like sentries. The child's toys littered the yard, and Dad built a small soccer field for their son to hone the boy's raw skills. Westlake Academy had a competitive team that won the state soccer championship for twelve and under the year before.

The Holders spent lazy weekends entertaining family or business clients, showing off mother's Texas barbeque and homemade pies. During football season, they never missed the Dallas Cowboys home games as Dad entertained clients in the firm's private booth on the forty-yard line. When there was time, the father took his son fishing and hunting.

Mom devoted her time to homemaking and designing the home interior. Texas flagstone adorned the outer walls, and handmade Saltillo tile gleamed throughout the interior. She selected Italian furniture, Navaho rugs, and various oil paintings, mainly by Texan artists—all amenities proudly showcased in the April 1983 edition of Texas Country Homes & Lifestyle magazine.

The parents astutely recognized that their son would live in a different world once he ventured beyond the safe confines of their cloistered suburban utopia. They encouraged their son to cultivate friends outside their social network and develop his budding social skills.

The boy invited a few soccer teammates from school to their house to play, and he was eager to share his vibrant world with them. So, they came on several weekends, swam, kicked soccer balls, shot baskets, rode bikes, and feasted on mom's hamburgers, hot dogs, ice cream, and homemade desserts. They saw "The Goonies" three times together. The boy now had three best friends: Miguel, Brady, and Juan. They were inseparable—for a while.

At school, the boy tried to make new friends but unconsciously did little to suppress his wealthy background—bragging about his big house, servants, vacations, clothes, and life. The young boy didn't know better and thought this was a way to win the hearts of his schoolmates. Over time, his three soccer friends grew tired of his constant pretensions and began to shun him, along with most other classmates. He attempted to hang out with them, but they responded with youthful disdain and hostility. Ostracized from most elementary school cliques, he became lonely and withdrawn. Miguel, Brady, and Juan maintained their own loyal cliques and never allowed the boy to enter their insular group. Being scorned by most in school devastated the ten-year-old boy. He would hear the taunts from the kids: 'Jeremy the Germ, Wormy Germy! Wormy Germy!'

On the school bus, the boy sat alone. 'Hey, Wormy Germy!' During the lunch hour, the boy ate alone.

In the school hallways, the boy walked alone.

Loneliness shackled him like a straitjacket, and he no longer invited the three boys to his home.

He now played soccer at home alone.

He now shot baskets at home alone.

Loneliness began to gnaw at his soul and turned it raw.

One day, he finally dared to approach Miguel, Brady, and Juan after school as they waited at the bus stop.

"Hey guys, wanna come this Saturday? We can hang out and play some soccer. I'll see if my mom can cook some burgers."

The boys gazed awkwardly at the ground. Miguel spoke first. "Nah. We got plans, man. My dad's taking us to see the Cowboys this Sunday. They got Seattle."

The boy asked, "How are your seats?"

Miguel responded, "My dad said we got the cheap seats. You know, the ones where we gotta stand up. I can't wait. Man, they got the best food!" Brady and Juan nodded.

The boy turned to Brady and Juan and asked, "You two guys going also?"

Brady said, "Of course. I wouldn't miss this. My parents can't afford to take all our family to a game, but they said I could go. Can't wait to eat all that food!"

Juan chimed in, "I'm gonna wear my Tony Dorsett jersey! Might get his autograph."

Miguel said, "No way you'll get that autograph."

The boy interrupted and said, "My dad does some legal stuff for the Cowboys, and he met Tony Dorsett once at a party a long time ago. He even got his autograph." The other three boys said nothing and looked down the street for the bus. Someone on the sidewalk yelled, 'Hey, Wormy Germy!'

Miguel said, "That's cool, man. Tony Dorsett was the best."

"Hey, why didn't you guys invite me to that game? My dad has a skybox on the forty-yard line. The owner sits nearby. I met him once. You didn't need to go to those cheap seats, standing all day. You'll get tired watching the game."

Miguel said, "We'll be OK. Those seats are good. My dad spent most of his paycheck to buy them a few months ago. We don't mind standing. We'll be all right."

The boy said, "My dad's skybox also has air conditioning when it gets hot. You'll have all the food you can eat, man. Not just cheap hotdogs."

Miguel interrupted, "We'll be good. I can eat fifty hotdogs." Juan and Brady nodded.

The boy said, "Well, I can eat a hundred!" The three boys laughed.

The boy was subdued and asked, "Hey Miguel, so why didn't you guys invite me? I would have paid for the ticket."

"My dad didn't have more to spare. I would have invited you if there were more tickets; there just weren't anymore."

The boy said, "You guys just didn't want me to come! That's it. Don't lie to me!"

Juan raised his palms and said, "Hey man, take it easy. Miguel just didn't have enough tickets, OK?"

Unsatisfied with the explanation, the boy said, "You guys just didn't want me. After all the times you guys were at my house playing, eating, and hanging out. And you don't invite me? My mom told me she made all that expensive food for you guys so you wouldn't have to eat only those darn baloney sandwiches and bean tacos!"

Miguel put his hand on the boy's shoulder. "Listen, we can still hang out a little at school. But we might not have time to visit your house for a while. My parents probably won't let me."

The boy, wiping the snot from his nose, said, "Screw you three. While you guys are standing and eating cheap hot dogs, look up at the skyboxes, and you'll see me giving you guys the finger. Screw you all!"

The bus finally arrived, and Miguel, Juan, and Brady climbed in. The boy waited and climbed in last, sitting alone in the front seat.

Someone in the back yelled, 'Hey, it's Wormy Germy!'

***

The three boys were exhausted when they returned from the Cowboys game. Their stomachs bloated warmly with hot dogs, ice cream, chips, and hamburgers. Their voices were hoarse as they cheered and yelled through four quarters of football. But their exhaustion was a good sensation, and they would reminisce about this childhood memory for many years like an old photo.

The boys returned to Miguel's house early in the evening, and Juan headed to his house on his skateboard about six blocks away.

He knew the neighborhood well and maneuvered quickly. He was five minutes from home.

As Juan glided along a row of bougainvillea, an unknown assailant knocked him off the skateboard, and Juan fell on his stomach. The attacker grabbed the skateboard and hammered Juan on his back, sides, and head. Before he blacked out, Juan could hear muffled cries from the assailant. The anguished voice of a young boy sounded vaguely familiar, but Juan couldn't identify it.

Two hours later, Juan woke up in a white hospital room. Through the gauze on his broken nose, he smelled only medicinal alcohol, and he could sense that one of his eyes also had gauze covering it. His head pounded from a fractured skull. Acute pain from his broken ribs returned, and he turned to see the I.V.s attached to his skinny arms. The frozen looks on his parents' faces showed fear, relief, and anger.

Juan's memory of that day never returned until thirty years later, when the assailant visited him in a nightmare, and he saw a face, the face of a childhood friend.

The boy mollified his parents when he lied and told them he went to the football game with his three best friends, and they were relieved, attributing the recent mood changes as temporary. They thought he would be the same cheerful boy as before.

They believed him when he told them the blood on his clothes came from a nosebleed when he accidentally slipped and fell during the game.

The mother began to doubt her son's story in the following years. Their son's behavior suddenly changed again, and it concerned them. No longer energetic, he became lethargic. No longer talkative, he became morose. Behind a closed door, they heard him whisper to himself repeatedly, 'Wormy Germy.' The three friends never returned. The boy's dramatic mood swings triggered minor episodes of violent tantrums. The parents consulted counselors and teachers. They hired psychiatrists. They prescribed psychotropic medications.

But the boy's violent proclivities seemed to dissipate with age as he entered college and began a successful legal career. The parents eventually accepted the notion that the boy's alarming behavior was a temporary phase that most adolescents go through. This rough growing pain would disappear with kindness and patience.

The Holders tragically—and conveniently—ignored the silent dormancy of their son's rotting soul.

CHAPTER 17

Sanchez relished the most mundane work in her apartment: laundry.

The mindless task whisked her away from her world of courts, lawyers, crime, office politics, and L.A. traffic. Laundry was her therapy. She placed all her whites for a new load of wash but held on to one particular piece—the pillowcase with the bullet hole. The hole was clean and innocuous, with heat marks framing an aesthetically perfect black circle, like a round photo frame. She held it tight, raised it with her outstretched arms, crumpled it, smelled it, buried her face, and wiped her tears.

She would let the load run twice.

***

The following Monday, Ed Ross met with Linda in his office at seven in the morning before his staff arrived.

"Linda, I have some connections with the California State Bar. You will receive an email and a certified letter advising you that the bar has received a complaint about you. I don't know the specifics, so we can wait until we receive more information. You have due process rights and will quickly know the basis for the complaint."

Sanchez said nothing.

Ross said, "From the administrative standpoint, I will do nothing until we get more information. It's pointless for me to ask you anything or guess the nature of the complaint. Plus, anything you tell me might compromise us if you ever have to respond formally."

"Damn, Ed, you're treating me like a criminal suspect."

"Lin, don't take this too personally. Let's just wait. Keep to your normal schedule. I know you have lots of work on your desk, and I'll see what I can find out."

"Thanks, Ed, I'll keep in touch. Am I free to go?"

***

The Holder dilemma created a force of nature that united Sanchez, Santos, and Whitten in this fiasco. The unique symbiosis created in this relationship formed a tight bond among them, and they began to realize their risks—known and unknown.

Whitten was now operating against his co-counsel.

Sanchez was investigating a case that she prosecuted.

And Santos was along for the wild ride.

If all the disparate events, including a murder, an attempted murder, and a deadly entrapment, were all linked to Jeremy Holder, then Holder was an extremely dangerous human being, maybe a psychopath. They not only had to find more concrete evidence to nail him, but they also had to look into this guy. Who was Jeremy Holder? What were his motives?

They could not underestimate Holder's resources, so they agreed to meet covertly in Irvine after hours in an apartment of Wallace's close friend, who was on a month-long cruise. The apartment was quiet and spacious.

Sanchez briefed them about a pending state bar complaint against her. She offered few details, but her gut told her Holder was involved. All she could do was wait. Sanchez also reviewed the lab tests on the cap with smoke residue that arguably came from Holder's grill.

She outlined her case like an opening statement. "First, Holder knew where Meza stored his cap, which he grabbed when he visited Mrs. Meza. He went to the Meza house at least once without Wallace. He probably smoked that cap in his barbeque pit to get the residue on it and create a smokey trail to the arson.

"Holder then hires his ex-client, Panchito Gonzalez, to plant the cap at the house after the arson. Let's be honest: L.A.P.D. was pretty lax at protecting that crime scene. Panchito probably made the easiest one thousand dollars in his miserable life.

"Something spooked him, and he took off to Calexico. Holder then hires another one of his clients, Kike Escalante, to kill Panchito. We thought the assailant dropped the Glock by mistake at the All-American Canal crime scene, but maybe the shooter left it there on purpose. The L.A.P.D. uses that particular Glock model, and maybe the shooter is trying to blame them. The shooter shot him first in the kneecap, so he was

135

probably trying to get information from Panchito. Holder wanted to ensure Panchito told no one about planting that cap."

Santos said, "We're dealing with a messed-up prick. Hey guys, how do we know Escalante killed Panchito? Maybe Holder did it."

Wallace and Linda both shrugged their shoulders.

Sanchez said, "I knew that guy was too glib. I just kept my distance from him. I always got bad vibes from him." She continued her train of thought, "Then the bastard hired someone to come to my apartment to kill me once he realized we were on to him.

"Finally, it would not surprise me if he filed that red herring with the state bar to slow me down or distract me."

Wallace briefed them on the visit to Eddie's Bar and showed them the tape that unraveled Sanchez's central piece of evidence in the trial, that cap. Santos muttered, "Damn, Holder is a psycho who lets his client get convicted with that pen drive in his hands. What for?"

Wallace sipped some freshly brewed coffee and said, "There must be a beef between Nico and Holder. When I spoke with Nico at San Quentin, he said they had no animosity. I can't go up there to visit him again 'cause Holder would certainly find out."

Linda said, "That pen drive gets Meza's conviction tossed, but we can't do that until we nail Holder."

They took an hour's break after Uber Eats delivered some Japanese sushi, and they ate quietly, each trying to process their predicament.

As they concluded their meeting, they outlined their next course of action.

First, Linda would keep a low profile and continue on a regular schedule, drawing no scrutiny of her work on the Meza case. Crime in Los Angeles never ended, and prosecutors had to pick up the endless supply chains of garbage like sanitation workers. She did not know where the bar complaint would lead, and she had to walk a very delicate line: At some point, she needed to publicly reveal her growing suspicions about Jeremy Holder, but she needed more facts to corroborate his involvement.

Linda was fully aware of a fundamental legal maxim: As a matter of law, the prosecution does not need a motive to secure a conviction. Prosecutors need to prove the *what* and how—not the *why*. The *what and how* variables of the trial equation are the underlying provable facts. But most juries will not convict without a motive. That's the *why* part of the equation. Missing one of those variables equals *not guilty*. To a prosecutor, hearing the words *not guilty*, sounds like someone scratching a chalkboard. If the evidence pointed to Holder, the question remained: *Why? Why set up your client and send him to death row?*

Second, Whitten would look at Holder's past to see if any clues revealed themselves.

Third, Santos would continue investigating any of Holder's previous cases to look for anomalies. He would be Linda's eyes and ears since all her other work kept her busy. He would also look for a forensic computer guy who might search for Holder's electronic footprints. Santos knew people.

Finally, they had to be discreet and not let Holder know this troika was covertly working to build a case against him. Before they left, Whitten handed Sanchez two tickets. "Hey Linda, these are for you. I have season Dodger tickets, but I can't go this Saturday. Take them. They're on the third base side. My wife and I have another commitment."

Linda said, "Thanks. I will, and maybe I'll take my mom. She became a fan since the days of *Fernandomania*. I could use the distraction."

***

Linda returned to her world of motions, arraignments, witness interviews, and trial preparation. She could set aside the Meza case temporarily since she trusted Santos and Whitten would follow the clues alongside her. The three were the only ones on the planet who could believe an astonishing story of a defense attorney trying to sabotage his client.

A defendant enjoys many rights, but one of the most basic and overlooked is the right to an attorney's effective assistance, embedded in the Sixth Amendment of the United States Constitution.

The operative word is *effective*, a quaint legal euphemism. The right does not mean that the only thing guaranteed under the Constitution is a licensed attorney next to you with a bare modicum of competence, articulation, and intelligence. Borrowing the term from Colonel Ollie North's attorney in a congressional hearing, a defendant needs more than "a potted plant" in a suit at the counsel table. While all trial attorneys make mistakes in a trial, the collective amount of trial errors could be catastrophic. If that screw-up was a pivotal reason for a conviction, and

137

the conviction would not have happened except the screw-up, then a defendant doesn't receive the full protection of the Sixth Amendment. A defendant wants an attorney who knows what they are doing. You don't want your brother-in-law's probate attorney to handle your murder case, just like you wouldn't want a podiatrist to perform your heart surgery—unless you want your well-manicured feet to look good in the casket.

Linda thought it was noteworthy that Holder, the trial attorney, was also one of the appellate attorneys. She learned that Holder volunteered to be appellate counsel, which is not the norm. He thrust himself into that role and convinced Meza that having the same trial attorney at the appellate level would be advantageous. That dynamic would minimize—and possibly foreclose—a serious inquiry into Holder's trial competence. Typically, the appellate attorneys might ask the trial counsel why they pursued—or didn't pursue—certain avenues in the trial. Monday morning quarterbacking. Trial attorneys might have to explain why their decision was strategic. Meticulous scrutiny of Holder's trial conduct might reveal the astonishing strategic decisions he made or failed to make to ensure Meza's conviction. But Holder, as both trial and appellate counsel, would effectively block any consideration of *effectiveness*, and he could smother any flame of incompetence.

The bar complaint against Linda worried her. Since the State Bar had only received the complaint recently, the Bar would not publicize an attorney's complaint unless the Bar sanctioned the attorney with a suspension or disbarment. Still, Linda knew that the ensuing state bar case was now public knowledge. Her only move was to wait, as her supervisor advised.

But she still had the uncanny feeling that those around her treated and looked at her differently. She felt like she was back on the first day at Saint Mary's Catholic School—shy, scared, and sensitive at the stares and whispers swirling around her.

More than one professional friend asked her, *Are you OK? Is everything well with you?* Even judges gave her an extra-long glance in court. Or maybe she was just paranoid.

Santos sat down with Linda and showed her anonymous entries on various social media sites that announced her disbarment, that the Los Angeles District Attorney would soon suspend her, or that she was the subject of an investigation by the California Attorney General's Office.

Her unknown enemies even splashed her photo across various social media platforms with misleading captions. All were fabrications. Vicious lies.

For the first time in her professional and personal life, she was losing something— control and a clear plan.

It only took a tiny seed to plant this frenzy of misinformation, and that seed was germinating in the rich soil of electronic gossip. *Damn you, Jeremy Holder.* The D.A.'s office received phone calls from nosy reporters and citizens. As if things could not get worse, Edward Ross "suggested" that she might consider taking some vacation time.

Linda told him, "But Ed, wouldn't that make things worse? Wouldn't it imply that I had done something wrong?"

"Look, Lin, the California State Bar works slowly. They only informed you that it received a complaint; that's all. Other than the petitioner and the State Bar, no one knows the nature of the complaint.

"I know it's difficult, but try to ignore all this garbage on social media. You're right; the person who complained to the Bar probably started the social media frenzy. Prosecutors get criticized every day about something. I'm sure you even get letters from the California Department of Corrections about disgruntled inmates blaming you. They always file frivolous writs, blaming the unscrupulous prosecutor for their conviction."

Linda said, "I just need to keep working, Ed. Please don't sideline me because of this gossip."

"And you're telling me none of this has anything to do with the Meza case?"

"I honestly do not know what the Bar complaint is about, and I won't guess. Once I know, I'll deal with it head-on."

"I know you will, Lin, head on."

"You're not making fun of my big head with that pun, are you, Ed?"

Ross looked closely at her head and said, "No, of course not. Hold off on vacation time and continue working as normal. Keep me informed, and we'll talk soon."

CHAPTER 18

The dreaded letter from the State Bar's Office of the Chief Trial Counsel arrived by certified mail at her office on November 30, 2023. The document was impersonal, succinct, and dry, courtesy of an A.I. robot or a dull bureaucrat. The letter outlined nothing concrete and extracted the salient portion of the State Bar Act—C.A. Business and Professions Code Sections 6000—that sounded ominous and intimidating:

"The purpose of attorney discipline is not to punish attorneys, but to inquire into the fitness of the attorney to continue in that capacity in order to protect the public, the courts, and the legal profession."

Sanchez immediately reviewed the letter with Ed Ross.

"Linda, the California State Bar receives about sixteen thousand complaints yearly. Most are frivolous, but I'm not telling you not to worry. Yes, worry. Let's take the same cautious approach."

Linda asked, "Am I sidelined in my work? You know I need to keep working. I have a large caseload that won't go away, and you're aware of the social media attacks. Those attacks reflect on the office entirely and on you politically."

"I'm aware of all that. Listen, let's do this. I will change your schedule to reduce your physical appearances in court. This reduced schedule will minimize any direct contact with other attorneys and maybe even the press and might snuff the burning embers before they turn into a full fire. Continue your work here in the office, and other attorneys can make your other court appearances without drawing too much attention to the change in your routine schedule."

"I don't like it, but I'll do it. You're probably right," Linda said.

***

Linda remembered: *unknown accusers summarily executed the hapless Mr. K.*

If a bar complaint merits further review after the initial intake, then the Chief Trial Counsel of the California State Bar will formally open an investigation. Sanchez prayed it would not go to the second phase. *Just let it die!* But if it proceeded with an investigation, she would know the details of the complaint and the complainant.

If the State Bar formally opens an investigation after the initial review, then Sanchez's duties are clear, and she will be obligated to:

"… cooperate and participate in any disciplinary proceeding pending against himself or herself."

If Sanchez failed to cooperate, such failure could be a separate ground for discipline. She wondered how Holder's actions and her investigation into him might factor into a state bar trial. Her mind wandered to the worst-case scenario: Maybe Holder did nothing wrong, the Meza case gets reversed on appeal, and Linda gets disbarred. What would she do without her license? Her past accomplishments, once proud, now felt meaningless; her present situation, normally stable, now felt wobbly, and her future, once bright, now looked foggy.

Sanchez needed to look for an attorney to represent her before the State Bar within a small niche of attorneys specializing in bar proceedings. She thought, *Attorneys representing other attorneys. What the hell? There's a lawyer joke in there.*

Linda felt dizzy with the Meza case swirling around in her consciousness. *Now* she got it: Kafka.

In undergrad, Linda's English Lit professor focused on Franz Kafka's *The Trial*. Sanchez read the novel, analyzed it, and wrote a term paper without fully understanding its underlying premise. Now she did.

"I get it now!"

She was *Mr. K.,* the narrator in Kafka's iconic novel. She was now the defendant, whom unknown prosecutors were chasing, murky ghosts in a horrible dream pursuing her relentlessly.

In the novel, *Mr. K,* the narrator, finds himself accused of a crime or crimes, but he does not know what he's charged with. He tries to mindlessly meander through the labyrinth of a bureaucratic maze to garner information but is more confused at every step along the way. The beauty of this nightmarish parody is that neither the reader nor the protagonist, *Mr. K,* ever discover the crime charged. The novel is surreal, thrusting the reader into Kafka's dreamlike world, the same world Sanchez was entering.

At the end of *The Trial*, the nameless accusers summarily executed the hapless *Mr. K.*

A dreadful sense of vertigo now engulfed Sanchez, and she was entering the realm of Kafka's world, floating aimlessly around in a surreal world. Off balance. Without clear direction. She wondered if she might face a fate similar to *Mr. K's*—metaphorically executed—and not knowing why. She needed to find her mental buoyancy, seeking a lifeboat on the horizon.

After she returned home to Santa Monica, she dozed off on her couch next to Wallie.

Hey Rob, I need to talk to you about these problems. I need you now.

Please tell me what to do. You always have the answer.

Please guide me. You always show me the way.

Please console me. You always make me feel better and whole.

Talk to me, babe. Please.

The dream ended with no response from the netherworld.

***

Throughout his career, Santos had cultivated many shady characters with particular skills in the murky underworld. He knew a lot of guys, superb specialists at his disposal through regular law enforcement channels—pathologists in homicide cases, actuarial experts in fraud cases, handwriting specialists in forgeries, chemists in narcotics cases, accident reconstruction experts in vehicle manslaughters, and psychologists in child and spousal abuse cases. However, the resources available to the L.A. District Attorney's Office were vast but not limitless.

The labyrinth of the Los Angeles underworld also provided a vast ancillary network of specialists touting their services. Most were not public servants, but they served an essential function. Many had superb skills that were unmatched anywhere. They developed their attributes and honed their skills not through formal education and jobs but in the streets and the prisons.

Santos knew a lot of guys, like Spike Smith (not his real name). The corny name sounded phony because it was. Santos first met him when he investigated a series of forgery cases, and Spike was a suspect. Although arrested, Smith avoided conviction primarily because he assisted   the police in other pending forgery cases.

But his forte, no—his sheer brilliance—was computers. He was born into the world of computers, numbers, and electronics. Smith's father was a successful computer engineer with Honeywell and Microsoft in its early days. Spike would observe and absorb everything his father did when working on computers, and he would often go with his father to the Microsoft building in Redmond, Washington. While kids his age played sports and watched video games, Spike spent his childhood around software engineers. Although his father was a computer genius, Spike's parents could barely balance a checkbook and spent without self-control. Threats of foreclosure, doctors' bills, and unpaid credit hounded the family.

His parents died in a traffic accident late in 1985, and therefore, they didn't reap the financial rewards after Microsoft went public in March 1986. Spike was an orphan at ten and shuffled into foster homes until emancipation.

Spike opened a computer repair shop within a drab mini-mall in the north end of the San Fernando Valley. He cared little about worldly accouterments since he rarely possessed any of them and mainly worked for rent, food, marijuana, and Comic-Con tickets. Santos also used his services in 2011 during a routine investigation of computer hackers breaking into bank accounts and sucking out money from unsuspecting victims. Smith helped him identify, arrest, and convict the culprits.

After hours, around seven, Santos entered Spike's storefront shop, *Gold and Gold Computer Repairs*, sandwiched between a Korean massage parlor and a small tax service. He knew Spike would be there since he lived in the back of the shop in a spartan studio large enough for a tiny hamster.

Looking for a place to sit, Santos said, "Hey Spike, I've known you all these years, and you've never told me how or where you got the name *Gold and Gold Computer Repairs.*"

Smith replied, "I hitchhiked to Mexico back in 1997 looking for ancient *cenotes* to swim in, and along the way, I smoked some strong hash in Sinaloa when I thought of the name, and it just sounded cool. Originally, it was supposed to be only *Gold Computers*, but I think my mind stuttered when I got stoned, so I kept both *Golds* in it. It sounded cool then, and I grew into it."

Santos asked, "Did you eventually swim in the *cenotes*?"

"Nah, I realized halfway down the Yucatan that I can't swim. I only stuck my toes into the *cenote*. It looked dark, deep, and frightening, man." Spike sat on his small cot and gestured for Santos to sit on a wobbly lawn chair Smith salvaged from a nearby dumpster. Computers of every make and model, electrical parts, wires, and computer magazines dating to 1980 cluttered the studio. The stench in the room wafted with a heavy amalgam of human body orders, stale paper, moldy furniture, and stale food. A refurbished refrigerator, circa 1957, stood in a corner that Smith stocked with only two types of drinks, beer and Mountain Dew—his only sources of water.

Santos gestured to the refrigerator and asked, "Does that thing work?"

Smith said proudly, "That's a 1957 Philco. Works like new. It only needed a few parts. Philco built those babies to last. When the nuclear holocaust arrives, I can still survive for a few months with my Philco. Want a cold beer or a Mountain Dew?" Santos licked his dry lips and nodded, and Smith retrieved two Mountain Dews.

Santos had been around Smith several times and was used to his eccentric quirks—he never made eye contact with other human beings, his eyelids twitched incessantly, he laughed randomly, and he could not concentrate on one subject unless that subject were computers.

"So, what brings you out here, Santos? I know it's not my pleasant company." Smith stroked his light beard.

"I *enjoy* your company, Spike. Your place has changed little since I was here last; that was right before COVID. That dried-up Jumbo Jack on the table was here the last time I visited a few years ago. I see you got a new coffee table. Salvation Army?"

"Nah, I traded with a homeless guy on Ventura Boulevard. I gave him an ounce of weed and five liters of Mountain Dew. It was a fair trade. So, how can I help you?"

"I need some information, that's all." Spike's eyes squinted with a confused dog look.

"OK. Let's see if I can help," Smith said.

"One of my associates is the subject of a character attack on social media. False rumors and innuendoes about her have appeared anonymously on social media and could hurt her career.

"We suspect the source of this crap is an individual named Jeremy

Holder, a local attorney. We just want to see if he might be the one spreading this garbage across the Internet. His information is easy to find on the California Bar website."

"Lawyers, they can't stay off the Internet. I've fucked with some of them before, professional pontificators," Smith said. "During COVID, all the internet traffic spiked. I enjoyed cruising around the Internet, randomly poking into people's lives. But COVID. There was some weird stuff out there, and that shit got more abnormal with COVID. People had too much time, too much loneliness, and too much suffering."

Spike grabbed a squishy black banana and peeled it. "Want some Santos?" Santos demurred and took a sip of his soft drink.

Santos said, "And if he's the one, I need your guidance in stopping this before it gets out of hand."

"I can probably block some of the stuff he's put out. But once that information is on the web, you can't turn it off or undo it. And if it's this prick, do you wanna take the offensive? I can screw someone up a hundred different ways—just pick a number, Santos. I can drain his bank accounts. I can even suspend his bar license. The State Bar will take a few weeks to correct the error, but his name will appear on the sanctioned attorneys' list. I can deep-fake a photo of him with Micky Mouse panties and a red bra, engaging in a carnal activity with Goofy, Pluto, and the seven dwarfs. I can impose his face onto some actor in a low-grade porn movie. We can even name the movies with cheesy legalistic motifs like *The Well-Hung Jury*, *Cherry Mason, Attorney at Law*, or *The Lincoln Voyeur*."

Santos said, "Catchy, Spike."

Ignoring his guest, Smith said, "And if someone is helping Holder with his computer entries, I'll get that guy too—you know the old saying, *kill two nerds with one stone*."

"Easy, Spike. I don't wanna go nuclear on the guy. Let's keep it limited to electric recon and guerilla warfare. We don't engage him in the open unless we have to."

Spike chugged the drink wryly and said, "I'll try my best, Santos."

CHAPTER 19

FROM JULIO

I don't resent my big sister too much. Yeah, she's a big-shot lawyer, and I'm the failure in the family. A felon. A high school dropout. Gang member. She had more opportunities. But that's not the complete picture. I know I'm as smart as she thinks she is. I could've been something, even a lawyer like her. I just needed a chance, and she took that away from me.

After our father left us, things got bad. I don't know why he left. He was cool. My dad always found time to play with me when we lived in the San Fernando Valley. We played catch after he bought me my first baseball glove. I played for two years in the Peewee League of Pacoima, and he helped the coach. That was fun. My dad also taught me how to swim so I would be ready when we went to the beach. When he came home from work, I would get his beer and help him remove his work shoes as he watched boxing on TV.

I came home from school one day, and he was gone. All his stuff was gone. I could still smell his Marlboros and foot powder, but he was gone. We had a small house, but it was our home. It seemed empty after he left. Screw it. I quit baseball, and I never went to the beach. Mom said he left because he no longer loved us and had a girlfriend. Linda took it worse than me. She was crying all the time and didn't want to eat. She stayed home from school for a month. I told my mom I was going to school, but I skipped a lot, and that's where I learned to love the streets. Independent. No one tells you what to do. And I made new friends on the street.

My mom seemed to spend more time with my sister after my dad left. She said Linda was "very delicate" and needed more attention. I guess she thought I was stronger.

Didn't she notice all my bed wetting after my dad left? But Linda was too "delicate."

Didn't she hear me crying in the bathroom? But Linda was too "delicate."

We stayed in the San Fernando Valley for another year, but my mom couldn't pay the rent. The house, with three bedrooms and a big backyard, was too big. Without Dad's income, the bills got too big. Mom worked as a babysitter, in a laundry, and many other shitty jobs. But Linda and I knew she wouldn't make it.

So, we had to move "into the city," to Los Angeles, to a crappy place named Boyle Heights. I thought the word "heights" meant we would live up in the hills, in the "heights." I anxiously expected a glorious view of Los Angeles above the stinky smog, away from the traffic, where you could see the bright stars at night and the ocean from the "heights." "Damn, was I stupid?"

OK, I learned the true meanings of two words: "heights" and "irony."

My mom found a small wooden house with one bath and a small backyard. Linda and I had to take a dirty bus that took forty-five minutes to get to our elementary school. Friends were hard to make, and most boys my age seemed distant. Kids smoked drugs in the back of the school, and ditching school was typical, even expected.

My mom told us to be home by five every day. My new friends made the adjustment smoother for me. I began to like Boyle Heights. It seemed exciting. There was always something going on. I started ditching school more and smoked my first pot at eleven. School was boring. What was the use of learning? I didn't need all that. My mom thought I went to school daily, but it was easy to forge report cards. I intercepted my truancy letters. The teachers didn't care too much about teaching or attendance. By three, the teachers' parking lot was empty.

Linda kept to herself while I had a group of new cool friends. I know she feared the new neighborhood and the new school. My sister knew I was skipping school, but she covered for me, kept her nose clean, and got good grades.

One day, my mom sat us down at the kitchen table and told us that she didn't like our schools. "Too many bad things there. Bad teachers. Bad kids." So, she wanted to get us into a safer Catholic school. She planned to send my sister first, and then when Mom saved more money, she would send me. I don't know why she wanted her to go first.

Mom couldn't see I was a small kid, and my only friends were "bad kids?" But she sent Linda first.

Couldn't Mom figure out I was ditching school? But she sent Linda first.

Couldn't Mom see that I missed my dad more than Linda? But she sent Linda first.

So, Linda went to St. Mary's Catholic School in Cypress Park, and I didn't. I can tell you that I never would have ditched St. Mary's. It was a beautiful mission-style five-acre school with lush green grass and flowers everywhere. All the kids wore clean uniforms. They even had a beautiful baseball field. I wished I could play on that field.

As I grew up, Linda and I grew further apart. I hardly saw her. We had different friends. I was always alone in the house with Mom working and Linda in school five miles away. I went to school less and hung out with my friends more. They became my family.

I was only fourteen when I was first sent to Los Padrinos—juvenile hall. On a dare, I stole some beer and chips. The Korean clerk showed me his pistol, so I threw all the stuff on the ground and took off. My mom got mad at me, but I think she expected it. She wished she could send me to St. Mary's, but "Mijo, no money. I can barely keep Linda in school." I wanted to go to Linda's school. I wished I could go to a regular school with no fighting all the time and all the bad things in my school and my neighborhood that I had to put up with every single day.

I only went to high school since my homeboys were there. We hardly went to class, but we hung out there. We got into a few fights, but nothing serious. I tried to move out when I turned eighteen but had no money.

One night, I was hanging out with my friends when a car drove by and fired a few shots at us. They hurt no one, but we got in a car and followed them in our neighborhood for about two miles, and my homeboy took a few shots at them. He missed them, but we got pulled over by L.A.P.D. They found the small pistol in the car, and I took the blame 'cause I was the youngest. I thought that made me tough. "Take it like a man." They put me on probation with three months in County, but I never snitched. I got mad inside because the gun wasn't mine, but my homeboys pressured me to take the blame.

Five years ago, my friends and I thought we could make easy money. So, we scored on five pounds of meth to resell it on the street. I stashed the stuff in the kitchen closet where my mom put all the cleaning supplies. I had hidden lots of things in the house before, and my mom never found it.

Linda found it. Since I was on probation at the time for an assault, my probation officer would visit the house weekly.

My mom asked Linda for advice. Linda, my big sister, told her to inform my probation officer. My mom refused, so Linda called him. The police arrested me, and the judge sentenced me to state prison for five years.

I'm not too mad at her, I guess. She is in law enforcement. But her brother? My homeboys got pissed at me, too, because I lost the stash of meth. They cut me out and probably want some payback from her or me. And it never helped my situation in the neighborhood that my sister is a district attorney prosecuting gangs. I don't think they're happy with her. In prison, I thought I would get shanked every day, but they left me alone. I even spent my time helping in the kitchen as a trustee, and I learned to cook. It relaxed me, and I was good at it. I hope someday I can be a chef.

I don't think my life would have been so messed up if I had gone with Linda to St. Mary's Catholic School when I was a kid. It's funny how minor events early in your life can have a big effect later in your life.

CHAPTER 20

Sanchez felt sidelined, despondent, and weighed down by all the surrounding threats. She understood that Ross's decision to minimize her court appearances was reasonable in reducing her contact with the outside legal world and diminishing all the gossip fueled by social media. She knew that Holder was behind this effort to slander her reputation, which took over twenty years to build, case by case, conviction by conviction. Now, social media was attacking her like a nebulous monster. Relegated to her office, Linda felt claustrophobia setting in. She read reports, researched, and prepared motions behind her desk. She rearranged her photos, bought a plant for her office, updated all her law books, and painted her fingernails.

Linda wondered if Nico Meza was also thinking of her at that moment as if the perverse cosmic universe had found a joint portal and merged their daydreams. Linda was suffocating in the stagnant air and needed to breathe courtroom air.

Sanchez entered Ed Ross' office unannounced and said nothing. Not surprised, he asked, "Lin, what is it? I've seen you walking down the hallway like a zombie. Have you checked your pedometer? Damn, you're probably logging in ten thousand steps a day."

"And I still haven't lost a pound, Ed. The only thing I'm losing is my mind."

Sanchez closed the office door behind her, cleared her throat, and said, "Ed, I need to get back into a courtroom. I'm dying in here. Don't you think keeping me sequestered in my office only draws more attention and gossip? People around here and at court wonder if you're demoting, suspending, or punishing me."

"Linda, some reporters have pestered me, and they're asking indirect questions about you. I can just brush them off and throw them a few crumbs." Ross closed his laptop and said, "I tell those reporters that prosecutors constantly get blasted on social media. And it won't get any better soon with the endless proliferation of social media. They need to be more sympathetic to us.

"Just wait until I start my campaign next year. Critics, pundits, defendants, defendants' families, lawyers, nut jobs, and politicians will go after me. I'm ready for that. That's what I'll sign up for when I announce my candidacy. I get it."

Linda was daydreaming and not listening.

Ross paused a few seconds to ensure he had her attention and said, "Linda, I realize you're not a politician; you're a lawyer. Maybe this is not fair. But what you're going through is part of the job. Think of it counterintuitively: If someone attacks you on any level and someone is trying to take you down, it probably means you're doing your job and stepping on someone's toes. So screw them. You are one of the strongest lawyers I know. Weather it out, and it will blow over."

"Boy, Ed, you're good. That was some silky bullshit. Smooth. I wish I could have recorded that and played it at my next A.A. meeting. My alcoholic A.A. family can always use a good laugh."

Ross laughed under his breath and said, "That sounded corny. I have to step up my rhetorical game before the election. But you know I meant it. You can't let these social media attacks consume you."

Linda said, "I know you make sense, but I don't feel better. I need to get into court and get back into the game."

Ross said, "Continue with your current caseload. But tomorrow, you can handle the arraignment calendar. Easy. I'm not demoting you; you're just taking the calendar temporarily. There's nothing you can do about the slanderous stuff on social media. It will blow over."

***

When Sanchez was a rookie prosecutor, most of her assignments involved arraignment hearings at the Central Arraignment Courthouse in Department 80. She appeared at these hearings where defendants would enter the vast labyrinth of the criminal justice system, the world of Kafka's *Mr. K.* She would argue bail, preliminary hearings, trial scheduling, and probation violation hearings. This arraignment calendar was a rite of passage for most young prosecutors. Although mundane and monotonous, Sanchez learned much and quickly transitioned to more substantive proceedings. That was twenty years ago.

So Edward Ross placed her back onto the arraignment calendar, back to *Single-A* ball. Entering the Central Arraignment Courthouse, Sanchez felt she was back on *terra firma*. Strolling through the courthouse hallways, she heard the familiar buzz: lawyers whispering to their clients, busy prosecutors reviewing their notes with nervous witnesses, families asking for directions, clerks walking quickly with files, prosecutors, and defense attorneys haggling like a Middle Eastern bazaar—a bunch of buzzing bees looking for that sweet nectar from the courts. She was back home with a keen sense of youthful invigoration. Jeremy Holder was temporarily a distant thought, a speck of nothing on the horizon.

As she entered Department 80, she sensed little had changed. The musty smell of the airless courtroom brought her home. The court faced the same litany of complaints—robberies, burglaries, carjackings, shootings, and everything in between. She would slice through the arraignment calendar like an old plow horse. The same stale arguments from defense attorneys: *No record! He's a good family man. She will lose her job if incarcerated. He has no money to afford any bail. We demand a Humphrey hearing as soon as possible!*

She walked into a time warp. But one thing had changed—most of the attorneys looked like they were still in their first year of law school. Their smooth baby faces showed no signs of depression, anxiety, hangovers, or cynicism—only youthful exuberance ready to change the world overnight. *Damn, I feel old*, she mumbled to herself. Even the newly appointed judge looked like a kid.

Linda's assignment included forty arraignments, and she breezed through the first twenty, like getting back on a bike. She knew few of the prosecutors in the courtroom, and they looked at her with awkward expressions, a mixture of confusion and reverence. *Why is one of the most experienced and revered district attorneys in the arraignment calendar, like Tom Brady, demoted to the punting team?*

The courtroom clerk bellowed, *Calling case number L-56203, People v. Steven Campos. One count of domestic violence and another count of possession of a controlled substance.*

The young public defender droned, "Your honor, my client will enter a plea of not guilty, but he cannot post bail, but he's no flight risk. He's lived at the same address with his parents for over ten years and has a pending job application. He is a good candidate for an O.R. release with strict conditions. We would be amenable to electronic monitoring."

The judge: "Miss Sanchez, what is your position regarding bail?"

Defendant Campos, a twenty-year-old man with tattoos up to his neck, turned to his attorney and whispered. The defense attorney then shook his finger at his visibly agitated client.

The annoyed judge asked, "Counsel, is there a problem? Mr. Campos, please do not interrupt this proceeding."

The judge said, "Miss Sanchez, you may con—"

"That bitch! That's the bitch I've been hearing about. I heard she's no good and is gonna lose her license!"

"Counsel, restrain your client, or I will." The judge's fatherly admonishments had no palpable effect on the angry defendant. He was now pointing his finger at Sanchez, twenty feet away. Two burly bailiffs began inching toward the adrenaline-pumped Campos, who ignored them.

Sanchez then turned to face Campos twenty feet away and stood her ground, bracing for anything, clutching her pen like a switchblade knife. She had dealt with these outbursts before, and court staff usually quelled any problems.

The defendant said, "That bitch messes with cases and cheats! She has a complaint against her right now. I saw it on Facebook! I don't want her in my case!" His wrist and ankle chains now began to rattle. "Get her the fuck out of here!" The young public defender, alarmed, stepped away from his client, allowing the two bailiffs to restrain and then tackle the defendant to the ground.

Campos yelled, "Fuck you, Sanchez!" as two burly bailiffs dragged him to a holding cell.

The judge sighed and said, "Let's take a brief recess. Welcome back to arraignment court, Miss Sanchez." Sanchez rolled her eyes and shook her head, still clutching her pen, locked and loaded.

Sanchez calmly said, "Your honor, before we recess, I will move to increase Mr. Campos' bail once the angry gentleman returns from his time-out." The public defender raised his arms in surrender.

***

Returning to court and dealing with the outburst exhausted Sanchez. She felt out of shape, like running a mile after being away from the track. But her return also energized her, and she looked forward to the week ahead in court.

Plopping down in her apartment in front of the television, she opened the Styrofoam plate of sushi and noodles. Her Glock rested nearby on the kitchen table. Halfway through an episode of "The Great American Race," Sanchez felt her entire body finally relax. The contestants were racing their way through the beautiful country of Slovenia. She began to daydream that she was there with the contestants in Slovenia, in another world, far away from Los Angeles, far away from the courts, far away from Jeremy Holder.

Almost dozing off, her cell phone buzzed to life. On the other end was an unfamiliar number, which may have been spam. "Is this Linda Sanchez?"

"Who wants to know?" she asked carefully.

"Oh, I'm sorry. My name is Frank Sanders, and I'm a Los Angeles Nightly Tribune reporter. I interviewed you one time a few years ago, that double homicide in Culver City. You sent the guy to death row.

"I just wanted to ask you a few questions, if possible."

Sanchez quickly googled Sanders on her laptop and confirmed this guy was legitimate and not some nut. "How the hell did you get this number?" Linda asked.

"I just googled it, and it came up. It's strange your number just came up. But I got lucky, I guess. I just wanted to ask you about the state bar complaint against you and whether the California State Bar will suspend you. It's on social media. Any comment?"

"No." She hung up and tossed the cell phone on the couch.

Another ring, "Hello? Is this that God-damned corrupt prosecutor? You were the prosecutor on my case a few years ago, and I spent two fucking years in prison. You know you people..."

She turned off her phone, quickly packed an overnight bag, and googled for the nearest Holiday Inn, hoping the hotel was pet-friendly and stocked with Ben & Jerry's.

CHAPTER 21

FROM RAMON

I met Linda when she was a rookie prosecutor after graduating from law school. I did not get to know her at first since the D.A.'s Office assigns most rookie prosecutors crappy calendars.

After a while in this office, many newbies evolve from fresh faces that quickly wrinkle and sag, idealists who turn into cynics, and workaholics who evolve into alcoholics. But if they persist, many become outstanding trial attorneys. The fortunate ones retain their idealism and their youthful exuberance. With all these young, zealous prosecutors, many get lost in the crowd, and few stand out. Linda didn't stand out upon her entry.

Linda Sanchez never worried about "moving up" in the ranks. Promotions in the District Attorney's Office were never her goal; it was merely a side effect. What she wanted was a challenge, a problematic prosecution to attack head-on. She got convictions that the supervisors rejected, abandoned, or ignored. She revitalized dead cases through tenacity, intelligence, and hard work. While other prosecutors were out of the office by five, Sanchez spent her after-hours pouring through case files, reviewing them, and rechecking them. While other prosecutors were relaxing on weekends, Sanchez was tracking down witnesses. While other prosecutors were asking their supervisors about promotions and pay raises, Sanchez's supervisors were asking her questions about her cases and often seeking her advice about their own.

I first met her during her third year in the office, about 2003 or 2004. It seemed like she was fast-tracked to take on more severe cases because of her excellent conviction rate. I was going through my divorce, and I couldn't outrun my drinking. Linda and I worked on a case with a defendant named Charles Griffin, a serial rapist who we charged with three rapes in West Hollywood. All the victims were petite blondes.

The D.A.'s office initially rejected these cases primarily because all the victims were street prostitutes. From a prosecutor's standpoint, you already have two strikes against you. However, Linda saw something that others didn't, so she persuaded the office to file the complaint, and she selected me to assist her even though she did not know me personally or professionally.

She knew his M.O.: pick up the victims on Hollywood Boulevard in his black S.U.V., drive to a nearby alley, tie them with plastic ties, rape them, then beat them before dumping them back on the streets like morning garbage. Sanchez found out Griffin had some outstanding traffic tickets, so she "arranged" to have his S.U.V. towed for unpaid tickets, which wound up in an impound yard. Then, she quickly secured a search warrant for the car, planted a camera and microphone inside, and promptly returned it to Griffin with an apology from the L.A. Police Department for towing the vehicle.

With a backup strike team, Sanchez placed a young-looking decoy cop on Hollywood Boulevard. After a few nights, Griffin took the bait and picked her up. After small talk and a discussion of money, he punched her and tied her. As he tried to rip off her blouse, we arrested him. Linda and the strike team were a block away.

Linda spent hundreds of hours on the case and never flinched at one goal: Get the son-of-a-bitch in jail. She worked with the three victims and built a strong rapport. I never saw a prosecutor invest so much of herself in a case.

Eventually, they all testified against Griffin, resulting in a sixty-year prison sentence. Her trial work was astonishing. She even convinced the three victims to escape the streets and seek a better life. She succeeded with two and got them into counseling and other lines of work in a different city. The two were reborn, and Linda saved them. I had seen dozens of jury trials, preliminary hearings, sentencings, and motions, but her witness examinations and rapport with the jurors were unmatched.

You can never fully appreciate how good someone is until you see that person up close.

We leaned on each other when our personal lives were in shambles. My divorce and, later, the death of her husband and unborn child drove us together. I began drinking and slowly crawling to a black cloud, but Linda guided me out of that dark place. In her, I found what I could not find in A.A., the church, or meddling friends. With her, I had a patient, strong, and trusting friend who led me back to sobriety and my life.

After her husband and daughter died in the car crash, she found bitter solace in alcohol. So it was my turn to pay it forward, and I dragged her away from the bottle. I was there for her many times when she asked for rides from bars and restaurants. I was there for her when I saw her arrive at work with a hangover she couldn't hide. Someone called her a "functioning alcoholic," but she was reaching a point where she was not going to function. In the throes of her alcoholism and self-loathing, I saw her at her worst, as she had seen me years before. When I was drinking too much, it was hard to look at myself in the mirror. I didn't recognize that asshole in the reflection. I'm sure Linda saw the same hideous creature when she looked at herself. With the help of her supervisor, Edward Ross, she went into rehab, went into A.A., and threw herself back into work. We have both not touched a drop since. When the temptation arises, we both remember the reflections of the creatures in the mirror.

Shared tragedy creates a necessary symbiosis for survival. Linda Sanchez is my friend, and I'm a better person because I know her. And I know her feelings are mutual.

CHAPTER 22

"Holder is behind all this, all right," Spike Smith said as he popped open a frosty Mountain Dew.

Santos met again with Smith for an update.

Spike Smith verified that the social media attack against Linda Sanchez originated with Jeremey Holder. Despite Holder's efforts to camouflage the source of the defamatory attacks, Smith quickly traced Holder's electronic footprints through his sophisticated search engines—most of them legal. Santos also knew Holder was the source of the internet attacks and the California State Bar complaint. Spike's technical brilliance corroborated that theory. But again, the question remained: Why was Holder sabotaging Meza's case?

Santos asked Smith how to abate or mitigate the impact of the internet attack on Sanchez. Smith was blunt. "You can't. I mean, the information is already out there on multiple electronic platforms. The genie is out of the proverbial bottle, and it's too late to pop the lid back on."

"What do you suggest?" Santos asked.

Spike's eyes lit up, and he said, "I can use a cool worm and fuck him up. He wouldn't be able to touch anything online for a while. Those neat little wormies can burrow through just about any electronic defense. Military grade, dude."

"No, let's not go all *Dr. Strangelove* on me, Spike. As I told you before, we only wanna engage in conventional electronic warfare, not nuclear annihilation."

"OK, well, I could block Holder from disseminating anything more about her, but he would probably know that Miss Sanchez has initiated a counter-intelligence operation targeting him. Then, this situation evolves into the proverbial *cat-in-mouse* dance. Then, he might resort to alternative tactics. This guy's a prick, and he's good with computers. What's his beef with your friend, Sanchez?"

Santos said, "It's a long story, and we're far from the ending."

Smith said, "These situations are bad. People use social media in the worst way. It brings out the worst in human beings: slander, electronic hostage-taking, payback, sexual deviancy. The meanness of the human species has continued to evolve. There's no limit to the way people can use social media. I can partially block the dissemination, but it's only a band-aid. The bleeding will continue."

"OK, Smith, thank you for your efforts. Do me a favor and continue checking out Holder and his background. Maybe something will come up out there in the electronic biosphere. We don't wanna take the offensive—yet."

"Cool, man." Smith finished his Mountain Dew, reached under a stack of old magazines, and grabbed the Styrofoam taco plate from the night before.

***

"Linda, I am delighted you returned for another session. You know I cleared you so you could return to work. Is there anything wrong?"

"No, I'm doing OK, Doctor Chambers."

"Just OK?"

"I'm good."

Chambers asked, "Are you still talking to your deceased husband?"

"We haven't talked in a long time. But I know we'll talk soon. It helps me."

"Linda, there are many examples of situations that trigger P.T.S.D. We covered this at length in our previous sessions. But I need to remind you that you had two major episodes in your life: the deaths of your family and the recent attack.

"You're a strong woman, but every person has their limit. Maybe we concluded our sessions prematurely. So, let me ask you again. Are you all right?"

"Doctor, I'm good. As far as the deaths of my husband and child, you told me that talking to my husband is therapeutic, and it is. I'm not delusional, and I'm fully aware they died, but their memories are still alive within me. They always will be. I feel good when I talk to Rob. I feel alive, almost normal.

"As far as the shooting is concerned, hell yes, I had a lingering reaction. But he's dead, and I'm not. That's all that matters. I saw that

159

bastard take his last breath on this earth, and I'm glad I did. Seeing him die gave me some satisfaction and solace. What's that cliché? Closure. I can cope with that. Is that weird, seeing a guy die in front of me and having no empathy?"

Doctor Chambers replied, "No, because the threat ended quickly. If he had survived, your trauma might have lingered."

Linda said, "If I need to talk to you about the shooting in the future, I know I can count on you."

Doctor Chambers said, "OK, so why are you here?"

"I have come here for many sessions so you can pick apart my brain. And I admit, at first, I didn't come here voluntarily. Well, now I want to pick apart *your* brain. I need to educate myself about something from someone with your expertise."

Chambers said, "OK, I'm listening."

"Doctor, what is a *psychopath*? I have done some cursory research, but I wanted your insight in simple terms."

Chambers said, "Hm. I feel like I'm back in med school, but here goes. I don't use the term *psychopath*. The psychiatric and medical communities will not find that term in the latest D.S.M., the mental health handbook, our version of the medical bible, without all the Jesus stuff."

Chambers took a drink from her thermos and said, "So, instead of the term *psychopath*, our profession refers to some people as having an *antisocial personality disorder*. But psychopathy just refers to a set of discernible traits. It's not a diagnosis, per se.

"The most common characteristics of psychopathy include lying, showing no remorse, behavioral problems that might have originated in childhood, insincere charm, cruelty with no empathy, and manipulating other people. These are just some of the general traits. You might know a person who has a few of these characteristics, but that person might not be psychopathic; they might just be an everyday asshole."

Sanchez said, "I've encountered a few of those. I'm a lawyer." Both laugh. "But doctor, if there's such a fearful person close to me, harassing me with a violent disposition who fits those traits, what can I do? Further, if this person has already tried to harm me physically, what can I do?"

"Run."

***

During a break outside Courtroom 80, Linda held the phone close to her ear and said, "Hey, ma, how are you? I just wanted to call you 'cause we haven't spoken in a few weeks. Everything good?"

"Yeah, *Mija.* I can't complain. I just came from church. I prayed for you. Have you been going to mass? You need to go more with everything you have been through."

"Yes, mother. I've been going every Sunday, like I told you." Her mother could tell she was lying. "Let's go together next Sunday, promise, OK?"

Rita said, "What are you doing right now?"

"I just came from work. It was a hectic week, but tomorrow is Saturday, and I thought we could go somewhere to eat. I need to relax and not think about work."

"Linda, I can tell from your voice that something is wrong. What is it? Tell me."

"I'm good, ma. It's just that I haven't seen you in a long time, and I just wanted us to spend some time together, that's all." Sanchez moved her cell phone away from herself so her mother could not hear her sniffling.

"I don't believe you. Linda, I can hear you, *mocosa.* Blow your nose. You sound sad. All right, let's go someplace tomorrow. You can surprise me."

"Good, just you and me, ma."

"Linda, Julio will be here for the weekend. I told him he could until he found a place. Let him go with us tomorrow, OK?"

Linda hesitated for a moment. "Julio is back with you? Well, that's your business. We talked about this. Yeah, let's bring him with us. I'd like to see him, too."

"Wonderful, *mija.* We never have time to be together like the old days."

"Ma, also, a good friend, a lawyer, gave me two tickets to the Dodgers game on Sunday. It's at one against the Giants, and I want you to come with me. They are season tickets, so they must be good ones. If Julio also wants to go, he can get a ticket there but won't be able to sit with us. But tomorrow I have a surprise for you, and I think you'll like it. Then, we can go to the Dodgers game the next day. Julio, too!"

"This is a treat! The last time we saw a game, I think, was five years ago, before COVID. We saw them against San Diego. Cory Seager hit two homers, remember?"

"No, ma, but I trust your memory. So, I want us to go on Sunday, all right?"

"Sounds good. So, who's this lawyer friend?"

"Just a guy I know from the court. We had coffee a few times. It's professional."

"Is he good-looking, *mija*? Invite him over, and I'll make him some *albondigas*. That's your favorite. I haven't made homemade tortillas in a long time, and I can do that too. Bring him over."

"Ma put the wedding plans on hold. He's happily married with two kids. I'll pick you both up at five tomorrow. And don't eat anything before I pick you up. Saturday night is all ours."

CHAPTER 23

FROM GEORGE CHAMBERS II

My name is George Chambers II, attorney at law. (The "II" means absolutely nothing. My father had a different name, but I added the "II" because without it, "George Chambers" has the cachet of an assistant manager from Wal-Mart. And in this legal business, the additional "II" projects an image of erudition and distinguished lineage.) My name also has a pliable component to it. When advertising in the barrio, I change the first name from "George" to "Jorge."

PARA TODOS SERVICIOS LEGALES LLAME LA OFFICINA DE JORGE CHAMBERS II

TEL: 213-C-H-I-N-G-Ó-N-

I have a few comments about Linda Sanchez. I know I'm not a part of this story, but hear me out.

I have over thirty years of trial experience. The California State Bar has certified me as a criminal defense specialist—the cream of the legal crop. With an office in Century City, you've probably seen my ubiquitous ads on many West/Central Metro bus stops in West Los Angeles. On those bus stop benches, that's my handsome face that many Angelinos have sat on.

So, back to Linda Sanchez. I tried my first case with that woman about eighteen years ago, a felony assault case. I knew little about her except that she had been with the D.A. for nearly five years. She projected no outstanding features when I first met her outside the courtroom. The word "nice" is one of the most bland, non-descriptive words in the English language. Linda Sanchez seemed nice—like a warm, vapid Hallmark movie; she was lovely—like a chilled glass of milk; she was nice—like a teenage Starbucks barista. She could pass for a Walmart greeter—nice.

My client's assault charge arose over a minor dispute with a frisbee in the park. My guy, a parolee, was enjoying a sunny day in the park with his girlfriend, and the victim, a middle-aged bookkeeper, was nearby with his two friends tossing a frisbee. Cool so far. But then the frisbee landed near my client and struck his girlfriend on the leg. She shook it off; it was just an accident. The victim approached my guy and his girlfriend to retrieve the frisbee and apologized to both. It wasn't a smug fuck-you-I-apologize apology—it was genuine remorse.

Most normal human beings in my client's position would have responded:

"Cool, no problem." Or "Watch out, man!" And that's where the situation would end. But my client lacked the niceties of politeness and common sense. After three years in a Level Four penal institution, he developed a mental G.P.S. that positioned him somewhere north of stupidity and south of imbecility. Instead, Mother Nature gave my client relentless aggression, and he punched, kicked, and bit the poor victim. The victim's friends tried to intervene, but not before my client partially bit off the victim's left ear and spit it out. Not sure if he was a Mike Tyson fan. Anyway, after my guy Tysoned the victim, the police quickly arrived, arrested my guy, and retrieved the left ear. I thought we had a potential self-defense case since the situation evolved into a three-on-one.

Before the trial, I was overconfident once I saw Linda Sanchez, a diminutive Latina attorney who looked non-threatening—nice. Not to be racist, but she looked like my housekeeper. I detected nothing aggressive about her. I had not skirmished with her in pretrial hearings or had any substantive contact with her. I barely skimmed her fifty-page trial brief the night before jury selection.

The trial then began with jury selection. I can bullshit with the best of them. I do bullshit for a living. It's a cultivated art form. I can bullshit my wife when I tell her I worked late. I can bullshit my girlfriend when I tell her I'll leave my wife. I can bullshit my clients when I tell them I'm working diligently on their case. I even bullshit myself when I look in the mirror and see a great attorney. But Linda's jury selection threw me off my game. The trial unshackled that beast and unleashed her with unrestrained vengeance.

During the jury selection phase of a trial, attorneys want jurors to like them. Attorneys try to slather butter on the jurors with sweet, creamy blandishments to curry favor. It's that simple. If I say so myself, glibness is my forte, especially during jury selection. My lips and facial muscles often cramp during jury selection because I smile and laugh too much and get lock-jaw. Sanchez had a natural, casual approach with the jurors, and they liked her in a way I envy. The closest thing to look for during jury selection is not the substance of their answers; instead, I look for their body language, which is more revealing. Their unspoken demeanor will tell you how they feel about something. It might be a subtle gesture, a movement on their lips, or a nod. Those are the best clues.

When Sanchez spoke to the jurors, I saw many smiles in that jury box. Some laughed with her. Some nodded like robotic bobbleheads in response to her comments and questions. Damn, Sanchez was like a conductor in front of a choir, smooth but not phony. Textbook. Her courtroom arsenal included a form of finessed, subtle bullshit—just plain talk like she was speaking to them at a P.T.A. meeting.

The courtrooms and trials are like a jungle. (Yeah, OK, that's a corny metaphor.) The Serengeti moved to the Serengeti courtroom—where lawyers wage battles for survival. Some attorneys are predators like cheetahs, lions, and hyenas. Then there are the helpless mammals like field mice, gazelles, and rabbits. I am a lion who loves to feast in court. I eat up hostile witnesses, especially cops. I devour other lame attorneys, especially the young ones. And I even nibble off a few parts from judges.

I initially viewed Linda Sanchez as a gazelle frolicking out in the Serengeti desert, and I would feast on her and tear apart her case. Self-defense, no doubt.

Then the trial began, oh Lordy.

I saw her examine witnesses like I rarely see in a court of law— stainless steel, straightforward, precise questions, all in a logical, sequential order. Empathy is an essential term in the trial attorney's word arsenal. You want the jury or the judge to empathize with your client, whether that client is a domestic violence victim, a defendant, or someone seeking a custody order. She turned the victim into a warm, defenseless human being, and the jury took the cue.

In boxers' parlance, I am like George Foreman. I lob heavy punches in court, trying to knock out a witness into submission. (Apologies for mixing my metaphors.) Sanchez had a different fighting style; she threw small jabs—a few jabs here and there would not win a boxing match or a courtroom battle. But when dozens of jabs fuse into a giant fist, they can be lethal. A jab here. A jab there, and your opponent will go down.

Jabbing was her style.

Sanchez: "Mr. Victim, how much do you weigh?"

Victim: "One hundred and ten pounds, ma'am." Jab.

Sanchez: "What do you do for a living?"

Victim: "I'm a bookkeeper, ma'am."

Sanchez: "Did you apologize to the defendant and his girlfriend?"

Victim:" Yes, ma'am. I was really sorry." Jab. Jab.

Sanchez: "How much do you think the defendant weighed?" Jab. Jab. Jab.

Victim: "At least two hundred and fifty pounds, I would guess. He is a big guy, and I wasn't about to fight him, believe me." Jab.

And her meticulous examination of the victim continued. Jab. Jab. Jab.

When my client testified, the slow-punching onslaught continued, and his knees, lips, and face quivered. Showing absolutely no mercy, she attacked my poor guy, disabled him, and slowly, methodically subdued him on the witness stand.

Sanchez: "So, Mr. Defendant, this one-hundred-and-twenty-pound bookkeeper was a threat to you?"

Defendant: "Yeah."

Sanchez: "This bookkeeper assaulted your girlfriend with a lethal purple frisbee?" Jab. Trying to duck the punch like a slow-footed boxer, my guy said meekly, "Yup."

Sanchez: "When you were in prison at Pelican Bay, you were in administrative segregation, correct, known as 'ad seg'?"

Defendant: "Yeah, so what?"

Sanchez: "Here's the 'so what:' Why were you in administrative segregation?"

The defendant mumbles something inaudibly. I mumble a weak objection. The trial judge either ignores me or doesn't hear me.

Sanchez: "The jury couldn't hear you. Let me ask again, why were you in ad seg?" Jab

Defendant: "'Cause they said I beat up a correctional officer, I guess."

Sanchez: "Good guess. What specifically were you accused of doing to the correctional officer?"

The defendant mumbles inaudibly.

Sanchez: "Sir, no one heard you. Could you answer the question so these fine people can hear you? What did you do to the correctional officer?"

"Bitch. I told you. I BIT THAT FUCKING C.O. IN THE EAR!" At that point, jurors seven through twelve in the front row closest to the witness stand moved back in their seats in fear like a receding wave.

Jab. Jab. Jab.

Sanchez: "I have your statement from the administrative hearing on the incident, the 115 hearing. An administrative officer asked you why you bit his ear. Please read this portion of your answer to the jury."

Defendant, turning to the jury, yells, "I bit the mother fucker 'cause he was harassing me, and he was an asshole."

Sanchez, in a motherly tone: "What did the C.O. do, assault you with a purple frisbee?" Jab. Jab. Jab.

My client continued to receive an endless barrage of jabs to his body, to his head, to his psyche.

The poor shmuck looked defenseless as his knees buckled, waiting for his inevitable demise. She bitch-slapped my client with lyrically smooth questions that hypnotically mesmerized him, and he just gave her the answers she wanted. Showing no mercy, she dangled the victim's bloody ear in the evidence bag in front of him like a hypnotist. My client wanted to vomit. I objected to her grandstanding, but the trial judge, enjoying his ringside seat, nonchalantly nodded no, swatting away at my objections like a pesky fly. I wish this were a boxing match—at least I could have thrown in the white towel.

Good lord.

Sanchez commanded that Serengeti, the boxing ring, or any other metaphor you care to use. The jury convicted him in less than an hour. When the clerk read the verdict, I expected that five-foot Latina cheetah across the attorney's table would gleefully burp after she feasted on a full stomach. After that first trial with her, I always settled cases with her to avoid jury trials. I'm not entering the boxing ring with that hungry predator lurking.

As a footnote to this debacle, I received a gift-wrapped box from Miss Sanchez a month after the trial. Inside, I found:

A note written in an elegant cursive style that read: "Well counsel, you know the old saying, 'Ear today, gone tomorrow.'"

I opened the box and found a gingerbread man with his left ear bitten off, attached to a purple frisbee.

Sanchez floats like a butterfly and stings like a bitch. Jab. Jab. Jab.

CHAPTER 24

Holder persuaded Meza to remain on the appellate team, and Meza discerned no ulterior motives by Holder, assuming Holder was acting in his best interests.

"Don't worry, Nico; you have a better chance on appeal with me as your appellate attorney because I know the case better than anyone. Don't forget, I'm one of the best in the business. Trust me."

Once Holder wormed his way onto the appellate team, his trial performance would avoid objective legal analysis and close judicial scrutiny.

Besides Holder, the appellate attorneys included Walt Barrington, from Barrington & Associates in San Francisco, and Jeffrey Montgomery, a sole practitioner specializing in appellate work from Orange County, both experienced appellate attorneys appointed by the State of California. Holder invited them to his Culver City office, and they feasted on his beef briskets with the *legally insane barbeque sauce*, coleslaw, homemade biscuits, chile, and lemon cheesecake. Holder wanted to entertain them with a feast that included a side order of glib Texas twang bullshit.

Barrington started the meeting and outlined the team's duties as he was licking his fingers. "I can look at the pretrial motions the judge denied. Our client made several admissions, but the court still allowed them in. We'll look at that issue more closely, and there might be some potential chain-of-custody issues. I expect to receive the last batch of the reporter's transcripts next week, and I will disseminate them to you as soon as possible." Barrington was a seasoned attorney specializing in death penalty appeals and worked briefly with the California Innocence Project through Stanford Law School. He had argued over ten cases before the California Supreme Court and two before the U.S. Supreme Court. "The transcripts are voluminous, so we'll be busy on this for a while."

Montgomery chomped his last piece of coleslaw and, turning to Holder, asked, "How about that prosecutor?"

Holder responded, "What about her?"

"Well, did she pull any shenanigans? Should we look at her also?"

Holder said, "This was my second trial with her. She's good, but I heard rumors that she recently had a complaint lodged against her with the state bar, but I don't know much else. She's a recovering alcoholic."

Barrington added, "We should keep our eyes and ears open. You don't think the bar complaint has anything to do with this case, do you?"

"I doubt it. I heard through the grapevine that this was her fifth death penalty conviction, and she bragged that she was now a member of The Nickel Choir," Holder said.

Montgomery shook his head and said, "The Nickel Choir. Those darn prosecutors are morbid. That's messed up. They're responsible for executing five human beings, and they brag about it."

Montgomery added, "I expect to visit our client in person in two weeks at San Quentin. I always like to talk directly to an appellant. Sometimes, you can pick up issues not addressed at trial by talking directly to the defendant." Holder and Barrington nodded in agreement. "I will also look at the jury instructions. Jeremy, didn't you ask for a couple of special instructions?"

Holder answered, "Yeah, I thought they were legitimate. I wanted the court to admit the violent history of Nico's wife, but he didn't allow them. Damn judge."

Barrington paused briefly, saying, "We can also explore that issue."

Holder quickly added, "I can go with you to visit Nico."

Barrington teased, "You're eager to go to San Quentin, Jeremy? It's not a nice place to visit. You seem a little too zealous to make the trip."

Holder said, "I know that place sucks. But I think it would smooth things out for Jeff. I built a great rapport with Nico, and I'll take you to a great restaurant in Chinatown for sushi right off Pine Street."

Montgomery said, "That might be a good idea so you can break the ice. I need to meet with him and establish a good working relationship. This appeal is going to be a long process."

After another hour of strategic discussions, the meeting broke up.

Before they left, Barrington asked, "Jeremy, is there anything we haven't covered? Did we outline all the issues on appeal?"

Holder: "No, we covered it all; trust me."

***

169

Nicolas Meza couldn't figure out how to kill himself.

Since his arrival on death row, isolation in a tiny cell twenty-three hours a day began to melt his brain. After his attorneys told him that appeals could take decades, he knew he would not survive San Quentin. Some others here had taken the easy way by self-execution. That option was looking more promising by the day. He didn't believe in God, but maybe suicide would be a way of redemption, as a way of evening things out for his worthless life. Rumors about Prop 66 transfers for him amounted to nothing. He was stuck here.

He had no contact with other guards unless they slammed his meals through the small bar opening, and he couldn't eat without a guard watching him. No contact with another human was the hardest thing about being here. He began to have imaginary conversations with his mom. *Hi, Ma. What did you do today? How's Uncle Tomás? I heard he got COVID. I miss your caldos.* He would have discussions with people he had never met—Lebron James, Selena, and Obama.

The cold walls whispered to him late at night. *Other inmates? Did guards make those sounds? Was it the wind? The ocean? Were the sounds only in his mind? Hungry monsters whispering from below?* Meza reminisced about his drug days. He snorted, injected, or casually swallowed most controlled substances ten times over. He knew that the drugs messed up his life and rarely made him feel better. But the isolation of a slow impending death was worse.

He could not use any utensils to slit his wrist or throat since the prison limited inmates to paper plates and cups along with a plastic spork. The clammy, tasteless prison food caused him to lose twenty pounds, and the starchy prison diet was not good for his diabetes. He had only seen two visitors, his mom and one of his attorneys. Seeing his mom was pointless since she only cried during the depressing visit.

His mind games were in full swing, and he only slept three hours a night, unable to discern whether he was asleep or awake—or somewhere in between. He slowly began to doubt his innocence: *Could I have murdered my son and his mother?* A jury thought so. And he even felt his attorneys had their doubts. Getting his conviction reversed through appeals was a long shot; even someone with a sixth-grade education knew that.

His depression deepened, his sanity quivered, and his options narrowed.

***

Max Prater had been a San Quentin correctional officer assigned to death row for nearly ten years; he counted the days until he retired to a small trailer with his wife near Portland, Oregon, but he would miss this assignment. His friends and family could not understand the attraction to the work, but Prater found every day sometimes enjoyable and always demanding. Keeping these condemned inmates safe was his primary duty, although he had seen his share of suicides and mental breakdowns from the condemned inmates.

He was on night watch on April 10, 2024, and the row was quiet two hours after supper. He heard a loud thump, but he couldn't locate the source. After the second and third thumps, he rushed to cell number 301, Nico Meza.

He saw the motionless inmate on the floor. Prater hesitated for a moment before opening the cell in case this was a ruse, but after seeing blood oozing out from Meza's ears, he rushed in.

CHAPTER 25

Linda arrived at her mother's home at dusk on Saturday night. East-side traffic—light and steady. L.A. weather—cool and windless. Linda's appetite—growling and impatient. Linda was eager to spend time with her mother and Julio. It had been several years since they enjoyed time together, especially since Julio's absence. This precious time with her family would be cathartic for her and take her mind off all the problems emerging along her dark horizons.

Her mother and brother blamed Linda for his arrest and conviction, and she had trouble rationalizing her reasons for turning him in; the tension between her duty as a district attorney and her loyalty to her family was taut. She still thought she did the right thing. Her mother supported Julio but understood Linda's reasons for turning him in. It was Linda's way of protecting both her mother and her brother. Maybe she could patch things up with them this weekend.

"Hi, Mom! You ready?"

"No, give me a few minutes, and I'll get a sweater. Will it be cold where we're going? You still haven't told me."

Julio quietly entered the living room and said, "Hi, sis. So, where are we going?"

"I wanted to surprise both of you, but just wear comfortable shoes and a sweater, OK?" Julio looked anxious and nodded his head.

They packed into Linda's car and hit the on-ramp on Freeway 60 heading east. The traffic was light, and the snaking lights from cars cruised comfortably at seventy miles an hour. At dusk, the sun-splashed the Los Angeles skyline with a kaleidoscope of brilliant colors painted with broad strokes of gold, red, and purple on the western horizon against a dark blue canvas from the moonless sky. Sparkling lights from the city below played a silent duet with the dull stars emerging in the heavens. Julio rolled down his window and inhaled sweet, fresh air with a slight hint of rain.

Linda's mother sat in the back, and Julio in front. Linda reached over to the FM radio and began listening to the soft jazz station. Julio asked, "Who's that?"

"Eddie Harris. Great sax. You don't like him?"

"It sounds cool. But I got to like some of that old-school jazz in prison. I didn't hang around with the Blacks too much, but I could hear some of their music. There was his old-timer, a lifer in a level four yard. The dude had been in about thirty years. He was in his sixties, I think. We talked a little. He was cool. They called him *Scape,* and most of the black inmates respected him.

"Anyway, he was over in the Level 4 yard, but I could hear his music, and I got to like it. He favored Charles Mingus, Coltrane, and Herbie Hancock. The younger Black guys played that urban rap shit. I could never go for it."

"And the Latinos? What did they listen to?" Linda asked.

"The young gang bangers in prison are very particular about their *rolas*, mostly that Sinaloa-cartel-tuba-*oompa-oompa* crap, the drug cartels' national anthem. The lyrics are stupid. They only sing about guns, women, cruising, and macho stuff. I don't think they were into the traditional Mexican music like the kind Mom likes. Isn't that right, Ma? You awake back there?"

Rita said, "I'm listening, *mijo.* I could listen to Vicente Fernandez and Jorge Negrete all day. I used to play their music for you when you were little. You guys liked it."

Linda said, "OK, Ma, I'll change the songs in my iTunes and put on some Vicente Fernandez! You know, I saw him about ten years ago at the Hollywood Palladium. Those fans adored him! And it didn't matter what age they were. Young teenagers and old ladies were throwing their panties at him, and he put on a two-hour show."

Linda put up the volume as they listened to *Dos Corazones* cruising along Freeway 60 toward Pico Rivera. "So, *mija*, where are we going?" Rita asked nervously.

"You'll see when we get there, ma, and I think you'll like it. By the way, Julio. Why did they call that lifer *Scape*?"

Julio said, "Because he escaped from the Los Angeles Men's Central Jail."

"And he got a life sentence for that?"

"Oh, I didn't mention. During the escape, he carjacked a car from a young family, a young mother with a child. The car rolled over on Interstate 5, and the mother and child didn't survive."

Linda shook her head and said, "*Scape*, you bastard."

"You know, sis, this doesn't mean much. I spoke one time with the guy. I think he honestly feels remorse for what he did. He told me when the husband gave his victim impact statement at the sentence, he wanted to cry and go hug the man."

Linda said, "And you believe that garbage, Julio?"

Thirty minutes later, they exited the freeway in Pico Rivera. Linda turned down the music and said dramatically, "Guys, we're gonna dance, eat, laugh, eat some more, and we're going to have a great time. Welcome to the *26 Avenue Night Market*."

As they parked the car, they saw an endless sea of food trucks lined up to the horizon, each unique.

Poncho's Fish Tacos

Far East Korean Kabobs

Lalo's Michoacán Birria

Sally's Churros

Fusion Mediterranean

The array of food was astonishing, reflecting most of L.A.'s cultures, with meats, vegetables, and desserts that were smoked, deep-fried, and barbequed. Thousands of Angelinos mingled among the food carts to sample the latest culinary offerings. Giggling children sampled the homemade *paletas, churros,* and Mexican *tamarindo con chile.* Elderly couples listened and danced like teenagers to the cumbias blasting throughout. Young couples strolled along the food trucks like they were in an art gallery.

In the highly competitive world of Los Angeles cuisine, the *26 Avenue Night Market* was ground zero, where blue-collar chefs created culinary masterpieces that found their way onto the menus of upscale restaurants throughout Los Angeles and beyond. These brazen cooks were like mad scientists creating food combinations in outdoor labs. This food nirvana is Los Angeles at its best.

As Julio and his mother gawked at the splendid enormity of this place, Linda said, "Tonight is *Cumbia Night*, and I hope both of you are ready to dance!" Near the center stage, a five-piece band was tuning up.

The three scouted and sampled the various food wagons. Linda and her mom visited the Vera Cruz fish tacos while Julio scouted the Korean fusion wagons. Wafts from the hundreds of food delicacies bombarded their nostrils as their taste buds percolated like sizzling frying pans. The three had not been this excited since:

Linda—when she passed the California bar exam and began her career with the L.A. District Attorney.

Rita—when she received her priceless green card and married.

Julio—when he completed his prison term in the California Department of Corrections without getting gutted like a trout.

Rita said, "Linda, I can hear your *tripas* growling even over this noise, *mija.*"

Linda ignored her mom and focused on the menu. "OK, Mom, let's get the red snapper fish tacos with the red tomato sauce and black beans. I'll get you a beer, and I'll get a Diet Coke. We can get some dessert later after we eat and dance a few cumbias."

"Linda, that's perfect." Meanwhile, Julio ordered his Korean plate with spicy beef kabobs a few wagons away.

They found a small wooden table near the musicians' stage, devoured their food, and sat back to enjoy the wonderful ambiance.

Julio scanned the food trucks and said, "Maybe someday I can get my food wagon, my business. I could cook all day like I did in prison. It's probably the only thing I was ever good at. I'll call it *JULIO'S CUISINE.*" His voice trailed off to a whisper.

Linda said, "Those fish tacos had about ten thousand carbs, but it was worth it. Damn, that Vera Cruz red sauce was terrific."

"Even better than my salsa Linda? I've been teaching Julio how to make my salsas. He learns quickly!"

"You make the best, ma. Julio can make some green salsa for me soon!" Linda then did something she had not done in a long time: She laughed not just to herself but out loud, a boisterous, unrestrained, belching laugh, and she felt good. Linda grabbed her mother's and brother's arms and yelled, "Let's go! I said we came all the way here to dance *cumbias*, and that's what we're gonna do!"

The three joined the throngs of others on the concrete dance floor and danced until they were all winded.

Rita said, "Linda, I can't go anymore. My knee is hurting, but it's a good hurt. I'm not as young as I used to be. Your father and I could dance forever when we were younger. We would go disco dancing, then listen to music at the Audio Climax."

As they returned to their table, Linda turned to Julio and asked, "Julio, are you OK? You want to go back on that dance floor and show off your moves?"

"Nah, I got too tired too. Damn, I'm out of shape. Are we ready to go?"

Linda said, "We're not going until we sample those *pupusas* over there. I'm hungry again."

Her mom said, "We'll take some of those *churros* and *tamarindo* candies back home."

Linda laughed and said, "We have a long day tomorrow: Dodgers versus Giants at one. I think Bobby Miller is starting, so we need to go early. And we gotta see Ohtani! Julio, are you coming with us tomorrow?"

"No, sis, I got stuff to do. Let's go home."

Arriving at Boyle Heights just past midnight, the trio felt exhausted but satisfied, not just because their stomachs were full but also because they had fun together. Linda could not recall the last time they had a family outing with so much fun, laughter, and food.

***

Early April. Sunday afternoon. Dodger Stadium. Blue heaven.

Above the stadium, light puffs of clouds glided gently below a deep blue sky, floating eastward like a caravan of shapeless white galleons, majestic and proud. Just above the right field fence, the San Gabriels looked so close Max Muncy probably could hit one over those snow-capped mountains. Noon sun provided soothing warmth but not blistering heat. Redolent stadium air bombarded the senses with wafts of barbeque, Mexican and Korean food, curry, kettle corn, hot dogs, and everything in between. Joyful noises of forty-five thousand fans melted into one monolithic soundscape of laughter, crying children, yelling, clapping, and periodic booing. Grown millionaires played like children in a backyard, never losing their youthful innocence and blissful joy. During the Star-Spangled Banner, Linda and her mom arrived and found Whitten's seats three rows behind the third base dugout. Nice.

Rita pointed up and said, "Linda, I never sat this close. When your father and I brought you guys, we were usually up in the right field bleachers with the rowdy homeboys. This is nice. We saw Fernando! That lawyer friend must like you, *mija*; maybe you should ask him out. I bet he's cute. Oh yeah, he's married."

Linda ignored the last comment and sat back, fully relaxed, savoring the moment. Linda brought her old softball glove, which she had used when she played second base with St. Mary's Bobcats junior varsity. (255. batting average, moderate power, speed that her coach described as *plodding*, with a throwing arm the coach described as a *wet spaghetti*.)

The game began slowly, with Bobby Miller in command, throwing a shutout into the fifth. Linda turned to her mother and said, "Ma, I'm hungry again, and I'm sure you are. I'll get something to eat. Dodger hot dogs?"

"Sounds good, but add a Coke with one of those chocolate Frosties. Leave your glove and binoculars. I might get lucky with one of Mookie's foul balls."

"All right. Be right back."

Linda strolled up to the crowded concession stand, bought enough food for a construction worker crew, and returned to their seats. Walking down, she saw both seats were empty and double-checked her tickets. She was in the right place.

Arriving at their seats, all she saw was her glove on her mother's seat. Strange. Her mother, with weak knees, would not go to the restroom alone without Linda's help. She looked around and waited a few minutes. She was about to ask for help from a stadium attendant when her phone rang.

"Hey, Linda!" She recognized that voice—the distinctive Texas twang.

With a look of apprehension, curiosity, and confusion, Linda asked, "Holder? That you? I'm at a ball game. I'm busy. I can't talk much. How did you get my private cell number? What do you want?"

Holder said, "You know when I was a kid, my dad had a season skybox for the Dallas Cowboys. I played a lot by myself in that skybox."

"Good for you, Jeremy. I'm sure you spent lots of time playing by yourself and playing with yourself in that skybox. Jeremy, I'm in a situation here and need to look for my mom."

"Funny one. Anyway, I have a skybox here at Dodger Stadium. I use it for clients and friends, and sometimes I come alone. There's nothing like watching the Dodgers up here and not being bothered by those rowdy Dodger fans. It's a great tax write-off. Gotta keep up that Holder tradition."

"Well, Jeremy. I'm sure you need lots of things to help you keep it up."

"Again, another funny one, Linda."

"Jeremy, I need to cut you off to look for my mom. See you later, you moron."

"Wait, Linda, I'm at the game right now! Look up here! You can see me at the skyboxes near Rick Monday's broadcast booth. I'll wave to you. Whitten has pretty good seats down there. Not a skybox, but good."

Fortunately, Linda brought binoculars for the game and scanned the rows of skyboxes in the upper levels behind home plate. Maintaining her focus on the skyboxes, she grew nervous and started to feel that damn pebble in her shoe. She finally spotted Holder near Rick Monday's booth, and he appeared to be windshield-waving to her with both hands like an awkward elementary kid posing for a class photo. Linda whispered to herself, *Idiot.*

As Linda adjusted the focus of her binoculars to get a clearer view, she noticed someone next to Holder.

Her mother. "Holder, what the hell is my mom doing up there? Let me talk to her right now!"

"Lin, she's good up here. I helped her up here. She's enjoying this incredible view. And the servers are getting her anything she needs to eat. She's munching on a dodger dog, nachos, and a cold beer. Damn, your mom can eat. Come up here. I spotted you guys in Whitten's seats down there, and I thought I would bring your mom up here to check out my skybox."

"Holder, you bastard. Let me talk to her."

"Linda, come up here to join us. I can get you some vodka. There's plenty of room in here. Just me and Rita. She told me her knee was hurting from all the dancing last night. Too many *cumbias.* Let her stay up here to relax." The stadium erupted in applause as Freddy Freeman hit a two-run homer to give the Dodgers a 2-0 lead. Linda could see the menacing smirk on Holder's face as he said, "Damn, that was about 430 feet! You know, I'm good friends with Freddy Freeman. He lives near me. Good guy."

Linda's voice lowered softly, afraid to agitate Holder. "Holder, I'll be up there right now. Let me talk to my mom."

"OK, I'll get her down there right now. She's in good hands. I'll take good care of her, trust me. By the way, Lin, you're a pretty good dancer. I can't dance too well, especially *cumbias*. But Julio. Damn, Julio can't dance worth a shit. They should violate his parole just for his shitty dancing display last night, maybe a disturbing the peace or artistic indecency or something."

"Holder, you prick, you were following us last night?"

"Nah, I was in the neighborhood and had a craving for some *pollo al pastor*. There's a food wagon there, *Sinaloa Pollo*, that I go to. Good stuff. Next time, maybe I'll take you there, and you can show me your dance moves and any other moves. Linda, you're light on your feet, and you have some really smooth hips—really smooth. But yeah, I saw you last night, but I didn't want to interrupt you since you were having a great time."

"I'll be right up there!" Linda rushed through the crowd and began climbing the stairs toward the skyboxes. A flurry of terrible thoughts bombarded her mind, but she didn't want to panic. She tried to keep a clear head about the situation.

What the hell was Holder up to? He wouldn't harm her mother at a baseball game. He was following them like a madman. Holder must have known that she was investigating the Meza case. She already concluded that Holder could have hired someone to kill Pancho and also kill her. As she climbed the stairs with these thoughts racing, her mild worry quickly turned to panic, then horror.

When she reached the elevators to the skyboxes, a security guard stopped her and asked for her ticket. She brushed past the guard as the elevator opened and closed the doors. *I can explain later*, she thought.

Exiting the elevator, she saw a crowd gathering with several security personnel and two officers from the L.A.P.D. rushing toward the center of the commotion. Elbowing her way to the center of the crowd, she saw a person on the ground, lying prone. Her mother. Next to her, Holder looked directly at Linda. She thought she saw a smirk.

Bending to hold her mother's hand, she asked, "Mom, are you OK?" Paramedics arrived to attend to her.

Grimacing in pain, her mother said, "I don't know what happened,

Linda. Mr. Holder escorted me back to you when I tripped on the stairs. There were many people, and I think someone might have accidentally pushed me from behind. I think I felt someone. It's a good thing Jeremy was with me because he called security right away. He was right behind me."

Glaring up at Holder, Linda said, "Right behind you."

The paramedics whisked her to the hospital while Linda returned to her seat to retrieve their belongings. As she left their seats, she glanced up at Holder's skybox. He wasn't paying attention to the game—he locked his eyes on her, not smiling.

***

Wallace Whitten thought the phone call was spam, but he answered when he saw the caller's location: Marin County, San Quentin.

"Mr. Whitten, this is Terry Oswalt, the assistant warden at San Quentin State Prison."

"OK."

"I know this is unusual, but I'm calling about your client, Nicolas Meza."

"Is he all right? I visited him a few months ago."

"I'll get to the point. Your guy tried to commit suicide a few nights ago, but he survived. The incident was quite messy, and he slammed his head against the wall several times until he fell unconscious. He sustained a fractured skull, a concussion, and a broken jaw, which explains why he couldn't call you."

Whitten said, "I was not his lead attorney in the trial; Mr. Jeremy Holder was, and he's also part of Nico's appellate team. Did you notify him?"

"No. Meza insisted that I call you and not mention the suicide incident to Mr. Holder. He was adamant about that point. He wants to see you alone as soon as possible and feels he cannot communicate with you any other way. I don't normally do this because I'm not a glorified messenger, but our primary duty in monitoring death row inmates is to prevent them from harming themselves—until the state executes them. We want them to be healthy when they die. And seeing you might appease him, so I just wanted to pass along this message. Let me know if you decide to come, and I'll expedite your entry."

"Thank you, Mr. Oswalt."

Whitten hung up the phone, rescheduled his court and office appointments for the week, and booked the first flight to San Francisco.

Two days later, Whitten entered Meza's bedroom in the San Quentin medical ward and saw his client lying motionless on a medical bed, gauze wrapped around his head like a mummy, with painkillers dripping into his arms. Meza's face sucked inward with sharp cheekbones sticking out like a corpse trapped inside thin skin, and angry, bloodshot eyes glared out from the gauze.

Meza sat up slowly, took a deep breath, and whispered, "Whitten, I'm glad you came, man. I needed to talk to you alone, without Holder." Whitten showed no response, still gawking at Meza's condition. "I know how busy you are, but after you hear what I say, I hope you'll understand."

"OK, Nico, I'm listening. But first, tell me why you tried to kill yourself by bashing your head into a cell wall."

"Whitten, can you think of any better ways to do it? I can't wait until I die of natural causes after all those years, no decades, of fucking appeals. I couldn't take it. I didn't give it much thought, and I just did it. But my mom always said I have a thick skull, so that's probably why I survived. I broke my jaw, but it doesn't hurt too much when I talk. These drugs are good, man."

"The nurse told me you'll be OK, but you might remain here for a while, and you'll need some mental health therapy. So why am I here?"

Meza said, "We can't communicate too much on death row 'cause they're constantly checking on us, and we can't talk to other inmates. But here in the medical ward, it's a lot better. I can talk to the medical staff. And I can bullshit with other inmates in here. There's a guy I spoke with here in the ward—Chris Allen. They call him *Shrek* 'cause he don't photograph too good.

You know, he's a little Forrest Gumpy. The jury convicted him of murder—three people in a liquor store robbery about two years ago, and that's what got him to death row.

"But in the penalty phase, his lawyer did very little. The guy told me his parents had school records showing he was always in those special ed classes. They used to call those classes other things, but you know what I'm talking about."

Whitten said, "That might have helped him avoid a death sentence. A jury might have given that some weight—or not."

Meza said, "Yeah. Now that I know how this court process works, I think his attorney messed him up." Pointing to his head, Meza continued, "Whitten, when you talk to this guy, you know right away he's slow. He asked his attorney to get all his school and parents' records. The only number he knows is sixty, his I.Q. score. When you talk to him, it's like talking to a six-year-old who flunked kindergarten. Slow. Shrek is slow, man. Poor guy. I thought they couldn't execute mentally slow people; at least, that's what I read here in the law library. And he told his attorney about all the times bullies in the foster homes raped and assaulted him.

"According to his story, he got lost and got a ride from a gang, and they wanted to initiate him. The guy told me he was in a car with three others; one guy got out with a mask and shotgun and went into the store. He heard three shots, and when the robber came back in the car, they drove off. Then, they gave him the shotgun and mask and dumped the patsy on the street. The cops arrested him right away and forced a confession from him. The dummy would say anything the cops told him to. He said he told his attorney about these guys and the make of the car, but his attorney just said he found nothing. I think his attorney purposely screwed him, Whitten."

"Well, I can contact one of the innocence projects for them to check it out."

"But Whitten, the important thing is this. Guess who his attorney was? Jeremy. Holder screwed Gomez, and I think he screwed me. Maybe Holder is just nuts. I don't know if he did it on purpose or if he's just a bad lawyer. I know I didn't set that fire, and I know I was at that bar during and after the arson—and I know I would never leave my Dodger cap anywhere.

"Gomez also told me Holder represented another guy here on death row; last name was Bards, I think, a Black guy."

Whitten said, "Wow, Holder has three clients on death row. I'll check into it, Nico, promise."

Meza's last comment was, "Whitten, I trust you. You were always good to me. You always showed me respect. And I bet if you look deeper into my case, you'll see Holder did some weird shit to get me convicted."

"Nico, I'll check it out. And I'll keep this between us."

As he left his meeting with Meza, Whitten knew he could not reveal some of the information to Meza about Holder.

CHAPTER 26

Patient Rita Ayala Sanchez remained at the U.S.C. Medical Center for one week after knee surgery. While their mother was recovering, Linda talked seriously with her brother. "Julio, I need you to take care of Mom. She'll be home in a week but will need your help and protection. Stay with her for a while."

Julio asked, "What do you mean, *protection?*"

Linda then outlined her general suspicions about Jeremy Holder and told him about Holder's connection with the shooter and that he followed them to the *26 Night Market*. Her clinically dry summation camouflaged her terror underneath. Julio looked skeptical, but he knew his sister was no alarmist.

To drive home her point, she told Julio, "I think Holder pushed Mom down those stairs. He took her up to that skybox and was probably spying on Wallace. I'll try to get copies of the camera videos from the stadium security to see how she fell. She said Holder was right behind her when she lost her balance."

Julio said, "The prick is a psycho. Let me talk to people I know who might pay him a visit."

Raising her palm, Linda said, "No, Luca Brasi. Take it easy. Take care of Mom, and I'll do everything else to understand this guy's motives. I don't have enough to open an investigation formally, but I know I'm close to getting this guy. And he knows I'm on to him."

"Sis, be careful, *trucha*. I got your back. I'll take good care of her, and I can practice my cooking with her. She can show me how to make chicken enchiladas."

***

Linda felt pincer forces surrounding her, exerting personal and professional pressures on her like a vice. Thinking like a prosecutor, she felt there was not enough evidence to connect him with murder and attempted murder, not to mention planting evidence in a death penalty case. She also knew Holder shoved her mother down the stairs. The missing link was: *Why? What motivated this guy to send a client to his death and then cover it up with murder?*

Linda, take a deep breath and think.

After the Dodger debacle, the vice kept getting tighter. She received another letter from the California State Bar—a formal investigation had begun. California recently enacted a new rule of professional conduct known in the legal vernacular as the *snitch rule*. Lawyers are now obligated to rat on one another when there is credible evidence that another attorney has engaged in misconduct, such as misappropriating a client's money.

In Linda's case, the rat was likely the Texas-twang-faux-hipster-barbequing rat, who probably complained that Sanchez had harassed Meza's mother. The State Bar framed the letter and the complaint in cryptically euphemistic terms and never clearly mentioned Holder. The complaint said the State Bar received credible information from a licensed attorney of undue contact and influence with a potential witness in *a pending appellate case.*

She made an appointment with Ed Ross that afternoon to brief him.

After reviewing the letter with Sanchez, Ross said, "The state bar now has taken this to a second level. Linda, when your drinking was growing out of control fifteen years ago, I wanted to minimize the damage to you personally and professionally.

"It was only a matter of time when your alcoholism would affect your work. And I sympathized with the personal tragedy in your life. You lost a husband and child. I probably would have drunk myself to death if that had happened to me. You took a month off work; you got back on your feet, went to A.A., and performed like one of our best prosecutors." Sanchez said nothing and clasped her hands nervously.

Ross continued, "Now, you have a formal investigation filed. I need to know a few things, Linda. You don't need to tell me details of these allegations unless you feel comfortable doing so. But I need to know if the complaint involves your work as a prosecutor." He waited a few seconds, then asked, "Are you drinking again?"

Sanchez looked away pensively, then said, "No, I'm not drinking, but I want to. Ed, I can never repay you for supporting me when my drinking was getting out of hand. I owe you. Without your support, I would be living in a tent under the 101 overpass.

"The bar complaint might be part of a more significant problem that I'm dealing with, potentially grave. I would never compromise my work nor place you and the office in a situation that would embarrass you. I need to fight, but I can't reveal any more details until I'm confident I have a clearer picture.

"I will deal with the State Bar head-on. I will retain a lawyer, a specialist, to represent me with the Bar, and you'll be the first to know when I have more details."

Ross looked skeptical and shook his head. He said, "OK. But you need to keep me in the loop. Up to this point, the bar investigations are confidential. However, if this complaint leaks to the press, we will discuss your options further."

"Yes, sir. You will have to excuse me, Ed. I have a lot of work to catch up on."

***

Sanchez returned to her office, sat down to think for a minute, and then grabbed her cell phone to dial Jeremy Holder's number.

"Hey Lin! How are you doing? How's Rita? She took a good spill. Tell her when she's back on her feet so you guys can join me for a game."

Sanchez ignored him and told him, "Listen, motherfucker. I know what you did to Meza, Pancho, and my mom. And what happened to your associate, Kike, huh? And I know you're the snitch with the California Bar. I will first ask for an immediate trial with the California State Bar and tell them everything I know about you and why I spoke to Meza's mother. I will also pursue an investigation using my resources with the D.A.'s Office. Go to hell, you pathetic psycho." Then she hung up.

Her response, along with the scope of her information, shocked Holder. With a calm smirk, he thought to himself, *BITCH.*

***

Ramon Santos began to explore Holder's past, searching for clues that might explain the emerging picture of a disturbed individual. Google and

185

Facebook offered minimal information—just his personal and professional background that was public knowledge. He came from Texas wealth, was an only child, was a successful attorney specializing in death penalty cases, and was a loyal alumnus from the University of Texas at Austin, both undergrad and law school. His first two marriages failed, one in Texas and one in California. He handled high-profile cases throughout the state and beyond and was in demand as a lecturer on the death penalty. The internet was replete with his images—a handsome, smiling face next to politicians, judges, celebrities, models, sports figures, and lawyers.

Santos cross-referenced Holder's family. His father, Brandon, was a successful lawyer and certified accountant with his firm, Holder & Associates, which focused on corporate mergers and taxation with offices in Fort Worth, Dallas, Houston, and San Antonio. Santos thought it was odd that Jeremy never worked in his father's firm. Maybe the elder didn't want his son to be too close to him or his clients.

Santos then focused his search on the University of Texas at Austin from 1991 through 1999, the years Holder would have been in college, undergrad, and law school, to troll for any relevant information. An interesting blurb appeared in an article in the *Austin Times* about a controversial racial incident in 1994.

A young student, Wilson Smith, joined one of the most prestigious fraternities at the college. He was the first Black student in the fraternity, and the fraternity welcomed his admission. According to the article, harassment against Smith began shortly after he joined the fraternity. Smith found vile graffiti on the walls and doors outside his dorm room. They vandalized his car and made telephonic threats to him about remaining in the fraternity. There were also rumors of an attempted attack on Smith.

On the horizon were threats of lawsuits, a tarnished reputation of a prestigious institution, and donor concerns. The university administration responded quickly to quell the imminent controversy and began an investigation; the university ultimately suspended two unnamed students for one year. The only reference to one culprit was that he was the son of a prominent Fort Worth lawyer. The Black student left the university and transferred to Howard University.

Following these clues, Santos traced Wilson Smith to Atlanta. After undergrad, Smith went to Emory University School of Law and became a public defender in Atlanta. Santos took some vacation time, booked a flight to Atlanta, and made an appointment with Wilson Smith, attorney at law, under the pretext that he was investigating a fictitious case.

Santos entered Smith's Atlanta office and said, "Mr. Smith, my name is Ramon Santos, and I am an investigator with the L.A. District Attorney."

Wilson Smith was tall, slender, with a beard, and well-dressed in a dark business suit. His eyes displayed a friendly, approachable nature, and he warmly extended his hand to shake Santos. Santos noticed office walls with family photos, two girls in school uniforms, baby photos, vacation photos, and a lovely wife. "Mr. Santos, how can I help you? I must cut you short since I have a two-hour motion hearing. You didn't say much to my receptionist about your visit. You're a long way from L.A., so I assumed it must be important."

"Mr. Smith—"

"Please call me Wilson."

"OK, Wilson, this visit will sound odd to you, but I will get to the point. I am in the middle of a sensitive investigation in Los Angeles, and you might provide information or context to some leads we're following. Could you tell me about the hazing incident at the University of Texas at Austin in 1991?"

Smith returned a blank stare, trying to recall a bad memory, and said, "Most of that stuff is behind me. That was a long time ago; frankly, I wanted to forget it. Besides, the local press in Austin documented most of the basic information about these incidents, which I'm sure you've reviewed."

Santos said, "I'm trying to get the names of the suspended students."

Smith squinted his eyes and asked, "Why?"

"Mr. Smith, I'm not trying to be coy, believe me, but I'm not at liberty to give you too much information."

Smith grimaced and said, "The two guys they caught doing this stuff to me were Robert Lynch and Jerry, no Jeremy Holder, yeah, Jeremy Holder. Both guys were rich pricks who got off too easy if you ask me."

"Can you tell me how all this hazing started?"

Smith said, "Hazing. That's a bland, innocuous word, a pleasant word. Hazing. It sounds like some minor prank of a middle-school kid, like stuffing someone into a locker. It was more than a hazing, Mr. Santos.

They ran me out of college. All that was missing were the tar and feathers."

Santos nodded and said, "I gotta rip off the band-aid from your scar, so please tell me what they did."

"Santos, I grew up in a mixed middle-class neighborhood in Atlanta. Most of my friends were White, and I frankly never felt victimized by racism. So, when I was a freshman at Austin, one of my childhood friends, who was also at UT Austin, convinced me to join a fraternity. He told me it was an excellent way to make friends and network for the future. Also, the keg parties were legendary. OK. So far, so good. So, I joined.

"I wasn't aware I was the first Black to join that fraternity, but it was no big deal. I'm no Rosa Parks. I'm just a regular guy who wants to make friends. Being the first Black in that fraternity was a big deal for liberal-minded folks, and the fraternity received praise for it. But I never sensed that I was some token. Those guys I met in the fraternity treated me well.

"Shortly after my acceptance into the fraternity, the shit began. At first, I thought I was the victim of random pranks in the dorms. I didn't move into the frat house because I wanted to stay in the dorm for the rest of the semester.

"First, someone put glue in the keyhole to my dorm room. *Ha ha,* funny. Then they sprawled the *N-word* on my door the same day they vandalized my car in the parking lot with the same black paint. OK, now this was turning serious. I slept with a baseball bat beside my bed; even my fraternity brothers distanced themselves from me.

"The clincher, the moment I knew I had to go, was this: someone entered my dorm room late at night. Now, I can honestly tell you I never experienced blatant racism in my life up to that point. No cop ever pulled me over for some pre-textual reason. But I heard stories from my parents and grandparents who grew up in the South. I listened to those horror stories of late-night visits from the Klan and the Jim Crow nonsense. And I knew that when that person broke into my dorm, my only course of action was to defend myself and then to run off that damn campus. I never returned. I wouldn't stay around and ask the guy what he wanted. The intruder's intentions were not friendly, and the bastard knew I was waiting with a bat. He rushed out.

"To its credit, the university responded quickly, partly because they had an image to maintain. But through witness interviews and video cameras, they caught Lynch and Holder and suspended the two for a year."

"Did you see the guy or guys who broke into your room?"

"No, it was too dark. The hallway was also dark, so the security cameras could not pick up anyone. He must have seen the bat, and I was ready to swing, so he backed off. I remember hearing something odd. Maybe it didn't mean too much. As the guy entered, I thought I heard him say something like *Wormy Germy*. It makes no sense. What the hell did that mean?"

Santos said, "That is strange. Maybe it meant nothing, or you heard something else. Do you know what happened to Lynch?"

"I heard he did not return to Austin. After his suspension, who knows? As far as Holder is concerned, his story is more interesting. So, the prick gets suspended and then returns to school. I heard through the grapevine that his parents put him in a mental institution for a few months to sort things out. The rich refer to these facilities as *rehabilitation and relaxation centers*. Where I come from, they're called *nut farms*. I don't know how you can rehabilitate racists, but Holder's parents put him in a facility outside of Dallas.

"I left the school shortly after the incident to get a fresh start. I made the right choice, and look where I'm at. I love what I do here at the Public Defender's Office. I work with great lawyers, and I'm back home, although I know I would have liked Austin."

Santos asked, "Did you ever see Holder after that?"

"No. I heard he became a bigshot lawyer in Los Angeles, rubbing elbows with celebrities. He has cases in several states. I forgot to mention the last thing about him I heard. After his undergrad studies, he could not enter the University of Texas Austin School because of the incident, although, in his defense, he had superior grades in undergrad.

"But eventually, the university accepted him—he got *the Green exception*. His father donated a lot of green to the law school; daddy donated two million dollars for minority scholarships, and all that money greased Jeremy's way into law school. Successful completion of his mental health treatment was also a condition of his acceptance.

"So, that is the end of my story. I liked the school and the city of Austin. I was losing my southern accent to a Texas twang, and I hope to take my family there for a visit. So now, let me ask you. I assume you're investigating Mr. Jeremy Holder. Can I ask why? Just curious."

Santos said, "He is the subject of an ongoing investigation. Nothing might come out of it."

"Mr. Santos, you flew from Los Angeles. Something big is going on. Maybe I don't want to know. I have enough crap to handle here."

"Wilson, my flight doesn't leave until this evening. Can you recommend any good places to eat?"

"Come back at five, and I'll take you to eat some down-home southern culinary feasting you can't find in La-la Land. It's a hole-in-the-wall, but those places are the best."

"I'll be here as long as I can treat. Wilson, thank you."

***

Jeremy Holder had good parents who wanted to give little Jeremy a well-rounded and healthy childhood. But they reluctantly sensed his moral compass was off center. He was subject to daydreaming and could not focus on even the most rudimentary tasks, such as coloring books or toys. They bought him a small dog when he was seven, a brown dachshund that little Jeremy enjoyed mistreating. The dog avoided him, scampered to a corner at the sight of him, and pissed copiously when the boy touched him. For the dog's safety, the parents donated it to a neighbor.

The parents were happy when their son made friends with three boys when he was ten, but for an unknown reason, that friendship ended abruptly. Jeremy withdrew into himself after that point and remained a loner into adulthood. The parents wondered whether something profoundly sinister had happened after his friendship ended with the three boys. Their son slipped into despondency after the three boys stopped visiting.

He had a few girlfriends as a teenager, but those relationships never lasted. When they asked their son about the girlfriends, Jeremy would shrug his shoulders and say nothing. They had sporadic contact with their son after he entered college, and they only spoke about tuition and rent. On the days he came home, he sequestered himself in his bedroom, on the phone or reading.

When the parents learned of Jeremy's involvement in the hazing

190

incident, they were distraught—but not surprised. Jeremy's disturbing proclivities raised two concerns for his parents: their son's internal mental health and the family's external reputation.

***

"Linda, you might get disbarred."

The words smacked Linda like a cold slap on her face as she sat in the office of attorney Byron Teague, a specialist defending attorneys before the California State Bar. After twenty-three years as a prosecutor, Teague had been a solo practitioner with a sterling reputation for five years. Ed Ross recommended him, which partially mollified Linda's fear of the California State Bar.

"Mr. Teague, I know the potential implications of the Bar's investigation."

Teague said, "I've read the complaint. The Bar must believe it has some merit; otherwise, they would not have initiated a formal investigation. Let's review your options. We can prepare a written response and see what they decide to do. They may close the case or set the case for a formal hearing. The implication is that you harassed Mrs. Meza after the jury trial. I realize she was not a witness in the case, and your contact with her might've been innocuous. But if she claims you harassed her in any form, the Bar could still sanction you. And if this goes public, it could tarnish your professional reputation and your office's. I assume your office is aware of this situation."

"I've briefed my supervisor, Mr. Teague. Here's what I want to do, and if you think you cannot help me, I can look for other counsel. I hope you understand. Or I might represent myself. Yeah, I know the tired maxim: *Someone who represents themself has a fool for a client.* I want to fast-track this case to a full hearing before the Bar, and I will stipulate that the proceeding can be a public hearing. Can I do that?"

Teague looked perplexed and said, "I can arrange this, but if I'm going to represent you, I need to know why you want to pursue this course of action."

Linda said, "What precipitated this Bar investigation was an anonymous complaint under the new *Attorney Snitch Rule.*"

Teague nodded and said, "Yeah, I assume one of Meza's attorneys

191

filed the complaint."

Linda said, "He had two attorneys. You can exclude Wallace Whitten. It was Jeremy Holder."

Teague sat back and said, "OK. Holder's the guy."

"Mr. Teague, I want the trial to focus on the complainant's veracity. It's that simple."

"Linda, that might work in a criminal case, but the State Bar trials differ."

"Mr. Teague, with all due respect, they are not different. If the source of the complaint has ulterior motives, then the Bar needs to know. I want full exoneration. I want it clear that I did nothing unethical, and that Holder is the one who should, at the very least, come before the bar. You can question Mrs. Meza; she will tell you I did not harass her. I just asked a few questions about her son. It was simply a follow-up visit after the conviction."

"Linda, I was also a prosecutor in Santa Clara County for over twenty years, and I must admit, your visit to Mrs. Meza was odd."

"Mr. Teague, let me present the following hypothetical. Let's say a prosecutor receives information after a conviction that the defense attorney intentionally set up his client for reasons unknown. The conviction was based not on the attorney's incompetence but on a deliberate act to get his client convicted. And then, the defense attorney realizes that the trial prosecutor knows.

"The defense attorney then takes steps to cover his tracks, steps that include the murder of a witness and the attempted murder of that same prosecutor. Don't you think that information is relevant?"

Teague looked stunned, sat back, inhaled, and said, "Damn. This story sounds like a Lee Child novel."

Sanchez continued, "I am in the middle of a highly secretive investigation of Mr. Holder, and he just wants me to quit. Now, we're playing *cat and mouse*. He wants me to get sidetracked away from the investigation. A bullet missed my big head by four inches, a bullet that Mr. Holder directed. So, can I stipulate to getting this public trial soon and skip all the preliminary steps?"

"OK, I'll prepare a carefully crafted stipulation and submit it to the Bar tribunal. Wow, I thought I had heard everything in this business."

"Mr. Teague, I fully understand the gravity of this situation.

Everything for me is at risk here—my profession, reputation, and future. Without my bar license, I have nothing to fall back on. There's no plan B. I have no other skills. Maybe I might try joining a dating website. There might be a sexual niche for a forty-something, unemployed, disbarred lawyer, a petite, chubby Latina who enjoys Trivial Pursuit marathons and Taylor Swift and talks to her dead husband. I might get some bites. What do you think?"

Teague still couldn't comprehend her humor. *Was it wry humor? Was it a warped display of self-deprecation or self-flagellation?* Teague finally said, "I can help you, Linda. Let's work together. I will contact the State Bar Investigative Unit and tell them about our request for a speedy public hearing."

CHAPTER 27

"Hi, my name is Linda, and I'm an alcoholic."

"Hi, Linda!"

Sanchez chewed the last bite of her stale donut, nervously set her black coffee on a nearby table, exhaled, and said, "God, I need a vodka. Right now. I would honestly settle for some cheap whiskey. I can taste it on my lips, my tongue, my throat, and in my stomach. You know that feeling when you take that first drink after you haven't drunk in a long time? That's the best drink, that first one, like an old friend who hasn't visited in a long time. You savor it before the second one and let it settle in. Your whole body relaxes and feels heavy and warm. That's what I miss. And I almost had that first drink. But I couldn't, just couldn't." A few supportive heads in the group nodded.

Elsa, the monitor and Linda's sponsor, asked, "So why didn't you?"

Linda looked annoyed and said, "I don't know."

Elsa said, "Linda, we're not here to help you feel sorry for yourself. We're here to support and listen to you but don't feel sorry for yourself. We're all tempted every day. I don't care what kind of stuff you're going through, but all of us here have gone through bad shit, some horrible shit. Feeling sorry for yourself won't help."

Elsa was sixty years old, but she looked eighty after years of alcohol, drugs, physical abuse, homelessness, and losing her two young children to the courts thirty years ago. Slightly overweight, with thinning grey hair, Elsa had ill-fitting dentures that poked out, but they were an improvement over the rotten, rusty teeth she lost. A liquor bottle had not touched her lips in fifteen years, and she was slowly repairing her tattered relationship with her children, now fully grown adults with their own children. Just beneath Elsa's sullen eyes was a decent human being seeking a semblance of redemption in her life. Linda was her human project that Elsa sought to protect and guide away from alcohol, temptation, and self-flagellation.

Linda said, "Elsa, I know we don't feel sorry for ourselves. I came because I need you and the group. I lost an important person in my life, more important than anyone except for my mother.

"I'm not here to cry but to tell you how selfish I was. Maybe that's why some of us have alcoholism; we're selfish and take our loved ones for granted." A few heads nodded. "Her name was Olivia, Sister Olivia. I had not seen or talked to her in about two years, but I received a text message last week. I didn't realize the message was from a nurse at a hospital in Pasadena. But I ignored the message because I was so busy dealing with personal things.

"Sister Olivia had been in the hospital suffering from breast cancer and passed away before I could return the message and realize what happened. The nurse called because Sister Olivia wanted to talk to me before she went to heaven. But I was too damn busy. I never got to speak to her to tell her how much she meant in my life and how I loved her like a second mother. But I was too busy.

"After I found out she died, I drove to a nearby liquor store, bought some vodka, returned home, and the bottle just sat there on my kitchen counter. Yes, I know that's a cliché. But staring at that bottle for an hour was tough. That was a few hours ago, and I came here."

Sanchez sniffled and said nothing more, out of breath. Elsa walked over, sat next to Sanchez, and bear-hugged her tightly, saying nothing except, "Let's all go home. I think we've had enough." Elsa sat with Linda long after the rest were gone and asked, "Is that bottle open?"

"I tossed it in the trash, and it broke, but I could smell the vodka. It smelled like sweet, warm honey."

***

Returning to Santa Monica after spending time with her mother and Julio, Linda felt relieved. Julio was taking good care of their mom and feeding her well.

Rita said, "Linda, Julio said he's gonna make me some *cabrón nada*. I never had it before."

Julio said, "Ma, I'm gonna make you *carbonara*. It's spaghetti with Italian bacon." Julio looked at Linda as she left and winked.

Her mother's recovery was progressing well, and she would walk soon.

As Linda approached the freeway on-ramp after her visit, she noticed the light indicator blinking—the battery. So she took her car to Arturo "Turi" Gomez, the mechanic, also known as Turi's Auto Body in Montebello. Even though it was late Sunday afternoon, she knew Arturo's shop would be open since he lived behind the garage. Turi had no regular business hours, only *as needed.*

Gomez had been in business as long as Linda could remember and was a barrio icon. He provided superb, affordable service and was discreet when repairing cars under questionable circumstances. Bullet holes? Arturo was the Michelangelo of bullet hole repair and could make any vehicle look better than before. It only took a power grinder, fiberglass cloth, fiberglass resin, and a brush in Turi's gifted hands, and bullet holes disappeared back into the car like melted ice. On the streets of East L.A., his moniker was *T-1000,* the killer in *Terminator 2* who self-repaired his bullet-riddled body.

In another universe, Turi could have been a wealthy plastic surgeon with those gifted hands. But instead of breast augmentation, he repaired hoods and fenders. Instead of facial microdermabrasion, he delicately smoothed dents. Instead of Brazilian butt lifts, Turi worked on rear suspensions.

Turi was off-limits among the warring factions in East Los Angeles. All respected him because he didn't discriminate between gangs, and his shop was neutral territory, an urban demilitarized zone. He never asked questions as long as nameless customers paid in cash in advance.

When the Sanchez family first moved to Boyle Heights, Linda remembered her mother taking their old Buick for repairs and general maintenance. They only heard, *Take it to Turi,* whenever their car needed repairs. She pulled into the driveway of the body shop and rang a rusted metal bell on the gate.

"Mr. Gomez?" she asked. Behind the gate was a small, pencil-thin man, about seventy, with white facial stubs peeking out of his brown, leathery skin. He wore rubber yellow flip-flops, and his crusty, gnarled toenails looked like they were trying to escape in ten different directions. Wearing a tattered brown robe stained with coffee, beer, and last night's refried beans, he slowly swung open the gate. Looking at her up and down, he put on his glasses and squinted.

He said, "You look familiar, but I can't picture you yet. My eyes aren't like they used to be—glaucoma—but you look familiar."

"Arturo, I'm Linda Sanchez. My mom is Rita Sanchez. We live in Boyle Heights. Don't you remember? I came here with my mom when we brought our car in, and when I was a kid, you showed me how to change a tire, remember?"

"Oh yeah. Your mom had a white Buick Skylark, and I put in a new radiator and belts. You're that bigshot lawyer. Your mom used to brag about you all the time. You had a kid brother, Julio. I haven't seen your family in a long time. How can I help you?"

"I need you to check my battery. The light icon blinks, and the owner's manual says I should check the battery."

"Linda, screw the manual. Check with me first, with Turi. OK?" His bony finger pointed to his bald head and said, "I got the *pinche* manual up here, *mija*. Let me open the garage, and I'll look at it." Linda pulled the car into the garage beside Arturo's tiny house and parked.

Arturo opened the hood, peered inside, and then drove the car over a car bay to lift it.

Once he raised her car, he examined it underneath and hoisted it down.

"Turi, why did you need to look underneath? Isn't it just the battery?"

Arturo looked worried and said, "It's not just the battery. Let me show you." He led her to the front of her car, lifted the hood, and told her, "Look."

Linda said, "OK. What am I looking at? You only taught me how to change the *pinche* tires. I never graduated to the advanced level of *Turi's School of Mechanics*."

Arturo giggled. "Look, the reason your battery is low is this." He pulled a small black device near the battery, nearly hidden. "This is a tracking device. You can buy these suckers anywhere. I used one for my kids when they borrowed the car as teenagers. You can't trust kids. The power of this tracker feeds off your battery and can drain it. That's why it was low. This battery is less than two years old. Is your husband keeping track of you?"

"No, my dead husband knows where I'm at. So, why did you look under the car?"

"To make sure there were no others. Someone's been following you. I don't wanna ask why—none of my business. But be careful and check your car more often, OK? I'll throw this away. I'll put in a new battery.

197

That's one hundred dollars, cash."

"Wait, Turi, do you have a plastic sandwich bag?"

"Yeah, why?"

"In need to put this tracker in there."

"Souvenir?"

"No, evidence."

***

From Jeremy Holder, (213) 555-9823

Hi, Linda. I hope all is well. B.T.W., I still don't know how Rita tripped. I'm at home enjoying the ocean view with your favorite glass of vodka. So, a toast to the great Linda Sanchez! L.O.L. I saw Rita at the hospital, and she looked good. When she returns to Boyle Heights, she promised to cook some mole con pollo for me. I volunteered to take her home. I am sorry I could not protect her from her fall. I think someone in the crowd accidentally hit her, and she lost her balance. Maybe some A-hole did it on purpose. There are lots of bad people in the world. But I am happy her injuries aren't severe. I once represented a client who pushed his wife down three stairs. She was FUBAR. You're wrong about me. You don't know me well, and I mean no harm to you. You might H8 me, B.C., for some things you think I did. Let's get together sometime and have a drink. Oh, my bad. I know you haven't drunk ever since your hubby and baby died. Are your A.A. sessions helping you? Maybe coffee will do. L.O.L.

Linda wrote: Jeremy, do not contact me or my family. I don't do messaging well, so I don't know most of your silly acronyms. I only know one: F.U. (L.O.L.!).

***

Wallace Whitten arrived early at his office expecting a busy work week of motions, client interviews, and a jury trial. He and his wife also planned to take their two young children to Legoland on the weekend. As he concluded his research for his upcoming motion, his receptionist buzzed him, "Mr. Whitten, you have a call on line two. It's Mr. Holder."

Whitten hesitated a moment, then picked up. "Hey, Jeremy. What's

198

going on? We haven't talked in a while. Any news on the Meza appeal?"

"The appeal is going fine. Listen, Bro, we should get together for lunch sometime."

Whitten grimaced and said, "Jeremy, I have a full plate this month. Let me call you, and we can set a time, OK?"

"Sounds good. We should include the spouses. You know, I realized Sara has never met your wife, Gina. They have much in common, and I think they would hit it off. So we can have a nice dinner together."

"Let's see. I'll talk to Gina."

"Another idea; we can go to a Dodger game. You and Gina can be our special guests in my skybox. The Giants are in town next month for a daytime game."

"Jeremy, we'll see. I have piles of work on my desk. Let me call you later."

"Cool, bro. I know you have those season tickets. Just give those away to one of your clients or another attorney. That's good marketing. But I think you'll like my skybox. Maybe you can meet some celebrities up there."

"We'll see, Jeremy."

Holder said, "On another more serious note, I got word from San Quentin that Nico tried to harm himself. I'm concerned about him; he's a good guy. I don't know the details of the incident, so I plan to visit him in the next few weeks. I can't imagine what it's like waiting on death row; maybe the stress is getting to him. Or perhaps he's trying to decide the menu of his last fucking meal. It's like when you're at a restaurant and cannot choose between veal or braised rib. Have you heard anything about his attempted suicide?"

"That's messed up, Jeremy. I heard nothing, but I will let you know if I do."

"OK, Wallace. Cool."

Wallace hung up and stopped to think for a moment. *Holder's a nut. Holder knew that Linda Sanchez had used my Dodger tickets. He probably knew of my visit with Nico. Holder likely concluded that he was helping Sanchez investigate him.*

***

199

Monday's workdays are the worst. The entire work week is ahead, and it seems you are off balance on Monday until you find your buoyancy later in the week. Whitten settled back home after a long workday on Monday and wanted to get home with his family and do nothing. His lovely wife, Gina, had a special dinner for the kids: pizza. Billie, the ten-year-old, and Mattie, their eight-year-old princess, were on their computers in the family study.

"How was your day, Hon?"

"You know, the usual. My jury trial ended. The rest of the week might be lighter, so you guys have me to yourselves. I can't wait to take the kids to Legoland." He pecked her on the cheek, and she smiled. "I got a call from Jeremy this morning."

Gina tensed and said, "What did the great Mr. Holder want? Did he get pissed because you gave two Dodger tickets to Miss Sanchez? I hope you don't get in trouble for that."

"Don't worry, it was nothing. Just some stuff about the Meza appeal. He also wants us to double-date sometime."

"Oh? I hope you didn't commit us. There's something about that guy. Gives me the creeps. I can't say exactly why, but the few times I've been near him, he gives me that side look, you know? I don't know if you pick up on his weird vibe, but I do."

"Well, babe, I don't expect to be socializing with him soon. Don't worry."

"That's good to know. It's almost nine. We should get the kids to bed."

Both entered the small study with their children. Wallace commented, "They sure are quiet in there. They must have exciting assignments."

As they entered, they saw their children with similar expressions as they were looking at their computer screens—wide-eyed with their mouths agape, with a mixture of confusion and curiosity. Gina went to their computer stations, looked at the screen, squinted her eyes to focus, and yelled, "What the hell? Kids move away!"

As Wallace moved closer to view the screen, he yelled, "Oh crap! What the hell?"

Their oldest child asked, "Was that Pops in the movie?"

On the screen was a pornographic vignette depicting a man who looked like Wallace with two young females engaging in a multitude of activities in a bedroom. The only sounds from the scene came from one of the female participants panting, *Oh, Wallace! Oh, Wallace!*

Wallace and Gina knew the video inserted a dubbed voice like an old Kung Foo movie with English translations. But the face was Wallace's.

Gina closed the laptops and said, "Kids, go to bed. That was not Daddy. Someone played a joke on us. Not funny."

Wallace just shook his head, knowing it was a deep fake and that they would have a long discussion with their children and a few sessions with a pediatric psychologist.

The next day, Jim, a friend, came at their request. Jim was an I.T. guy who explained that cropping a face in this movie is easy. "Elementary kids can do it," he said. "Sometimes, it's a prank. Sometimes, the motivation is more sinister. Some guy who gets dumped puts his ex's face in a fake video where she appears to be servicing the offensive line of the L.A. Rams. This movie was fake. It's easy with A.I. face swaps."

"Jim, thank you for your time."

Wallace told Gina he would take the two computers to another I.T. guy he knew worked freelance for the District Attorney, Spike Smith. Wallace glimpsed a snippet of Holder's depravity—Holder knowingly exposed the fake porn image to the Whittens' two young children. While Wallace was aware of the seriousness of the situation, he still didn't want his wife to understand the full scope of the danger.

Gina asked, "Spike Smith? That can't be a real name. Is he legit?"

"Let's just say it is. He's very discreet."

"Wallace, this doesn't sound like a simple prank. Some nut planted this garbage in our children's computers for a reason. Do you have enemies I should worry about?"

"I defend accused murderers. But I can't think of someone who would do this," Gina said pensively. "Whoever did this is some sick bastard."

Wallace said, "Time for early Christmas gifts for the kids—new computers."

Gina turned to her husband and said, "I knew right away it was a fake. You know how?"

Wallace smirked and said, "OK—I'll take the bait. How did you know it was a fake, babe?"

"Because that dude on the video had your face, but below the waist, he had a piece like a Budweiser draft horse, babe. Sorry, no offense."

Wallace said, "No offense taken. It was probably someone's idea of a bad joke."

Gina said, "Yeah. But don't erase that tape. We might save it for a rainy day with a nice Chablis and some Barry White." She looked at him with an exaggerated, sensuous smile and said, "Or we could see it again tonight, rain or no rain."

***

They met in the South Coast Plaza parking lot behind an Old Navy store. It was nearly six p.m. when Holder pulled next to an old Honda.

A voice from the Honda asked, "You got it?"

Holder exited his car, approached the driver, and handed him a brown shopping bag from Old Navy. "It's all there, Trigger. Ten thousand. I'll keep this burner phone. Call me when you got him, 'cause I wanna hear him."

"Hey, man, you sure this is the right address? And the dude's name is Whitten?"

"Yeah, Trigger. That's all you need to know. And we'll never meet again after the next time I talk to you."

"Cool."

***

Linda and Julio brought their mother home after ten days in the hospital. Rita, a stubborn woman, wanted to be in her home despite Linda's desire to find an apartment in West Los Angeles.

"Linda, I want to be in my home. Julio is here and can take care of me. The doctor is nearby, and I can get a ride to my appointments from the neighbor."

"Ma, I can take you. And Julio can borrow my car if he needs to. You're not staying here alone, do you understand?"

"I been here alone for a long time. I'm fine. I'm safe." They sat in the small living room of the Boyle Heights house. Rita sat in a large recliner with a walking cane nearby. Linda and Julio had stocked the refrigerator with plenty of food.

Julio said, "Ma, I learned to cook in prison. I was a trustee for a while in Centinela prison, and they put me in the kitchen. It made the time go by. But I like to cook, and I can cook for us here. No problem, Ma; Linda will come after work and on weekends to help. You'll like my Hawaiian chicken, or I could do some pozole or paella. We'll be good."

"Thank you, *mijo*. I'm going to bed. Linda and Julio, thank you." She slowly hobbled to her bedroom and closed the door. Within minutes, they could hear her resounding snores.

"Julio, you've got to be very careful here. Never leave Mom out of your sight. You have Santos's phone number. Call him anytime, day or night, if something comes up. You can trust him. We're trying to build a case against this bastard, but he's still loose and might harm one of us. We'll get him with more evidence."

"You don't think you guys can arrest him now?"

"No. I want to make his arrest solid. The case is too crazy for someone to believe, but once the evidence comes in, you can't argue against the evidence. That sounds stupid, but we must get him the right way. I never go to trial unless I have everything lined up."

"Lin, you know what your problem is? You play by the fucking rules. Some people don't.

"You need to think outside your protective little box. This guy tried to kill you. He's playing by *his* rules. Maybe *we* should also play by his rules."

"Look, Julio. Trust that I know what I'm doing. I'm not going to do something irrational. I know this guy is a psychopath. What I need from you is just to focus on Mom's safety. Get someone from the neighborhood you can trust to help you, but we have to keep this to ourselves. Holder seems to know lots of people."

"Yeah, that hit man Escalante. He's the worst. Holder convinced him to kill you, so he must have a lot of juice to convince that *vato*."

"Julio?"

"Nothing. Just a paper I was looking at."

"It seems like it's an application for culinary school, Julio. It looks like you started to fill it out. Are you applying?" she asked.

"Nah. It's too expensive. They want ten thousand dollars for the two years. I thought about it. The school is not too far, but it's too much money."

"Julio, listen. Remember what I told you when we were kids, and I was trying to teach you how to ride a bike? I told you just get your tiny butt on the bike, don't overthink, and peddle 'cause I knew you could do it. Now, I'm telling you the same thing. Fill out the damn application, 'cause I know you can do this. I will pay for the costs, but don't fuck it up, OK?"

Julio stared at her with the same glass-eyed look he had when he first peddled a bike and said, "OK, Lin, I won't fuck this up, I promise. I can get my food truck in two years and be in business. Linda, I don't know what to say. Thank you."

"Julio, I have to go now. You don't have a car. Let me know if you need me to pick something up for you. These groceries should last. I have to keep checking my car. Someone put a tracker underneath my hood. Turi, the mechanic, found it. I'm sure it was that bastard. He knew we went out to eat, and he knew Mom and I were at the Dodger game. Be careful and keep your eyes open around the neighborhood. I'll see you."

"Hey Linda, I love you, sis."

"I love you too. Give me a hug, you little prick." They embraced and held each other like they were kids long ago—when five-year-old Julio learned how to ride a bike.

***

Trigger slithered slowly through a residential part of Long Beach. In the early evening, the streets were quiet. Household lights were flickering off as folks were going to bed. His G.P.S. display indicated he was close. Holder had only given him the address and the name—Whitten.

As he cruised by, the G.P.S. said in a soothing voice, *You have reached your destination.*

He looked at the location and saw a pleasant-looking white and blue house with a small front porch. Only one light upstairs was on. An elderly couple walking a dog gave him an extra look. The bikes on the Whitten porch told him that this was a safe neighborhood, and the target had young children. Since the target lived in a cul-de-sac, he sensed that too many neighbors were nearby. He needed to complete the task at another time when the target's family was gone. After all, he took pride in his professionalism.

CHAPTER 28

Sanchez remembered the first case she prosecuted with Holder as the defense attorney, searching for something retrospectively about him or the case that might have been unusual. She was in her fourth year as a prosecutor, and she charged Holder's client with an assault.

The defendant, Darnell Beck, a parolee, had assaulted an older woman in a wheelchair. Beck, at six feet and two hundred pounds, and the victim, at five feet and one hundred pounds, were just hanging out on a slow summer evening in Compton when he picked up a nearby tree branch, swung at her, and fractured her jaw in two places. When the police responded, Beck still clutched the thick branch and proudly flicked it over his head like an Aaron Judge home run celebration. During the interview with the police, Beck, with his foggy brain loaded with meth, cocaine, and cheap wine, told the police he hit her because she looked at him *the wrong way, like she was mad-dogging me.* The prison walls followed him, and in prison culture, he argued vainly, mad dogging justified a quick pre-emptive response. "That's just the way it's done," Beck said.

Because Beck had a strike on his record, he was looking at a decades-long sentence. Now that she was getting a clearer picture of Holder's current psychological makeup, she recalled some unusual behavior by Holder that she discounted at the time but now offered a different context.

First, she found him flirtatious. Both were married then, and she discounted Holder's conduct as harmless banter. He wanted to discuss the case after hours at a nearby café because they *might relax after a few glasses of wine and find common ground to settle.* When they met in court during pre-trial proceedings, Holder was too touchy-feely with her, stroking her hand and shoulders whenever he could. Linda's antenna was slow to pick up the signals this crude moron was sending. But eventually, she did and kept her distance.

The other odd thing she remembers was Holder often, in her presence, casually made racial jokes. She ignored them and discreetly told him they were inappropriate in any conversation. Holder did not limit his racial tones to Blacks. Assuming she would laugh along with him, he also made stereotypical jokes about Mexicans. Trying to maintain her professionalism, she denounced him with subtle threats to the State Bar, which he probably took as a joke. He wasn't the first attorney to utter crass jokes before her. So, with time, Holder's propensities faded away in her memory bank.

She also recalled how Holder referred to Beck not as *my client* or *the defendant* but as a *scumbag*. Most defense attorneys embellish their clients' good character or minimize their lousy conduct, whether they are speaking to a prosecutor, a judge, or a jury. Holder did little of that.

Although Sanchez knew Holder had a good reputation as a criminal defense attorney in Texas and California, she only saw him as a lukewarm advocate. Holder mentioned little of Beck's mental health history, schizophrenia, and commitments to state mental institutions throughout the trial—including, and especially, during the sentencing hearing.

Before the trial, Holder made superficial efforts to settle and failed to argue potential mental health defenses. He wanted to fast-track the case, a track that led directly to a conviction. During the trial, Holder filed half-assed motions, using poor research, and conducted little productive examination of witnesses. With barely a whimper from his attorney, the court sentenced Willis to a maximum term of confinement.

Holder promised to file a notice of appeal but failed to do so. Beck, with a third-grade education and severe mental issues, never understood this. Holder only advised him *we lost the appeal, bro.* An appeal that might have scrutinized Holder's shallow efficacy never saw the light of day.

Then, Linda attributed Holder's conduct to gross incompetence. Now, she realized it had little to do with incompetence.

***

Sara was a glittering gem.

As a teenager growing up in Fresno, California, Sara Miller had a tough childhood, as her single mother struggled to pay weekly bills working as a waitress at a truck stop café. Sara had no siblings, and making friends in their trailer park was a challenge because of her shyness.

Showing little interest in school, students taunted her when teachers repeatedly sent her home with lice. Her mother never thought of shaving her hair, which was luxuriously thick and soft. She was slightly bow-legged and taller than most of her cruel peers, who made fun of her thick reading glasses and height. *She looks like a blind Big Bird! Hey, Too-Tall Sara, how far can you see up there?*

Around age fifteen, she began to wear contact lenses, bathed more than twice a week, jettisoned her braces, and developed a keen self-awareness of her astonishing beauty. Her facial baby fat melted away, and she grew nearly six feet tall with a lithe frame. The heavens sculpted exquisite high cheekbones that framed an explosive smile with sparkling green eyes. A stunning young woman emerged from the stifling cocoon of her impoverished youth, and her suppressed beauty emerged like a chrysalis. Once Mother Nature set the gorgeous butterfly free, she caught the attention of modeling agents who convinced her to ditch high school to pursue modeling. Sara Miller enjoyed a mediocre modeling career, and it was over once she turned thirty. By then, her mother's addictions—alcohol, gambling, drugs, and men—sadly depleted most of Sara's earnings.

Her agent reminded her, "Sara, it's hard to find work in this business after thirty! You had a good run, but they're recruiting girls just out of high school." At the ripe old age of thirty-one, her career inexorably went downhill as she slid from the pages of fashion magazines to Porsche car dealership commercials to sporadic local ads for air conditioning companies.

Sara then pivoted to another career as a wellness coach and Instagram social media influencer, offering advice on *wellness and wholesome, healthy lifestyles.*

You are only as good as you feel!

My advice when you wake up in the morning? Drink a full cup of coffee, look at yourself in the mirror, smile, and then take a long walk on the beach.

Tell yourself at least five times a day how beautiful you are.

If someone is mean to you, treat them with patience and kindness.

These philosophical gems included layers of filtered photos of Sara frolicking on a sunset beach, cuddling up with a fluffy cat on a couch, or sitting cross-legged with a tight business suit behind an executive desk wearing phony horn-rimmed reading glasses with hundreds of leather-bound books she never read or would never read behind her.

Her following peaked at three thousand—just enough to live in a small studio with a steady diet of canned beans, hot dogs, and raman noodles. When her agent suggested soft porn as an alternative, she fired him and told him, "I can't do porn because my mom would see the tattoo on my butt."

The agent asked rhetorically, "So, your major concern about doing porn would be your mom seeing your tattoo?"

"No, I don't do soft porn or hard porn. I don't even know the difference. Porn is porn, soft or hard."

So, the over-the-hill model and social ex social-media-influencer contemplated her next career move without an agent, with her fading youthful beauty, and with only a limited education—two evening classes, one for her GED (she never passed) and another for stained-glass art (she got a generous B+) at Santa Monica City College—she had few career options.

She found a part-time job with a high-end food catering business servicing upper-class clients—movie industry people, investment bankers, West side realtors, Instagram celebrities, and lawyers. Jeremy Holder hired her company for an office Christmas party when Holder was crawling out of his second marriage.

During the Christmas party, Holder spotted Sara for the first time as she was arranging a table of prosciutto-wrapped figs, Greek yogurt cones, and pecorino meatballs. She appeared to examine each sample like Sherlock Holmes, looking for clues. Holder continued staring at her across the room as she sampled the figs and meatballs. Then, when Sara thought no one was looking, she swiped a few meatballs into her side pocket with a satisfied look.

Holder approached her and smirked, "You didn't like the figs?" She said nothing and blushed with a startled face. Holder was stunned at her beauty as she looked up at him—soft green eyes, flawless glowing skin, and a thick mane of silky brown hair cascading languidly over white shoulders. He quickly pivoted into flirtatious mode and asked, "Don't you want more meatballs for the road?" He extended his hand and introduced himself.

She smiled and was unsure if his question was sarcasm or something else. (It was something else.) The only retort she could think of came from her low reservoir of blandishments from her days as an influencer, and she said, "A small piece of bread is the only nutrition you need to be happy and healthy."

Not comprehending what the hell she just said, Holder looked at future wife #3 and smiled at her. "No, it's cool. I know you were just sampling the food to ensure it was good for us. You're just doing your job."

She asked demurely, "Please don't tell my boss. I need this job. I'm between modeling assignments."

Holder said, "You're a model? I thought I recognized you! Wait, two years ago, I was looking for a new Porsche. I buy a new one every year. And I saw a commercial from the dealership in Culver City. Was that you? Holy shit. I bought that Porsche because of you and that commercial."

She said, "No, you're bullshitting me."

"No, really. In the commercial, I remember you standing in the back of a red Porsche Boxster wearing a matching red mini-dress, with your back to the camera, leaning over the car, and saying, *West side Porsche. Get behind this baby, and you'll enjoy a thrust in heaven.* I loved that pun!"

She asked innocently, "It was a pun? Oh."

Holder grabbed a handkerchief and wiped her lower lip. "Looks like you left some of my crab cakes on your lip. Hope it was good."

"I'm so embarrassed, Mr. Holder. It was a pun? I like your accent, Texas."

"Yup. Born and raised. You ever been there?"

Sara said, "Yeah, my dad took us to Dallas when I was young. We went to the place where he said Kennedy died."

"JFK?"

"Huh?"

Holder said, "Dealey Plaza in Dallas is where they killed JFK, John F. Kennedy. In Dallas."

"Really?"

Holder said, "Isn't that what you just said? Your father took you to Dallas to visit the place where Kennedy died."

Sara paused for a long second, waiting for the spool in her head to stop spinning, and said, "Oh. I thought my dad was full of shit, and I was so confused because I thought Kennedy died in a plane crash over the ocean. He was so cute. I don't remember any ocean near Dallas. I wasn't too good at geography."

"No, not John Jr., Jon-Jon; I meant President John Kennedy, the father. In 1963, Lee Harvey Oswald, the lone gunman, assassinated him in Dallas."

Sara asked, "You think this Oswald guy also killed John Jr.?"

"I doubt it." Now visibly annoyed, Holder said, "But it's possible if you ascribe to the *super magic bullet theory,* then the same fucking bullet could have blown JFK's brains out, wounded Governor Connolly, then entered a time portal, and thirty-six years later returned in 1999 to whack John Jr. two thousand miles away while he was flying a plane near Martha's Vineyard."

Sara grimaced, said nothing, arranged a serving tray, and returned to Holder's guests. Her spool kept spinning. As she walked away, Holder asked, "Can I take you out for a drink sometime?"

Sara stopped, tapped her butt, and said, "Yeah, and you might get behind this baby and get a thrust in heaven." Holder knew she was #3.

Pursuing Sara Miller began as soon as Holder's divorce from wife #2 was final.

Their courtship was brief, culminating with a picturesque wedding ceremony at sunset on the cliffs of Carmel, California. They settled into a blissful marriage with a busy social schedule, entertaining clients and L.A. glitterati. Jeremy's busy law practice kept him away from home, but Sara kept busy re-decorating their house *to remove the stench from wife #2.*

Lacking any frame of marital reference, Sara thought it was normal when Jeremy carefully outlined his rules that included their domestic and social schedule:

She needed to call him whenever she stayed out past six, although he installed a tracking device under the hood of the Mercedes 500 SL.

Under no circumstances would she allow a man into the house alone.

Jeremy did not allow Sara to enter his upstairs study except to clean it when he was present.

Sara received a generous monthly stipend for clothes, salons, and spas, with the caveat that she retains all receipts *for my accountant.*

She had to give Jeremy all her friends' names and cell numbers.

Sara had to have his suit, ties, shoes, and underwear with compatible color patterns laid out every evening for his work the following day.

No dirty dishes in the kitchen, and all hand towels changed daily.

When he was home on weekends, he needed a ham sandwich on wheat with lettuce and Monterrey Jack cheese at noon with a cold glass of milk. The sandwich had to be sliced at 45-degree angles. On the side: one pickle and one jalapeno. (Sara later learned that Jeremy's mother always prepared his sandwich this way when he was a boy.)

The new Mrs. Holder was blissfully happy in her world of domestic nirvana, confined to the role of a devoted wife who managed an organized household and spent quiet evenings at home and peaceful mornings strolling along the beach. Sara's innate submissiveness, raw exterior beauty, and harmless dry wit provided a soothing narcotic that mollified and stabilized Holder's impulsiveness, mood swings, and suppressed another dormant trait—violent outbursts. Sara only saw a funny, generous, and wonderful man through the distorted prism of her myopia. Moving from her tiny studio apartment in Torrance with a view of a littered parking lot with homeless people pissing to a spacious cliff-side manor in Pacific Palisades with a view of the Pacific Ocean probably clouded her near-sightedness like delusional cataracts.

Although she had little interest in Jeremy's work, she often wondered why he represented so many criminal defendants, especially those facing the death penalty.

"Why can't you represent realtors, bankers, or white-collar persons? That way, your practice is much cleaner."

Holder's answer was short, "Sara, babe, please don't ask me about my practice or clients. You'll never understand, and it won't make sense in your pretty little head. Besides, most realtors and bankers I know are bigger assholes and crooks than my other clients. Let's not talk about this anymore. I just want you to pay attention to the house and me. Love you." He then gently patted her on the head like she was a pet chihuahua.

The new Mrs. Holder was upstairs one day when Jeremy was away for the weekend, attending a lawyer's convention in San Francisco. Although expressly forbidden from entering his private study, her curiosity—usually comatose—temporarily revived and flickered to life like an old light bulb. She snuck into the study by picking the lock like her mother taught her to snoop around. *What was the secrecy?*

She knew his laptop was in a locked desk drawer. She saw some discarded medicine bottles in a trashcan and closely examined them. She whispered to herself, spelling the pill bottle label, "Ris… per… done. Risperidone. Follow the doctor's instructions. Prozac. Te… gre… tol. Tegredol." Sara believed Jeremy's doctors prescribed these meds for his allergies and thought no further. Poor guy. He suffers so much. The study was immaculate, with rich oak paneling that glowed softly from the illumination of the Tiffany & Co. desk lamp. Childhood photos lined the walls, including Jeremy with his parents in Paris, Hawaii, and at a football game.

One photo depicted Jeremy with three childhood friends. All wore red soccer uniforms with a trophy, all smiling. Jeremy stood out since he was taller than the other three and lighter-complected. In the photo was a skateboard with wheels that had a unique design—a red lightning bolt. As she focused closely, she saw a small piece of paper sticking out behind the photo, and she carefully pulled it out. It was an old news clipping about a young boy who suffered a vicious attack. The authorities stated that an unknown assailant struck the young victim with the latter's skateboard as the victim returned home one evening after a football game. The authorities found no suspects.

Slowly scanning the room, something caught her attention on his large executive desk—a metal paperweight. She knew what it was as she picked it up and examined it. As a young girl, before her innate beauty engulfed her, Sara was a tomboy. She played multiple sports and was better than most young boys her age. One of her favorite activities was riding her skateboard.

Whenever a part of it broke, she would repair it herself since her mother could not afford to buy her a new one. She could take apart a skateboard with her eyes closed. The metallic paperweight on her husband's desk was the wheel of an old skateboard with a unique design— a red lightning bolt in the center.

The musty air in the study grew chilly, and she left shivering. Sara was trying to process some things she saw upstairs.

Who were those boys in the photo?

Why did Jeremy want to keep all this stuff private?

What were those pill bottles? Jeremy only told me he takes vitamins and some mild pills for insomnia.

Was he involved in that old incident of that poor boy's beating?

Why all the secrets?

Her doorbell then blared, and she scampered downstairs to answer it. As she opened the door, she saw a beautiful woman, about a youthful forty, tall, with green eyes, dressed in a sharp business suit with a cashmere sweater. Sara knew the visitor hadn't purchased her splendid outfit at a weekend rack sale. Her outfit was fit to form a woman who looked like she spent time on a fashion runway years ago. Even her sunglasses looked expensive.

"Hi, Sara. My name is Madeline Thorpe. My previous name, before my divorce was final, was Madeline Holder. I'm Jeremy's ex. May I come in?" Caught off-guard, Sara let her in with no thought. "May I sit down? I see you've done some remodeling; you have exquisite taste, Sara."

Still confused, Sara said, "Let me get some coffee; please sit." Sara's nervous eyes darted toward a manila envelope perched on her visitor's lap. "I met Jeremy during your divorce but never attended the court hearings."

"The judge ordered the record sealed, and the hearings were all closed. Jeremy is a stickler for privacy. I knew he was out of town, so I took a chance to visit you. If he saw me here, he would kill me," Madeline said.

"That was a joke, right?"

Madeline said, "Yeah, a joke. Anyway, I'm here to talk to you. You seem like a sweet, loving person any man would be lucky to have as a wife. But I just wanted to tell you about my experience with Jeremy and our two-year marriage because I don't want you to go through what I went through with him."

"Excuse me, Madeline, but there's no point in attacking my husband, which I think you're about to do. I love Jeremy very much and will do everything possible to make this marriage work."

"Sara, at first, I fell hard for him. He's good-looking, witty, on-the-surface rich, and has that Texas accent. We met at an art exhibit in Bel Air and were engaged for only two months until his first divorce was final. The honeymoon in Maui was magical. That was the best part of the marriage.

"Although I learned he had odd habits, I didn't think twice about it. Don't we all have personal habits that might seem strange? I got used to his rigid domestic rules, and they did not seem too strange at first since this was his house. He's the king of his castle! He probably outlined those same rules to you, right?”

Sara nodded in agreement. “He was also very secretive. Half the time, I didn’t know where he was, even when he went away for days. I attributed that to his busy law practice, but it was strange when I asked about his trips. He was just vague and dismissive without giving me any concrete information.

“I also suspected he had money problems, but you couldn’t tell because he was so pretentious with his wealth and lifestyle. I don’t think his law practice brought in the money to live here. How many criminal defense attorneys live in Pacific Palisades? I learned later that he had depleted his trust fund, and his parents quit supporting him. This house is heavily mortgaged. I suspected he had another source of income outside his law practice.”

“Miss Thorpe, with all due respect, what’s the purpose of this visit? Just to tell me how shitty your marriage was? Are you done?”

“Almost, and I’ll leave, but I wanted to share this with you.” Madeline opened the manila envelope and extracted several glossy color photos. “Look closely at these, Sara. This is me after Jeremy beat the crap out of me two years ago. These are selfies I took since the cops were never called. After the beating, Jeremy took me—no, he dragged me—to a plastic surgeon he knew in West Hollywood to repair my broken jaw and nose. He patched me up like new, and I told friends I had done some cosmetic work. That night, I couldn’t call 911 because I could not talk, and I was in so much pain. The main reason, though, was Jeremy pulled out a gun, pointed it at my head, and told me not to tell anyone what happened. He did this as he was pinching my broken nose before I fainted. I learned later that Jeremy was off his meds and was acting strange, pacing up and down frenetically all night. He turned into a monster. That monster is still in this house with you. LOOK AT THESE PHOTOS, SARA. CROP YOURSELF INTO THESE PHOTOS BECAUSE THAT’S WHAT WILL HAPPEN TO YOU! When Jeremy married you, he just traded his victim for a newer model, and you’re the newest model.”

Sara quietly said, “Kind of like he was buying a new Porsche.”

“What? Sara, when you said *I do* to Jeremy, you took a vow of domestic submission. Till death—your death—you might depart, Sara.”

Sara looked at all five photos as bile crawled up her throat like a warm volcano. She asked, “Why did he beat you?”

"That day, he was late for court. I forgot to arrange his suit, clothes, and shoes for that day. But he got really pissed when I neglected to remove the tags on his shirts from the dry cleaners. The first blow knocked me to the ground; then, he dragged me to the closet to arrange his clothes. Once I did that, I thought it was over. But the beatings continued."

Sara tearfully asked, "What should I do?"

Madeline quickly grabbed the photos, stood up, and said, "Run. Run and hide. Just take a few items of clothing. Do not go to a shelter because he will track you down. Take out enough cash to hold you over. Do not use credit cards. Get a few burner phones. Go somewhere safe. But run." Madeline embraced her, then left.

CHAPTER 29

"Mr. Teague, I have a confession—I am a fool."

Linda was in Teague's office reviewing her upcoming trial. Teague surprised the Office of the State Bar Counsel by seeking a speedy trial despite perfunctory overtures from the State Bar prosecutors to settle expeditiously. The prosecutors proposed a quiet, confidential reprimand with no actual suspension and no negative impact on Linda's job. Teague surprised the bar prosecutors when he informed them that Sanchez wanted a speedy trial and would not accept any proposed settlement. "I think of that old maxim about a defendant who represents himself—that defendant as a fool for a client. Well, I'm that fool, but I want to represent myself when I go before the State Bar next week," Linda said.

Teague leaned back in his leather chair, squinted, and stared closely at her. "I think I've gotten to know you a little these past few months, and I know I can't convince you to change your mind. I just want to make sure you want to go solo for reasons other than my representation. If it is, I'll refund your retainer."

"No. Absolutely not. You are a superb attorney; that's why I hired you. I know attorneys are the worst clients. As a class, attorneys are opinionated, self-centered, egotistical, and demanding—idiots." Teague laughed. "But seriously, attorneys come to you for help when the state bar is after their bar ticket.

"But the reason, or reasons, I want to represent myself has nothing to do with you. I want to go to that hearing alone because these allegations between the complainant and me, Jeremy Holder, are deeply personal. This complaint is a threat to my livelihood. He has made a spurious complaint against me, my reputation, my profession, and everything I have worked for. If I get disbarred or sanctioned, I don't want to blame my attorney—I will blame only myself.

"I want to look him in the eye and question him under oath. He must know we're closing in on him. I want to see him sweat. I want to hear that annoying Texas accent when he denies anything I've uncovered about him. I want to squeeze his Texas nuts to force him to plead the Fifth. And I want the State Bar Trial Counsel to know I did nothing wrong when I spoke to Mrs. Meza. This trial has to get out in the open. Our investigation is still pending, but he's the one who filed this complaint, and he is the one who will suffer the consequences.

"I have confidence in my legal skills in court, just as I have complete confidence in yours. But this is too personal, and I have to do this myself. I can't wait to put that arrogant, psychotic prick on the witness stand."

Teague leaned across his desk to extend his hand. "Linda, good luck. I will advise the trial counsel's office that I am withdrawing from the case. Keep in touch if you need anything."

***

"OK, Spike, why the hell are we here?"

Santos, Linda, and Wallace stood in Spike Smith's (not his real name) grubby office, looking for places to sit among boxes, magazines, computers, paper plates with week-old food residue, computer parts, and various bongs. Linda, who had never been to *Gold and Gold Computers*, asked, "Was this place ransacked? I can call 911. Did the cocaine bear come in here? Is this why you brought us here? Mr. Smith, you give hoarders a bad name. You need help, Mr. Smith, or whatever the hell your name is."

Smith laughed and said, "I already like you, Linda."

Smith had sent a cryptic message to all three so he could speak to them in person.

Because of the frantic nature of the message, all three dropped everything and drove to the San Fernando Valley to see Smith. Linda was preparing for her trial before the California State Bar scheduled for the following week, and Santos and Wallace set aside their busy schedules to meet Smith. A faint waft of marijuana masked the office's odor of mold and sweat. Linda and Wallace looked around the office for a spot to sit.

Smith said, "You guys know my life is a constant fuckup. Too many drugs, alcohol, and tragedies, but Santos knows one thing about me. I know my shit with computers. I trained with the best software engineers and probably could have been one of the top engineers at Microsoft, Apple, or Facebook. But I'm not. I never wanted to be. No regrets.

217

"A few months ago, Santos asked me to find info on this dude Jeremy Holder to search for any of his electronic footprints in cyberspace. This guy is a piece of work; I mean a piece of work like Norman Bates.

"First, I confirmed that he was the source of the false rumors about you, Miss Sanchez. Those rumors stopped disseminating on the internet once he knew we were on to him. Then, I kept fishing in the cyberspace ocean—that sucker's deep, man."

Linda spotted a pot of cold coffee beside an insecticide spray and interrupted, "Mr. Spike, can you get me a blond pumpkin latte, *venti*, please? How long has that coffee been in that pot, Spike? It looks like Valvoline oil. I think something alive is floating on top. You're not a Starbucks guy, are you?"

Smith ignored her and continued, "So, I began a deeper search of Mr. Holder and his activities floating out there among the cyberspace constellations. As Santos knows, I sometimes help law enforcement when they seek a geofence warrant from a judge. You guys know what a geofence warrant is—it's when you want to trace someone's movement through cellphone pings within a certain perimeter. Google needs a warrant from a judge because it might be over broad and include information from innocent persons within the geofence's perimeter. Cops might toss the electronic net too far and ensnare little innocent guppies, not the sharks. Someone like me, who is familiar with the process, might search a person's activities without that pesky search warrant. And I did— no more info about how I did that. Plausible deniability for you three.

"To make a long, boring story short, the bottom line is Holder has been stalking all three of you for the past six months and has been within a hundred-yard radius of your homes and offices. I eliminated random activity, so it is apparent that he was near your locations when you were within the electronic radius, within the geofence. The prick was within the geofence during Miss Sanchez's attempted murder and may have monitored the killer. When that guy shot at you, Holder parked his car three blocks away. So check your vehicles for tracking devices. I gave Santos three top-of-the-line instruments to scan cars and homes for trackers or hidden cameras.

"And here's a clincher. I continued searching for Holder's electronic footprints and found some other interesting stuff."

Linda said, "I need a liter of vodka right now."

Smith continued, "There are chatrooms in the deepest, darkest corners of the internet galaxy. Many are fringe groups, the usual assortment of nuts. I'm half Jewish, and occasionally, I will look at some of these antisemitic hate groups, but most are likely harmless. Lots of hate floating around. I sometimes forward these postings to other groups who monitor them.

"But after a deep search of Holder, I found a chat room in which I believe he was participating and had been participating for several years. And that's why I brought you here to share this stuff." Smith flicked on the computer screen for all to view.

"In this chat room, he goes by the name of *Daffy*. I printed some salient portions of Daffy's comments from the preceding five years to get a flavor of Daffy's opinions. I estimate this chat room might have about a dozen assorted nuts.

"As you can see, Daffy doesn't like people on the fringes of society, and it's more than just racist and antisemitic. He mentions the death penalty and how too many politicians are just too cowardly to implement the death penalty. He praises those five states that still currently have the death penalty: Texas, Missouri, Florida, Alabama, and Oklahoma."

Foxy: Those girlie politicians are too afraid to do the right thing and fry some of those scumbags.

Daffy: I agree. Some of these people aren't human. They kill, rape, and maim, and yet they live in prison with a warm bed, food, and clothing. All states should have the death penalty. California got too soft and liberal, and now they have a moratorium on executions. The states execute them with a soothing chemical that relaxes them before their hearts go out, unlike their victims. They go to sleep like pussycats with no pain. I miss the old days when the states shot, hung, or electrocuted degenerate scumbags. Those were the days.

Mod Man: I don't understand why their appeals take so long. Why not just try them, convict them, then execute them? Seems simple.

Daffy: I agree. But these scumbags have all the legal protection. Most on death row die of old age, or they take the cowardly way out and just commit suicide—no mercy for any of them.

After an hour of reading some of these excerpts, Wallace could only say, "Wow."

"Are you sure that Holder is *Daffy* in this chat room?" Santos asked.

Smith replied, "I am as positive as I can be. I traced *Daffy* directly to Holder's home computer. He's never changed it, probably because he feels comfortable that authorities could never trace him. This chat room closed about three months ago, and I can't speculate why.

"Maybe the members sensed something. The F.B.I. constantly monitors these chat rooms and any other fringe groups. Somewhere in hell, I bet J. Edgar Hoover wishes he had today's technology when he was alive."

Sanchez said, "Holder might be a racist, but is that the only reason he might be setting up his clients?"

Smith interjected, "My opinion, after reviewing this crap for hundreds of hours, is that, yes, Holder is racist. But he also expresses utter contempt for others who, in his opinion, deserve to be executed, including those with mental disabilities and those people who live on the fringes—the homeless, drug addicts, and those that society just tossed away. If this were 1930s Germany, Holder would probably use the term *vermin*."

Wallace said, "You know, Holder also has tried death penalty cases in those five states mentioned. We might look into that. I got a tip from Nico Meza about another Holder client, Chris Allen, who is on death row, and I'll return there to see him. Holder might have botched that case, as well. I can check it out without arousing too much suspicion."

Santos said, "We all have to be vigilant with this guy. He installed a tracker in Linda's car. He knows we're after him, and he's feeling trapped."

Linda said, "I have my State Bar trial next week. I'll see how his S.O.B. handles himself on the witness stand. I'll be ready. Mr. Smith, or whatever the hell your name is, thank you for your help and insight."

"Bernie Watson."

"What?" Linda asked.

Smith said, "My true name is Bernard 'Bernie' Watson."

Linda said, "Honestly, I don't know which name sounds more ludicrous—Bernie or Spike."

Wallace said, "Shoulda stuck with Bernard."

Linda smiled and said, "This was fascinating—and disturbing. Well, Bernie, you're one hell of a computer geek. I hope you never work for—or against—the U.S. government or any government. You're a scary bastard."

"I'll take that as a compliment. This conversation never happened. Now you guys can leave. Santos, leave my standard fee before you go. I need to smoke a joint and read some new comics. Gotta go to Camarillo Beach tonight for the grunion run!"

***

Linda knew that the State Bar Court maintains confidentiality of attorney complaints until and unless the Bar files formal charges. Most lawyers subjected to bar complaints cower in fear since a complaint can ruin a lawyer's reputation, practice, and marriage. Most complaints wither on the vine, and some cases end with a stipulated resolution. Linda's hyper-aggressive response to the potential complaint was unusual but not unreasonable, considering her goal was to expose Holder if she had to. She wanted more evidence against him before presenting it to the State Bar Court, and she also needed more corroboration before submitting a recommendation to Ed Ross.

In the informal discussions between Teague and the State Bar investigators, it was apparent to the Bar that Linda wanted to attack the complaint and the complainer head-on. She was in attack mode. After a few weeks, the Bar reviewed the complaint and notified the "anonymous" attorney that Sanchez sought a public hearing quickly.

***

HEARING DEPARTMENT OF THE CALIFORNIA STATE BAR
COURT OFFICE OF THE CHIEF TRIAL COUNSEL
LOS ANGELES, CALIFORNIA

IN THE MATTER OF LINDA SANCHEZ

State Bar No. 254-N-521

Sanchez sat alone on one side of the counsel table and glanced at the two prosecuting attorneys at the other end. They looked serious. In front of her sat the hearing department judge who would preside over her case, a friendly-looking guy ten years past his retirement age. He had fat jowls that jiggled when he spoke, with a rich baritone voice.

The proceeding was hauntingly surreal. Linda was *Mr. K.*

The parties completed all pre-trial matters, motions, and stipulations and were ready for trial. Linda could feel and hear her heartbeat and vexing whispers in her head.

Disbarment. Suspension. Reputation.

All these thoughts swirled in her mind. Usually comfortable in a courtroom, Linda felt weak and insignificant, like she was on a rowboat in a stormy sea, seeking her inner buoyancy.

The trial judge cleared his throat, glanced at Linda, glared at the prosecutors, and announced the case. "Counsel, good morning. I will be brief. I have a statement from the chief complainant that I will read for the record."

April 28, 2024

Dear Members of the Chief Trial Counsel of the California State Bar:
In the Matter of Linda Sanchez,

I respectfully withdraw this complaint vis-à-vis Miss Sanchez. In my zeal to protect a client's interests and preserve the integrity of our court process, the complaint I filed was premature, and I lacked critical information when I filed the complaint.

Now that I completely understand all the salient facts surrounding these serious allegations, I respectfully withdraw my complaint. This incident was a misunderstanding, and Miss Sanchez, who has a sterling reputation, did absolutely nothing wrong in this case.

I humbly offer my sincerest and deepest apologies to this board and Miss Sanchez in particular.

Respectfully,

[Name redacted.]

"I will enter and register this letter as part of the record and order this proceeding sealed. This matter is closed."

Turning to the State Bar prosecutors, the hearing judge said, "Next time, counsel, do your homework before dragging an esteemed member of the Bar through this. Thank you."

The lone donkey at the counsel table rose, said nothing, and left.

***

Linda quickly set up a meeting between her, Santos, and Ross to advise Ross about the Bar's dismissal. More importantly, Linda thought the time was ripe to give Ross a clear picture.

Linda laid out the events precisely, logically, and coherently. Santos was at her side to provide additional insight.

Ross sat listening, mesmerized, as Linda concluded her summation, and sat back on his chair and said, "So, we have a guy who goes off the rails, gets his client convicted, murders his associate in the arson, sets up a prosecutor to get killed, tries to get that same prosecutor disbarred, a guy who's friends with L.A.'s elite?"

Linda said, "Yup."

"Linda, look. This story is wacky. Hell, I've been to the guy's house. Great barbecue. He has lots of friends. If it were anyone else who laid out this story to me, I would just discount it with little thought. But I trust both of you. Keep after him. We will keep it confidential. But I need a trusted undercover cop from L.A.P.D. near your apartment and your mom's house. I will request extra time and get other prosecutors to cover your calendar if you need spare time. You don't have any trials coming up."

***

"Miss Sanchez, I need your help."

Linda was relaxing in her apartment, watching *Game of Thrones,* the third season, cuddled with a fresh pint of *Ben & Jerry's* Brownie Batter Core. She expected to finish the series a few years after her retirement. The caller's voice sounded vaguely familiar. Linda's senses were dull after binge-watching and seeing the Dragon Queen, Daenerys Targaryen, torch King's Landing with her dragon. Just as she was nodding into a deep nap, dreaming of riding a dragon and torching West Los Angeles without mercy, her phone rang.

"Mrs. Meza, is that you?"

"Yes, Miss Sanchez. I'm Nico's mom. I talked to you a few months ago, remember? I need your help."

223

With the fading image of her dragon torching L.A., Linda said, "Mrs. Meza, are you OK? What's wrong? I probably should not be talking to you. The last time I spoke with you, the State Bar wanted to disbar me."

"Miss Sanchez—"

"Call me Linda."

"OK, Linda. I'm so sorry I got you in trouble. But I wasn't the reason for the complaint. Mr. Holder found out and came to talk to me. I told him you did nothing wrong and were very nice and respectful, but he told me you should not have contacted me. Holder also told me he would file a complaint with the Bar. I asked him not to, but he ignored me and got mad. The people from the State Bar also contacted me and gave me a paper, a subpoena, to testify. They did not even talk to me because I would have told them you did nothing wrong. I'm sorry. But I was so relieved to find out the bar dismissed the complaint. *Gracias a Dios*."

"So, why are you calling me?" Linda asked.

"I wanted to talk to you about this paper I signed with Mr. Holder. I should have told you before."

"OK. What kind of paper?"

"I don't know. Mr. Holder took it after I signed it and never gave me a copy."

"Look, Mrs. Meza, just tell me from the beginning about this document."

Meza told her when Nico was first arrested, Holder visited her and told her he would represent her son. He outlined his extensive experience in the death penalty cases nationwide. The court did not appoint him, but he would handle the case privately. "How will we pay you?" Mrs. Meza asked him.

"Miss Sanchez, he used big words, so I had a hard time understanding him. At the home visit, Holder explained that he would represent Nico but that Nico and I could pay him later with a *deferred payment*. Holder prepared a power of attorney for me to sign documents. He explained that this document was unique, like a life insurance policy, but that part of the monies would pay his attorney's fees and to survivors.

"Linda, I thought this was odd, but I trusted what he said. I only have a sixth-grade education. He would not get his attorney's fees paid until Nico died, and his survivors would also get a part of the money. This seemed like a good deal because Nico would have a great attorney. But he never left or sent me a copy of that paper. Since it was a ten-year policy, Holder said he might never get paid, and his work would amount to a free legal service."

"What was the amount?"

"Three hundred thousand dollars."

"Look, Mrs. Meza, I never practiced probate law. But I can tell you that sometimes an attorney will get his client to sign a document called an *assignment* where the attorney receives payment once he completes the legal services. For example, property or cash bail could satisfy the attorney's fees. But I have never heard of a life insurance policy for attorney's fees if that's what it was."

Linda's epiphany hit her like a lightning bolt—*the attorney will get paid when his client dies naturally or—by execution?* Holder's strange proposal was slowly sinking in. "Do you remember anything else about this document?" Linda asked.

"Well, it was about five pages long. Miss Sanchez he thinks I'm a stupid woman, but I know a few business things. I used to handle payroll for my late husband's landscaping business, and I have a good memory. This name was at the bottom of each paper; I think he's an insurance guy. I might have misspelled the names."

Linda said, "Let me get a pen and paper to write this down."

"The name I remember is:

"Walter Cooper

"Walden Insurance Agency 2410 Bradley Street, # 2301 Pacoima, CA

I'm pretty sure I got the information right. I never heard from Mr. Holder again about this paper."

Linda asked, "Is there anything else out of the ordinary about hiring Mr. Holder?"

Mrs. Meza said, "Yes, come to think of it. Holder knew of Nico's health problems. You see, diabetes runs in our families on both sides. My husband and his brothers all had Type 1 diabetes, and most died in their thirties. Nico's diabetes was bad and getting worse. I don't think he will live past his thirties, and they came close one time to amputating one of his legs. Prison food will kill him. Holder knew about Nico's condition and asked me about it, I guess, to confirm the condition. Why would he be so concerned about Nico's health? I assumed it might help his sentencing, but I don't know. It was odd."

"Mrs. Meza, I will look into this, I promise. Do not tell Mr. Holder about this conversation."

***

Wallace Whitten sought to investigate Nico's tip about another inmate on death row, Chris Allen, AKA: "Shrek," but he did not want to speak with him directly to avoid a blip on Holder's radar. Wallace learned through the public court files that Allen lived in several foster homes most of his life. His parents abandoned him to social services when he was three, likely to avoid the social stigma of raising—what they considered—a deformed child.

Until he was fifteen, Allen crawled through an endless labyrinth of rough foster homes where he endured vicious beatings, unbearable taunting, and profound loneliness. The endless parade of foster parents assigned to him lacked the resources, experience, and empathy to provide any nurturing environment for a soft boy in a hard world. Big for his age, he fought back against his various assailants and spent many years of his youth in juvenile halls and camps.

At fifteen, the social workers finally placed Chris in a loving environment with foster parents, Dora and Gil Allen, in Pasadena, California, both retired special education teachers who had three others placed with them. The new environment was nourishing on several levels, and Chris finally found a home where he was safe and well-treated. The Allens exposed their foster children to museums, libraries, and aquariums around Pasadena, opening a broader and brighter world to the four boys in their custody. Although debilitated mentally and emotionally, Chris Gomez became less introverted and became attached to his foster brothers, who looked after him.

Before he left the foster system through emancipation, the Allens formally adopted Chris, and he was now Christopher Allen, shedding his old skin from his rudderless life to begin a renewed future.

Wallace meticulously reviewed the initial police reports, including Chris' initial statement. On the eventful day of his arrest, Chris left his home in Pasadena on the L.A. Metro to venture to the beach alone, trying to assert his independence. Chris neglected to tell his parents until he

226

arrived at the beach, and his concerned parents told him to return home as soon as possible. Confusion and panic set in when Chris boarded the wrong return bus and disembarked near Silver Lake at dusk. A car cruised by with three young men and offered him a ride. This fateful decision would radically alter his life.

Quickly realizing Chris' mental frailties, the three youths hatched a plan to rob a liquor store and set Chris up for the blame. As the car stopped, one of the three exited. Chris, seated in the back seat, heard three shots as the other boy ran from the store and jumped into the car. As the car sped away, Chris froze with fear. The three boys laughed as they counted the money from the robbery—eighty dollars and a bag of *Fritos*. They ordered Chris to hold the shotgun as one boy slipped a ten-dollar bill and a black ski mask into Chris' pocket and took his cell phone. Chris said nothing and thought they would kill him.

They drove about four blocks, pulled to the curb, and kicked Chris out to the curb as he held the shotgun and mask. Police responded quickly and arrested him after the 911 call from the store. The result: Three people died, including a young mother buying baby formula along with her newborn child.

This calamitous bus ride to the beach brought Chris Allen straight to a special circumstances murder charge, Jeremy Holder, and death row. With Allen's limited mental limitations, the experienced cops quickly extracted a full confession using their repertoire of intimidation, the power of suggestion, sleep deprivation, and a few slaps to the face. His adoptive parents lost contact with him for two days until they saw him behind plexiglass with murder charges.

Whitten's trained legal eye combed the case transcript, and he came to several conclusions:

-Holder did little to verify Allen's original story to the police, such as locating the three individuals who provided a ride to Allen.

-Holder failed to analyze the fibers on the mask and gun to determine if another individual handled one or the other.

-Holder did not explore Allen's history of abuse and special education classes, including psychological evaluations.

-Holder never had his client evaluated to raise possible mental defenses. At the very least, such information before the judge and jury might have prevented a finding of death in the bifurcated portion of the trial. At a minimum, Allen should have received life without parole.

-Holder was also the lead attorney on Chris' appeal.

Linda had already briefed Whitten about the other bizarre development—the life insurance. So, he drove to Pasadena to visit the Allens.

After Whitten arrived and explained why he wanted to speak with them, it became apparent that Holder hardly talked to the parents to explore background information about Chris and showed little interest in verifying Chris's story. The Allens preserved three bankers' boxes of documents about Chris's background, including special education classes and psychological evaluations. Chris's reading and comprehension levels froze by the third grade—his I.Q. consistently tested at ninety.

Mr. Allen said, "We offered to let him take the files, but Holder was oddly dismissive and told us it wouldn't help our son's case."

Whitten said, "Mr. and Mrs. Allen, how often did Mr. Holder visit you about Chris' case? And did you hire him, or did the court appoint him from the death penalty panel?"

Mrs. Allen said, "Shortly after the arrest, he came to our house and told us he was one of the most qualified lawyers in death penalty cases. We confirmed that through our research. And he said not to worry about the money since we could pay him after the trial, but he didn't elaborate. We thought this was strange, but we're not experienced in this sort of thing. We don't have that kind of money. We're on fixed incomes with teachers' pensions. But he had us sign a document that he said would cover his attorney's fees in the future. He never left a copy, but it seemed like some sort of life insurance policy."

Mr. Allen said, "Holder was also familiar with Chris's health problems. You see, Chris has *hypertrophic cardiomyopathy*. That's a mouthful, I know, but it means he has an enlarged heart. Holder knew this when we first spoke with him, and he told us health issues might help in court."

Whitten asked, "Tell me about Chris's heart condition."

Mr. Allen said, "The previous foster homes failed to treat it with medication and a proper diet. We took him to a great cardiologist at the U.C.L.A. Medical Center, who told us his heart condition was poor, and he feared Chris might not make it past the age of thirty. We told Mr. Holder this. Of course, we never told Chris this information. Prison is the last place for Chris—especially with his severely damaged heart."

Whitten nodded and said, "Yes, it is strange that Holder knew this before he entered the case."

Mrs. Allen said, "But there's one other thing. Maybe it means nothing. But I got a strange call right after Mr. Holder entered the case. A man called us and asked some odd questions about whether we had a copy of a document Mr. Holder had left. I did not know what he was talking about, so he hung up. Our phone records incoming calls, and I jotted the name down somewhere. Lemme get it." She went to a small study and returned with a small notepad. "The call came from 'Walden Insurance Agency' in Pacoima. Does that mean anything?"

"It might, ma'am. I need to leave for now, but I promise I will be in contact with you. And please don't reveal this to anyone. Good day."

On the freeway, Whitten called Linda to brief her of the conversation with the Allens. "So, what's the con, Wallace? Holder gets these marginal defendants facing the death penalty, has them take out insurance policies ostensibly for an assignment for attorneys' fees, then screws them with minimum representation. He knows he can't collect. California has put a hold on executions indefinitely. But he can still collect if they die prematurely. What the hell?

"But other states where Holder has taken death penalty cases are still executing. No moratorium. We need to check that. We must still connect the dots, but they are getting closer."

"Lin, he's one messed-up dude."

"Let me go with Santos to visit this insurance guy and shake the tree. I have a feeling some low-hanging, rotten conspirator fruit is gonna fall. Let's meet later this week."

CHAPTER 30

As Whitten returned home, he retrieved his cell phone messages. A message from San Quentin arrived that afternoon.

"Hello, Mr. Whitten, this is Terry Oswalt, assistant warden from San Quentin, calling.

"We spoke several months ago. I'll try to catch you later; I know how busy you must be. You called a few days ago about visiting Christopher Allen. Bad news—he committed suicide two nights ago. Call me if you want, but I can't provide many details. Thank you."

Whitten returned the call. "Mr. Oswalt? Thank you for calling. I appreciate it. I was not Mr. Allen's counsel, but I only wanted to speak with him about a collateral matter. When did he commit suicide?"

"We found him two nights ago during a check. Poor guy probably lost all hope. I never spoke with him, but the staff told me he was a very quiet inmate. There were no outward signs of suicidal tendencies that my staff observed. He had been here two years last month."

"Can you tell me how he killed himself?" Whitten asked.

"He somehow got access to a small wood chip. He probably picked it up somewhere in the yard. There was some construction just outside the prison yard, and the wood was strong and sharp enough to slice through skin, and he cut his own throat."

Whitten said, "Damn. I just met his adoptive parents. Nice people. Have you told them?"

"I called them yesterday."

"Did your staff notice anything unusual about Allen recently? Anything?"

"No. My trained staff tries to discern any unusual conduct from the inmates. Mr. Allen recently had a visit from his attorney, Holder. They met for about an hour last week. Nothing unusual."

"Mr. Oswalt, thank you once again."

After he hung up, Whitten imagined the last conversation between Allen and Holder. *Was there something there to connect Holder to the timing of the suicide? And what about the insurance?* More questions lead to more questions. He needed to compare notes with Linda and Santos, and they agreed to meet at Linda's office for convenience and security.

***

"Is Holder cashing in life insurance on condemned clients he sold out?"

Linda got right to the point. Santos and Wallace were in her office on Temple Street after hours. Only the hypnotic drone of vacuum cleaners and light traffic was audible. A fresh pot of strong coffee was brewing nearby, and Santos brought some pastries. Wallace briefed them about his discussion with the Allens and Christopher's suicide, along with Holder's recent visit with Allen at San Quentin. Linda continued, "We know Holder took out insurance policies on at least two of his clients, one of whom is now dead. He was waiting for them to die of natural causes or suicide because California won't resume executions for the foreseeable future. He cherry-picked his defendants who might die prematurely from health conditions or—in other states—by execution."

Wallace said, "This might sound way off, but Holder may have convinced Allen to kill himself. I don't know how. I don't think he can collect the insurance of someone who commits suicide, can he? We need to research that issue. I think Holder provided the means for Allen to kill himself. The warden told me Allen slit his throat with a small piece of wood, but they couldn't compare the piece with anything in the institution." Wallace rose from his chair, began pacing, and said, "Could Holder have smuggled a sharp piece of wood that would not appear on a metal detector? Holder could conceivably have convinced Allen that there was no way out and the only option was suicide. Allen confessed to a double homicide two hours after his wrongful arrest, and Holder certainly has a more sophisticated power of persuasion than a street cop."

"Hey Santos, you're too quiet. What's on your mind?" Linda asked.

Santos was musing about the discussion, then said, "Linda, I've dealt with a lot of bizarre shit in this business, but this. Keep your eyes and ears open, and make sure your weapons are always nearby. Wallace, do you carry a concealed weapon?"

"I never thought I needed one, despite my profession, and my wife would never allow it. So, she bought this for my protection." Wallace

231

leaned over and pulled out a brass whistle from his pocket. Linda and Santos glanced at the whistle for a few seconds, and they almost fell out of their chairs laughing.

Linda said, "What the hell will you do if Holder comes after you with a weapon? Blow the whistle like you're a school proctor? *HALT RIGHT THERE, MR. HOLDER*! Or maybe you can disable him with a clean shot to his nuts?"

Wallace laughed, shook his head, and blew the whistle meekly, belching mostly spittle from the brass weapon.

Wiping a tear, Santos said, "Linda and I will visit the insurance guy tomorrow for more information. Hey Wallace, put that whistle back in the holster 'cause it might go off, and you might hurt someone with it. Are you licensed to carry that thing?"

Linda choked to get her words out and said, "I think I tinkled."

***

Linda knew the states currently imposing the most death penalties were Texas, Missouri, Oklahoma, Virginia, and Florida—where Jeremy Holder had a law license. She would review particular cases where Holder was the attorney, the outcome, and whether Holder had prepared any insurance policies with his representation.

Linda googled Walter Cooper and the Walden Insurance Agency in the San Fernando Valley. In business since 1995, it looked like a modest business operation, with Cooper likely the sole proprietor. He handled the standard policies—life, auto, and home—with the motto:

We treat you like family and serve all your insurance needs under one roof.

Santos and Linda arrived unannounced at Cooper's establishment early in the morning.

The modest office was near a busy street in a drab mall sandwiched between a Lowe's Department Store and a Starbucks. They entered the office, where a young receptionist with a frozen smile greeted them behind a cluttered metallic desk. She quickly put down her cell phone and fingernail file and sat up. In her mid-thirties with long brown hair and a pleasant, dry disposition, the receptionist, sounding like a worn-out tape recording, said, "Hi, welcome to the Walden Agency. How can I help you? Are you looking for coverage?"

Linda responded, "After what I've been through, I should probably increase my life insurance. Is there coverage for assassinations?"

With a confused look, the receptionist said, "Oh, Miss or Mrs., I assume you and your husband are married. Our policies will fit any situation and are quite flexible. May I make an appointment with Walt, Mr. Cooper?"

Linda looked over the receptionist's shoulder and asked, "Is he in now? We'd like to see him if he has time this morning."

"I'm sure he can make some time for you. We just returned from his Rotary Club meeting. He's the vice president of the Pacoima Rotary."

"Well, that's quite impressive. And your name?" Linda asked.

Pointing to her brass nameplate, the receptionist said, "My name's Brenda Striker. I'm also a notary public in case you might need one later. Glad to meet you. Please have a seat. And your names?" Her frozen smile showed no signs of thawing.

"My name is Linda Sanchez, and this is Ramon Santos."

Brenda buzzed the intercom and said, "I'll see if he's available. Hey Wally… Mr. Cooper, can you see two people now?"

On the other end, a muffled voice behind the closed door said, "Brenda, see if they can make an appointment for Tuesday. We have that thing scheduled this afternoon, remember?"

Lowering her voice, Brenda said, "Oh, I forgot about that thing." She turned to Linda and said, "Can you return on Tuesday?"

Linda said, "First, Brenda, there's no need to use the buzzer. I can hear Walt in the next room. It's only twenty feet away." Forming a pair of bunny ears with her two hands, Linda said, "Second, that *thing* you two lovebirds are planning can wait. Third, we need to speak with Walt now."

From the other room, Walter said, "Who are they?"

Linda marched to Walter's office door and banged impatiently. "Hey Walt, my name is Linda Sanchez. I am a deputy district attorney from L.A., with my chief investigator, Ramon Santos. We need to speak with you."

There was a brief pause on the other side of the door, then, "What is this about?"

Santos said, "Jeremy Holder, Walt. Life insurance, Walt. Death insurance, Walt. Felonious activity, Walt."

There was a longer pause, and then, "You're not from the Insurance Commission?"

Santos said, "No, Walt. We just want to talk to you. This won't take long."

The voice on the intercom said, "Brenda, take an early lunch. Before you go, cancel all my appointments today, will you, hun? And we'll postpone that *thing*, OK?"

As the office door slowly opened, Linda and Santos entered, and they saw a corpulent, balding man just north of sixty with a round body that sagged. Perched on a flat nose were thick glasses framed by soft green eyes that blinked incessantly, with a slightly hunched spine, probably from working in front of a computer screen for most of his adult life. Linda thought—*Paul Giamatti without a personality*.

The office was tiny and cluttered, not Spike-Smith-messy, but close. Heavy metal file cabinets bloated with disorganized files hovered along one wall behind Cooper's executive desk. The office was littered with photographic snippets and mementos of Walter Cooper's simple life—a dour-looking wife flanked by two dull-looking sons during various vacations, plastic plaques from various business clubs, chamber of commerce certificates, and certificates from the California Insurance Commission. A pair of golf clubs rested along a wall.

"Please sit. It was Miss Sanchez and Mr. Santos? I assume you're not looking for insurance?"

Linda said, "I told Brenda I might need some assassination insurance in the future, but that's not why we came. Jeremy Holder."

"What about him?"

"Well, we know he's taken out some policies through you. And before you tell me your records are confidential, let me give you more context about this visit—depending on how you want to play it, Walt."

Linda and Santos then briefed Cooper on the general parameters of their investigation and Holder's odd activity. Cooper listened intensely, and his eyes stopped blinking with an increasing look of fear and dismay.

Linda looked intensely at Cooper and said, "We know he took out policies through you in at least two cases, Nico Meza and Chris Allen. Why? Why would a lawyer take out life insurance on his clients and sabotage their cases, thus sending them to death row when he might never collect? California has a moratorium on executions. Is it even legal to take out a policy on an inmate's life?"

Cooper dropped his head and muttered, "Missouri."

Santos asked, "What about Missouri?"

Cooper: "It's true. I prepared insurance policies for Meza and Allen. But I also prepared one for one of Holder's clients from Missouri, Jerome Willis, who received a death sentence in 2006."

"So, what happened to him? Did Holder collect?" Linda asked.

Cooper cleared his throat and said, "He died on death row from throat cancer. Holder cashed it in. On the policy, there was a small assignment to Willis' wife in the policy, but Holder received the bulk of it, nearly three hundred thousand—tax-free."

Taking a few seconds to let that information soak in, Santos then asked, "Is it common to take out policies on inmates, especially those on death row? Holder also took out policies on guys with severe medical conditions. You must have had some crooked doctor approve the application without review from the Medical Information Bureau, right? And then sweet Brenda notarizes everything for you."

Cooper looked down and said nothing, partially sniffling. Sweat began to spread under his armpits.

Linda added she was investigating Holder's death penalty cases in Oklahoma, Florida, Missouri, Mississippi, and Texas. "Mr. Cooper, we're going fishing where the live fish and the   soon-to-be-dead fish are."

Cooper said, "I did nothing illegal. Unconventional, maybe, but not illegal. Most people can get life insurance unless they have some type of terminal illness, engage in risky behavior, or during war. And yes, life insurance can cover death by execution, as long as it's not during war."

"Does a death sentence qualify as a terminal illness?" Linda asked.

Cooper ignored or didn't hear the question and continued, "My policies are solid. Most folks aren't aware that policy coverage even includes suicides as long as the suicide occurs over two years after coverage begins."

Santos said, "Mr. Cooper, did you know that Chris Allen died two weeks ago? He had been on death row a little over two years and committed suicide. He slit his throat with a piece of wood one day after a visit from Holder. I checked through my sources, and they cannot trace where that piece of wood came from, but Holder is a suspect. He somehow put pressure on Allen to kill himself and provided the means to do it.

Holder visited just two years after he took out the policy on Allen. Coincidence? Holder will then collect, right?"

Cooper looked down and said, "Holder. Dear Lord. I have been on vacation for a few weeks and haven't checked my mail, but Brenda mentioned something about a message from San Quentin, probably confirming Allen's death before the five-hundred-thousand-dollar payout. Oh, God."

In a soothing voice, Linda said, "So, Holder collects if the insured dies naturally, by execution, or suicide. Walt, we'll need more information about these three policies, OK?"

Cooper said, "But I have done nothing wrong. These files are confidential, and I am ethically obligated to protect my clients. I should call my lawyer. You might have heard of him; he's well known in L.A. Ever hear of George Chambers II?"

Linda said, "OK, Walt, you can play that way. If you do, here's how I'm going to play it. First, I will get an emergency search warrant for your office and clean out your files. I have a forensic computer engineer named Mr. Smith who will dig into any files you've hidden. He's a computer driller. The search will be methodical and slow, so your office might be closed for a few weeks. You can temporarily set up a table selling insurance outside the Lowe's store, between the Salvation Army and *Save the Whales* tables. I'm sure sweet Brenda will like that.

Second, Mr. Santos knows people. He might drop an anonymous tip to the Los Angeles Night Tribune about an ongoing investigation into your business. Mr. Santos also knows people with the California State Insurance Commission who might be interested in your dubious dealings with Mr. Holder, not to mention the crooked doctors you used to bypass your clients' medical conditions. Holder's clients had severe medical conditions. Coincidence?"

"Third, I will refer this case to the white-collar division of the D.A.'s office to consider charging you with conspiracy. If your conspiracy involved a deliberate agreement to hasten the death of a human being, this could be a conspiracy to commit murder. Mr. Smith might also see if you received any kickbacks from Jeremy Holder beyond your standard commission. *Kickbacks,* Walt! I am guessing you used a friendly notary to get these signatures, probably that sweet, innocent Brenda. Prison, Walt. They might even demote you from the Pacoima Rotary vice-presidency,

Walt. It's your call, Walt, and we will consider your cooperation in the future."

Cooper said, "Come back tomorrow, and I will make copies and a pen drive available. I will also have attorney Chambers here to work out an agreement with you."

Linda said, "OK, Walt. We'll be here at seven sharp. Hey, Walt, do you know of any good sushi around here? See you tomorrow. Scouts' honor, Walt, and we promise not to let your missus know about this. And don't let Mr. Holder know of this visit. Hey Ramon, sushi?"

***

"Mr. Holder? Walt here. Yeah, I know you want to keep our contact to a minimum. I got a visit from a district attorney. Yeah, that was the one. Sanchez. She was asking a lot of questions about our policies. I need to talk to you about what they were saying about you. OK, I'll meet you here in about an hour. We also need to discuss the Chris Allen policy. We should be alone."

CHAPTER 31

Gossip travels with the speed of light in the L.A. legal echo chamber.

Whitten heard that the Los Angeles Innocence Project centered at U.S.C. had also started an investigation involving Holder and wrongfully convicted defendants. Whitten learned from a connection that the scope of their inquiry had expanded to Missouri and Texas, where Holder had tried and lost death penalty cases.

Whitten's acquaintance at the project, a law school friend, was unaware of the life insurance policies and the various violent episodes involving Holder; Whitten did not want to reveal those facts just yet. The Innocence Project had terrific resources, but Whitten wished to keep the information tightly constricted to him, Santos, and Sanchez. The walls around Holder were dissolving like sand.

***

Cooper sat behind his executive desk, nibbling on potato chips, deep in thought, staring at his cell phone screen, waiting for Holder.

"Oh, Amy, I wish you could be with me now. I really need to talk to you. You look beautiful tonight. I want to ravish you. I just need someone to talk to. Amy, I might be in trouble."

The voice from the cell phone said, *"Oh, Walt, baby. You're always nice to me. I will do anything for you. You know that. Do you want me to put on something else? I know you like this outfit, your favorite. I can be a good listener. You're the sexiest man I know."*

Holder drove to the San Fernando Valley and entered Cooper's office at eight. The surrounding mall was quiet this Wednesday evening, and Cooper's interior lights were dim. Holder entered the office, sat down, and relaxed while Cooper seemed jittery behind his desk. In his nervous condition, Cooper failed to notice that Holder was wearing black gloves.

"Hey babe, is there someone else there?"

Holder interrupted and scolded Cooper, "You know, Walt, try dating an actual flesh-and-blood girlfriend. That chatbot app isn't real, dude."

"Hey babe, why is that person being so mean?"

Holder grabbed Cooper's phone, peered into the pixelated image, smiling at him, and said, "Not bad, Walt. You're going for the naughty schoolgirl with pixie tails. A real classic." Holder squinted at the image and said, "Does she have *Walden Insurance Agency* written on her chest? Walt, you're sick, man. Amy, listen. Walt has to go now. But I'm sure he will call you shortly."

Cooper whispered, "Come on, Jeremy, I paid for another two days."

"OK, Amy, my bad. Walt can't afford you anymore. Goodbye."

"Walt, until the next time, my love. Think of me." Amy exited with a sensuous air kiss and faded away like pixel dust into the internet cloud like a fleeting chimera.

Walter said, "Jeremy, lemme bring her back up." He then clicked the app, and Amy's lovely face reappeared. *"Hi, babe! I missed you, sweet. Oh, Walt, why did you cut me off? Did Amy do something wrong? I can change clothes like the outfit I wore yesterday."*

"No, babe, you're beautiful. Just stay on until I finish talking to my friend here. Say hi to Jeremy."

"Hi, Jeremy. If you're Walt's friend, then you're my friend!"

Jeremy rolled his eyes, shook his head, and said, "This is too fucking weird, even for me. Can't you turn her off?" Cooper shook his head.

Cooper briefed Holder about the visit from the D.A. and was open to suggestions from Holder. "Walt, we need to remove those three files. Do you have any hard files in these cabinets?"

Amy interjected, *"I don't understand you. Could you repeat it? Did you say hard? Is that code?"*

Holder moved away from Amy's view on the cell phone and stood behind Cooper as they glanced at the screen with the files uploaded. Holder inserted a pen drive, downloaded the files, and instructed Cooper to erase the file from the computer.

"Hey Jeremy, what do I tell that D.A.?"

"Think of something, Walt. But don't tell them I was here; you better not speak to them without a lawyer."

"Lawyer? I can dress up like a lawyer if you want, Walt. Anything for you. How about an 'Allie McBeal' lawyer with a miniskirt and briefcase, Walt? Anything for you, babe."

Holder then quickly put his hands around Cooper's neck and held onto his neck with all his strength. With a sedentary lifestyle, a weekend golfer like Cooper was no match for Holder. Cooper began to lose consciousness and saw his drab life flash before his eyes—his childhood in Maine, his dull family, his mediocre insurance business, and Amy, his non-existent, smoking-hot A.I. girlfriend dressed like *Ally McBeal*. He began gasping for air, trying to talk.

"Walt, I did not understand what you said. Did you say help? Please repeat what you said, my love. I can't see you."

At that moment, thirty miles northwest of Los Angeles, near Reseda, sixty kilometers below the surface, the earth began to quiver like jelly. The instability triggered the Pico Thrust Fault Line, the same fault as the 1984 Northridge earthquake. The fault line shook violently through the San Fernando Valley.

Inside the office, Holder froze as the violent shaking increased like a freight train. He released his grip, and Cooper gulped a large pocket of air. As the shaking continued from the 5.9 land tsunami, Holder panicked and sprinted out of the small office. Cooper froze and remained sitting at his desk as an enraged Mother Nature shook the floor below with undulating waves of raw power.

At that moment, Cooper remembered that he failed to secure the heavy metal shelves as they began to sway like drunken sailors. One finally collapsed on Cooper, crushing his head. He died instantly. Meanwhile, Holder tripped on his way out as another file grazed him, lacerating his face and breaking his collarbone. With Cooper's computer, he hobbled out to the parking lot, driving to the nearest hospital. As Holder fled the office, he heard Amy one last time, *"Oh, Walter. What did you say? Is your friend leaving? Now we can be alone again. Walter, are you still there? Walter?"*

The emergency personnel accepted Holder's story that he was the victim of the earthquake and patched him up. The final tally: broken right collarbone, crushed nose, and deep facial lacerations, but his psychosis remained unharmed.

The external pressures encircling Holder from without and the internal ones slowly leeching from within coalesced, and Holder surrendered to them. The delicate thread between reality and insanity gradually unraveled as he clung for hope but slipped toward despair, as he grasped for normalcy but fell toward insanity. The alignment of these unworldly forces hastened his steep descent into dark madness.

Leaving the hospital, Holder limped to his car, crawled into the seat, popped some oxycodone, and sped home to Pacific Palisades. He then activated his G.P.S. tracker.

In Pacific Palisades, Sara thought about her discussion with Holder's ex-wife. His odd behavior had not assuaged her growing anxiety about her new husband since they began their marriage, and she knew the nascent marriage would not last past the honeymoon. Sara's growing fear and self-preservation forced her out of her bubble of naivete and self-delusion. She knew her safety was at risk, and her only option was to run.

The ex-fashion model thought: *What is a tasteful outfit for an abused spousal escape?*

Her sartorial decision complete, she snatched all her jewelry and assembled her escape-from-the-psycho-husband-in-manic outfit: a navy-blue crepe knit polo dress from Scanlan Theodore with a matching gold chain from Tiffany's, Christian Louboutin white pumps to run fast, along with a Louis Vuitton tote bag and luggage to fit enough cash and credit cards to survive for a year.

As Holder entered his house, Sara opened the door and screamed, "Who the hell are you? I'm calling the police!" She tried to slam the door shut, but he blocked her. She didn't recognize him under the facial gauze and sling hanging languidly. His left eye was a fat purple blotch bloated with pus.

Holder pleaded, "Sara, it's me! I fell in a store, and some stuff fell on me during the earthquake. Didn't you feel it?" Holder noticed the heavy suitcase near her as his head cleared. "Where the hell are you going? You never asked my permission for a trip!"

"I told you I was going with some friends to Big Sur for the weekend, but you probably forgot, remember? What the hell happened to you? Jeremy, you look like the Elephant Man. *I am not an animal!"* She laughed nervously under her breath.

Holder skipped around her and darted to his study to retrieve his handgun and silencer.

Sara remained downstairs and wanted to make sure her frenetic husband was well. When he returned, she noticed the handgun in his waistband and tried to stop him. "Where are you going, Jeremy?"

"None of your fucking business!"

"Don't go, Jeremy! Whatever you think you're about to do, I don't care, but stop to think a minute." Blocking his path at the front door, she told him, "Stay here, and we'll talk. My trip can wait."

Holder said, "You weren't going on any fucking trip, were you? After six months of marriage, you're just going to abandon me, right? No way." He grabbed the gun, but before he raised it, Sara punched his face. A direct hit from the Louie Vuitton tote bag to his broken nose caused him to buckle, and he collapsed to his knees, withering in pain. She then raised her arms like the Karate Kid and kicked his broken collarbone with her Louboutin pumps; she heard a sharp crack like a chicken wishbone. Her self-defense training during Pilates classes finally paid off. She ran to her Mercedes-Benz sanctuary, nervously opened the garage, and started the engine.

The Louie Vuitton tote bag and Louboutin shoes were undamaged, thank God.

Holder fumbled for his gun and silencer but realized his broken collarbone disabled his right side. Aiming with his weak left hand at the Mercedes speeding off the driveway, he fired and hit an oak tree. Sara sped onto the street, swallowed by the warm L.A. night, heading to an unknown future, to safety.

Holder mumbled to himself, "I'll deal with her later. Now, I'm going hunting for the Mexican bitch, once and for all." After popping more painkillers, he checked the G.P.S. tracker blinking red on a map and drove off in his Porsche, heading toward Boyle Heights.

***

"Ma, I already told you. I'm going to stay with you here. I explained why Mr. Holder is dangerous, and I don't want you here alone. Santos will check on us tonight. He and I are going to the San Fernando Valley tomorrow morning for some pressing business. I told Julio he could borrow my old Toyota Corolla for a few days 'cause he's going to the Coachella festival with his friends."

They were in her mother's living room. Julio and Linda came ostensibly to check on their mother after the earthquake. Julio nodded in agreement and told his mother she would be safe. "That guy won't come

242

by here, ma. I need to get going and return in a few days, but I left you some vegetarian pasta I made, my recipe." He hugged and kissed his mother, then hugged Linda and left.

Julio knew Holder had placed another tracker on Linda's old Toyota. With the help of Santos and his network of underworld contacts, Julio had also placed trackers on Holder's two vehicles. Julio knew that Sara Holder usually drove the Mercedes, and he could see the blip on the screen. Mrs. Holder was barreling toward San Diego to the edge of the G.P.S. screen. The second blip on the screen showed Mr. Holder's Porsche was now racing, as he expected, toward East Los Angeles. Julio drove in the general direction of Santa Monica, creating an impression on Holder that Linda was returning to her apartment.

***

Ten miles away in Long Beach, Trigger slowly parked his car two blocks from his target—the Whitten household. Trigger knew that Mrs. Whitten left with their children, so now was the right time. Trigger slinked onto the Whitten property and gently knocked on the front door. Wallace opened the door and darted back in fear when he saw the black revolver with a silencer in Trigger's hand. They said nothing, returned inside, and sat in the living room across from one another.

Whitten focused on the gun and stuttered, "I don't have too much cash, but I can get some. Please, whatever you're gonna do, do it now before my family returns."

Still pointing his gun, Trigger said nothing, raised his left index finger to his lips, and mouthed to Whitten, *be quiet*. Trigger dialed his cell phone.

"Hey, it's me. Yeah, I'm right here with him. You wanna talk to him?" Trigger passed the phone to Whitten.

On the other end of the line, "Hey bro, you let me down, man. You're gonna pay, fucker."

"Jeremy, what the hell? Don't do this, please."

"Give the phone back to my associate," Holder said.

"Go to hell, Jeremy!"

Trigger grabbed the phone and told Holder, "OK, wait." Trigger moved the phone away and raised his index finger again, signaling

243

Whitten to keep quiet and calm. Trigger raised the barrel of the gun to the ceiling and shot twice. "OK, Holder, it's done." Whitten remained on the couch, doing his best not to faint, pee, or scream, and gazed up at the two bullet holes in his ceiling.

***

Since Holder's home was near Santa Monica, Julio knew Holder would be waiting near Linda's apartment. Holder was now turning onto Broadway Avenue near the Santa Monica beach heading east, and Julio was on the 10-freeway heading west, the former two miles from Linda's apartment, the latter ten miles away.

As Julio passed the 405, he kept driving west and exited on Broadway. Holder was now waiting two blocks from Linda's apartment. Julio dialed his cell phone and said to someone on the other end, "OK, it'll be in about half an hour."

As Julio approached Linda's apartment, he spotted the Porsche on a dark side street, lying in wait like a silent predator. Pretending to see Holder for the first time, Julio revved the engine, quickly made a U-turn, lurched onto the 10 freeway, and then merged to the 405 northbound.

Julio knew Linda's old Toyota was no match for a thundering Porsche, the slow-footed gazelle trying to outrun the cheetah in the L.A. Serengeti. Julio figured Holder, thinking Linda was driving, would wait for the right moment to strike. The traffic was light and steady, and Julio spotted Holder prowling in the rearview about five car lengths behind in the slow lane.

Julio exited onto Sunset Boulevard eastbound, heading past the north entrance to U.C.L.A. and the south entrance to Brentwood. Julio's mind, pumped with adrenaline, thought for a fleeting moment—*this was the same route taken by OJ Simpson the night he murdered Nicole and Ron— allegedly.* Julio saw the Porsche gaining in the rearview and was now directly behind him. As Sunset Boulevard curved just past the Brentwood gate, Holder saw a moment to fire a clear shot with his weak left hand. PING! He hit the trunk, and Julio almost lost control.

Julio quickly sliced along Sunset Boulevard, passing The Roxy Theater and approaching West Hollywood. Holder was in close pursuit, with a broken collarbone, immense pain, and a slow explosion of anger inside him. Traffic was light as they now approached West Hollywood. Approaching Hollywood Boulevard, Julio quickly reeled onto a side street. PING! It blasted Julio's passenger door. *Too close!* The side street was pitch black, away from the illumination of West Hollywood. Holder closed three car lengths behind him.

Julio quickly entered a vacant lot, shut the lights, and stopped. Holder carefully parked fifty feet behind, trying to assess the situation and waiting for Linda to exit. Holder fired two more shots from the silencer but missed, striking the rear of the Toyota. At that moment, the bright headlights of four vehicles next to Julio lit up, illuminating and blinding Holder. To Holder's shock, Julio emerged from Linda's red Toyota.

As Holder exited his car with his gun drawn, he heard a voice from a silhouette behind the headlights. "Don't even think of it, Mr. Holder. Drop that gun. I have five pairs of weapons trained on you now." Holder meekly dropped his handgun.

Holder pleaded, "Who the fuck are you all? Think before you do something stupid. If you want money or my car, we can negotiate!"

Julio approached Holder, and the shadowy group encircled Holder. Julio said, "Jeremy, this is Hector Allen. His nickname is *Foster Boy* 'cause he spent most of his life in foster homes. He didn't turn out like his adoptive parents expected, and some say he's a powerful street lieutenant of the Sunshine Project crew. *Allegedly.* All rumors.

"Before the Allens adopted him, he lived in their foster home in Pasadena with his foster brother. You might know him, Christopher Allen. They call him *Shrek*, your ex-client." Holder showed no reaction.

With five trained assassins flanking him, Hector Allen intervened, "Mr. Holder, your currency is worthless to me, but your debt is priceless. Chris was the only brother I ever had. I protected him 'cause I knew he couldn't protect himself in the real world. When I heard of his arrest, I thought he would get out of that jam 'cause he had a great lawyer, Jeremy Holder. But you fucked him up, Holder. You sold him out. And when I heard that he committed suicide and that you probably convinced him to do so, even supplying a piece of wood to do it, I knew you had to pay. I know who I am and regret some things I've done on the street and in prison. But you, Jeremy, are a sick fuck. You did this for life insurance? You owe us a debt. You owe my brother Chris a debt."

Julio turned to Hector and asked, "Are we good? Is *my* debt clear?"

Hector nodded and said to Julio, "Now get the hell out of here. This is not on you. You and your sister won't have to worry. Get that car fixed. Go to Turi's and tell him to give it a quick paint job with a different color—besides red. Julio climbed back into the Toyota, revved the engine, and slowly drove out of the vacant lot, swallowed by the black water of the L.A. night, heading toward Turi's Auto Body Shop.

***

Trigger's cell phone rang at the Whitten household in Long Beach.

On the other end of the line, Foster Boy Allen told Trigger, "It's done. All cool homes." And he hung up.

Trigger reached into his coat pocket and retrieved a wad of cash—ten thousand dollars—and handed the money to Whitten, saying, "Here. Take your family on a nice vacation. I didn't earn it. And get those holes fixed. The missus might get pissed."

Trigger rose, placed the revolver in his waistband, and calmly exited the front door.

Trigger took pride in his professionalism. After all, Jaime "Trigger" Allen was a loyal member of the Sunshine Projects crew, a lieutenant of Hector *Foster Boy* Allen, and a former foster brother of Chris Allen.

***

From the Los Angeles Evening News, dated May 7, 2024:

Another tragic story last evening. In West Hollywood, unknown assailants gunned down a prominent Los Angeles attorney, Jeremy Holder, in his car. L.A.P.D. has not offered many details of the incident, but Mr. Holder may have been the victim of a lethal carjacking as he was driving his sports car, a late model Porsche. This incident may have resulted from road rage, as anonymous sources reported a chase along Sunset Boulevard involving another vehicle, with speculation that this incident was a gangland-type shooting.

Holder was a legal expert in death penalty cases, having practiced in Texas, California, Oklahoma, Missouri, and Florida. His spouse, Sara Holder, was not available for comment.

In the ensuing months, national newspapers, the California State Bar, and the Los Angeles Innocence Project opened investigations into Jeremy Holder's cases in Missouri, California, Florida, Oklahoma, and Texas. The Los Angeles Police Department and the F.B.I. didn't find the killer or killers of Holder, but rumors began to proliferate that it might have been *gang-related*. Investigations would also peruse Holder's death penalty cases and any individuals connected with the insurance payouts.

Julio returned Linda's car to her a week after Holder's premature demise. He explained to Linda that he "got into a fender bender at Coachella, but Turi fixed it up like new, even with a new paint job—metallic silver." He also mentioned in passing that he heard Holder "got *Sonny Corleoned*." Linda, Santos, and Whitten received recognition from the L.A.P.D., the Judicial Council of California, and the Los Angeles Innocence Project. With a promotion, Linda was now a senior attorney in the Los Angeles District Attorney.

***

"Is this for real?"

Nico Meza glanced at the icy, restless San Francisco Bay. A diffused sun hung languidly low on the western horizon, greeted by the Pacific Ocean waiting below. A sailboat glided gently across the tranquil bay just past Alcatraz, skimming the water, almost levitating. Across the bay, the astonishing old-world beauty of San Francisco welcomed a heavy fog nestling comfortably, snuggling the Trans America Pyramid like a light blanket, its pointed top piercing the blanket like a spear. The cable cars Meza heard in his dreams were now distinctively real.

Stern-looking guards opened the gates of San Quentin, the same gates Meza had entered a year before. He stopped nervously, peered at the guards for tacit permission, and they motioned him to exit.

He recognized four familiar faces on the other side, the free side: his mother, Wallace Whitten, Ramon Santos, and Linda Sanchez, all beaming with smiles. His crying mother carried a box, quickly opened it, and removed his lucky L.A. Dodgers cap.

Linda said, "Put that lucky cap on, and never take it off." She and Mrs. Meza embraced him.

Meza said, "No, Miss Sanchez. I don't need this cap for luck." He tossed it into the bay, quietly swallowed by its deep black water.

EPILOGUE

Two months after Holder's death, Linda returned from a two-week vacation in Maui with her mother and Julio. Her mother fully recovered from her injury, and Julio would begin culinary school in the fall. Catching up on her phone calls, she saw one from Ron Lacy, the prosecutor she met in Oklahoma, who accompanied her to view an execution at the "Big Mac."

She dialed early on the morning of her first day at work and heard a vaguely familiar voice at the other end, sounding slurred and tired. "Mr. Lacy, Ron Lacy. This is Linda Sanchez. Yes, it's been a long time. I clearly remember you. How's your retirement going? Lots of fishing, I hope. You sound tired."

Lacy answered, "Well, little lady. Good to hear from you also! You kicked up quite a hornet's nest with that Holder prick. They also began an extensive investigation here. Oklahoma has executed none of Holder's ex-clients, except one." He took a slight pause. Linda heard him slurp a drink. He then slurred, "Well, I just wanted to call you to congratulate you in person. All of us in the Nickel Choir need to stick together. I'm on my porch looking out at the beautiful hills around here, sipping my special coffee before I take my afternoon nap. It's a beautiful day, Linda." His voice sounded wistful, melancholy, and weak.

Linda continued listening, sensing Lacy wanted to vent. "That's good, Mr. Lacy."

"Hey, Linda… member Marlo Crawford? The last guy I convicted. We saw his execution, member? Well, Holder was his defense attorney, and he messed him up. Holder, that sick fuck, paid off eyewitnesses who falsely identified Crawford. Then Holder collected on a two hundred-thousand-dollar life insurance policy with a crooked insurance agent in Altus. Crawford was innocent, Linda. Fucking innocent."

Linda could hear Lacy crying on the other end. "I convicted him and sent him to death. We saw an innocent guy executed—no, murdered. Linda. Murdered!"

Lacy paused for a few seconds, waiting for Linda's response. For a few seconds, there was none. Before he hung up, the last thing Lacy heard was Linda's beastly, bloodcurdling scream that rang in his ears, haunting him in his dreams until the day he died.

"NO! NO! OH GOD, NO!"